The Mystery of the Unlocked Cave

by GARETH GAUDIN

ORCA BOOK PUBLISHERS

Library and Archives Canada Cataloguing in Publication

Title: The Monster sisters and the mystery of the unlocked cave / Gareth Kyle Gaudin.
Names: Gaudin, Gareth Kyle, 1973– author.

Description: Series statement: Monster sisters; 1

Identifiers: Canadiana (print) 20190066822 | Canadiana (ebook) 20190066849 |
ISBN 9781459822269 (softcover) | ISBN 9781459822276 (PDF) | ISBN 9781459822283 (EPUB)

Subjects: LCGFT: Graphic novels.

Classification: LCC PN6733.G38 M66 2019 | DDC J741.5/971—DC23

Library of Congress Control Number: 2019934055
Simultaneously published in Canada and the United States in 2019

Summary: In this graphic novel for early middle readers, two young sleuths must figure out why their sleepy seaside town is being overrun by monsters.

Orca Book Publishers is committed to reducing the consumption of nonrenewable resources in the making of our books. We make every effort to use materials that support a sustainable future.

Orca Book Publishers gratefully acknowledges the support for its publishing programs provided by the following agencies: the Government of Canada, the Canada Council for the Arts and the Province of British Columbia through the BC Arts Council and the Book Publishing Tax Credit.

Cover and interior artwork by Gareth Gaudin
Colors by Jim W.W. Smith

ORCA BOOK PUBLISHERS
orcabook.com

Printed and bound in China.

22 21 20 19 • 4 3 2 1

To the real Monster Sisters, Enid and Lyra.
Thanks for everything, kids.
Extra-special thanks also to Bronwyn Lee Gaudin,
co-creator of those real Monster Sisters.

Hello, and welcome to the first volume of The Monster Sisters. I'm the Perogy Cat, and I'll be your host and narrator throughout the series. I really like telling stories, and the story I'm about to tell you is pretty fantastic. I hope you enjoy it.

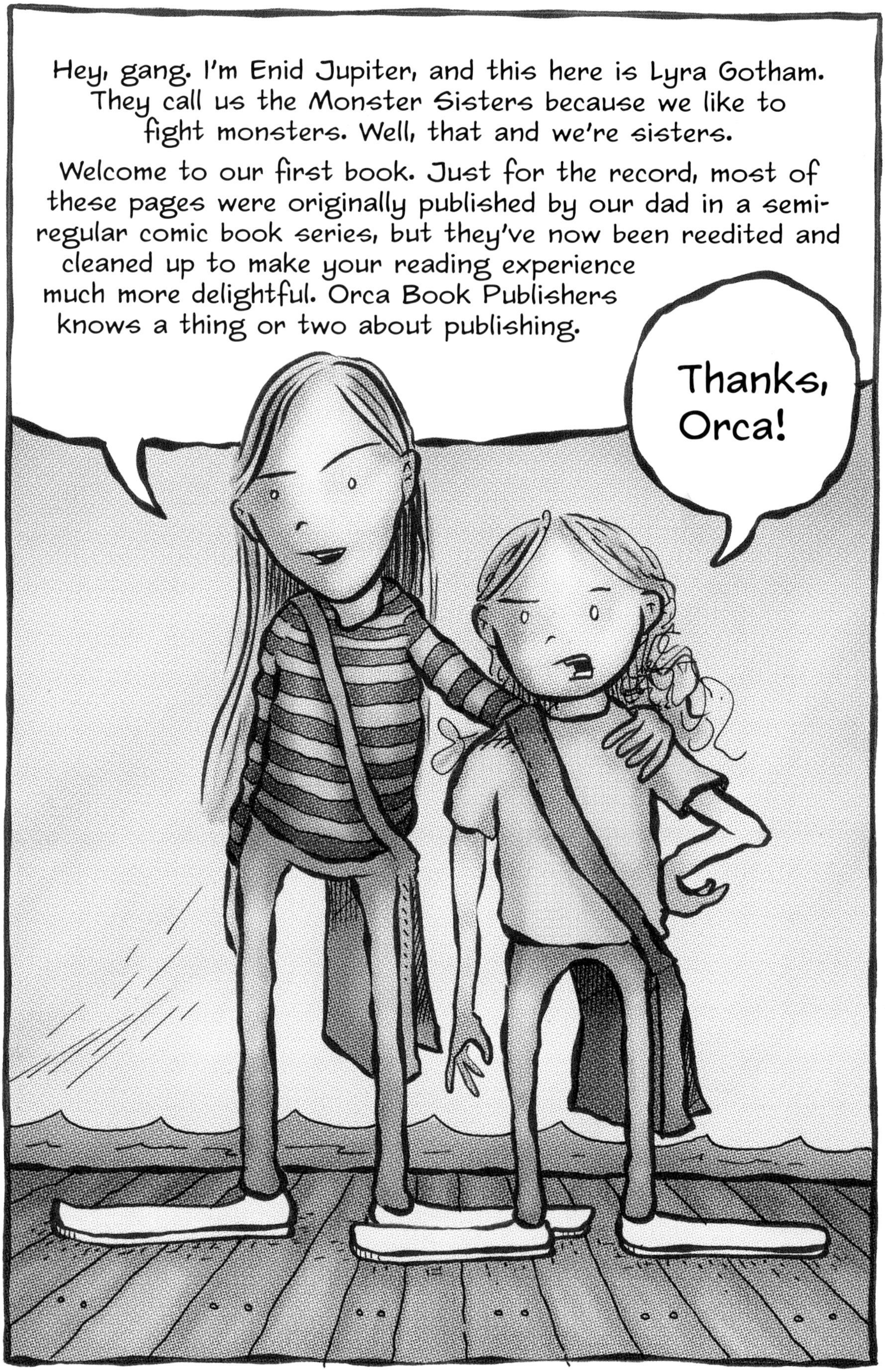
Hey, gang. I'm Enid Jupiter, and this here is Lyra Gotham. They call us the Monster Sisters because we like to fight monsters. Well, that and we're sisters.
Welcome to our first book. Just for the record, most of these pages were originally published by our dad in a semi-regular comic book series, but they've now been reedited and cleaned up to make your reading experience much more delightful. Orca Book Publishers knows a thing or two about publishing.
Thanks, Orca!

CONTENTS

CHAPTER ONE

THE MONSTER SISTERS

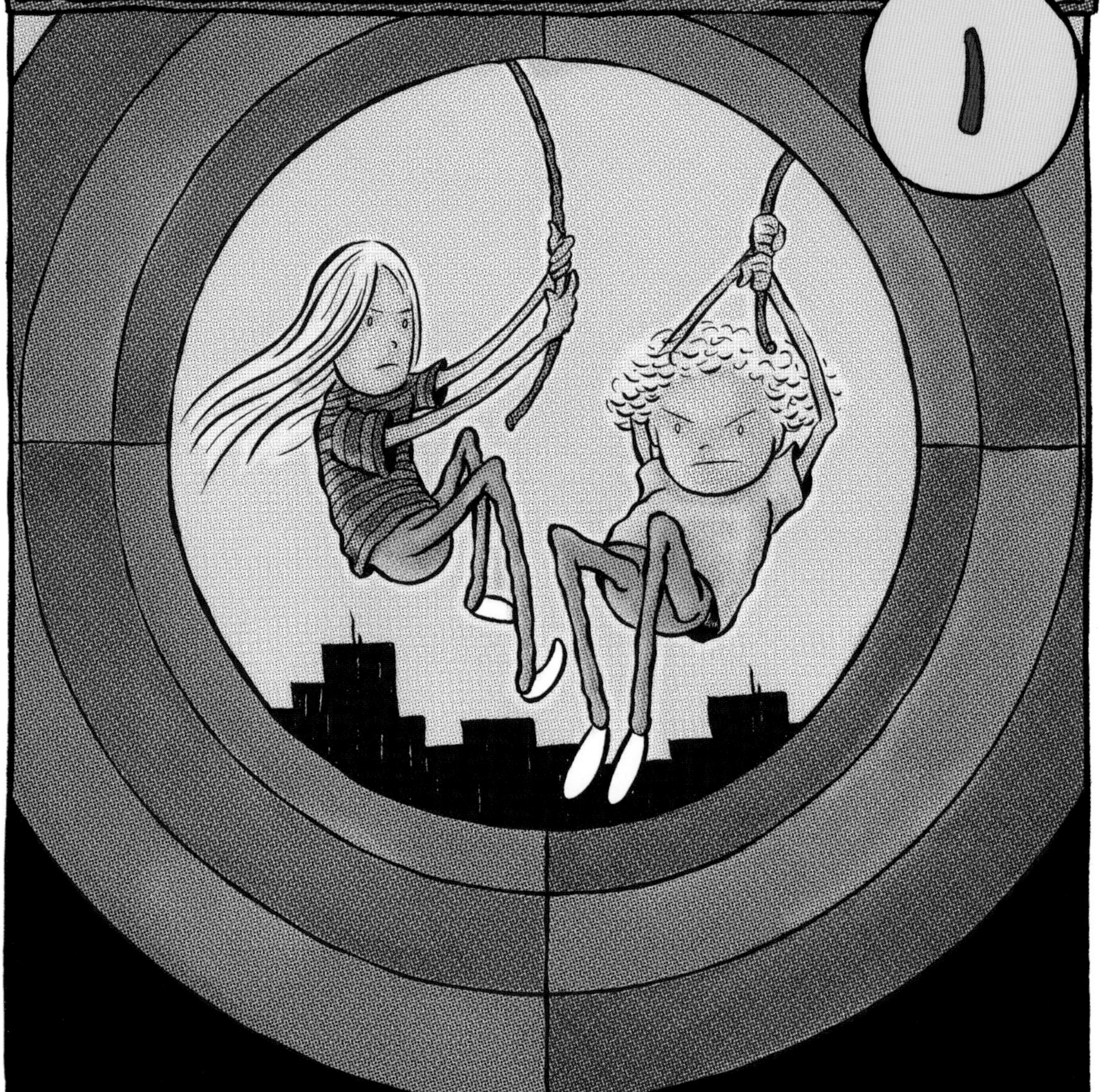
1

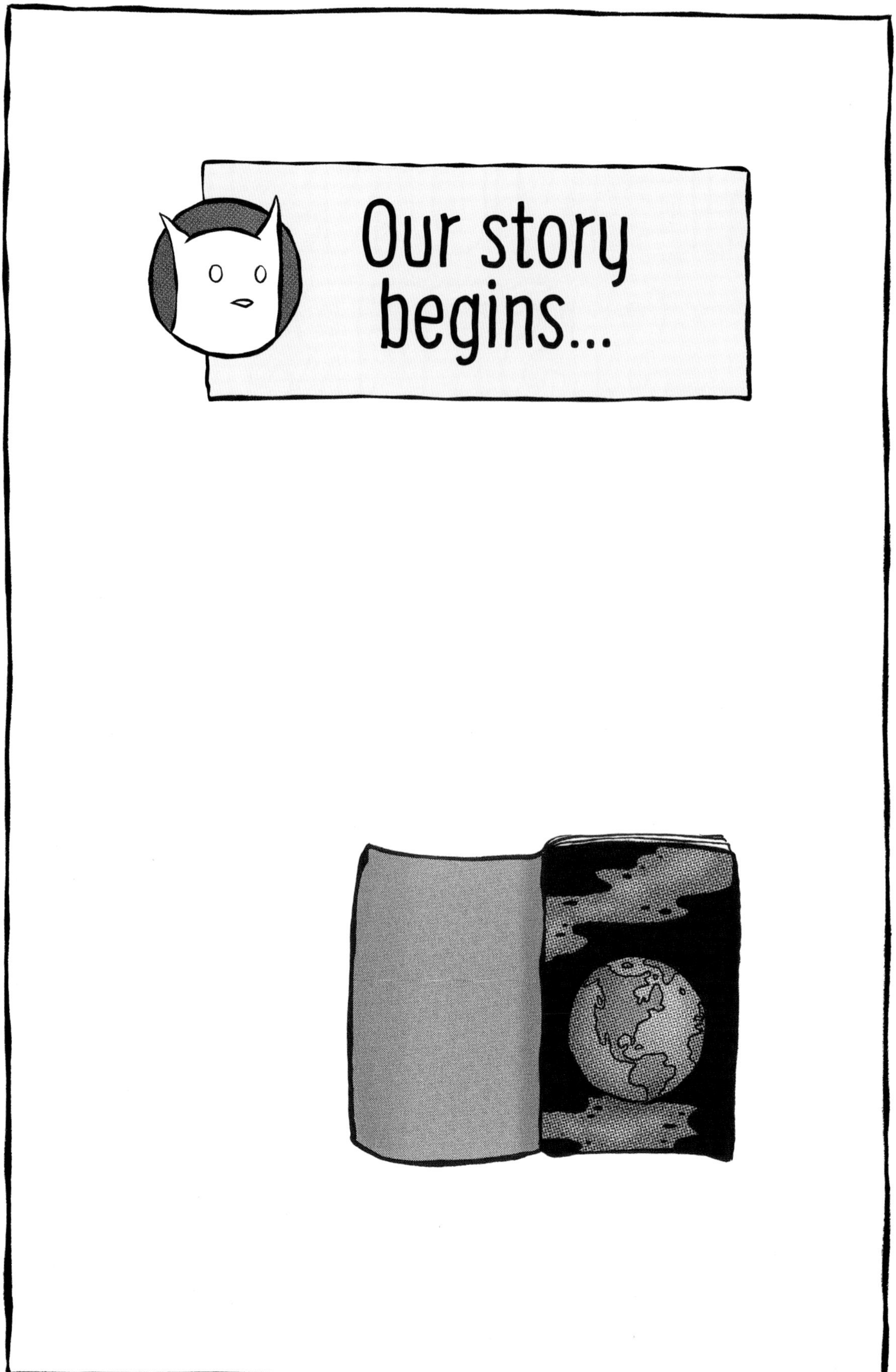
Our story begins...

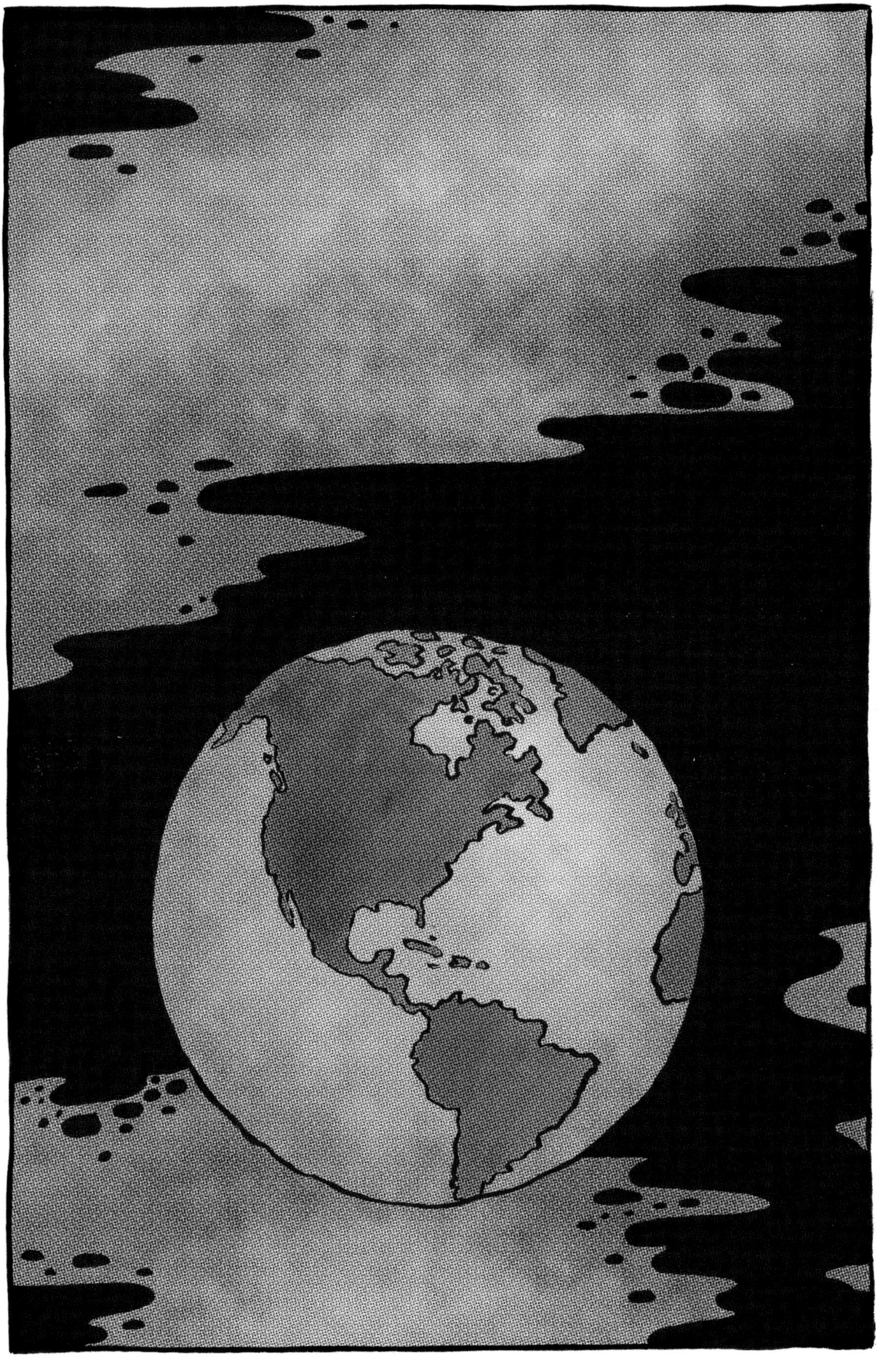

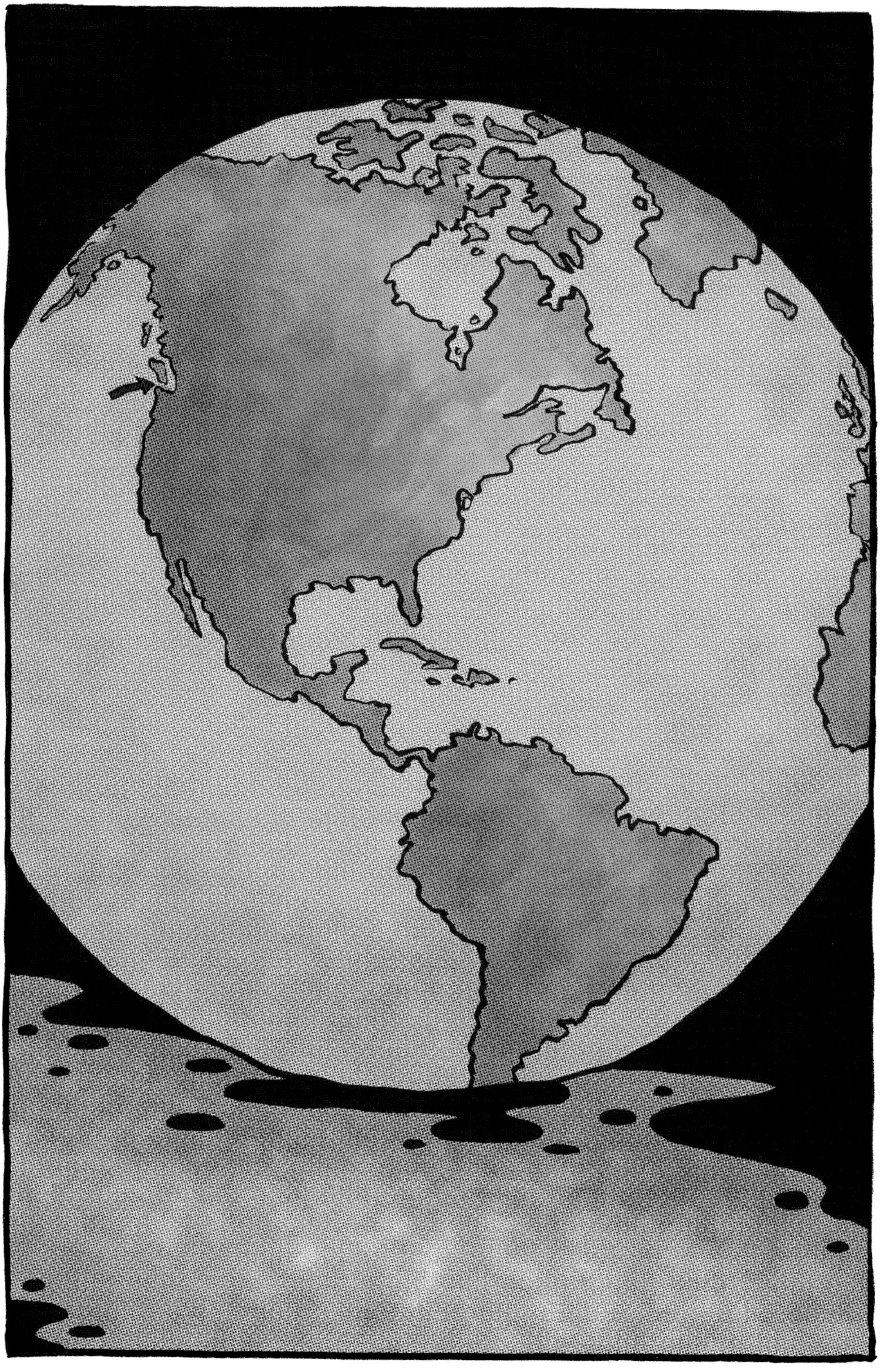

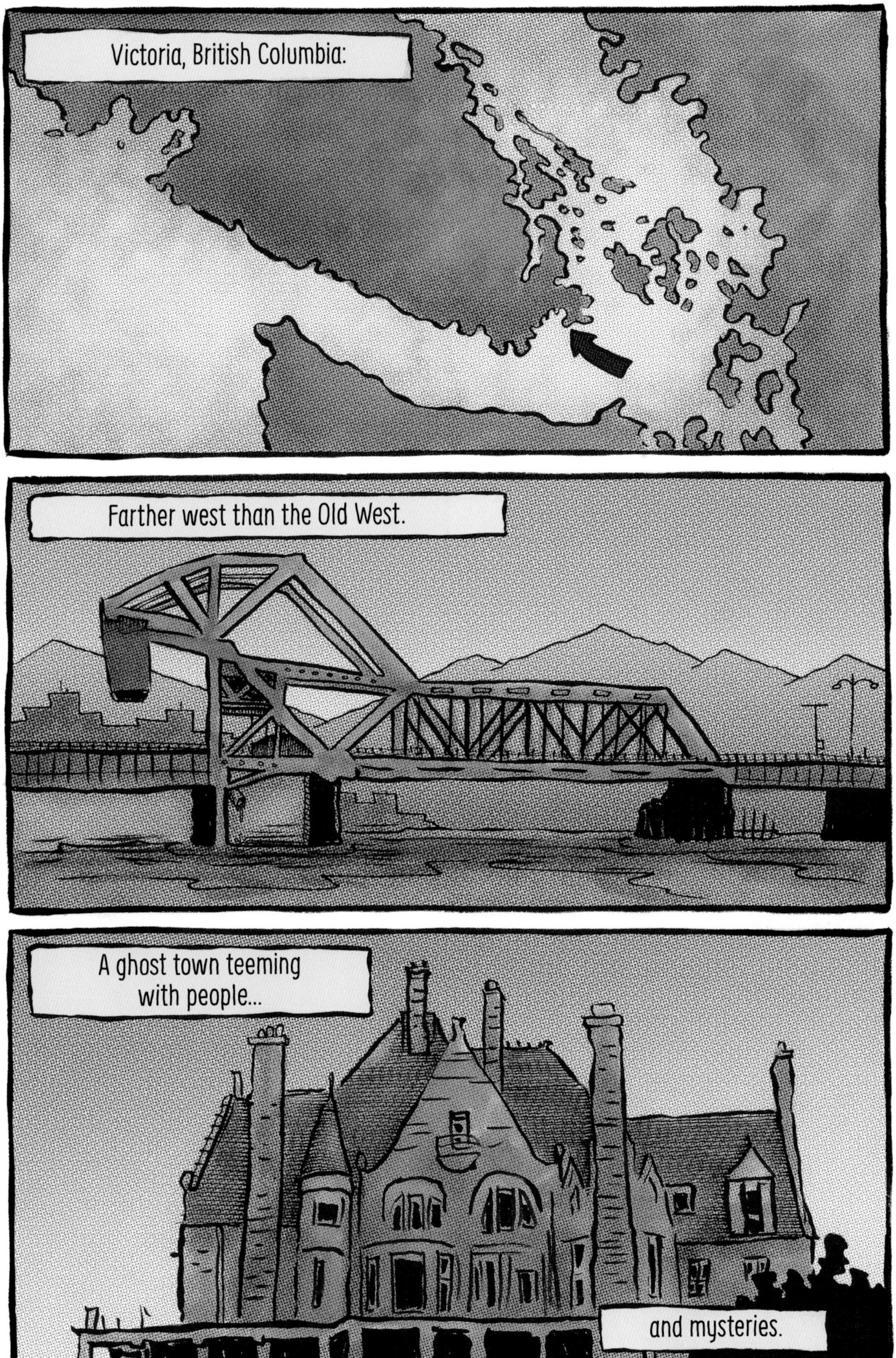
Victoria, British Columbia:
Farther west than the Old West.
A ghost town teeming with people...
and mysteries.

Victoria, BC:

A capital city on the southern tip of Vancouver Island.

Surrounded by the Salish Sea.

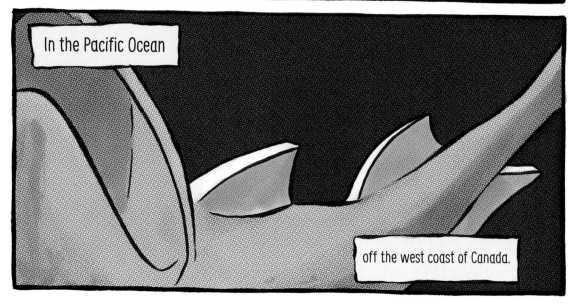

In the Pacific Ocean

off the west coast of Canada.

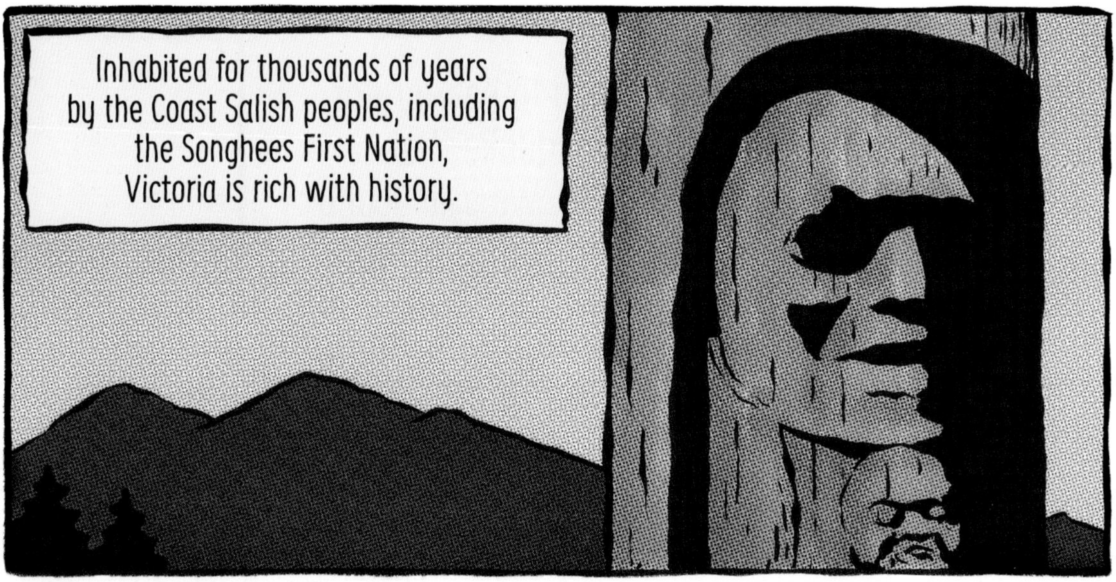
Inhabited for thousands of years by the Coast Salish peoples, including the Songhees First Nation, Victoria is rich with history.

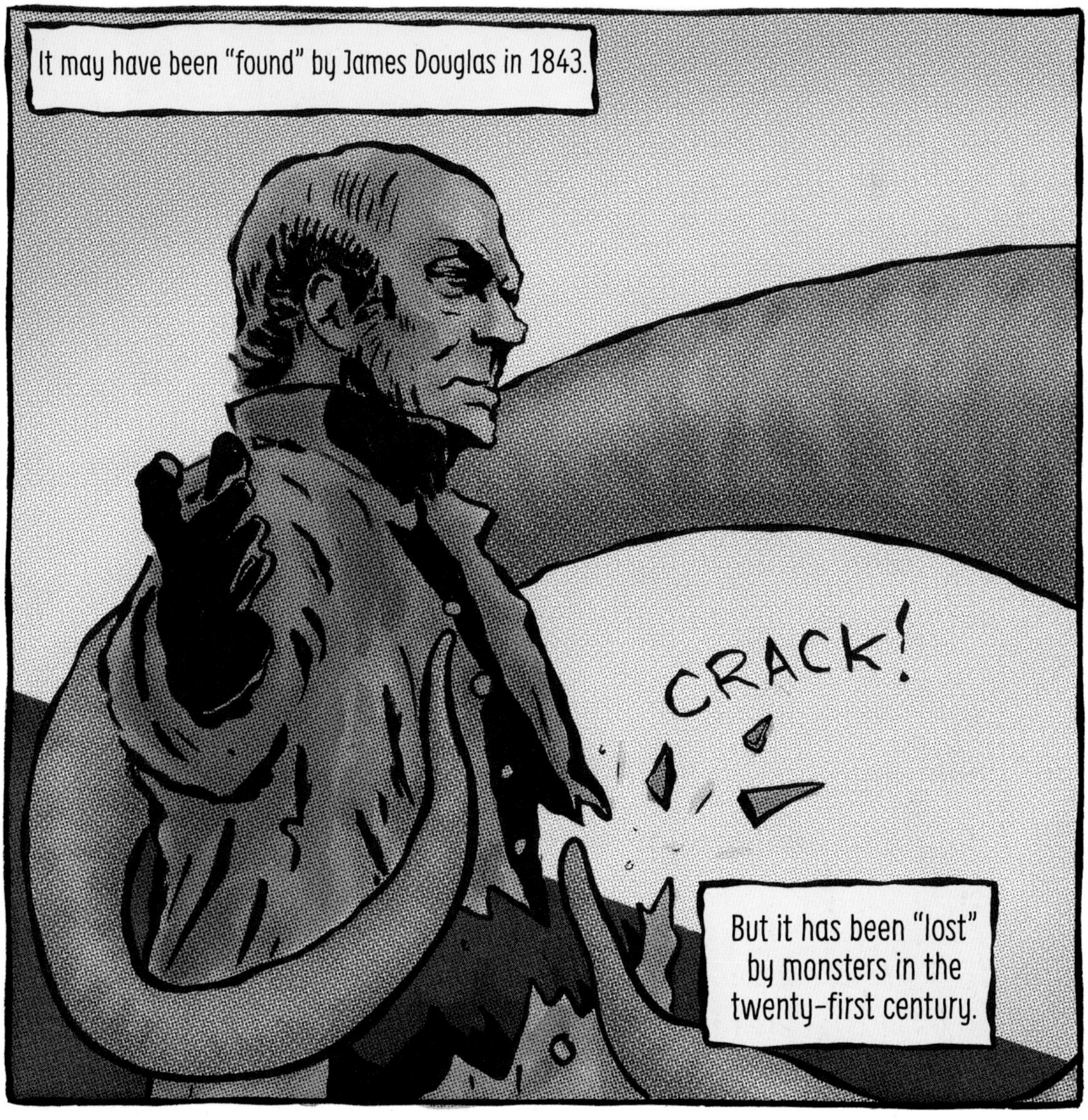
It may have been "found" by James Douglas in 1843.
CRACK!
But it has been "lost" by monsters in the twenty-first century.

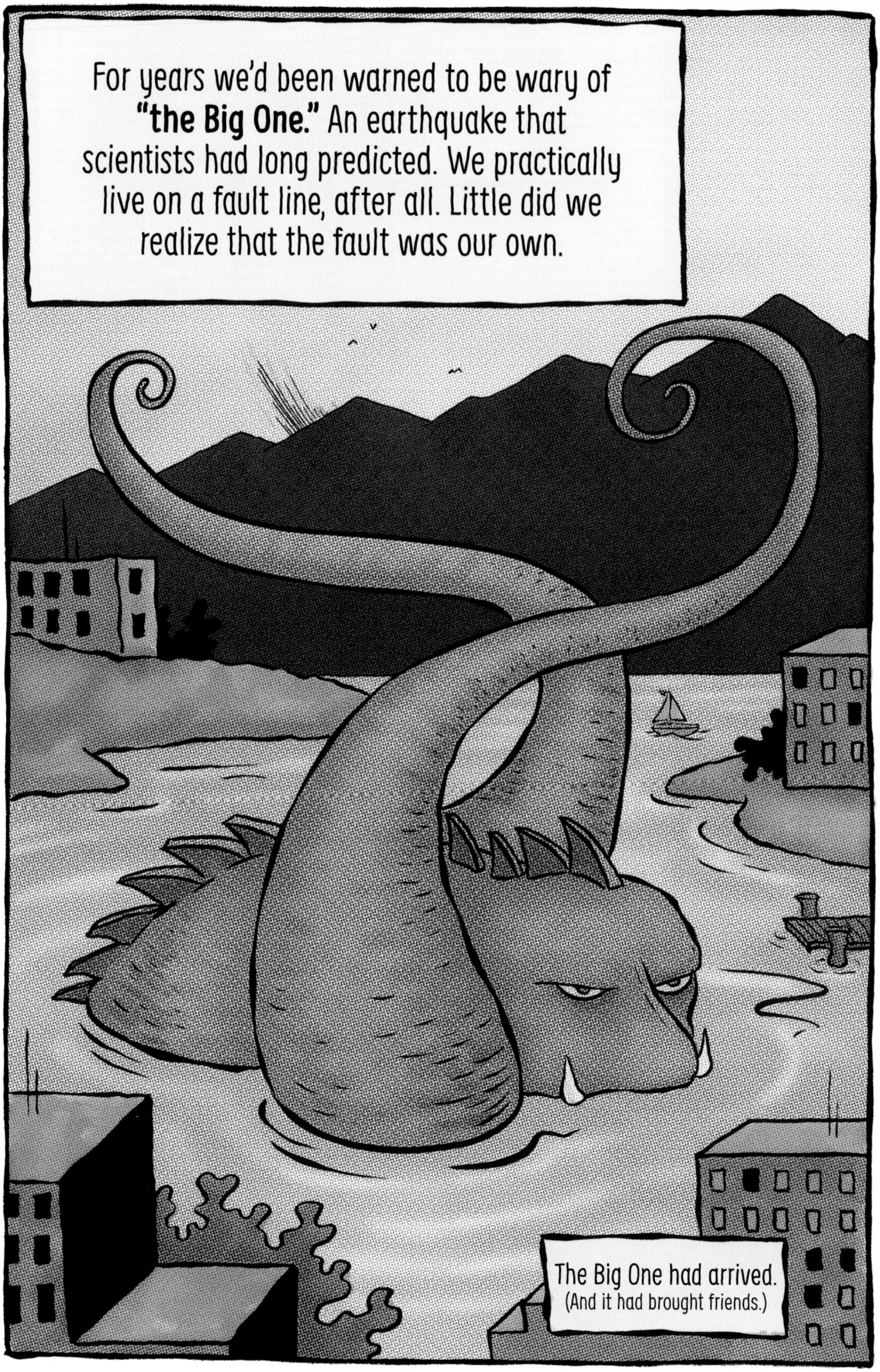
For years we'd been warned to be wary of **"the Big One."** An earthquake that scientists had long predicted. We practically live on a fault line, after all. Little did we realize that the fault was our own.
The Big One had arrived.
(And it had brought friends.)

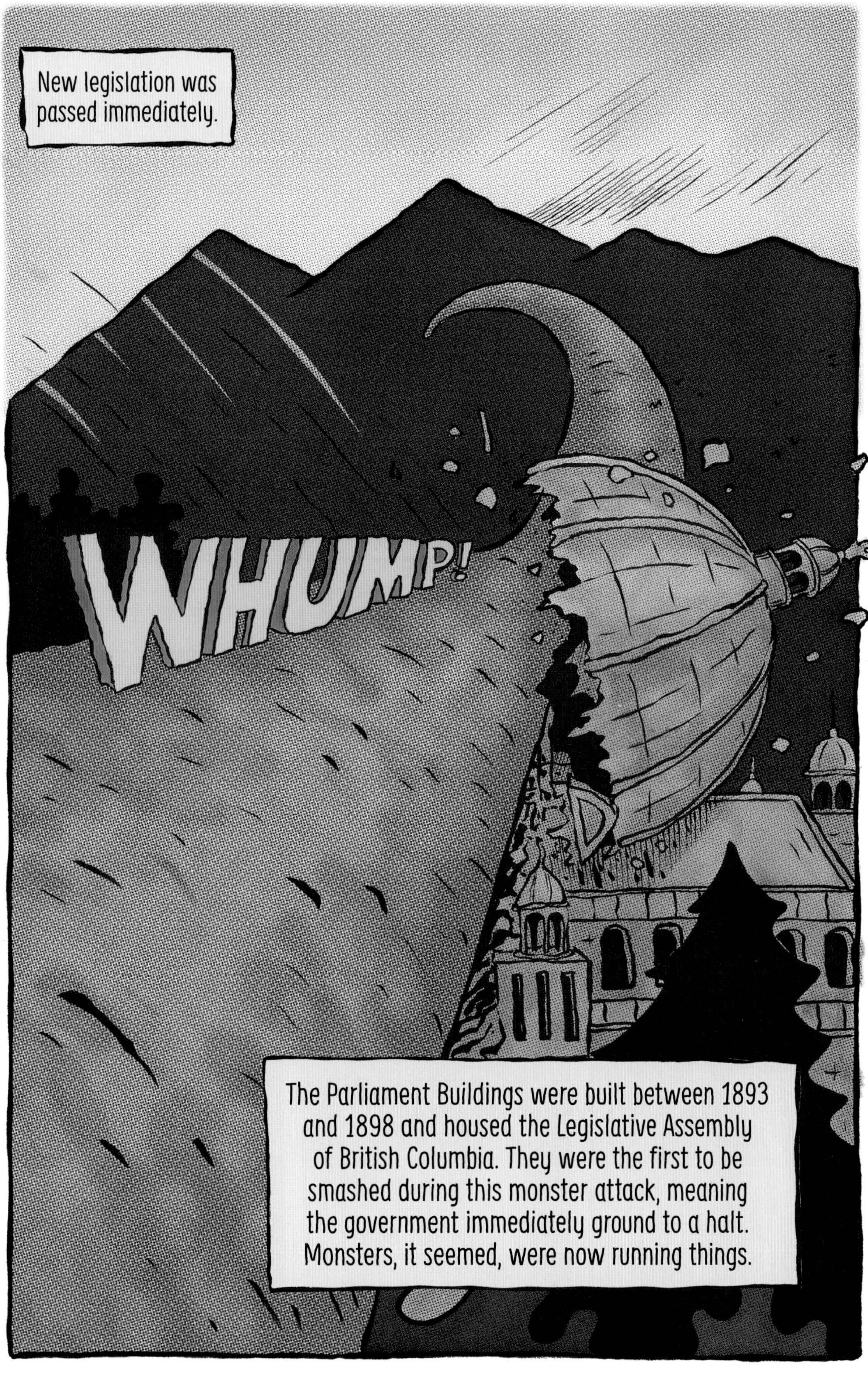
New legislation was passed immediately.
WHUMP!
The Parliament Buildings were built between 1893 and 1898 and housed the Legislative Assembly of British Columbia. They were the first to be smashed during this monster attack, meaning the government immediately ground to a halt. Monsters, it seemed, were now running things.

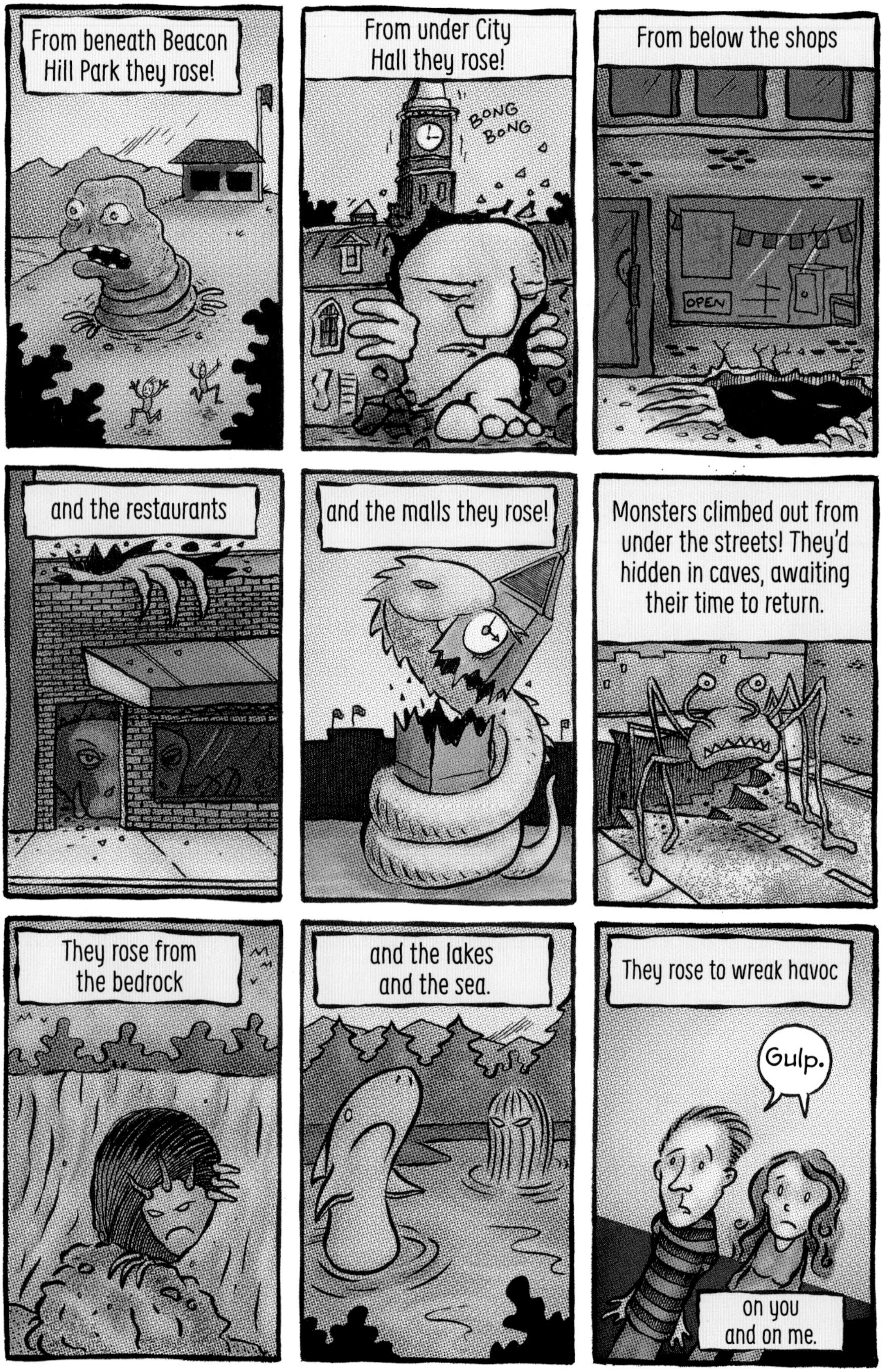
From beneath Beacon Hill Park they rose!
From under City Hall they rose!
BONG BONG
From below the shops
OPEN
and the restaurants
and the malls they rose!
Monsters climbed out from under the streets! They'd hidden in caves, awaiting their time to return.
They rose from the bedrock
and the lakes and the sea.
They rose to wreak havoc
Gulp.
on you and on me.

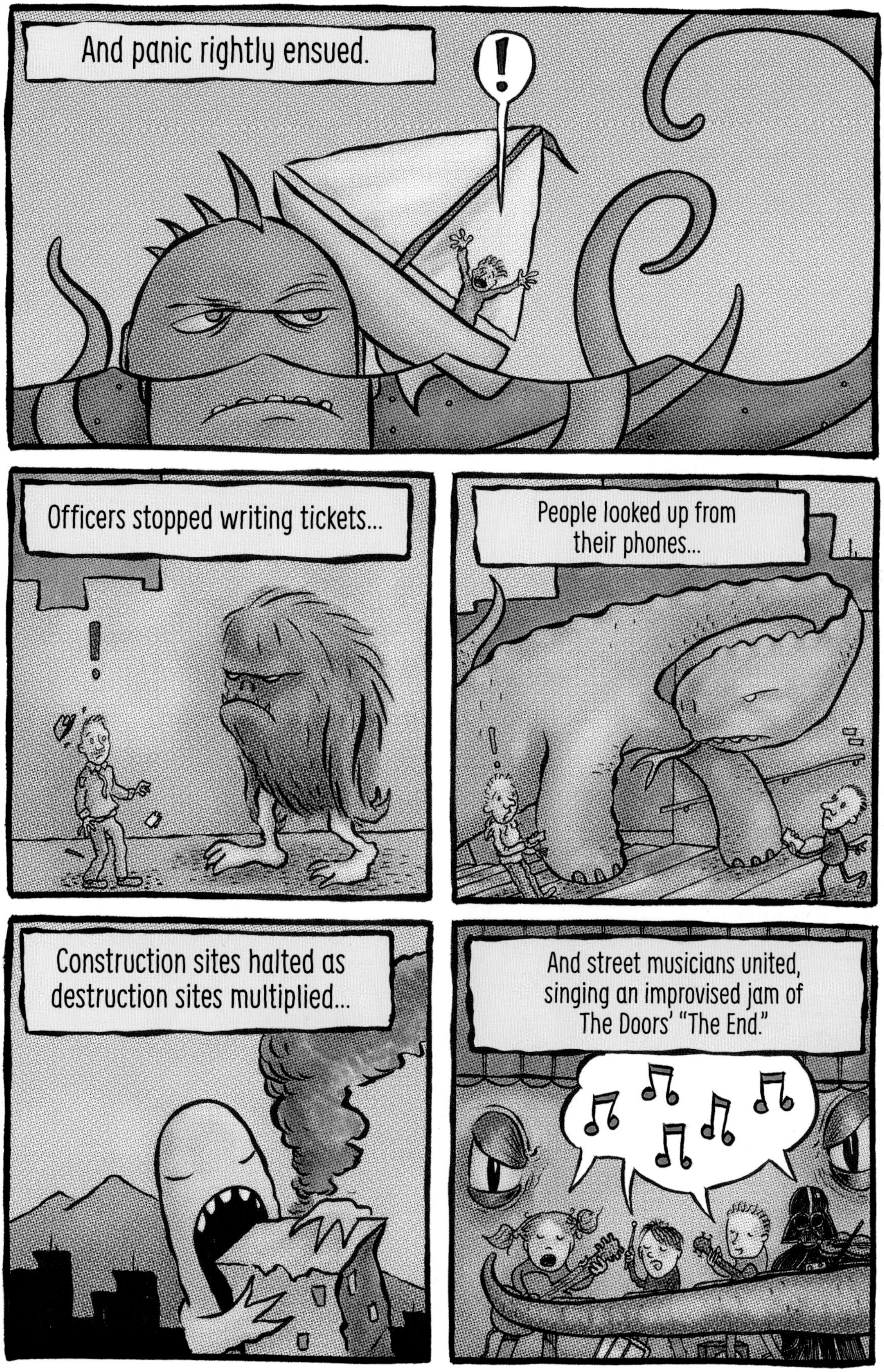
And panic rightly ensued.
!
Officers stopped writing tickets...
People looked up from their phones...
Construction sites halted as destruction sites multiplied...
And street musicians united, singing an improvised jam of The Doors' "The End."

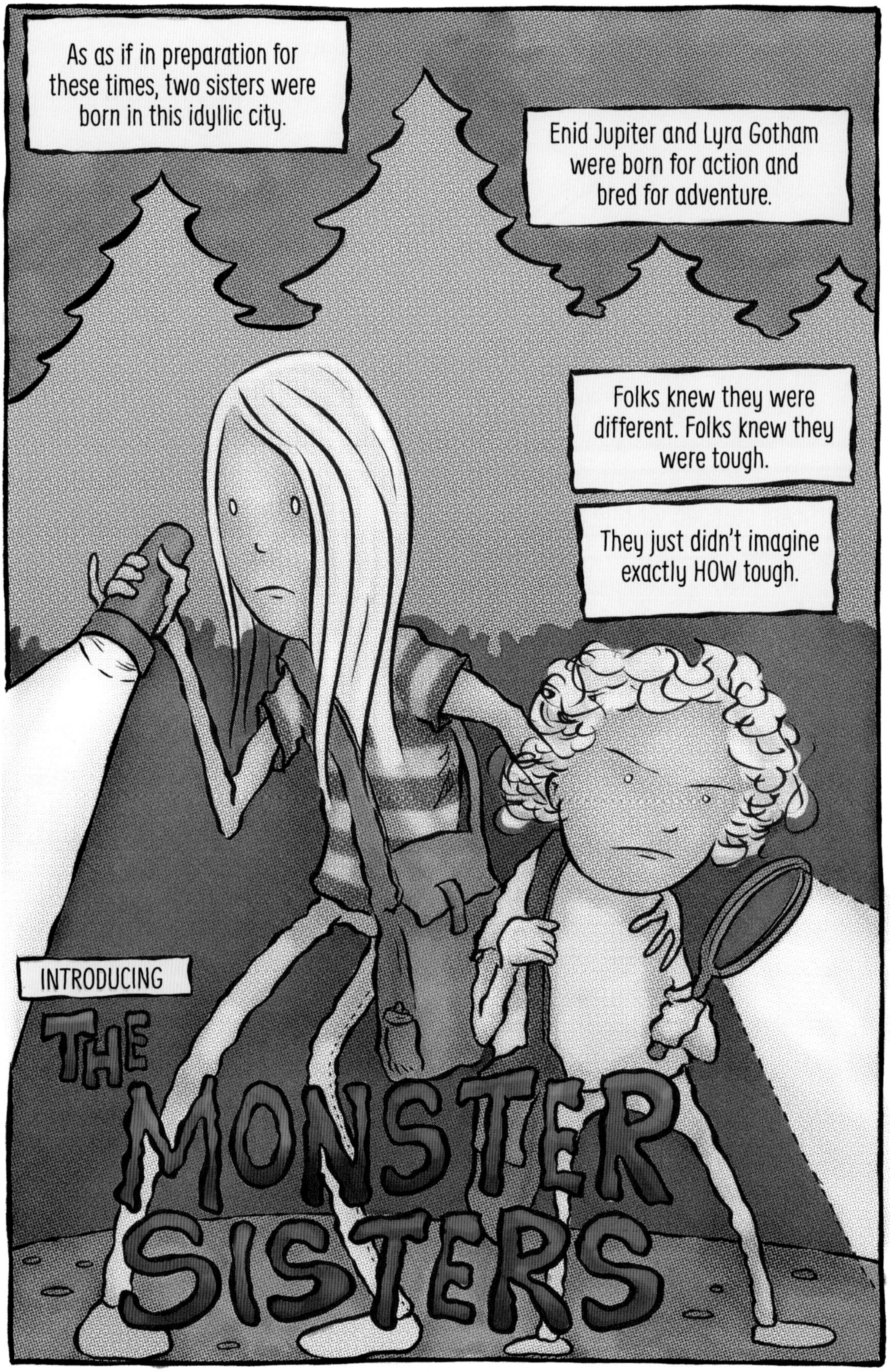
As as if in preparation for these times, two sisters were born in this idyllic city.
Enid Jupiter and Lyra Gotham were born for action and bred for adventure.
Folks knew they were different. Folks knew they were tough.
They just didn't imagine exactly HOW tough.
INTRODUCING
THE MONSTER SISTERS

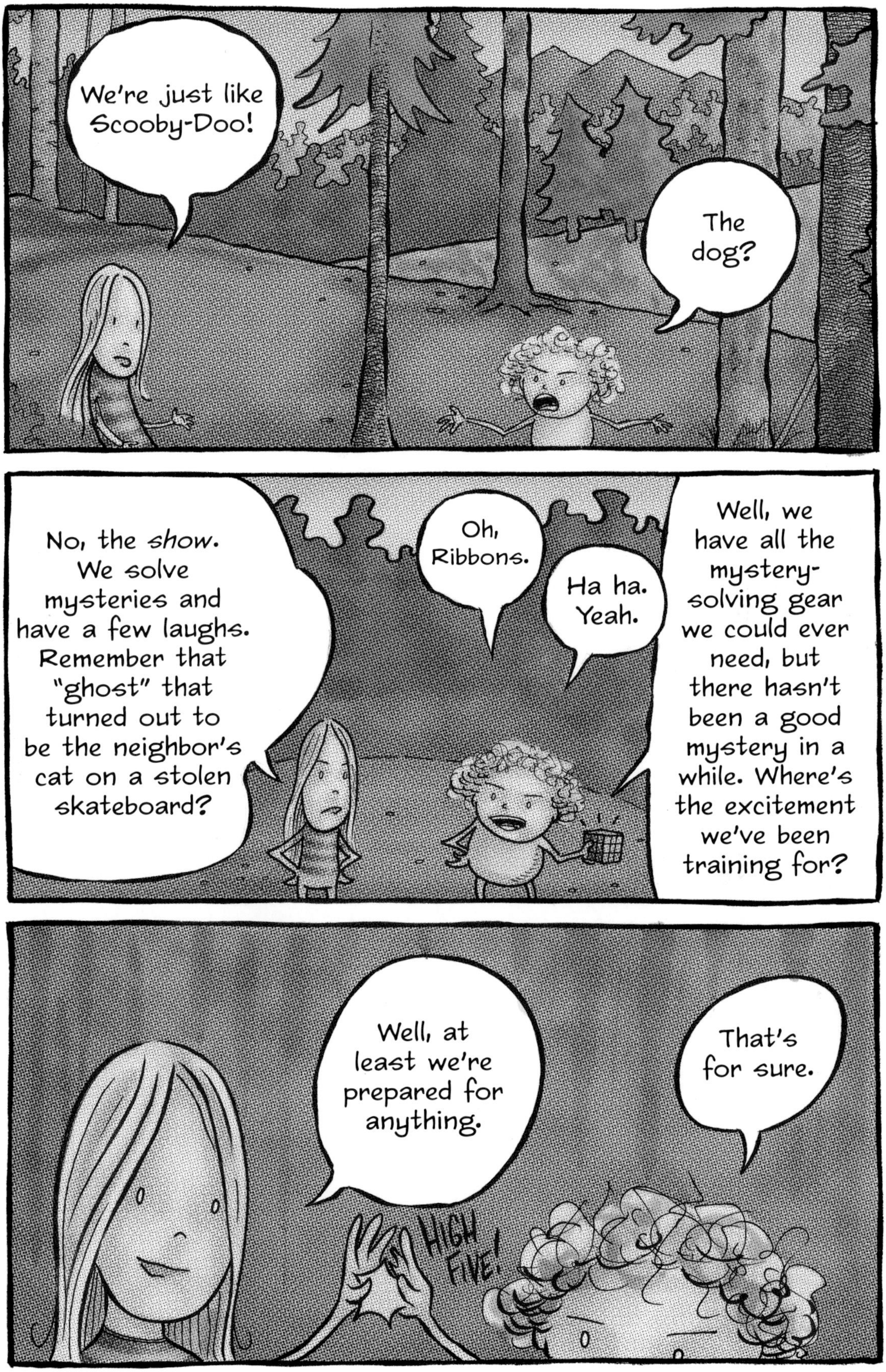
We're just like Scooby-Doo!
The dog?
No, the *show*. We solve mysteries and have a few laughs. Remember that "ghost" that turned out to be the neighbor's cat on a stolen skateboard?
Oh, Ribbons.
Ha ha. Yeah.
Well, we have all the mystery-solving gear we could ever need, but there hasn't been a good mystery in a while. Where's the excitement we've been training for?
Well, at least we're prepared for anything.
That's for sure.
HIGH FIVE!

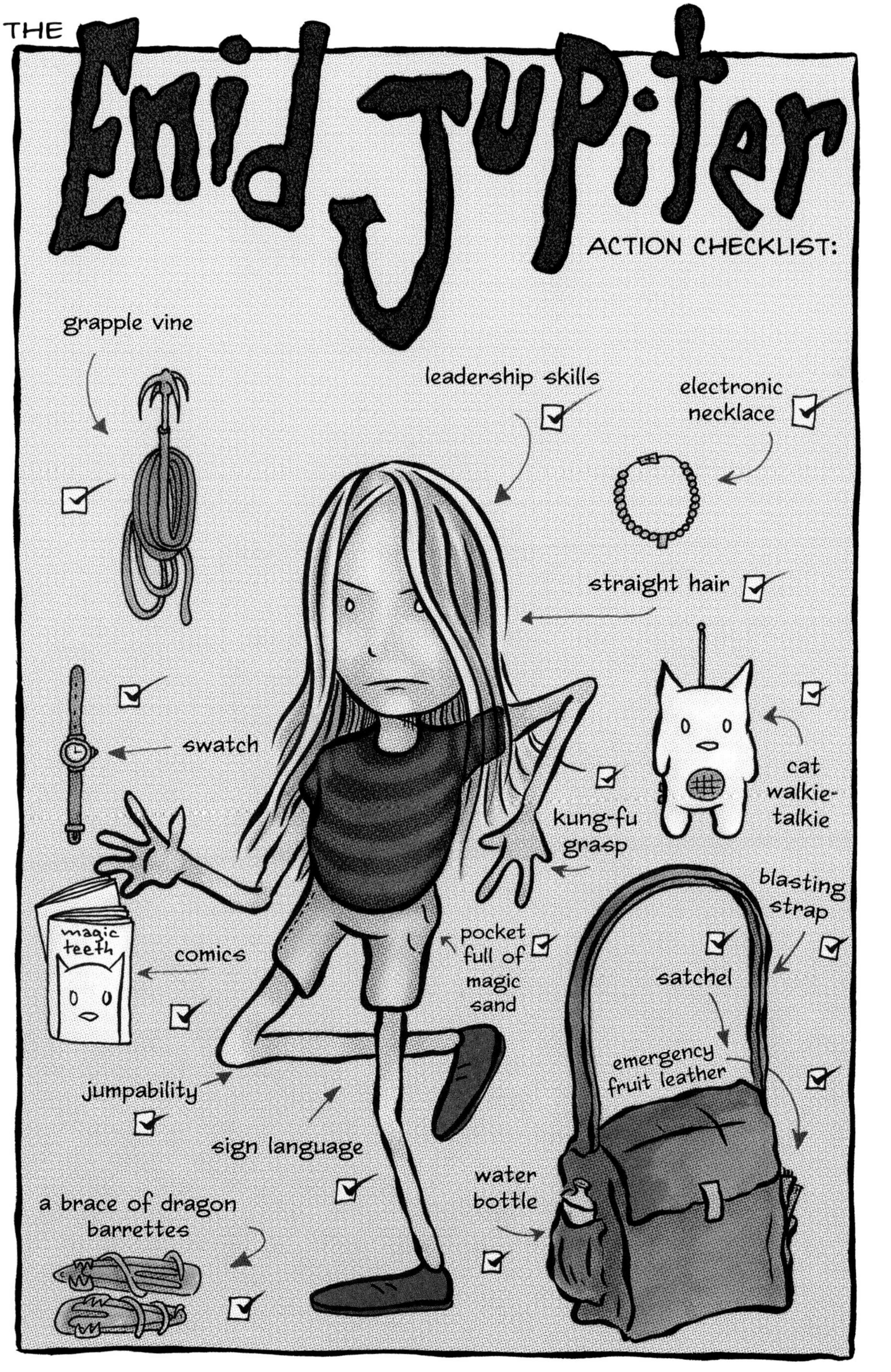
THE Enid Jupiter ACTION CHECKLIST:
grapple vine
leadership skills
electronic necklace
straight hair
swatch
kung-fu grasp
cat walkie-talkie
blasting strap
magic teeth
comics
pocket full of magic sand
satchel
emergency fruit leather
jumpability
sign language
water bottle
a brace of dragon barrettes

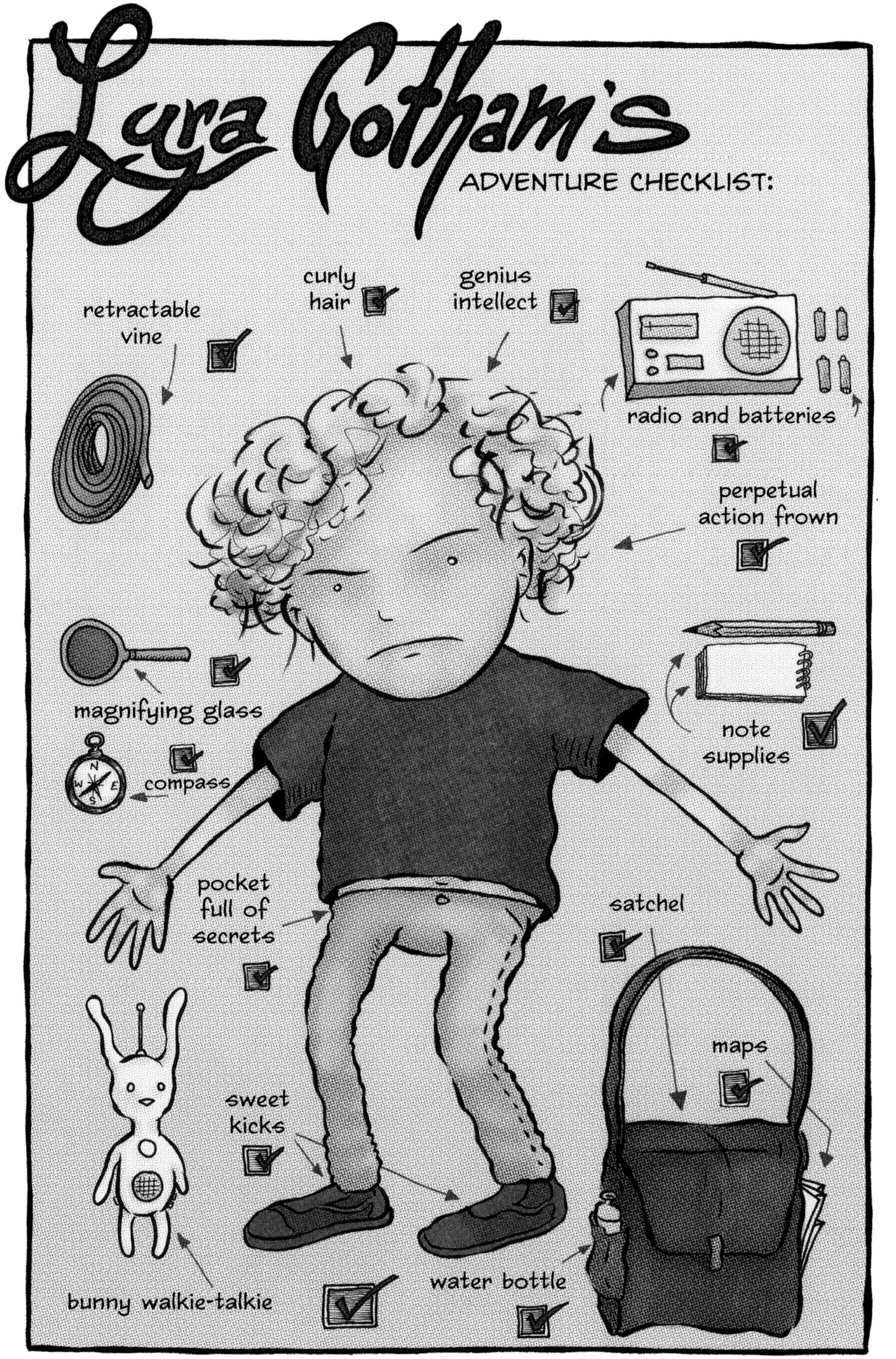
Lura Gotham's
ADVENTURE CHECKLIST:
curly hair
genius intellect
retractable vine
radio and batteries
perpetual action frown
magnifying glass
note supplies
compass
pocket full of secrets
satchel
maps
sweet kicks
water bottle
bunny walkie-talkie

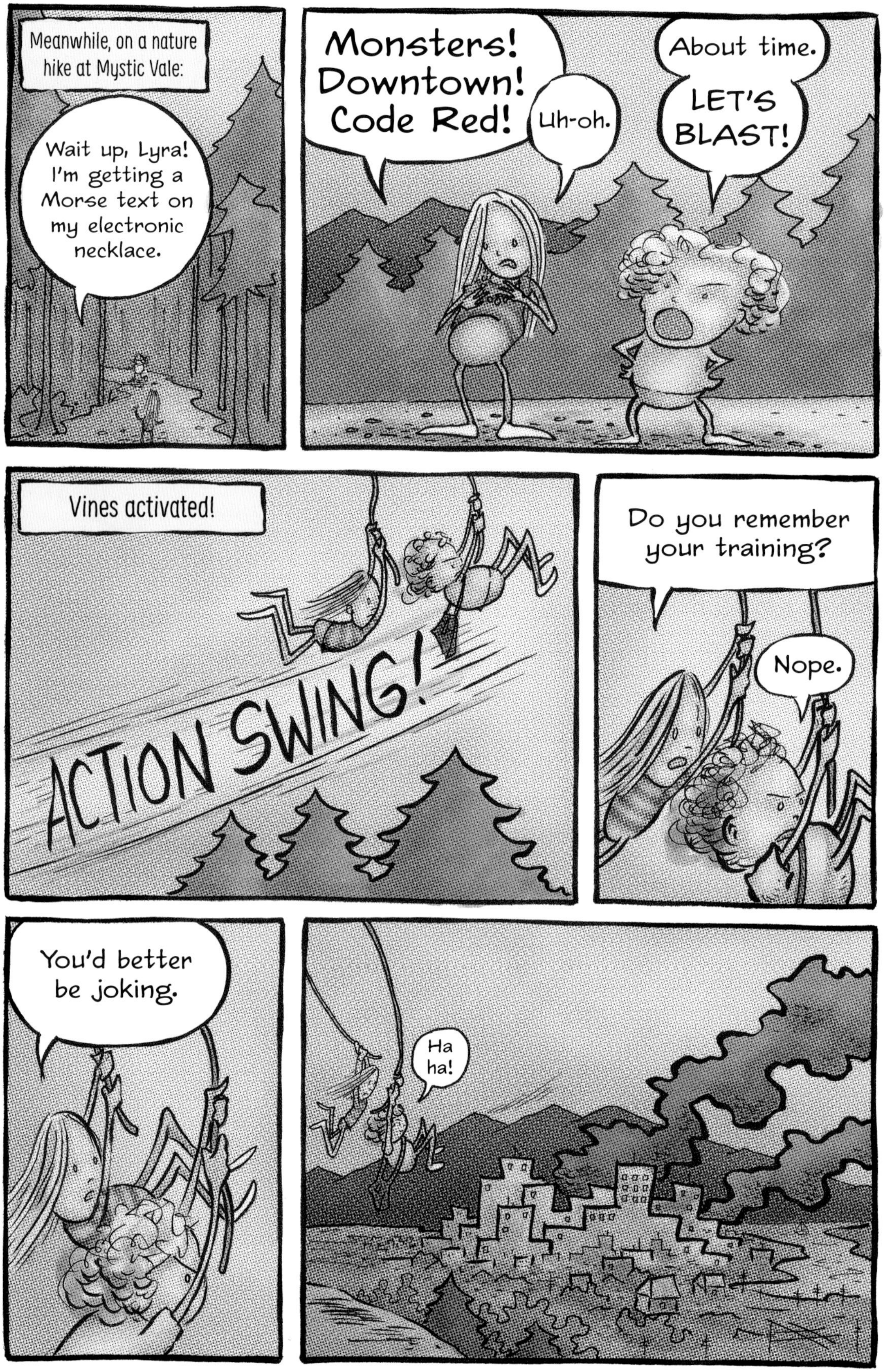
Meanwhile, on a nature hike at Mystic Vale:
Wait up, Lyra! I'm getting a Morse text on my electronic necklace.
Monsters! Downtown! Code Red!
Uh-oh.
About time.
LET'S BLAST!
Vines activated!
ACTION SWING!
Do you remember your training?
Nope.
You'd better be joking.
Ha ha!

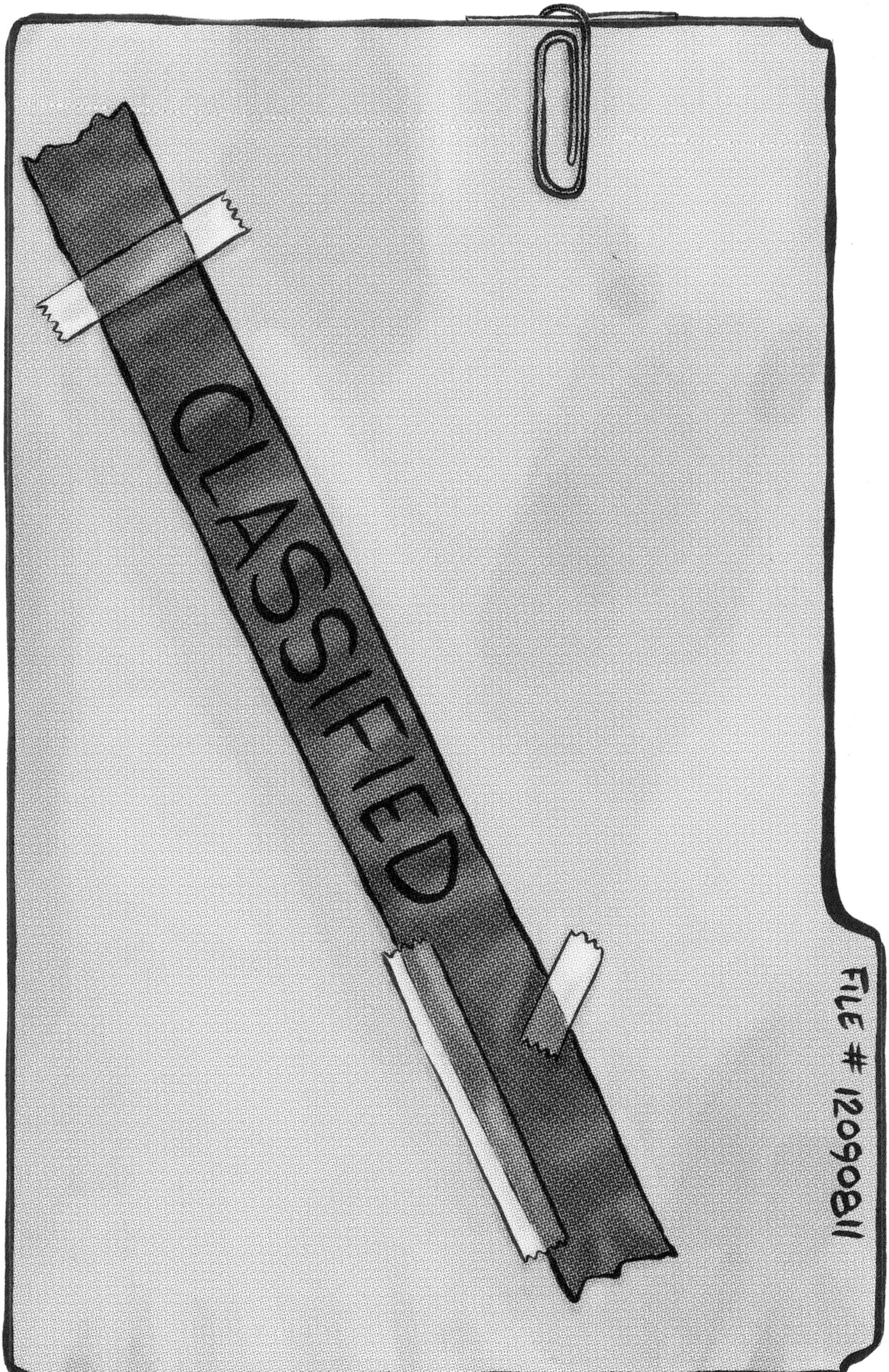
CLASSIFIED
FILE # 12090811

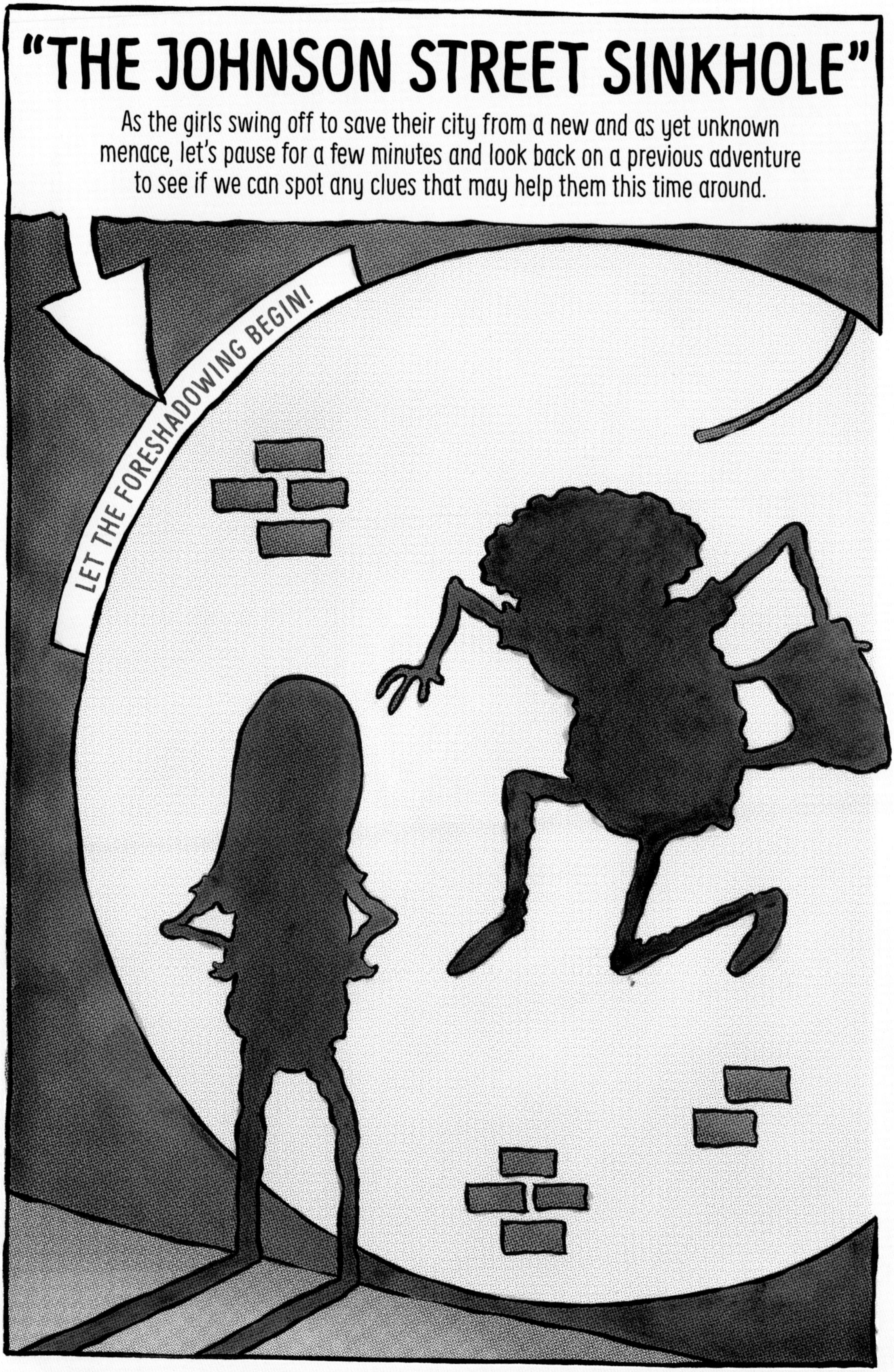
"THE JOHNSON STREET SINKHOLE"
As the girls swing off to save their city from a new and as yet unknown menace, let's pause for a few minutes and look back on a previous adventure to see if we can spot any clues that may help them this time around.
LET THE FORESHADOWING BEGIN!

Police tape doesn't apply to those who can walk underneath it without stooping.

Just because I made that up doesn't mean it isn't true.

My sister and I arrive on the scene at exactly midnight, and the city is silent with curfew.

The radio reports were right. A sinkhole formed at the intersection of Johnson and Douglas Streets about an hour ago, but nobody will do anything about it until morning.

DO NOT CROS

Lyra and I love getting a jump on the authorities.

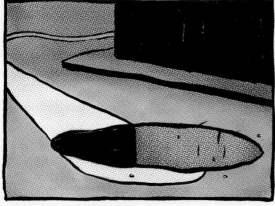

Speaking of jump...

Are you ready?

BAG TOSS!

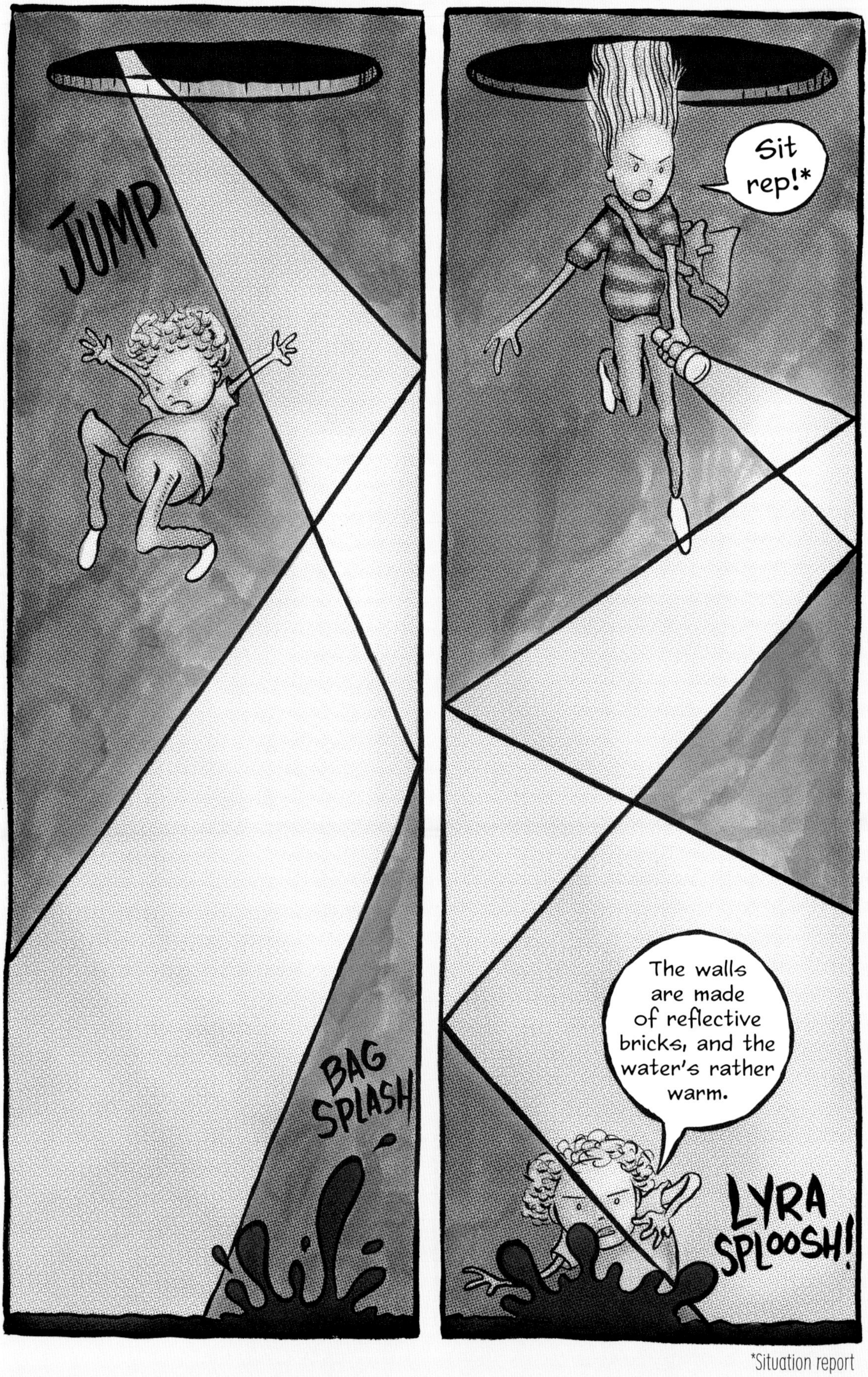

JUMP
BAG SPLASH
Sit rep!*
The walls are made of reflective bricks, and the water's rather warm.
LYRA SPLOOSH!

*Situation report

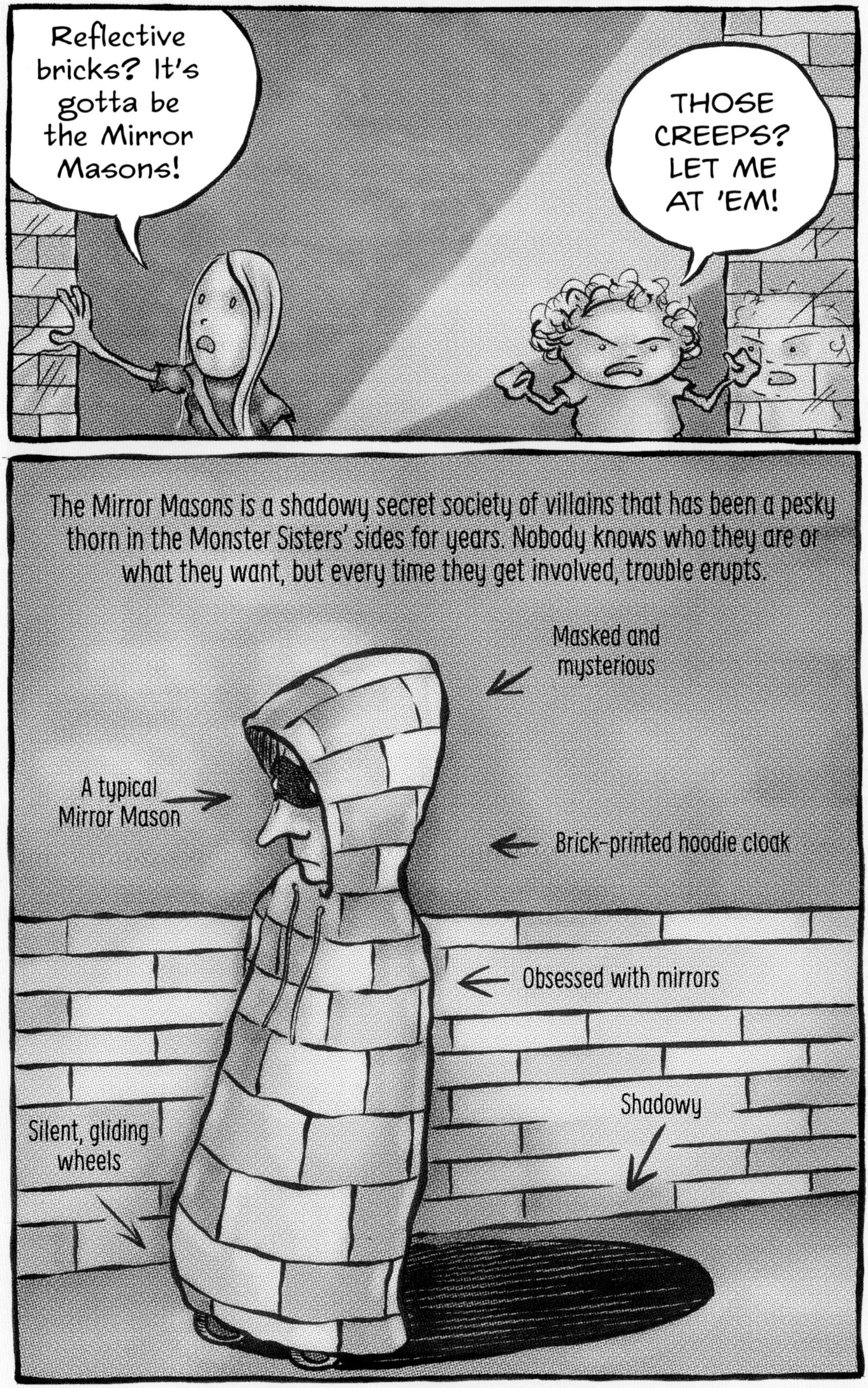

Reflective bricks? It's gotta be the Mirror Masons!
THOSE CREEPS? LET ME AT 'EM!
The Mirror Masons is a shadowy secret society of villains that has been a pesky thorn in the Monster Sisters' sides for years. Nobody knows who they are or what they want, but every time they get involved, trouble erupts.
Masked and mysterious
A typical Mirror Mason
Brick-printed hoodie cloak
Obsessed with mirrors
Silent, gliding wheels
Shadowy

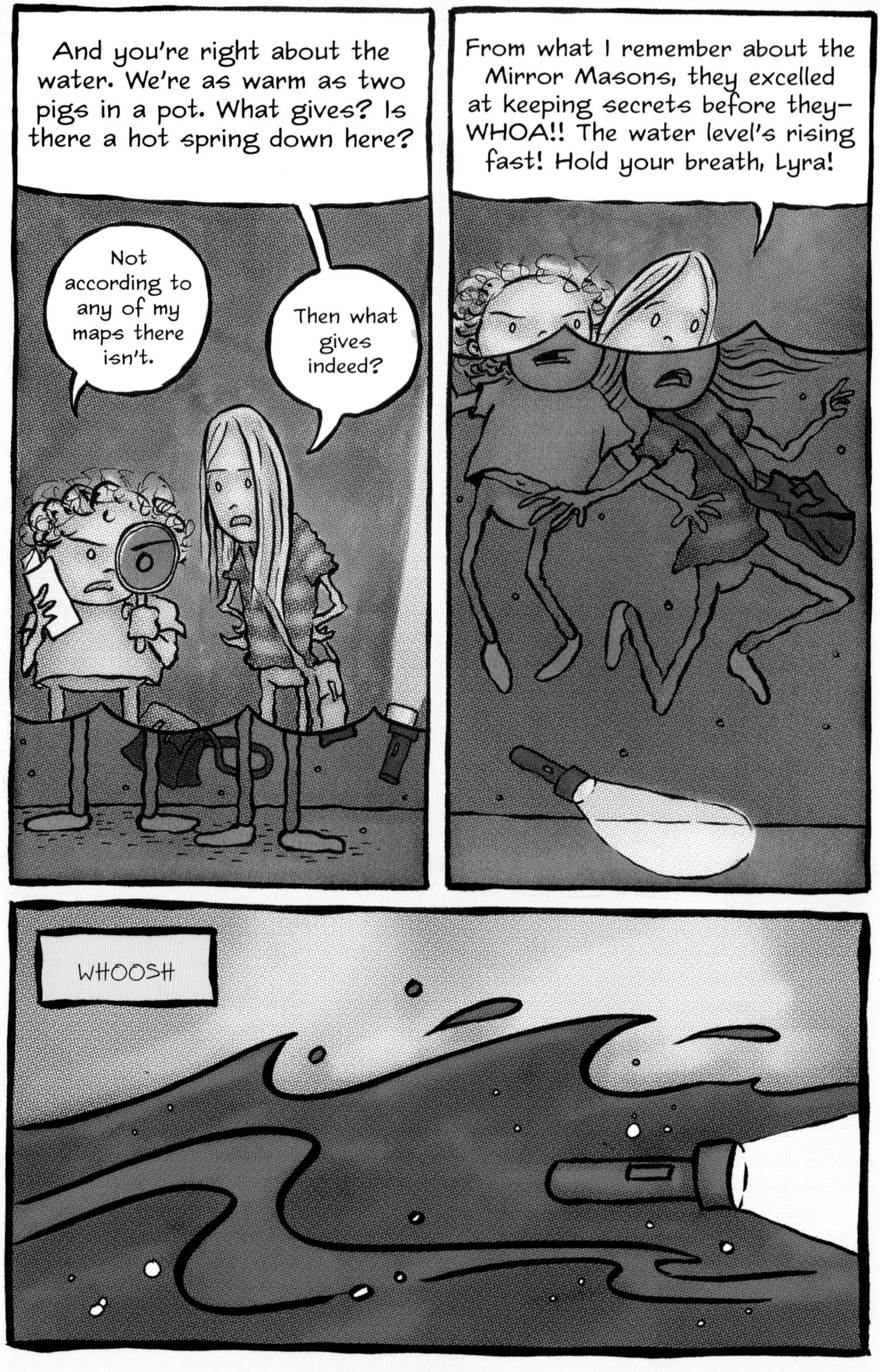
And you're right about the water. We're as warm as two pigs in a pot. What gives? Is there a hot spring down here?
Not according to any of my maps there isn't.
Then what gives indeed?
From what I remember about the Mirror Masons, they excelled at keeping secrets before they—WHOA!! The water level's rising fast! Hold your breath, Lyra!
WHOOSH

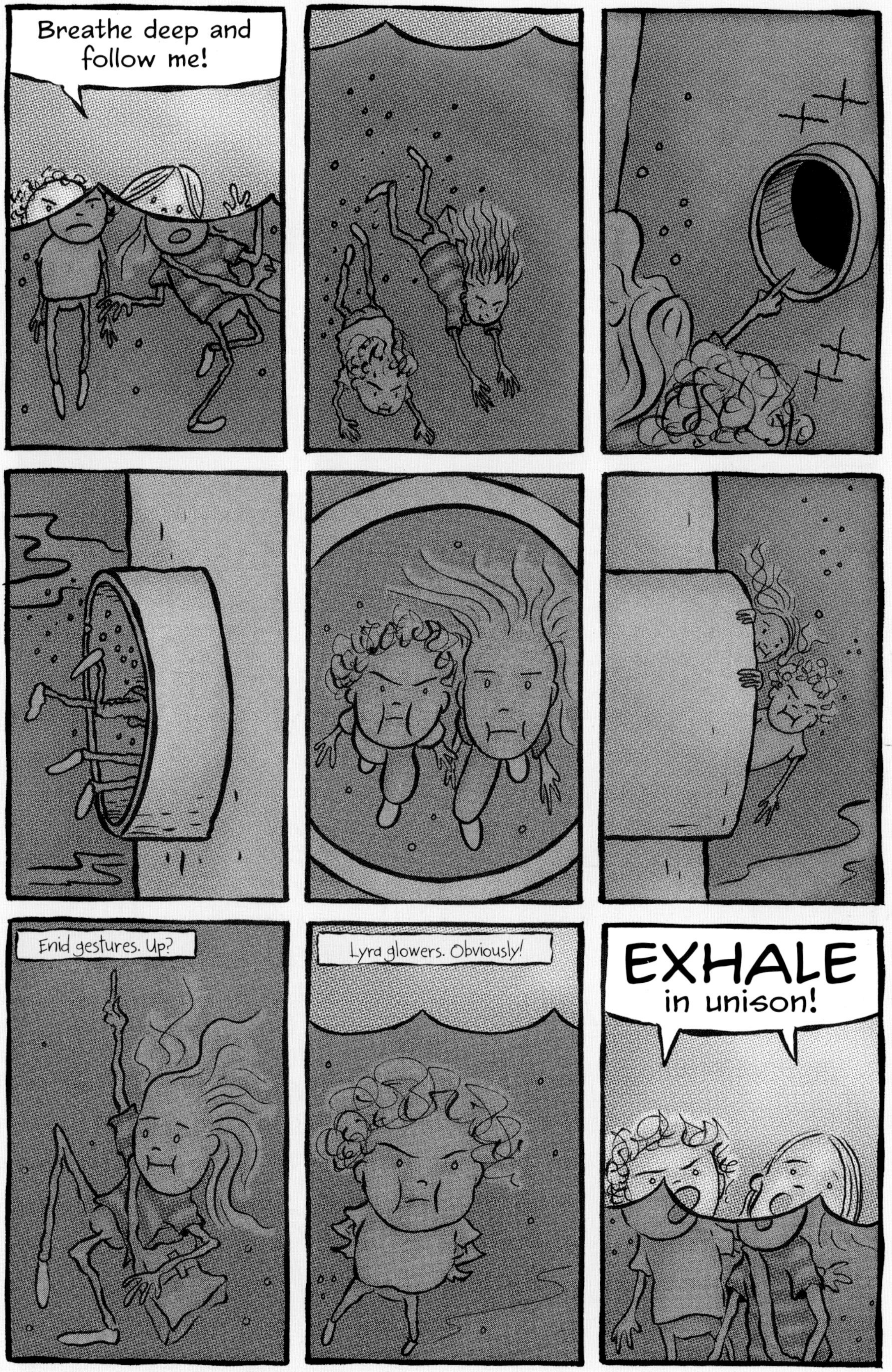

Breathe deep and follow me!
Enid gestures. Up?
Lyra glowers. Obviously!
EXHALE in unison!

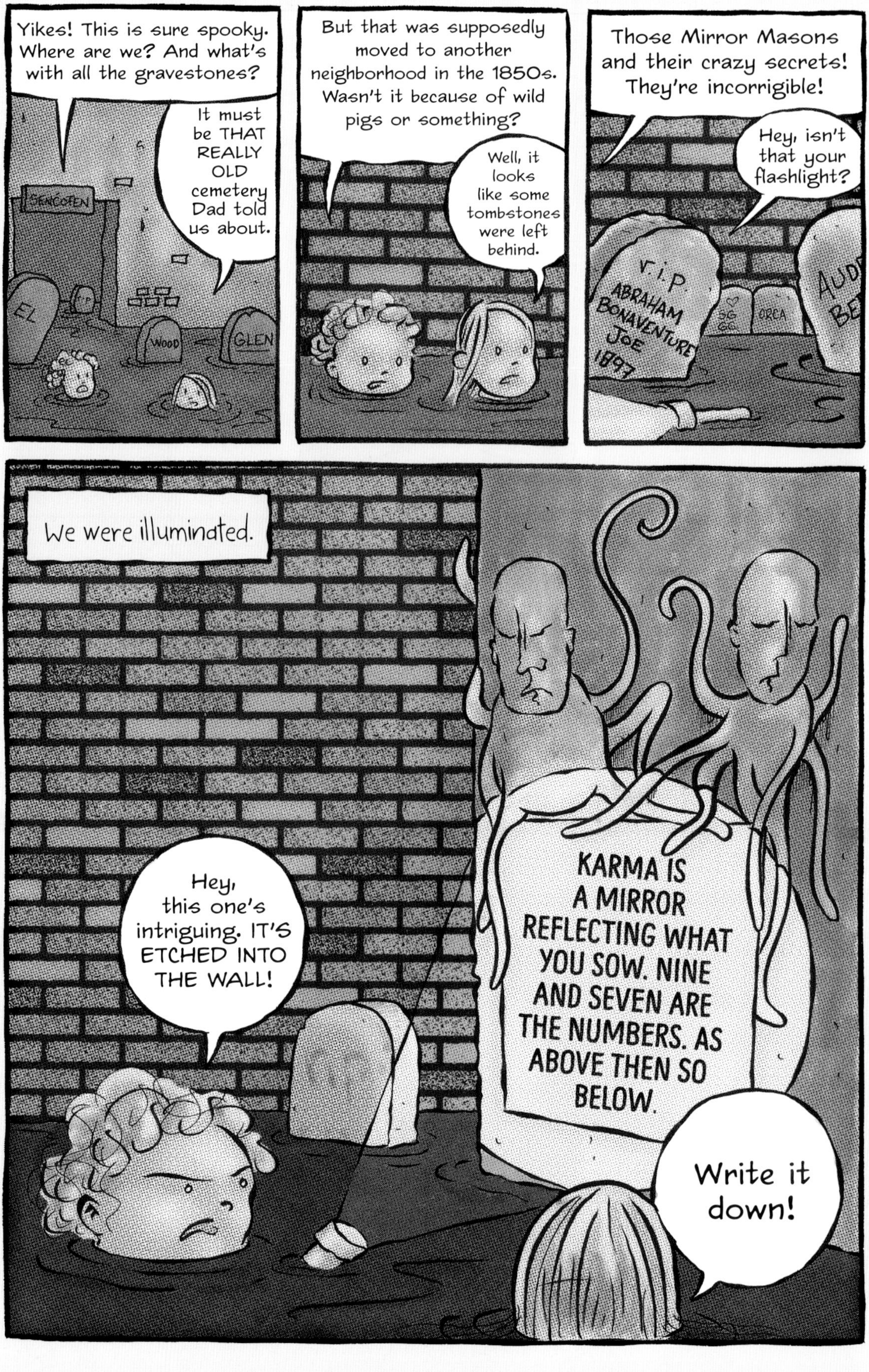
Yikes! This is sure spooky. Where are we? And what's with all the gravestones?
It must be THAT REALLY OLD cemetery Dad told us about.
But that was supposedly moved to another neighborhood in the 1850s. Wasn't it because of wild pigs or something?
Well, it looks like some tombstones were left behind.
Those Mirror Masons and their crazy secrets! They're incorrigible!
Hey, isn't that your flashlight?
r.i.p. ABRAHAM BONAVENTURE JOE 1897
ORCA
We were illuminated.
Hey, this one's intriguing. IT'S ETCHED INTO THE WALL!
KARMA IS A MIRROR REFLECTING WHAT YOU SOW. NINE AND SEVEN ARE THE NUMBERS. AS ABOVE THEN SO BELOW.
Write it down!

AND IN THE NEXT CHAMBER:

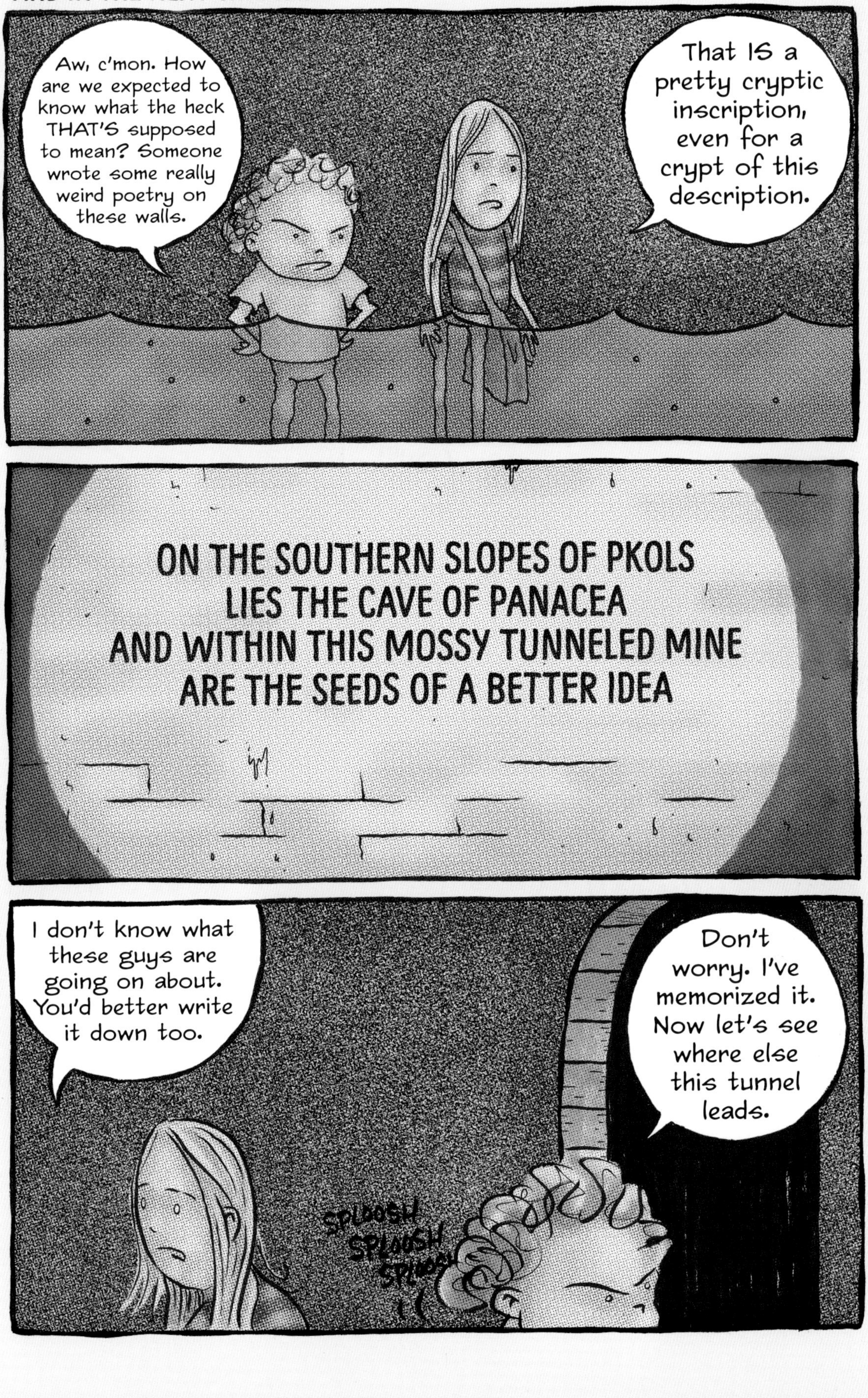
Aw, c'mon. How are we expected to know what the heck THAT'S supposed to mean? Someone wrote some really weird poetry on these walls.
That IS a pretty cryptic inscription, even for a crypt of this description.
ON THE SOUTHERN SLOPES OF PKOLS
LIES THE CAVE OF PANACEA
AND WITHIN THIS MOSSY TUNNELED MINE
ARE THE SEEDS OF A BETTER IDEA
I don't know what these guys are going on about. You'd better write it down too.
Don't worry. I've memorized it. Now let's see where else this tunnel leads.
SPLOOSH
SPLOOSH

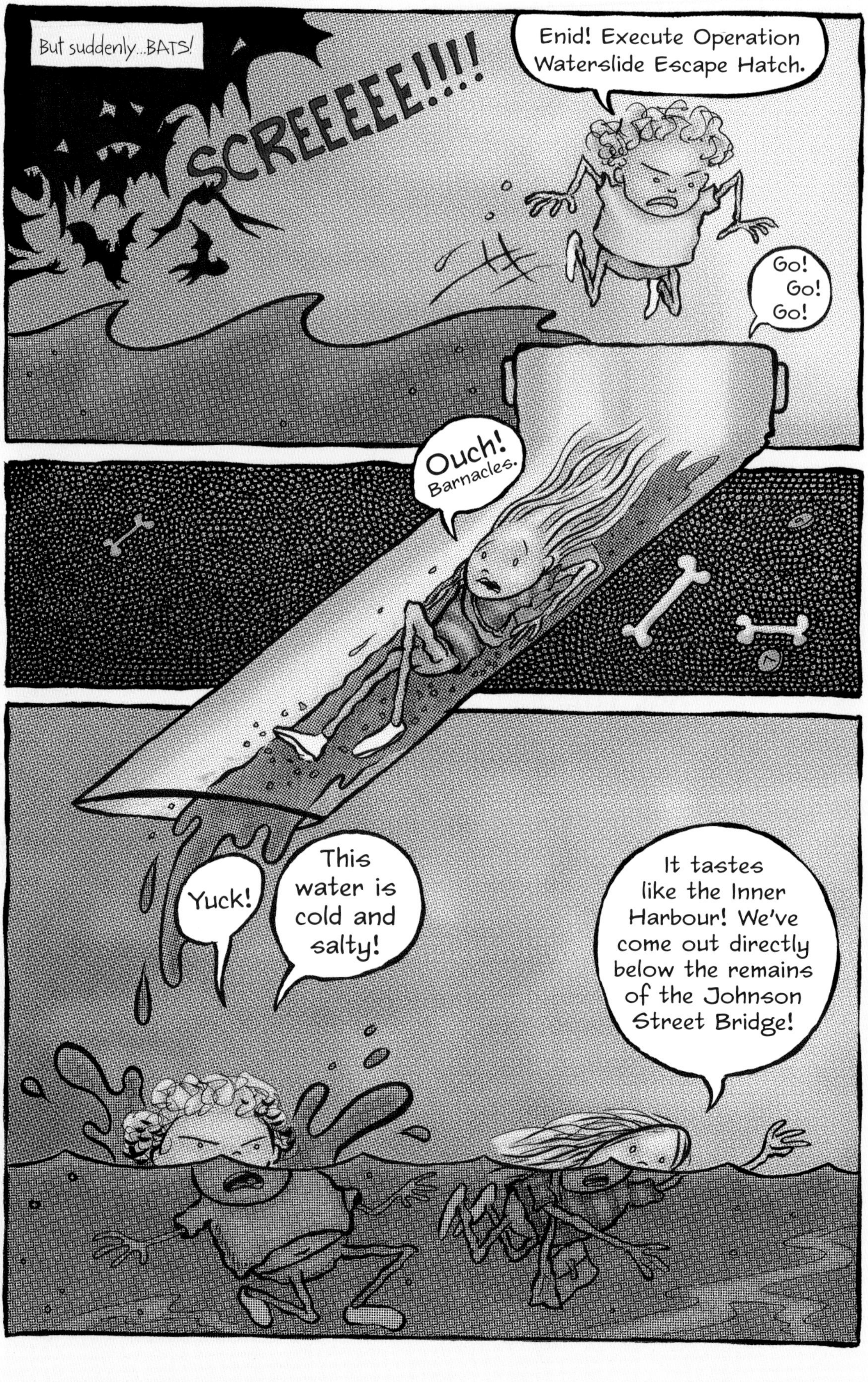
But suddenly...BATS!
SCREEEEEE!!!!
Enid! Execute Operation Waterslide Escape Hatch.
Go! Go! Go!
Ouch! Barnacles.
Yuck!
This water is cold and salty!
It tastes like the Inner Harbour! We've come out directly below the remains of the Johnson Street Bridge!

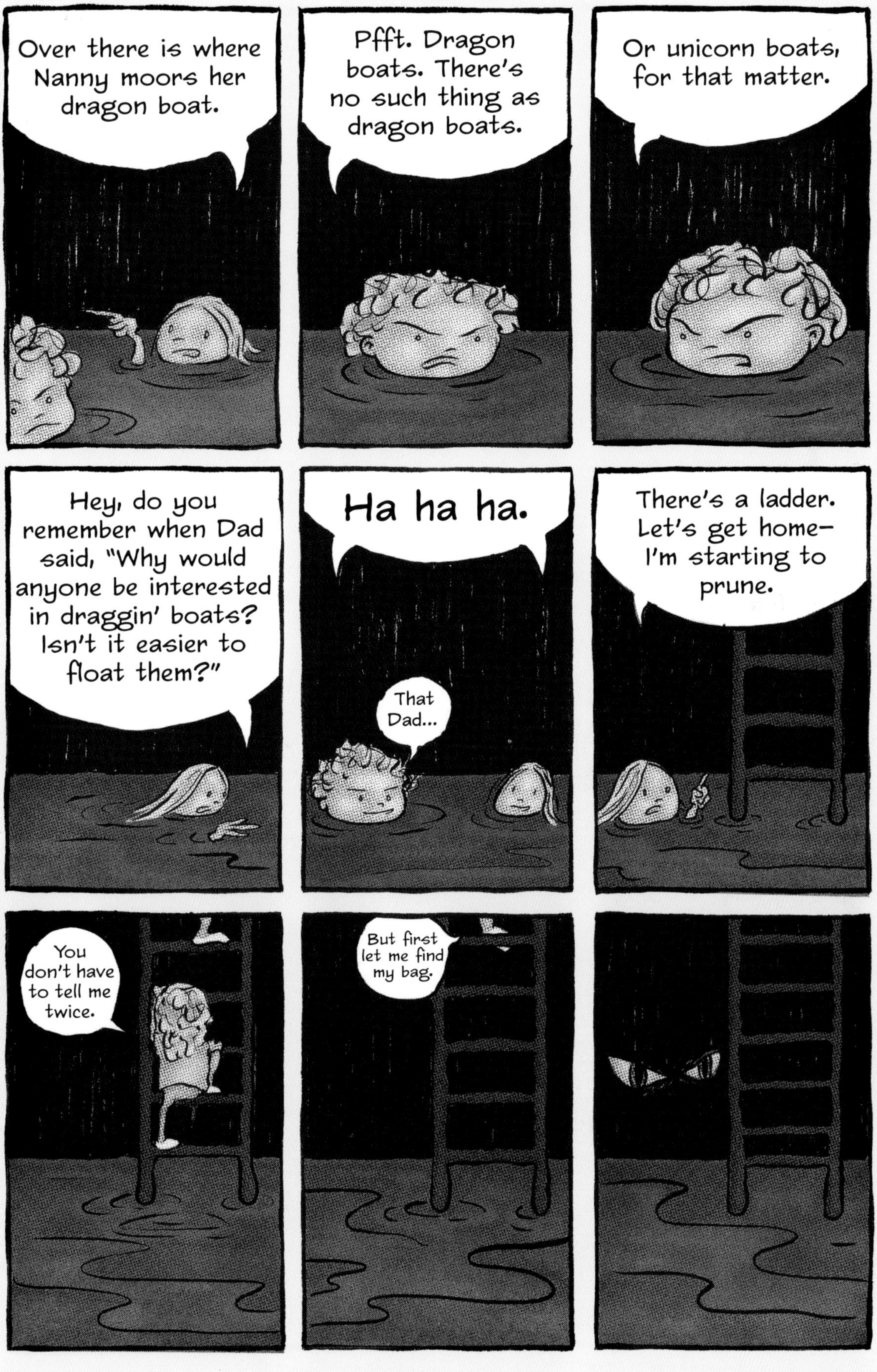
Over there is where Nanny moors her dragon boat.
Pfft. Dragon boats. There's no such thing as dragon boats.
Or unicorn boats, for that matter.
Hey, do you remember when Dad said, "Why would anyone be interested in draggin' boats? Isn't it easier to float them?"
Ha ha ha.
That Dad...
There's a ladder. Let's get home— I'm starting to prune.
You don't have to tell me twice.
But first let me find my bag.

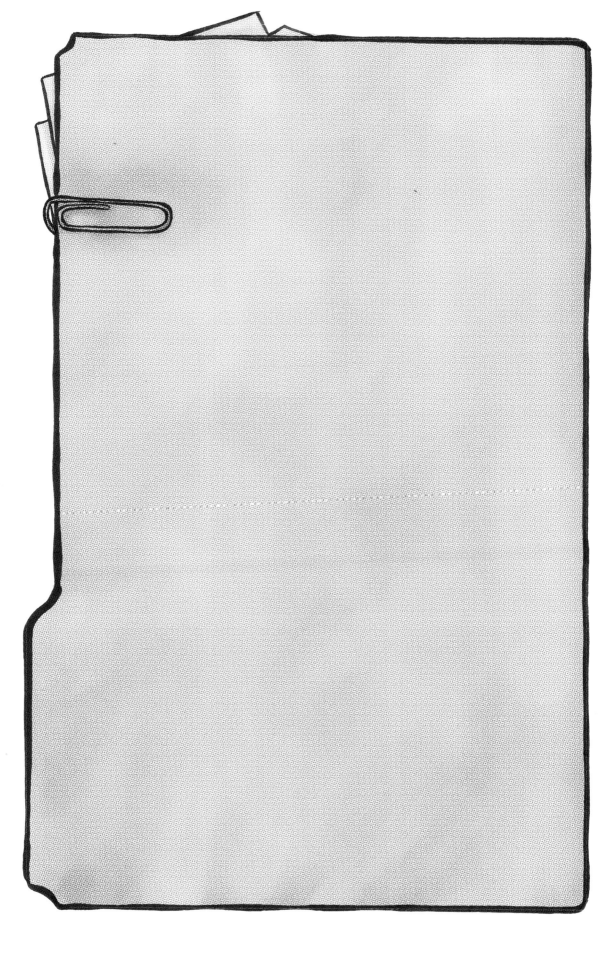

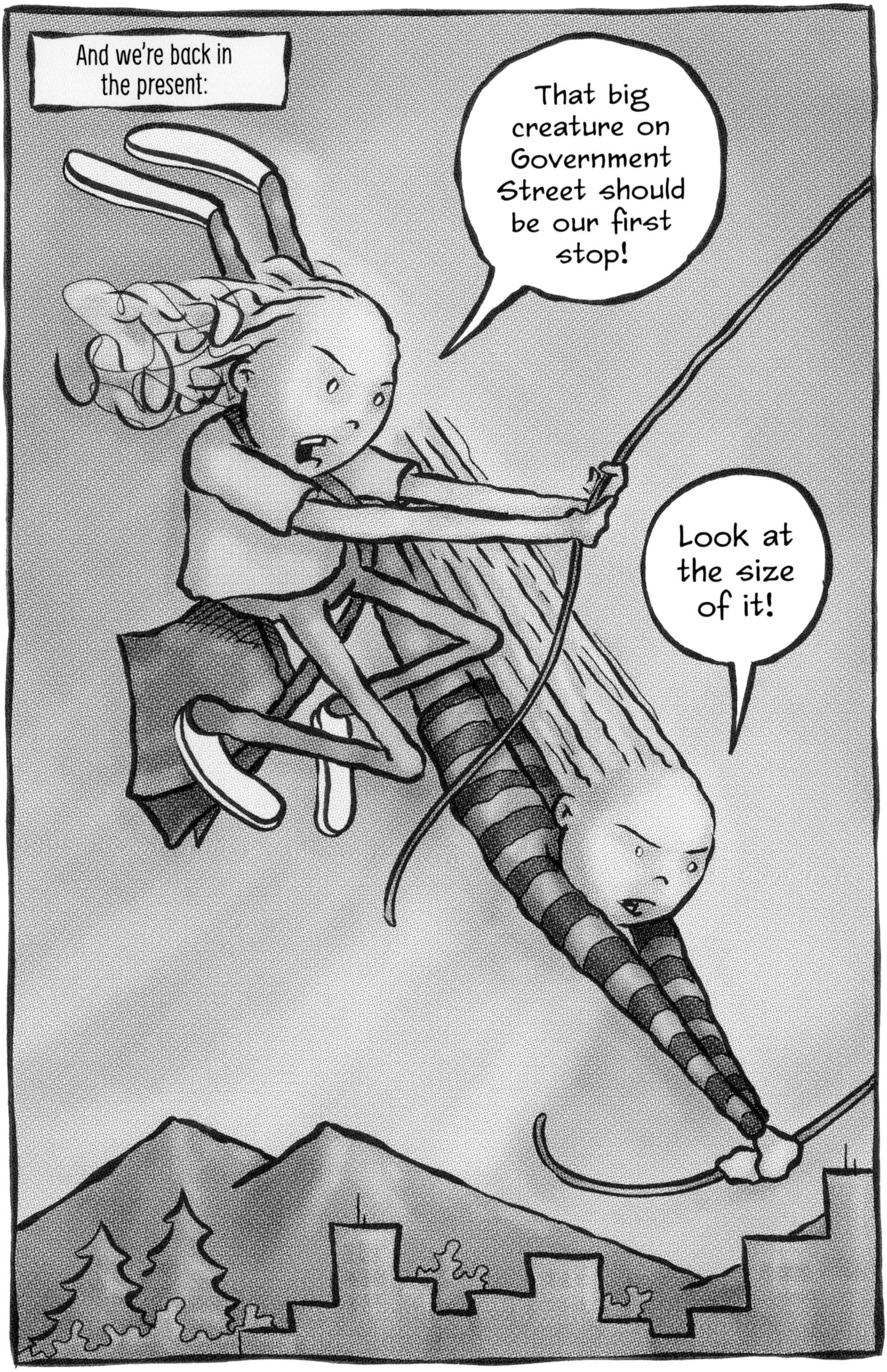
And we're back in the present:
That big creature on Government Street should be our first stop!
Look at the size of it!

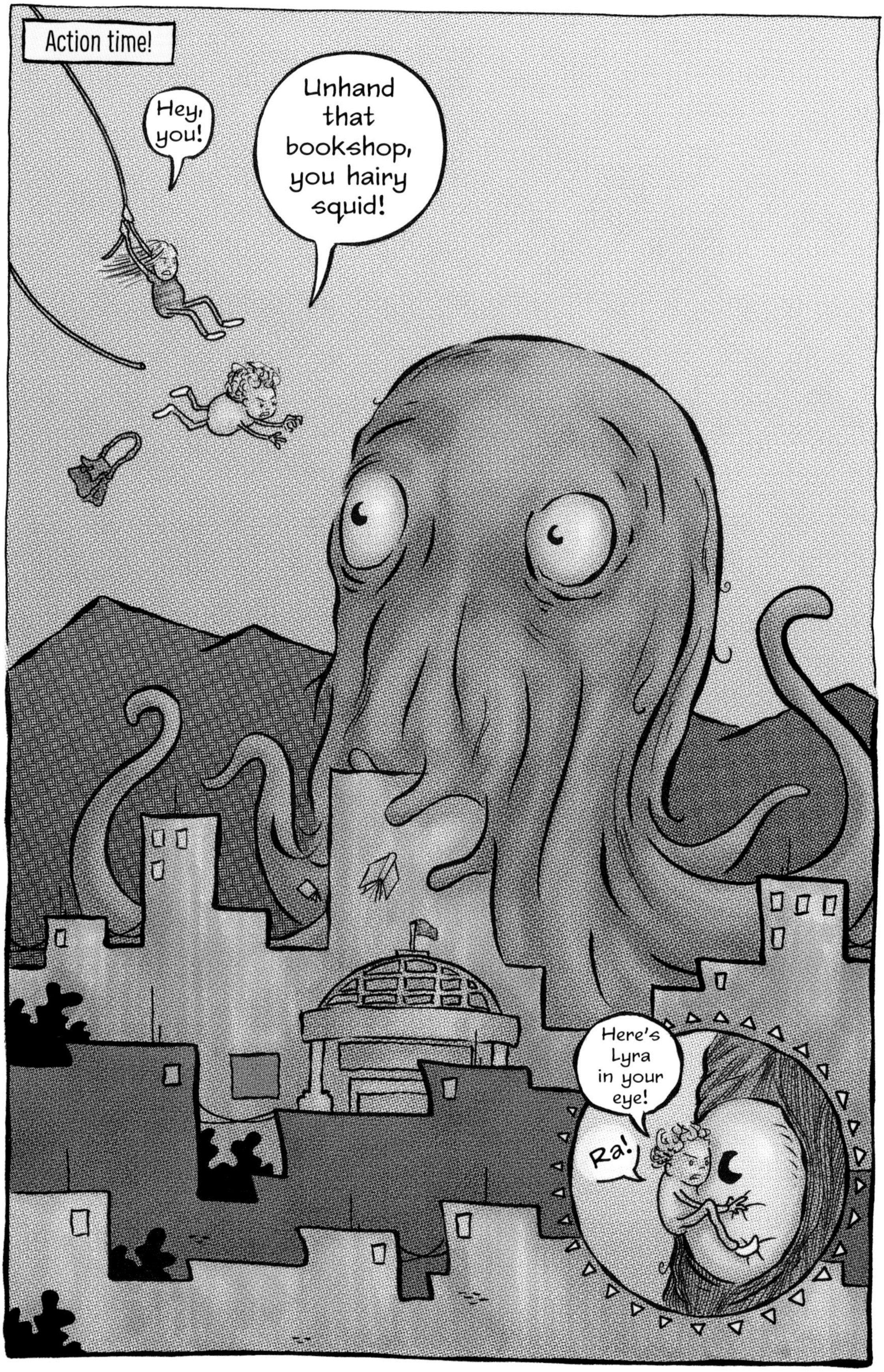
Action time!
Hey, you!
Unhand that bookshop, you hairy squid!
Here's Lyra in your eye!
Ra!

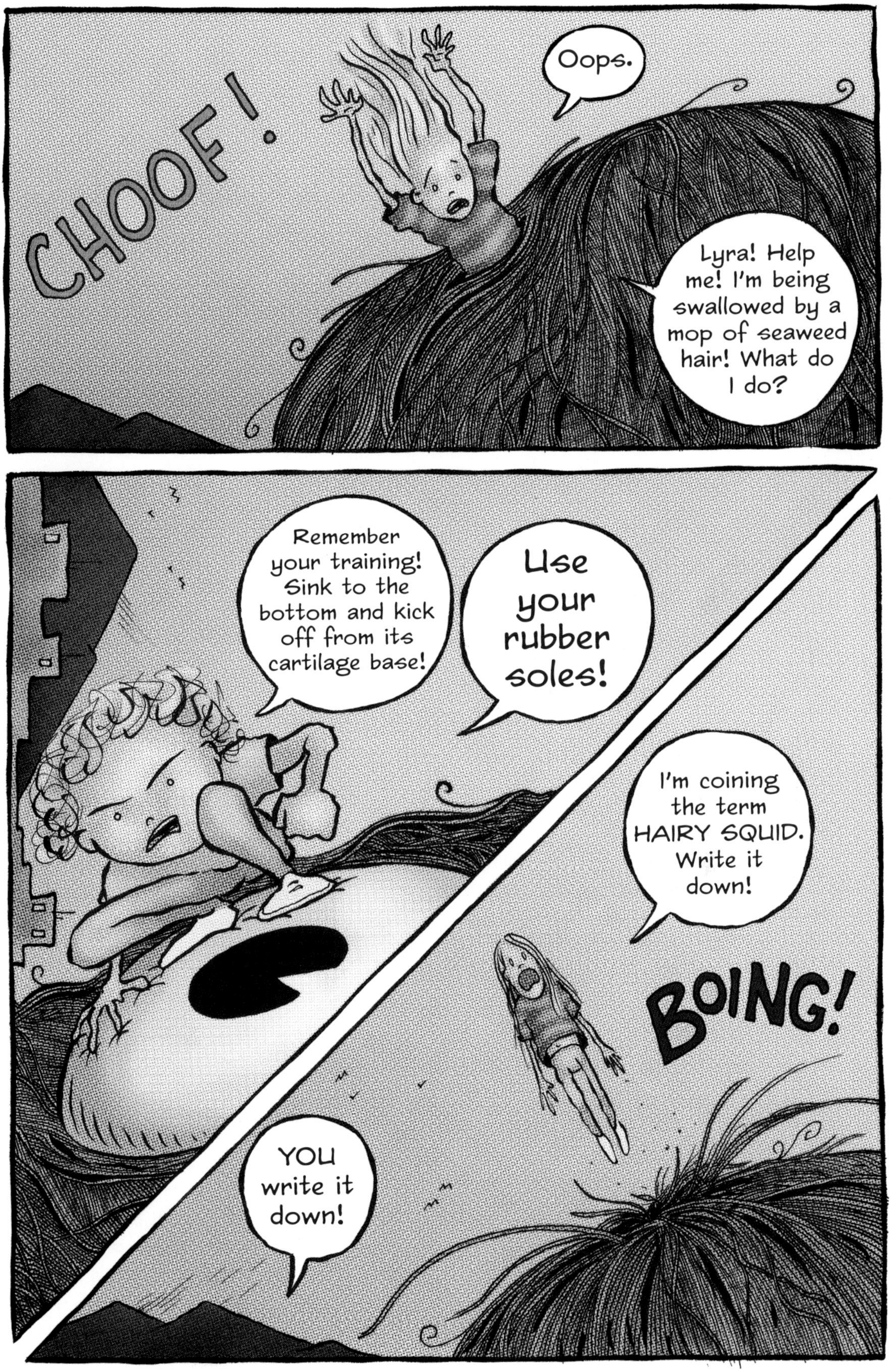
CHOOF!
Oops.
Lyra! Help me! I'm being swallowed by a mop of seaweed hair! What do I do?
Remember your training! Sink to the bottom and kick off from its cartilage base!
Use your rubber soles!
I'm coining the term HAIRY SQUID. Write it down!
BOING!
YOU write it down!

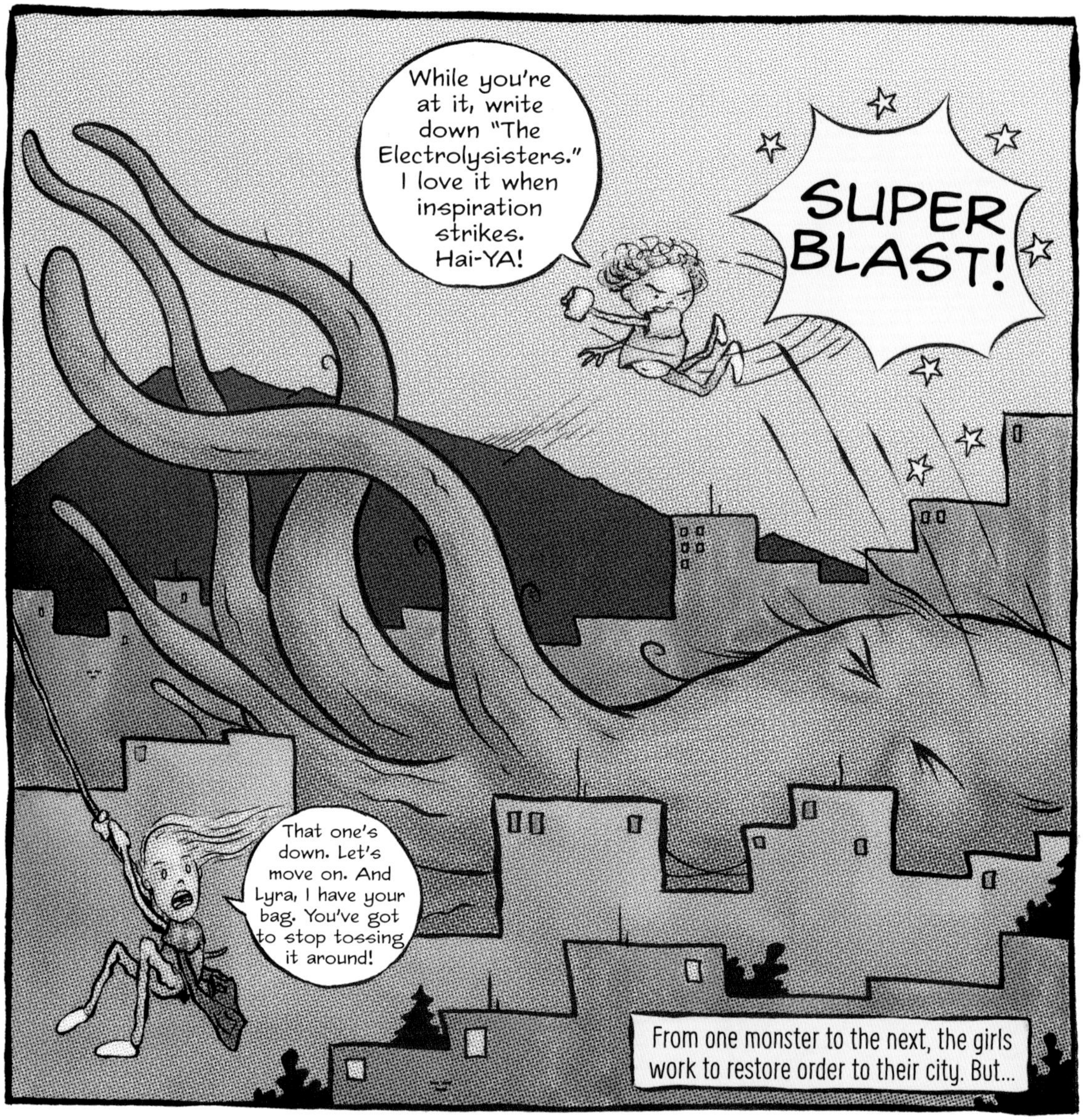
While you're at it, write down "The Electrolysisters." I love it when inspiration strikes. Hai-YA!
SUPER BLAST!
That one's down. Let's move on. And Lyra, I have your bag. You've got to stop tossing it around!
From one monster to the next, the girls work to restore order to their city. But...

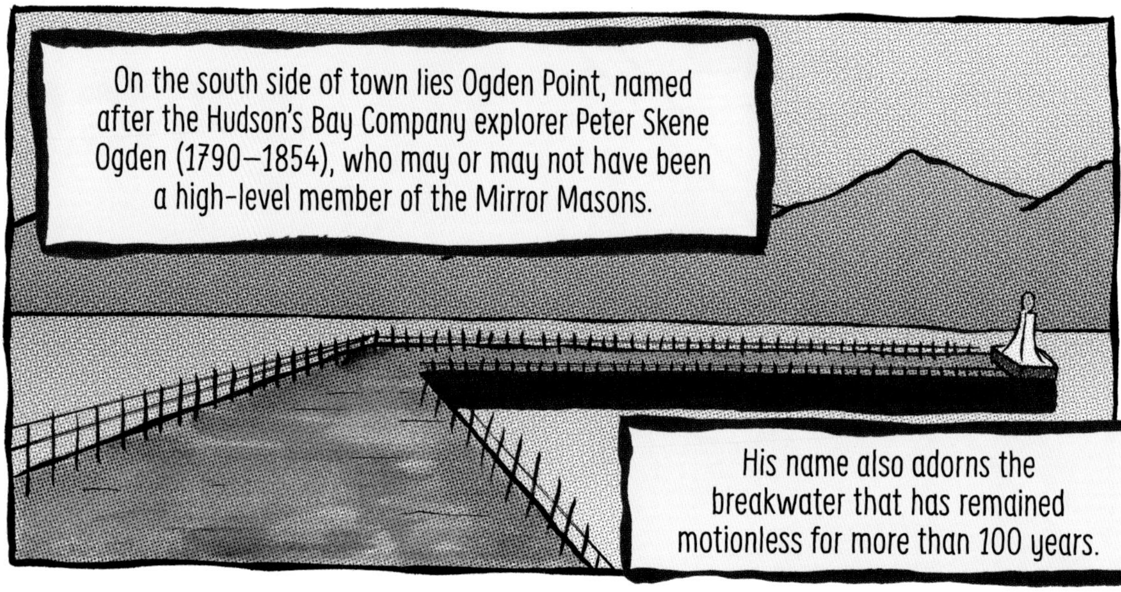
On the south side of town lies Ogden Point, named after the Hudson's Bay Company explorer Peter Skene Ogden (1790–1854), who may or may not have been a high-level member of the Mirror Masons.
His name also adorns the breakwater that has remained motionless for more than 100 years.

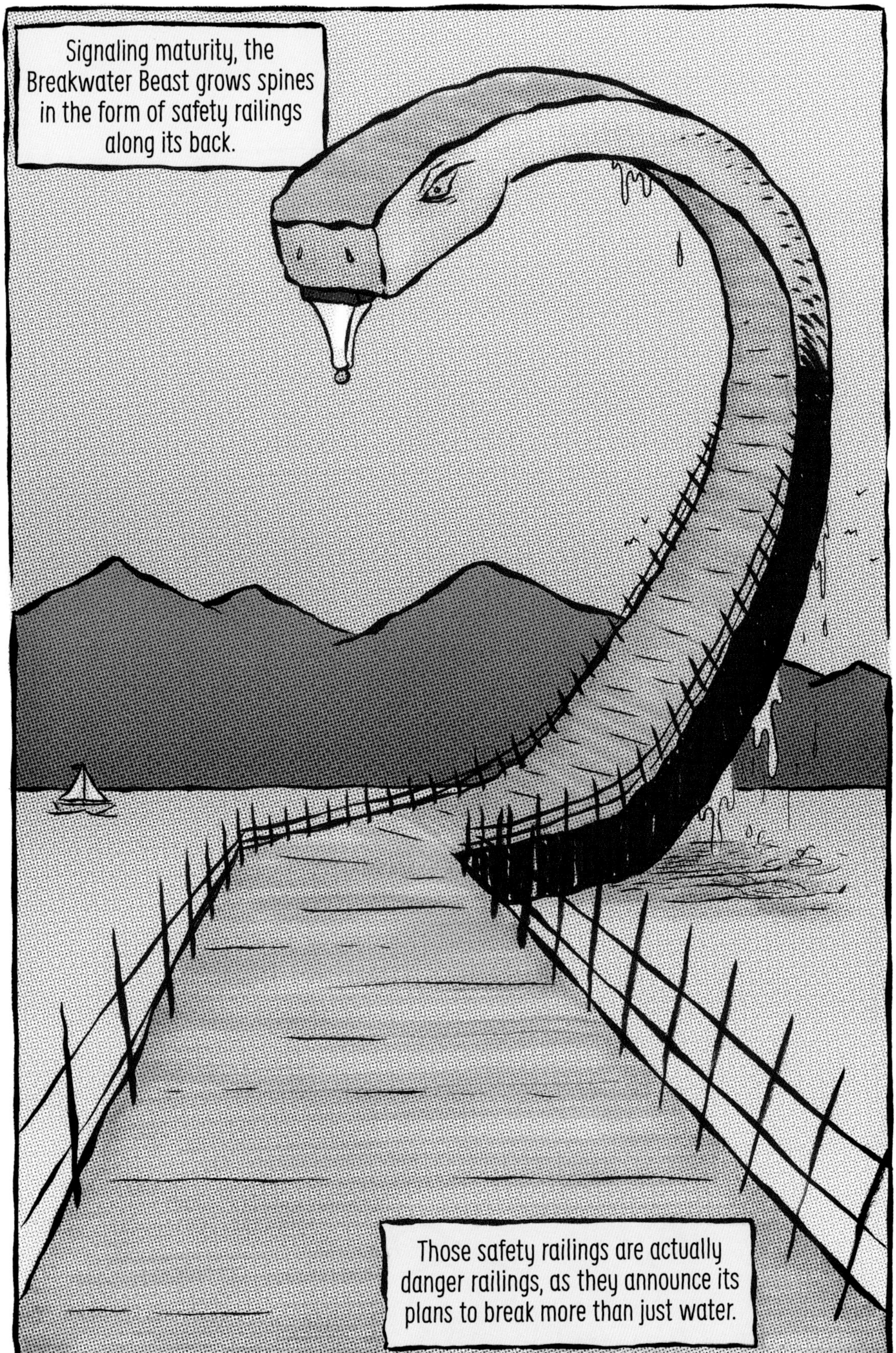
Signaling maturity, the Breakwater Beast grows spines in the form of safety railings along its back.
Those safety railings are actually danger railings, as they announce its plans to break more than just water.

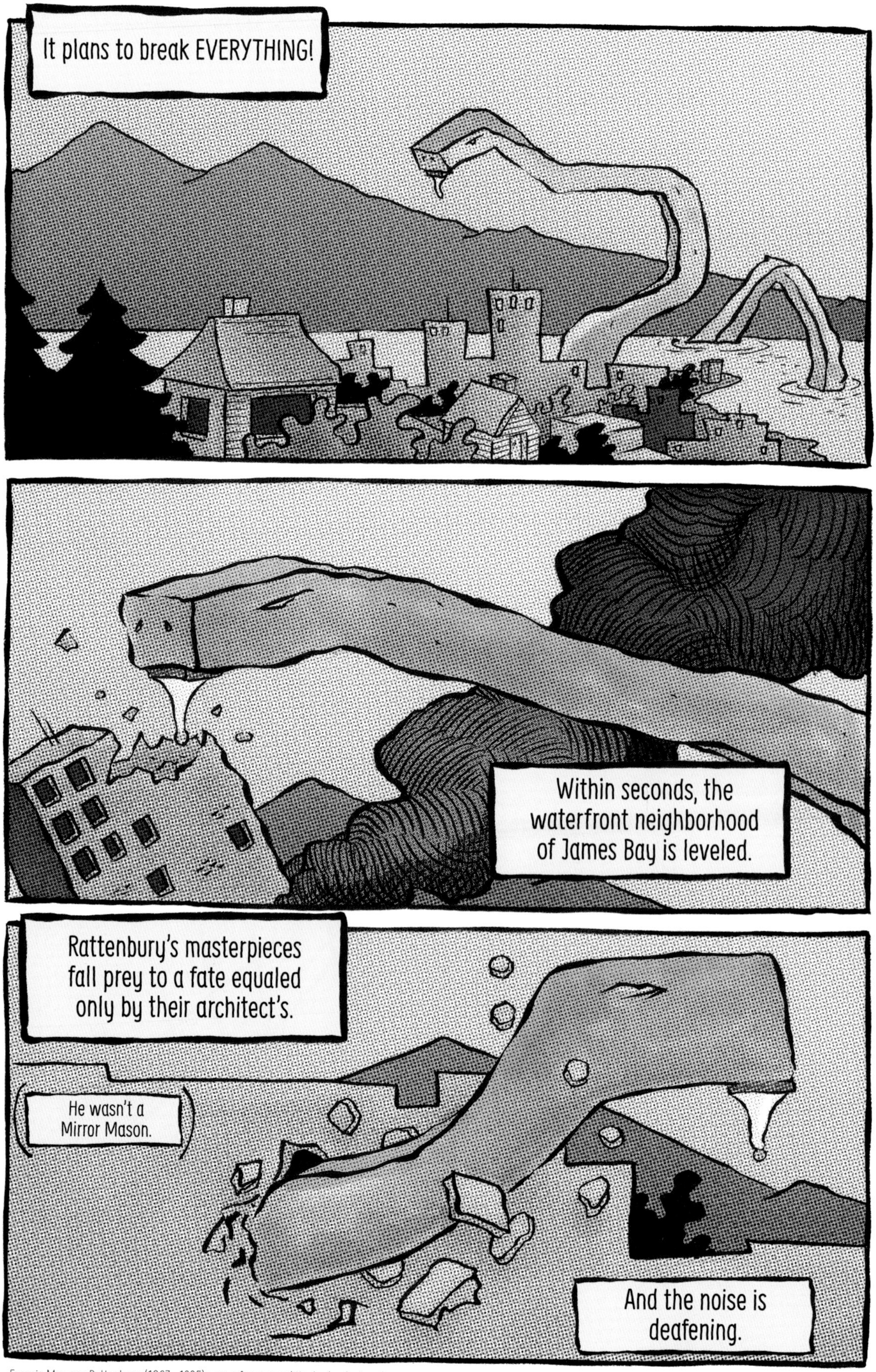
It plans to break EVERYTHING!
Within seconds, the waterfront neighborhood of James Bay is leveled.
Rattenbury's masterpieces fall prey to a fate equaled only by their architect's.
He wasn't a Mirror Mason.
And the noise is deafening.

Francis Mawson Rattenbury (1867–1935) was a famous architect who designed many of Victoria's finest buildings (including the Parliament Buildings and the Empress Hotel). His life was cut short by circumstances still shrouded in mystery and intrigue.

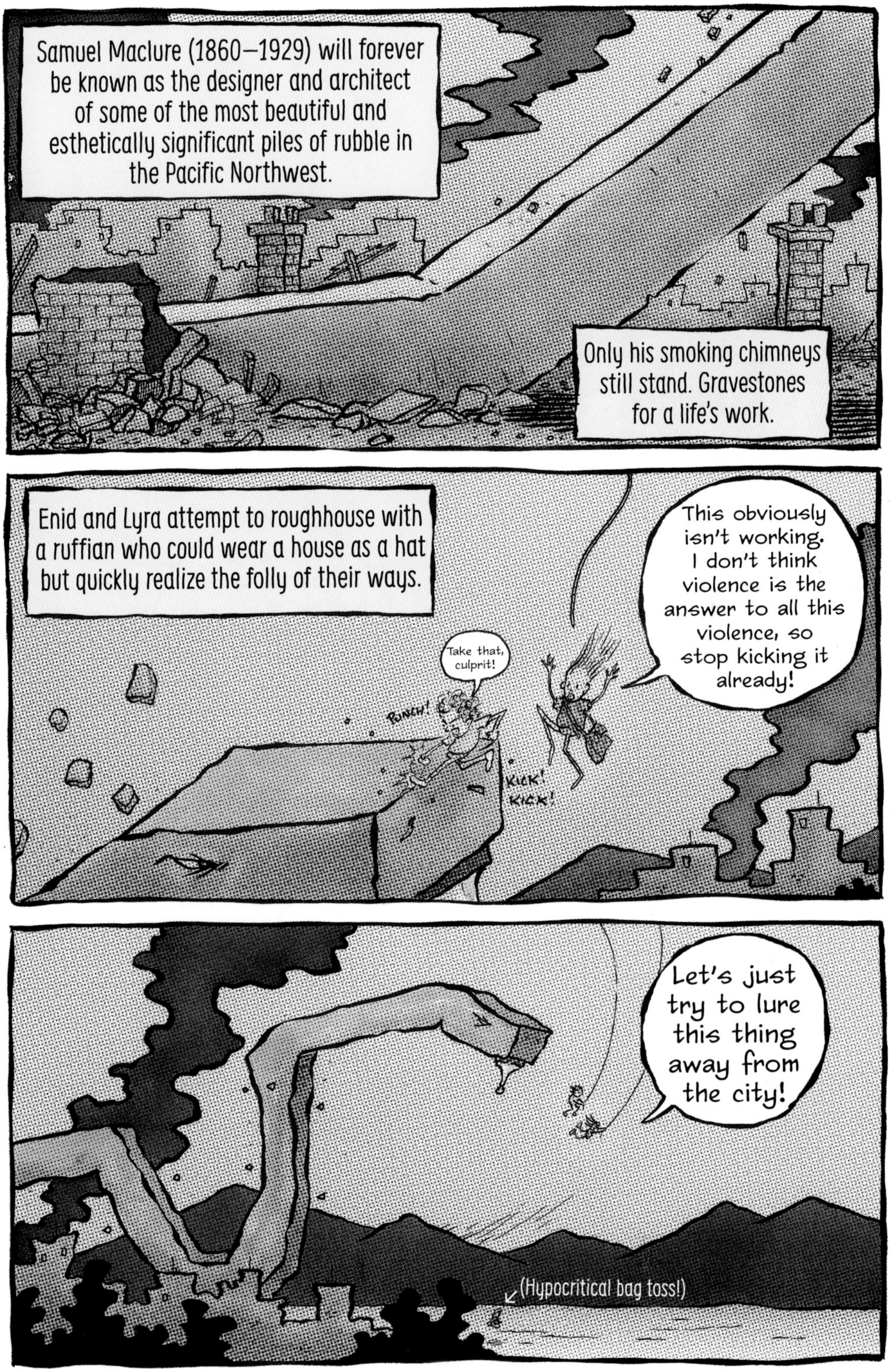
Samuel Maclure (1860–1929) will forever be known as the designer and architect of some of the most beautiful and esthetically significant piles of rubble in the Pacific Northwest.
Only his smoking chimneys still stand. Gravestones for a life's work.
Enid and Lyra attempt to roughhouse with a ruffian who could wear a house as a hat but quickly realize the folly of their ways.
Take that, culprit!
PUNCH!
KICK! KICK!
This obviously isn't working. I don't think violence is the answer to all this violence, so stop kicking it already!
Let's just try to lure this thing away from the city!
(Hypocritical bag toss!)

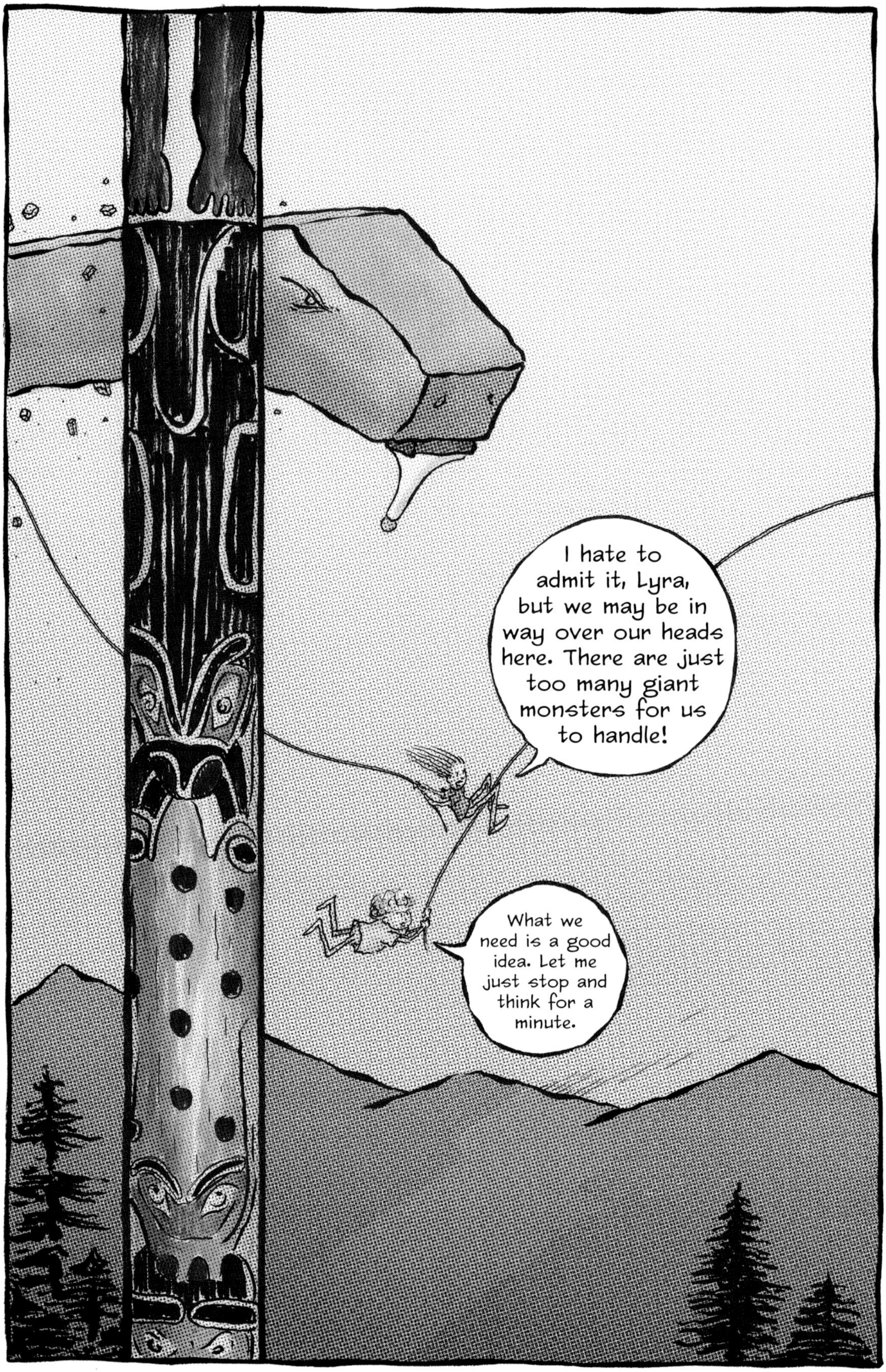
I hate to admit it, Lyra, but we may be in way over our heads here. There are just too many giant monsters for us to handle!
What we need is a good idea. Let me just stop and think for a minute.

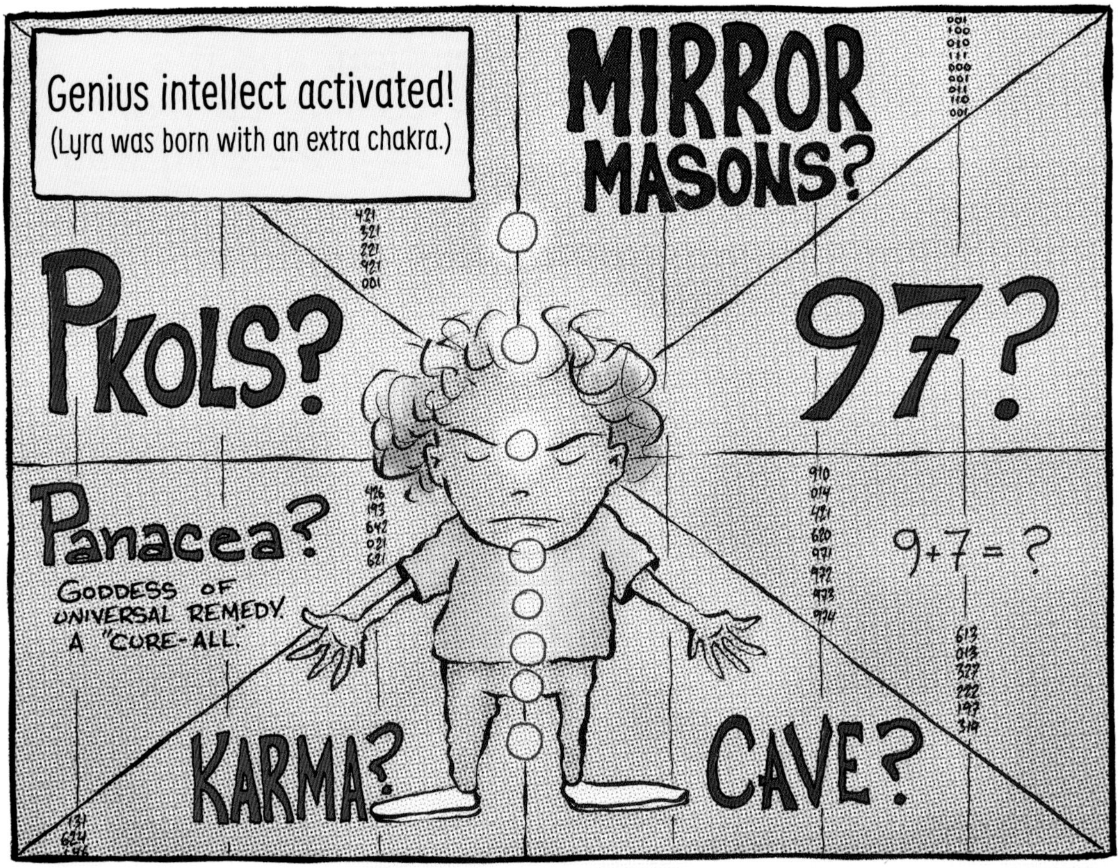

Genius intellect activated!
(Lyra was born with an extra chakra.)
MIRROR MASONS?
PKOLS?
97?
Panacea?
GODDESS OF UNIVERSAL REMEDY. A "CURE-ALL."
9+7=?
KARMA?
CAVE?

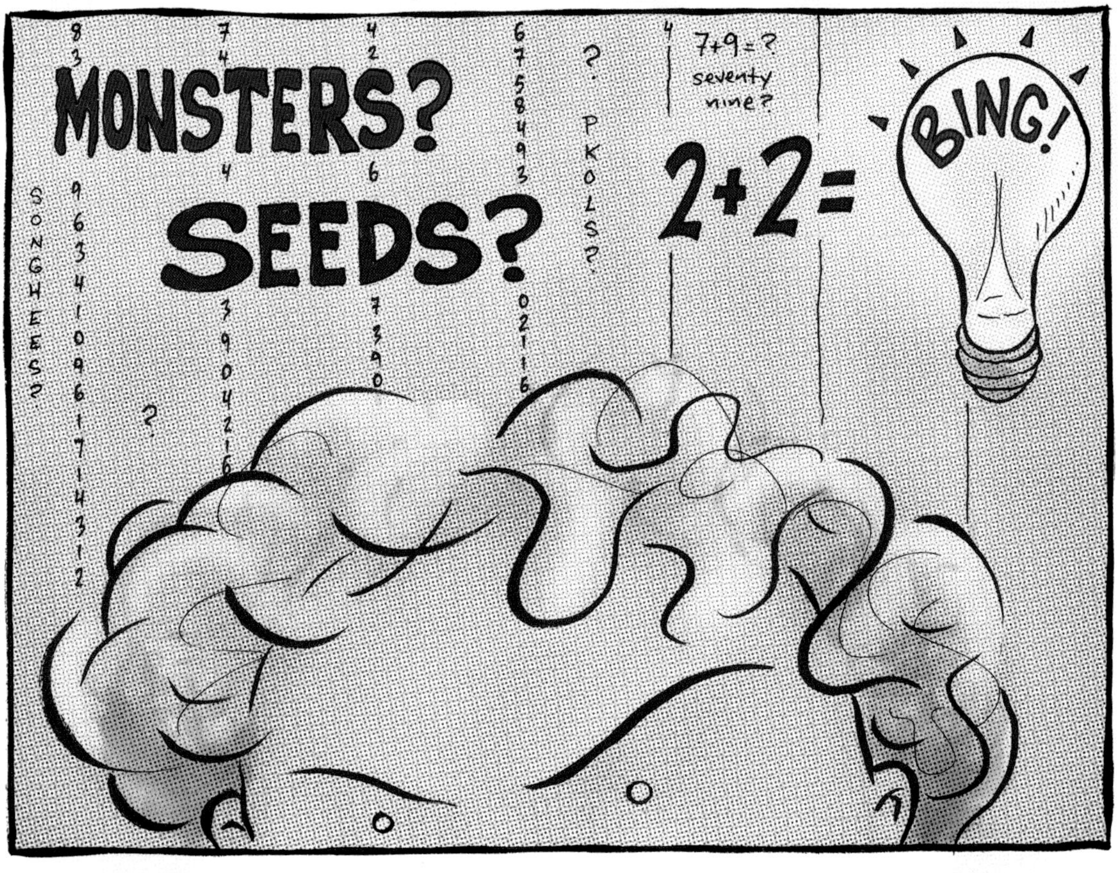

MONSTERS?
7+9=? seventy nine?
SEEDS?
PKOLS?
SONGHEES?
2+2=
BING!

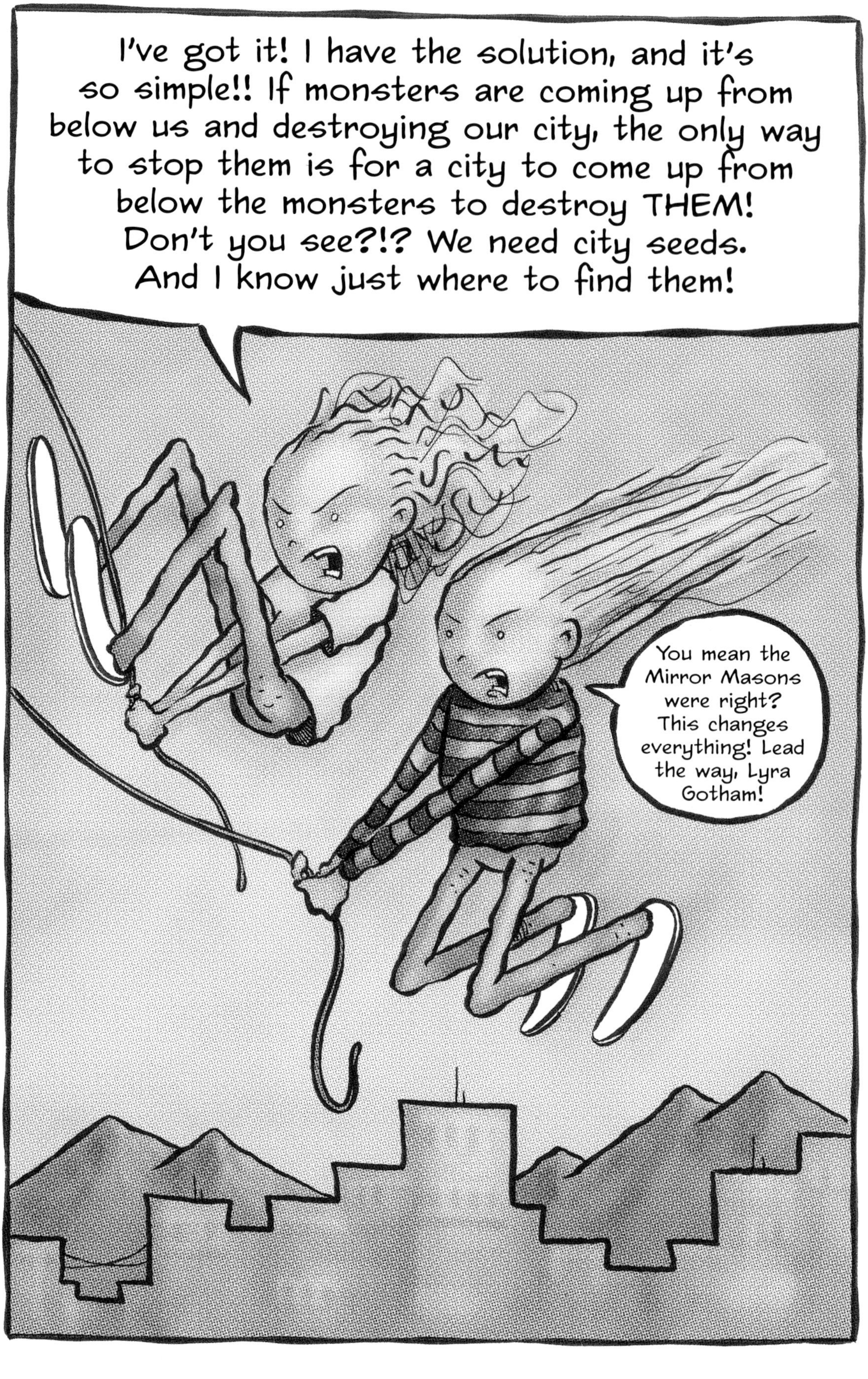
I've got it! I have the solution, and it's so simple!! If monsters are coming up from below us and destroying our city, the only way to stop them is for a city to come up from below the monsters to destroy THEM! Don't you see?!? We need city seeds. And I know just where to find them!
You mean the Mirror Masons were right? This changes everything! Lead the way, Lyra Gotham!

CHAPTER TWO

ALL THINGS MUST BLAST

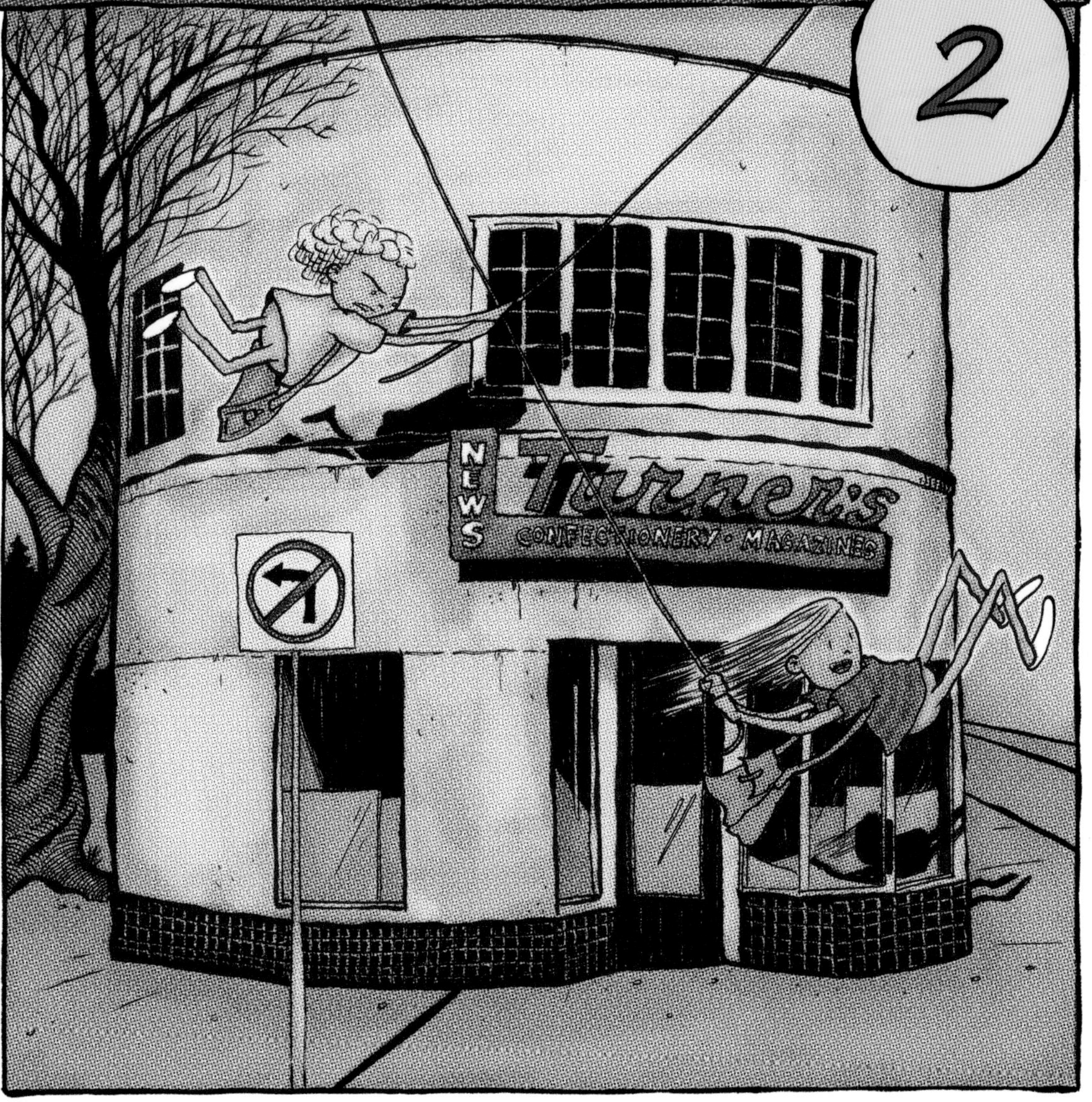

2
NEWS
Turner's
CONFECTIONERY · MAGAZINES

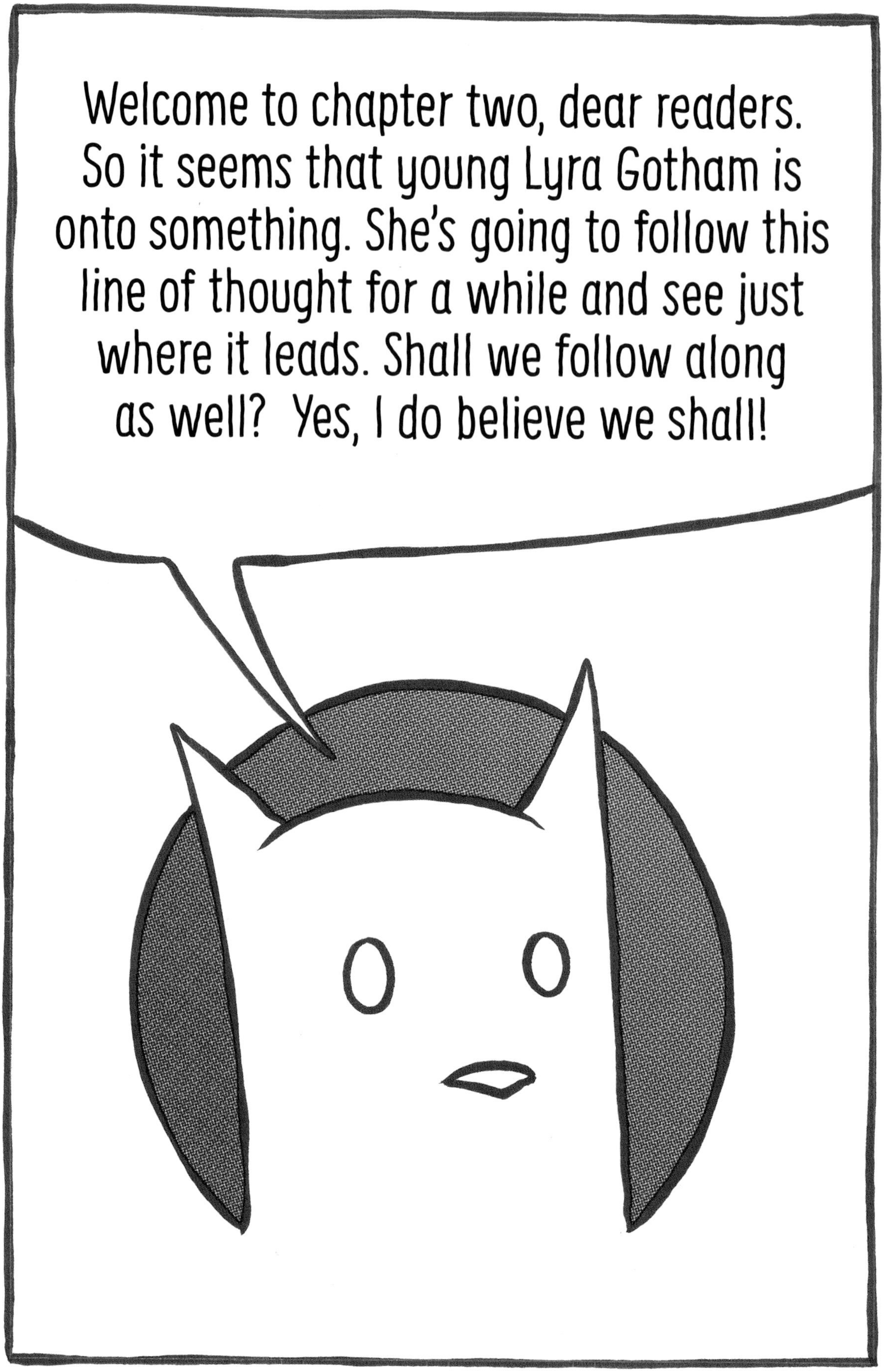
Welcome to chapter two, dear readers. So it seems that young Lyra Gotham is onto something. She's going to follow this line of thought for a while and see just where it leads. Shall we follow along as well? Yes, I do believe we shall!

We've got to get to PKOLS pronto!

Where is that?

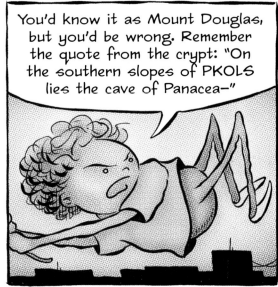

You'd know it as Mount Douglas, but you'd be wrong. Remember the quote from the crypt: "On the southern slopes of PKOLS lies the cave of Panacea—"

Who's Panacea?

She's the goddess of universal remedy, and she'll cure what's ailing the city.

But let me finish! "And within this mossy tunneled mine are the seeds of a better idea." I believe if we find this hole in the mountain, we'll also find exactly what we need.

Seeds of a better idea?

Yeah! City seeds!

That's a better idea than monsters.

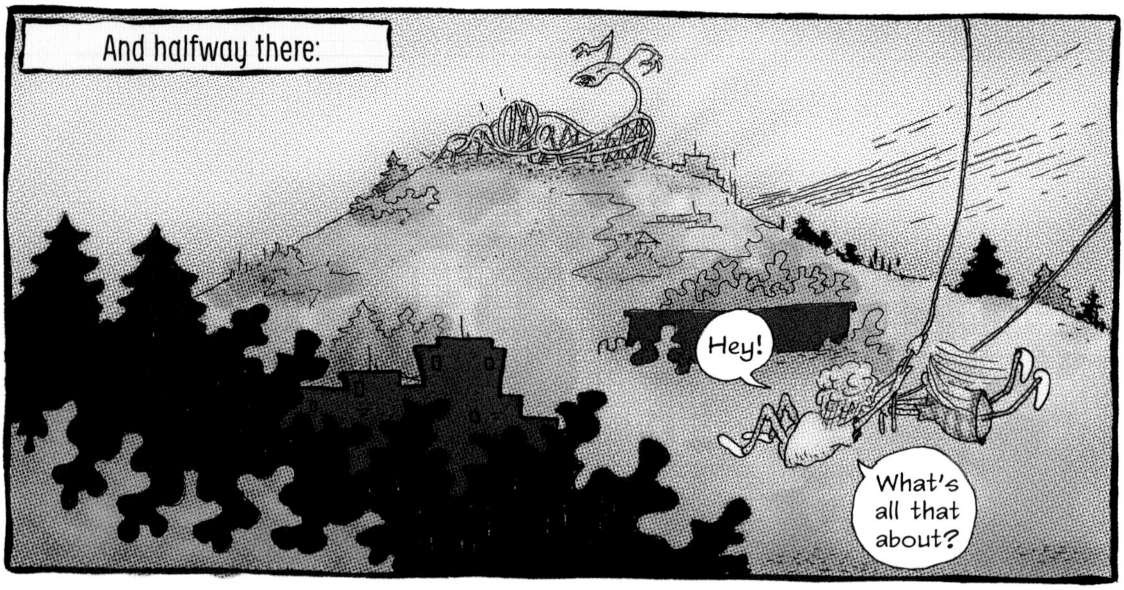
And halfway there:
Hey!
What's all that about?

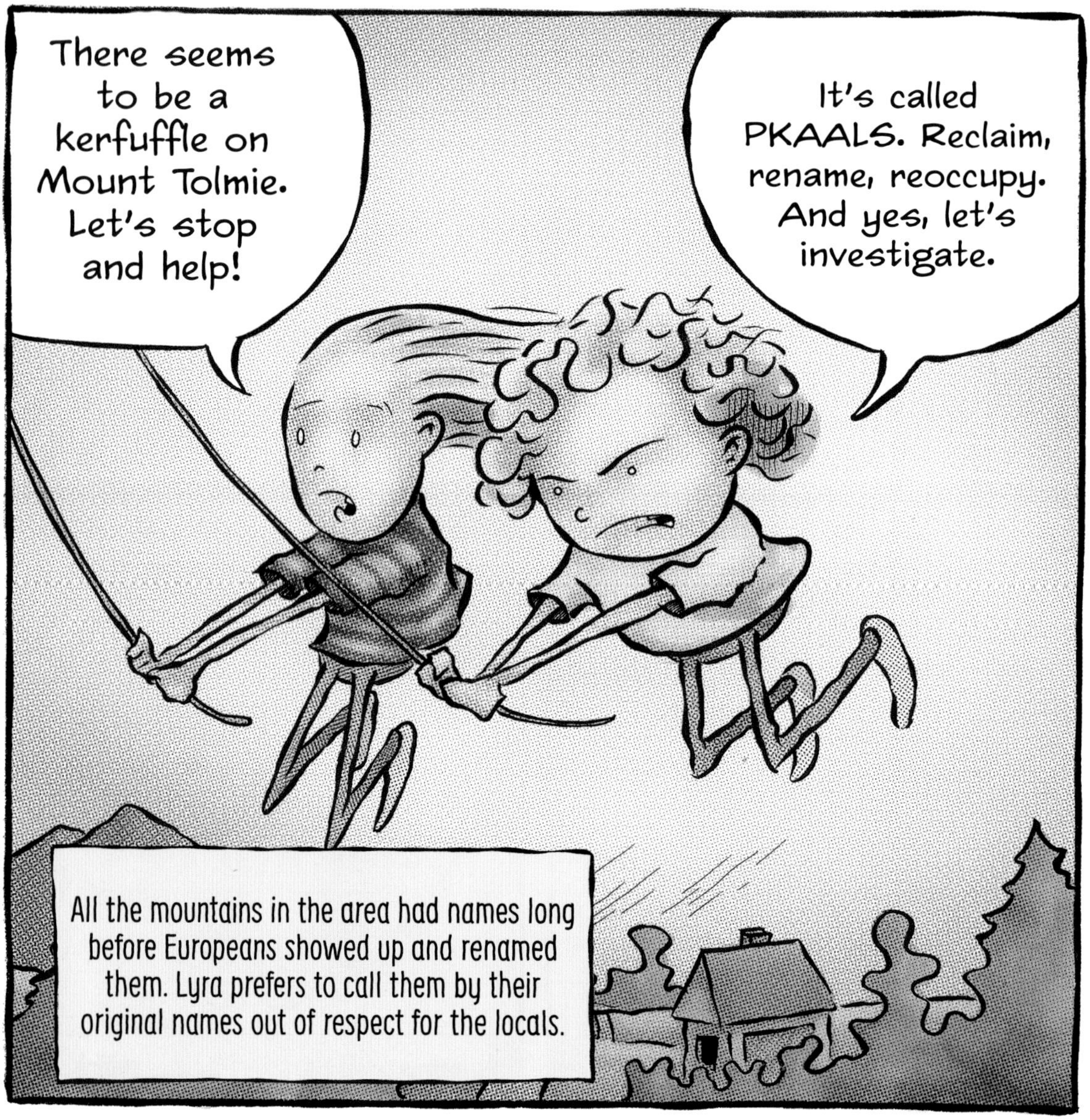
There seems to be a kerfuffle on Mount Tolmie. Let's stop and help!
It's called PKAALS. Reclaim, rename, reoccupy. And yes, let's investigate.
All the mountains in the area had names long before Europeans showed up and renamed them. Lyra prefers to call them by their original names out of respect for the locals.

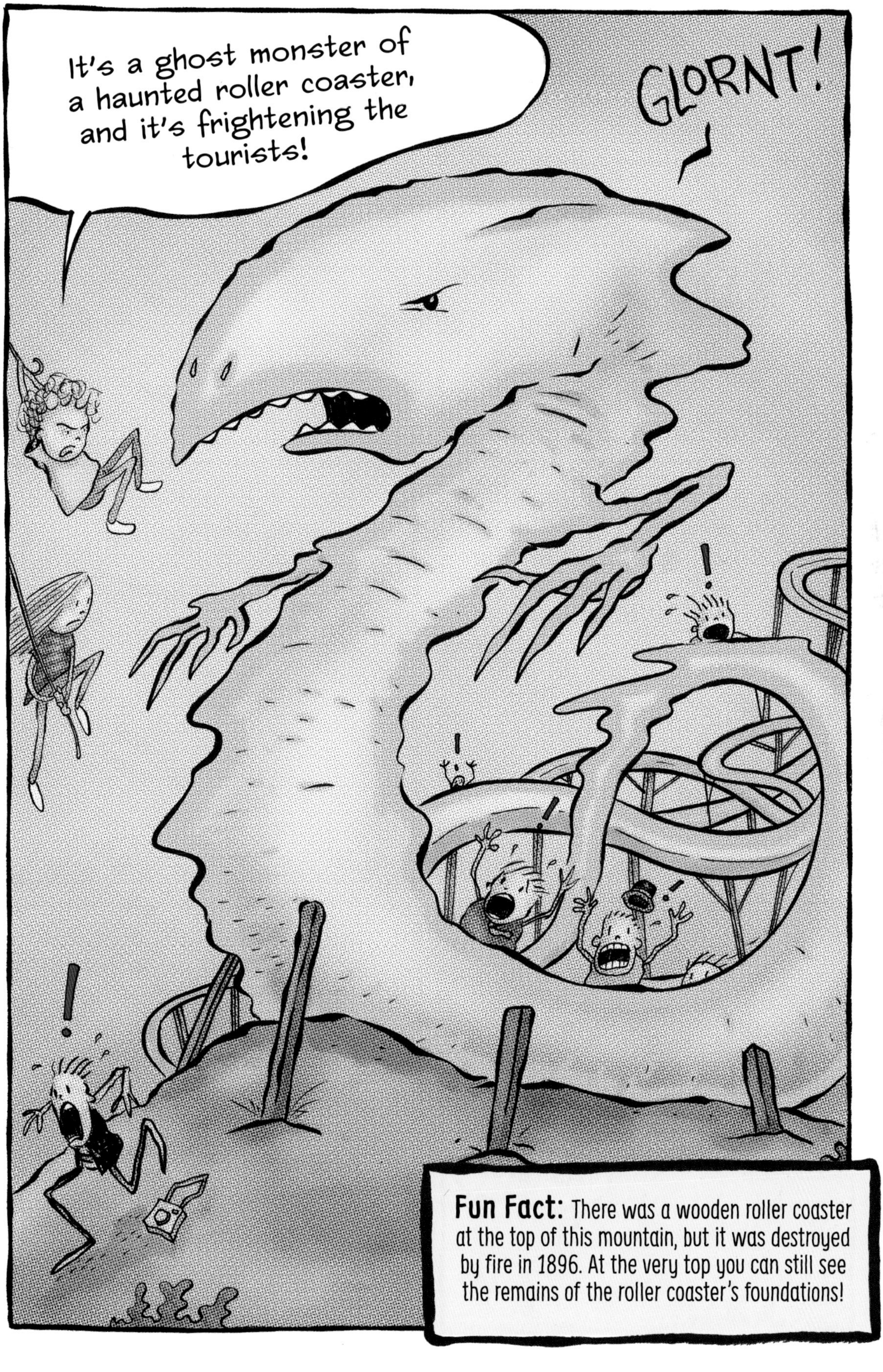
It's a ghost monster of a haunted roller coaster, and it's frightening the tourists!
GLORNT!
!
!
!
!
!
Fun Fact: There was a wooden roller coaster at the top of this mountain, but it was destroyed by fire in 1896. At the very top you can still see the remains of the roller coaster's foundations!

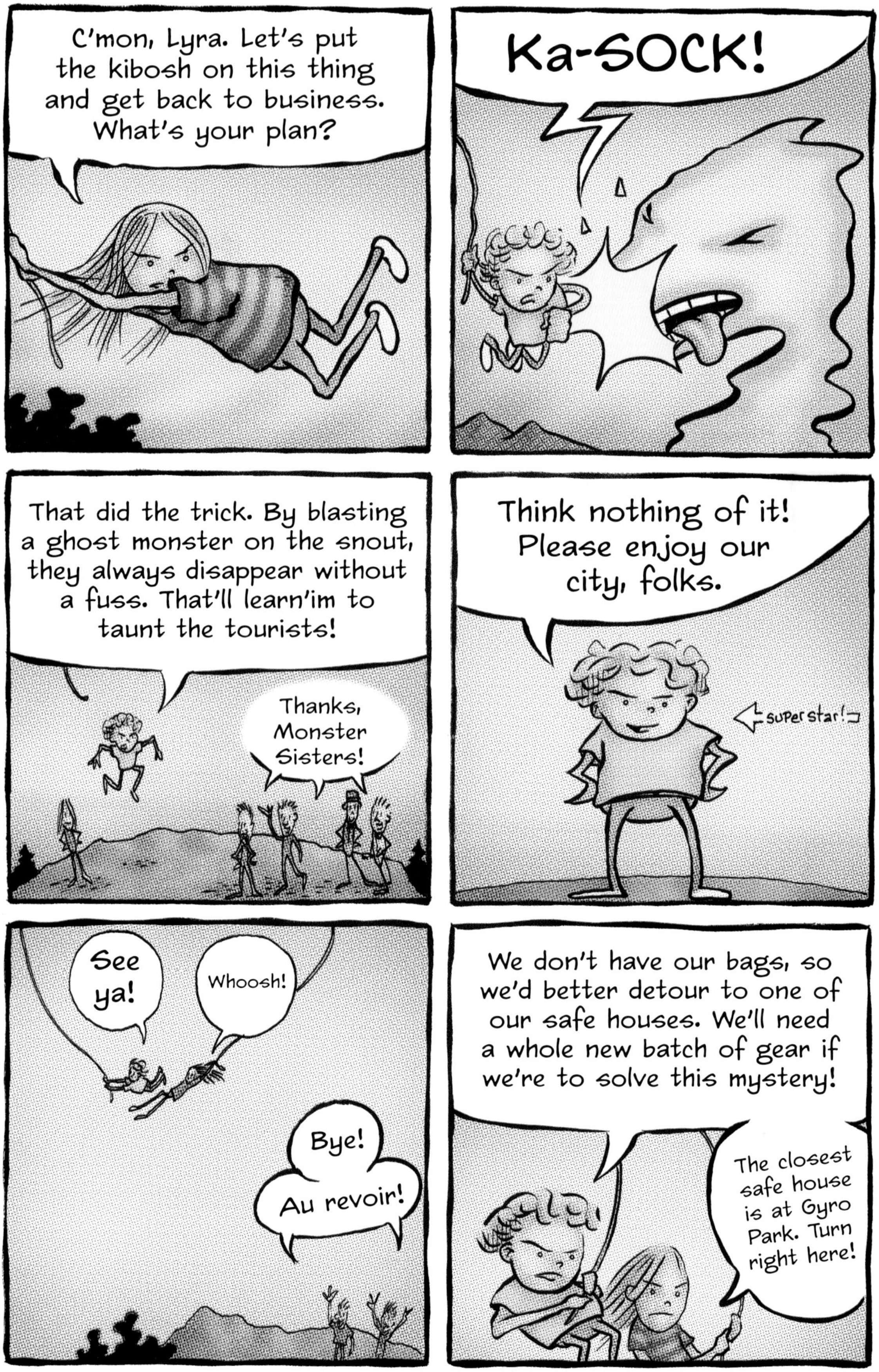

C'mon, Lyra. Let's put the kibosh on this thing and get back to business. What's your plan?
Ka-SOCK!
That did the trick. By blasting a ghost monster on the snout, they always disappear without a fuss. That'll learn'im to taunt the tourists!
Thanks, Monster Sisters!
Think nothing of it! Please enjoy our city, folks.
super star!
See ya!
Whoosh!
Bye!
Au revoir!
We don't have our bags, so we'd better detour to one of our safe houses. We'll need a whole new batch of gear if we're to solve this mystery!
The closest safe house is at Gyro Park. Turn right here!

Gyro Park. Home since the 1950s to three giant stone sentinels:

The Cadborosaurus!

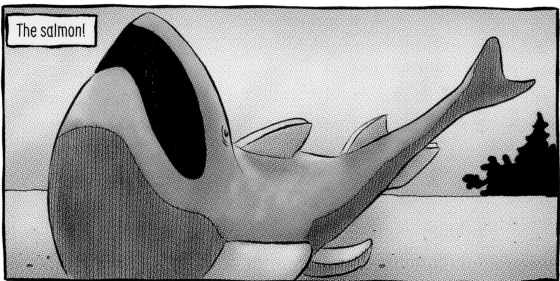

The salmon!

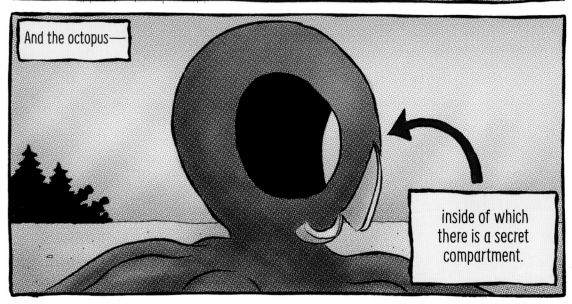

And the octopus—

inside of which there is a secret compartment.

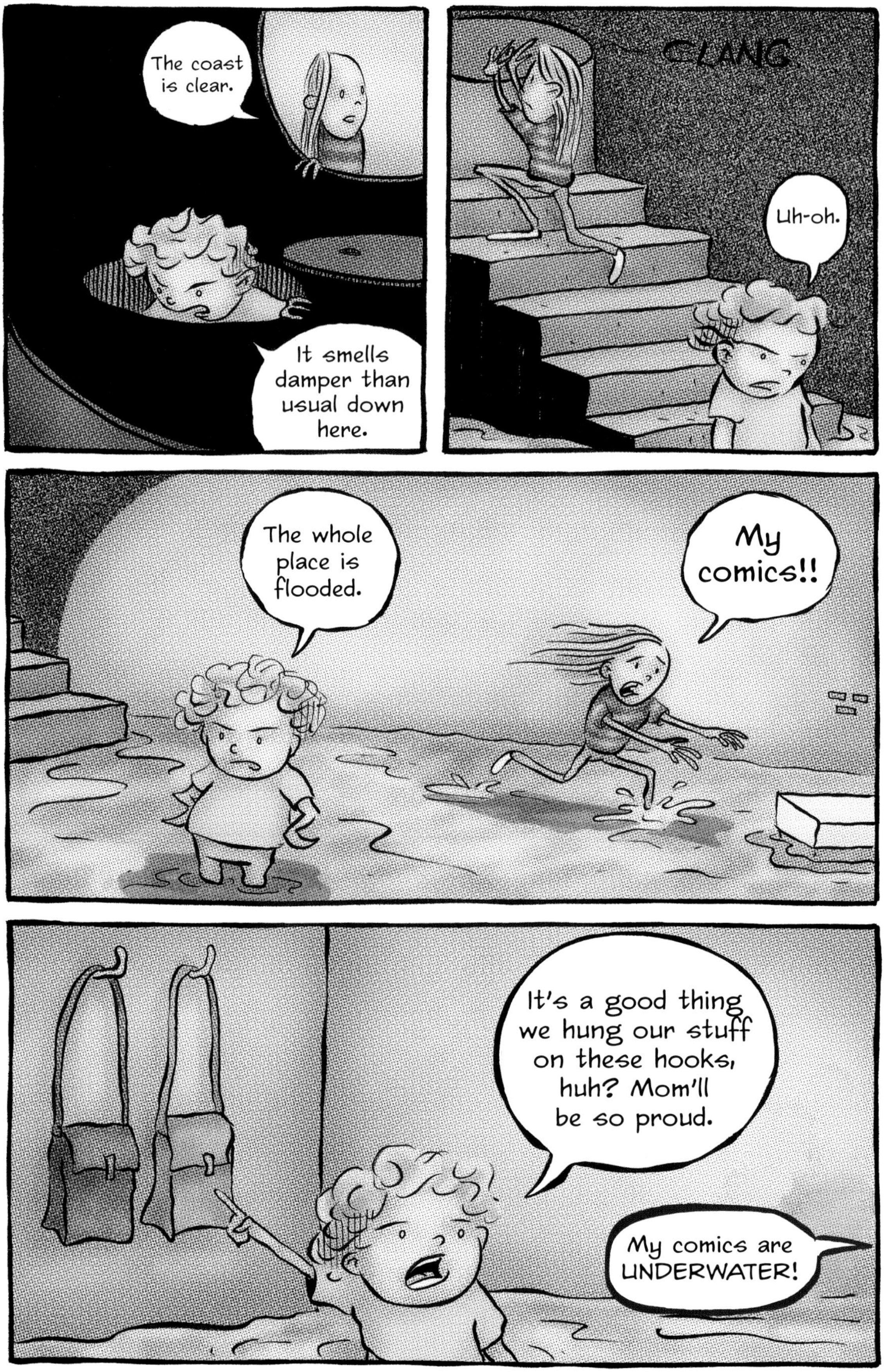
The coast is clear.
It smells damper than usual down here.
CLANG
Uh-oh.
The whole place is flooded.
My comics!!
It's a good thing we hung our stuff on these hooks, huh? Mom'll be so proud.
My comics are UNDERWATER!

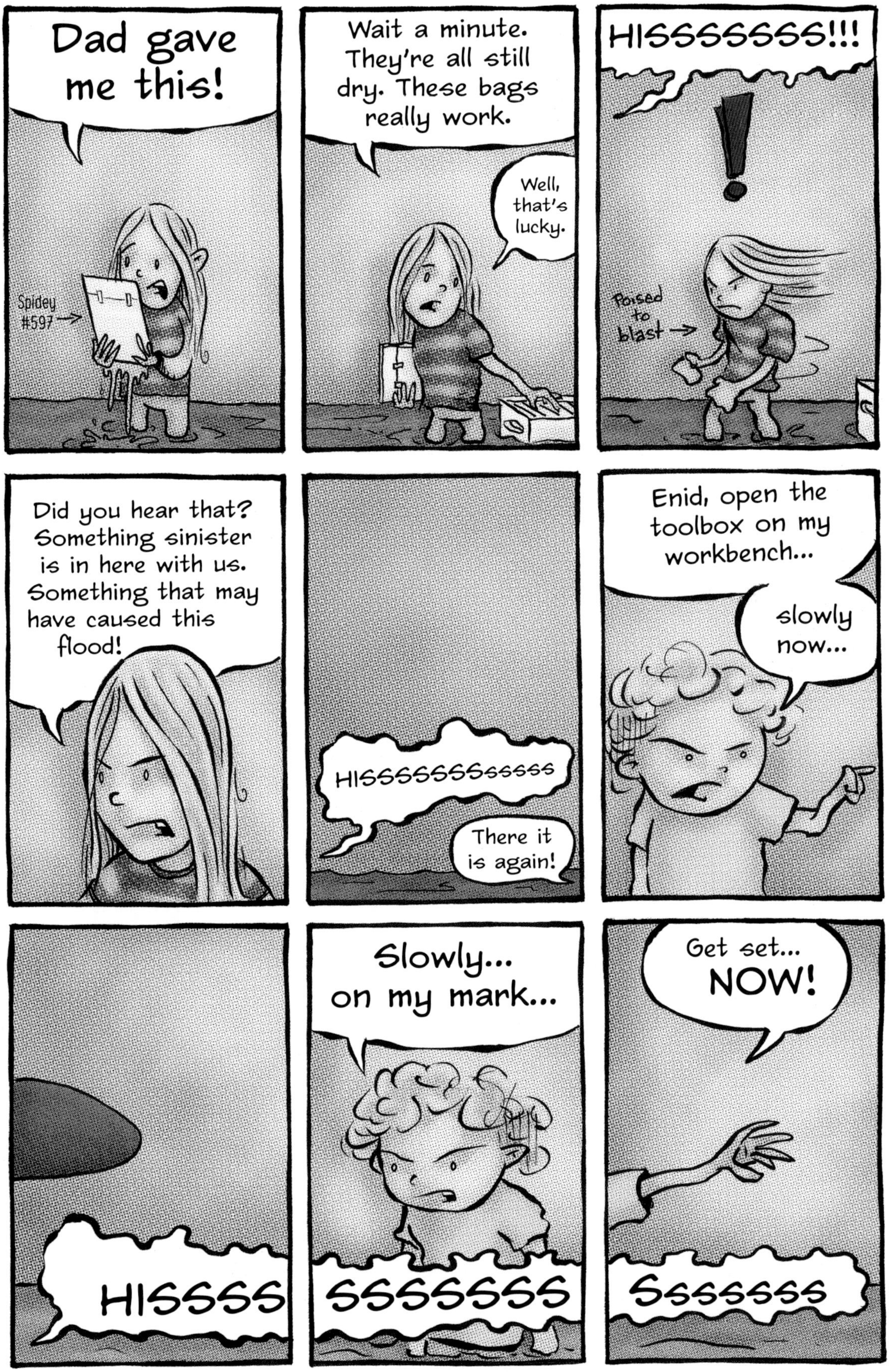

Dad gave me this!
Spidey #597
Wait a minute. They're all still dry. These bags really work.
Well, that's lucky.
HISSSSSSSS!!!
!
Poised to blast
Did you hear that? Something sinister is in here with us. Something that may have caused this flood!
HISSSSSSSSsssss
There it is again!
Enid, open the toolbox on my workbench...
slowly now...
HISSSS
Slowly... on my mark...
SSSSSSSS
Get set... NOW!
Sssssss

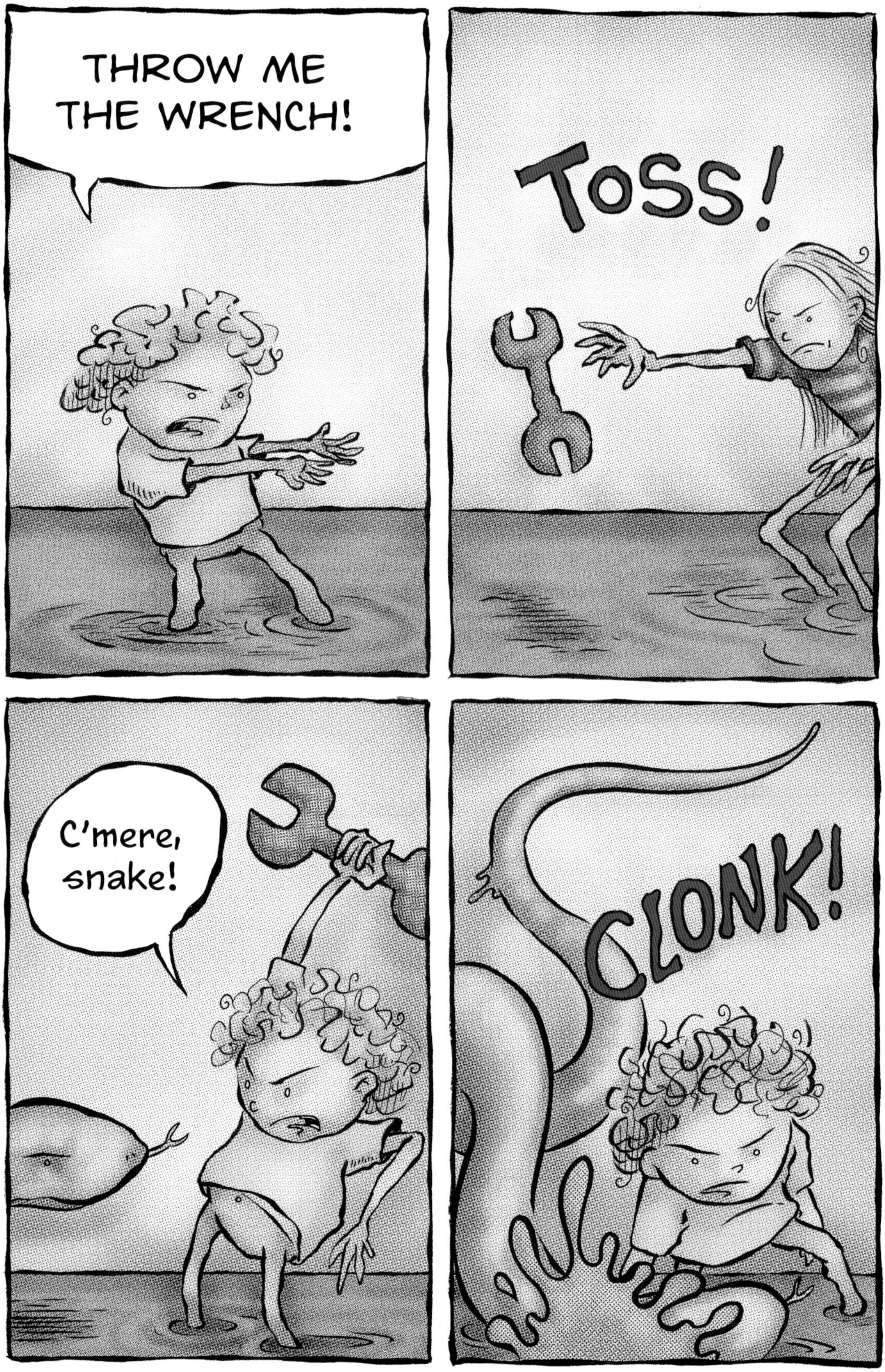
THROW ME THE WRENCH!
TOSS!
C'mere, snake!
CLONK!

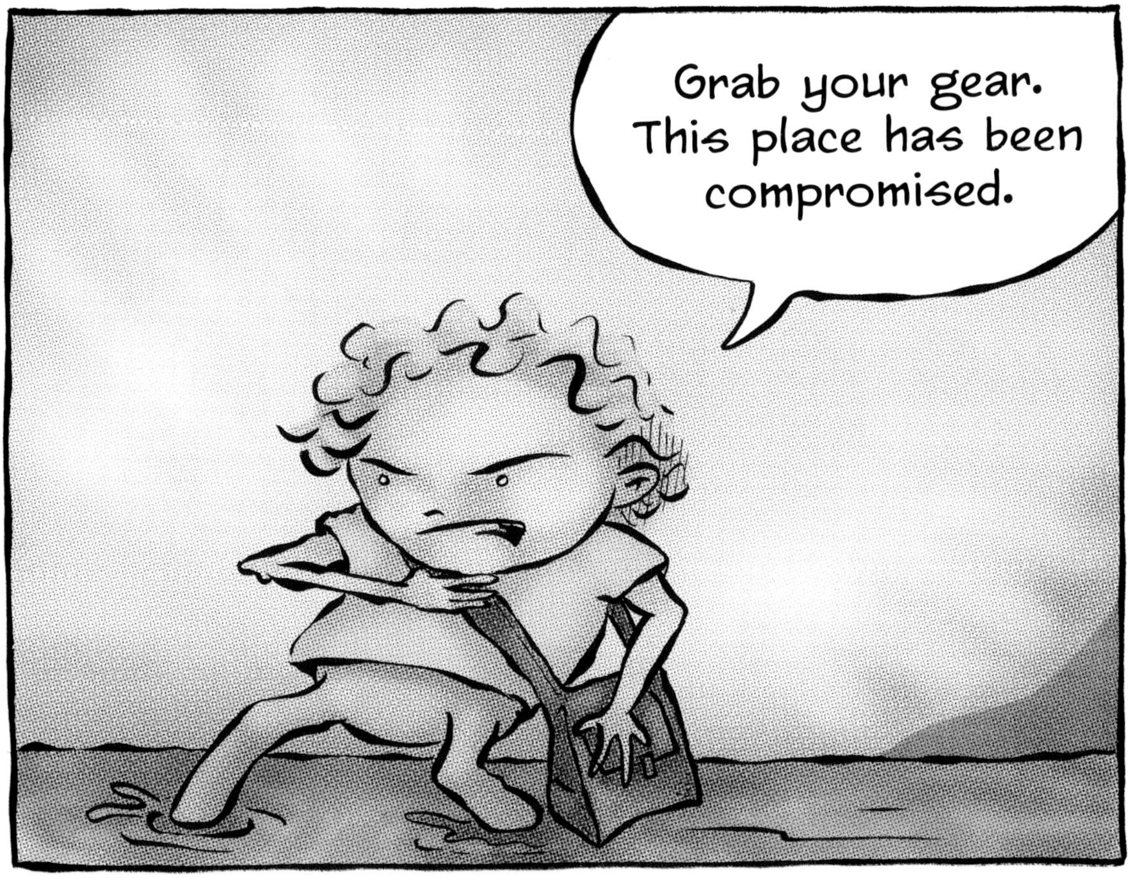
Grab your gear. This place has been compromised.

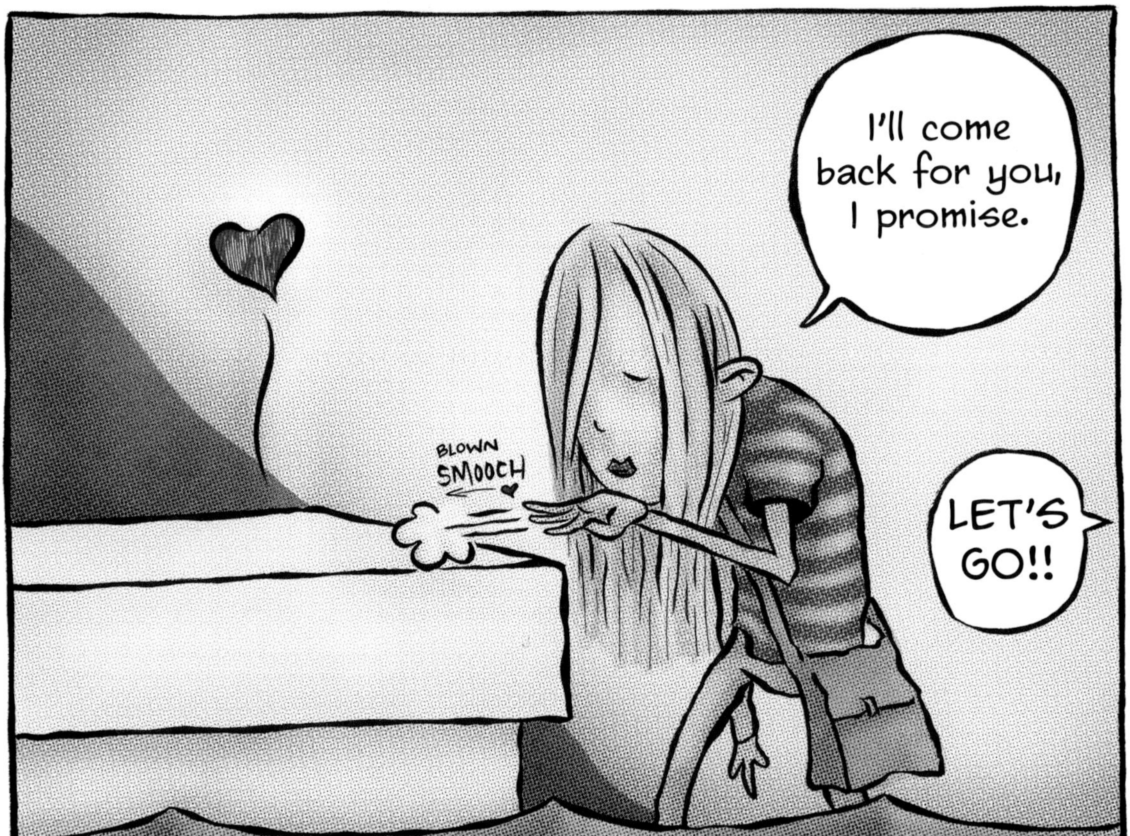
I'll come back for you, I promise.
BLOWN SMOOCH
LET'S GO!!

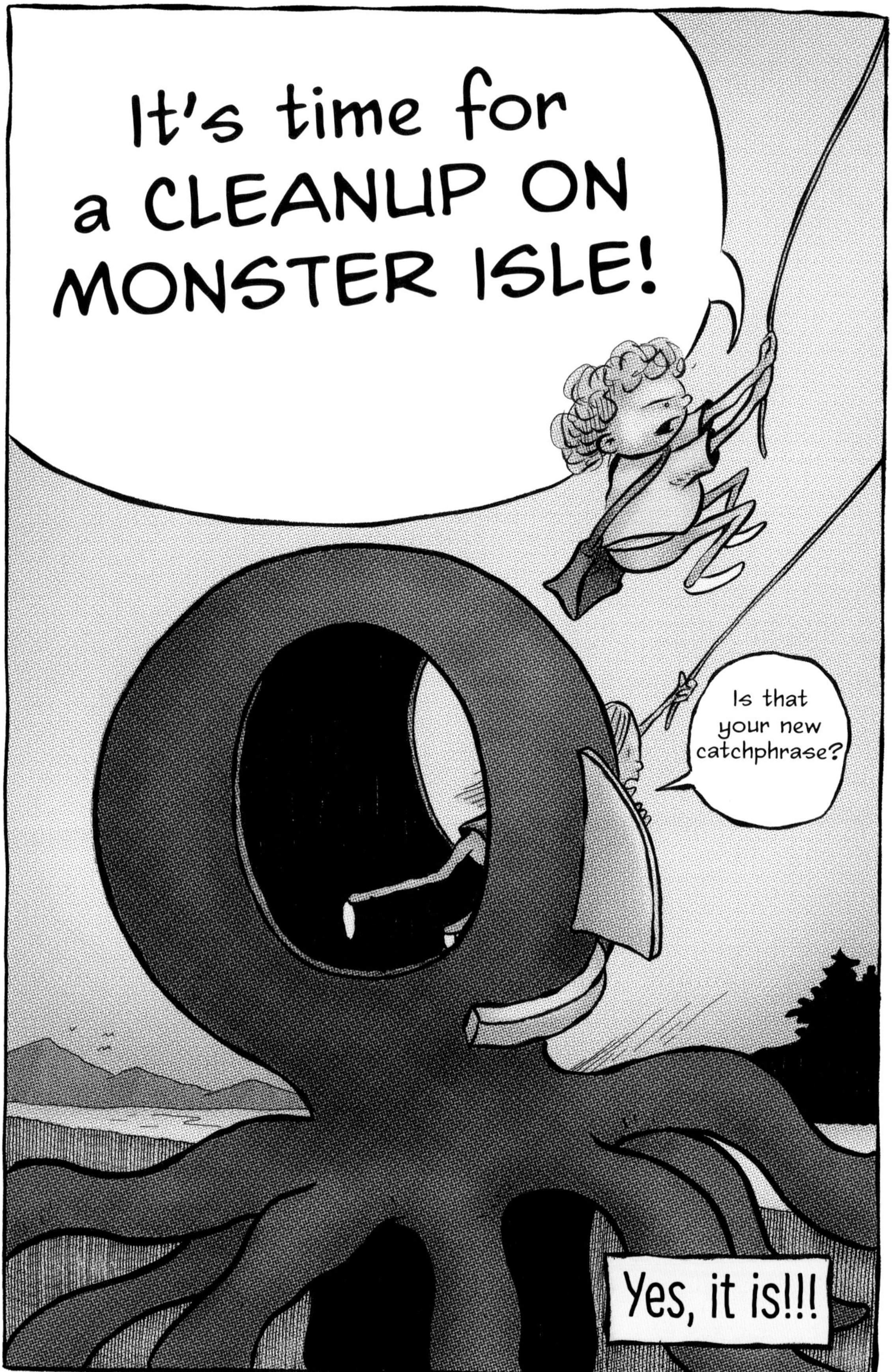
It's time for a CLEANUP ON MONSTER ISLE!
Is that your new catchphrase?
Yes, it is!!!

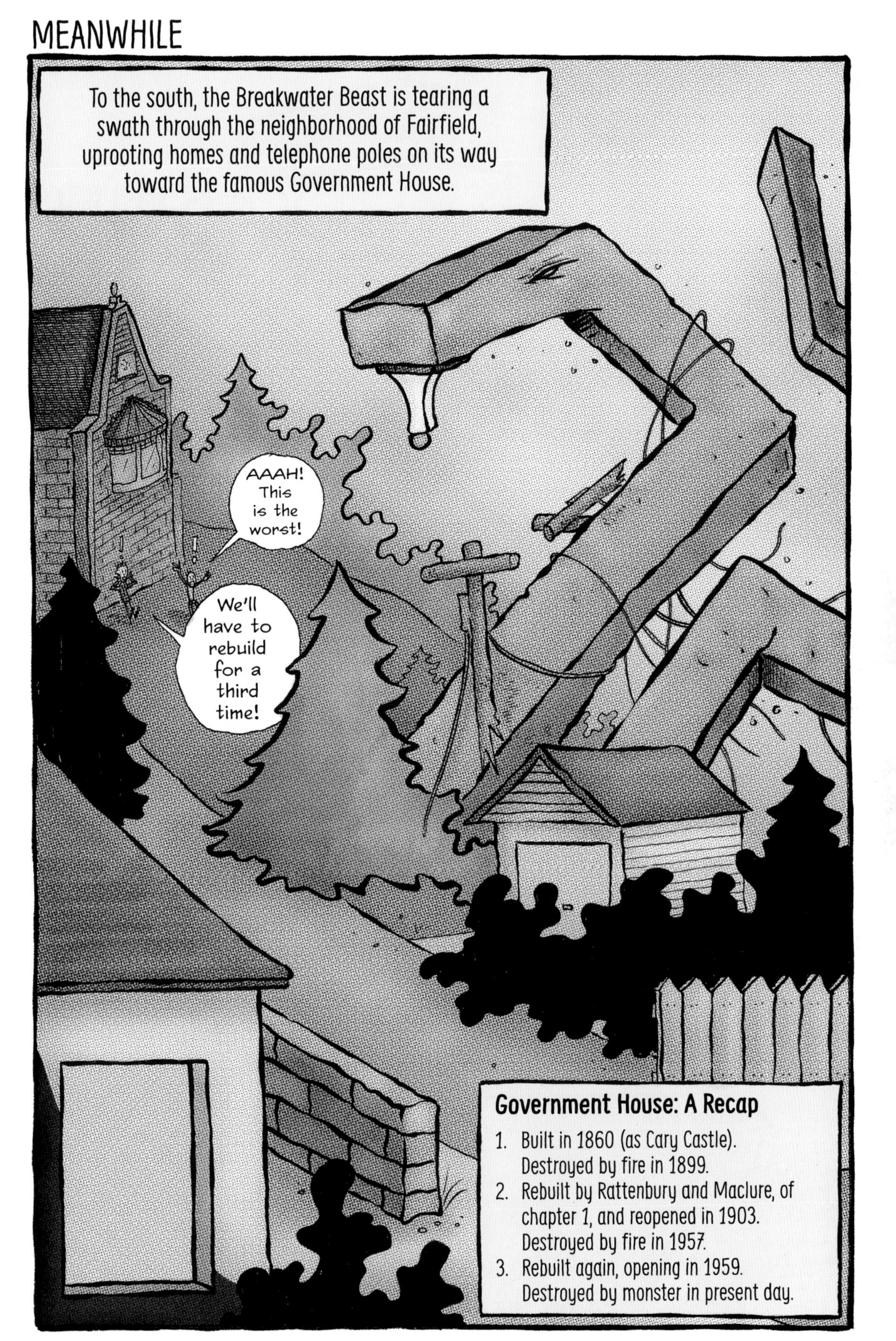
MEANWHILE
To the south, the Breakwater Beast is tearing a swath through the neighborhood of Fairfield, uprooting homes and telephone poles on its way toward the famous Government House.
AAAH! This is the worst!
We'll have to rebuild for a third time!
Government House: A Recap
1. Built in 1860 (as Cary Castle). Destroyed by fire in 1899.
2. Rebuilt by Rattenbury and Maclure, of chapter 1, and reopened in 1903. Destroyed by fire in 1957.
3. Rebuilt again, opening in 1959. Destroyed by monster in present day.

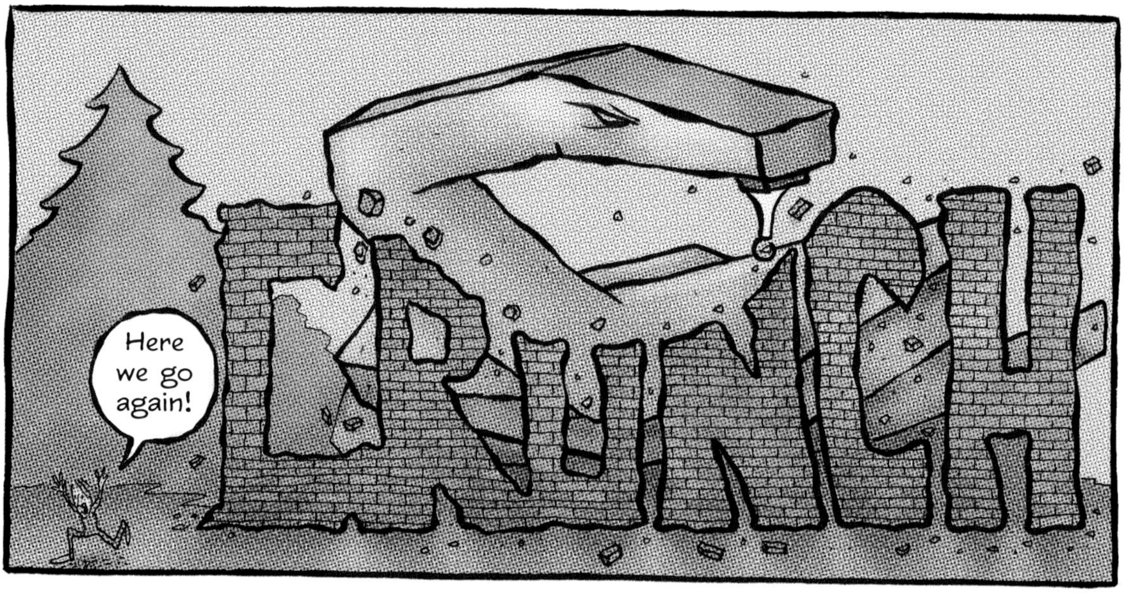
Here we go again!
CRUNCH

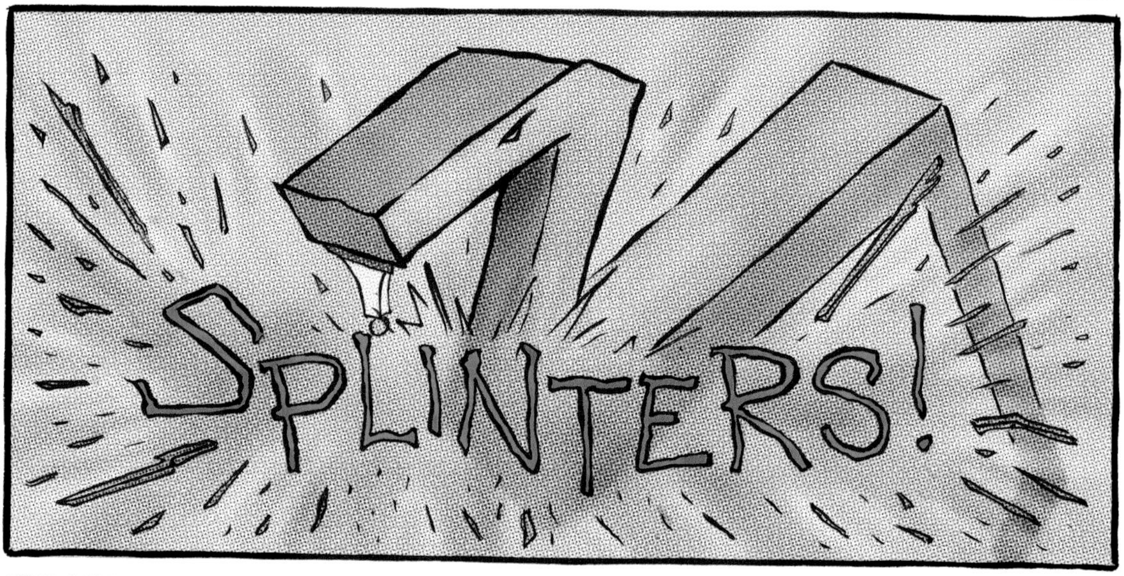
SPLINTERS!

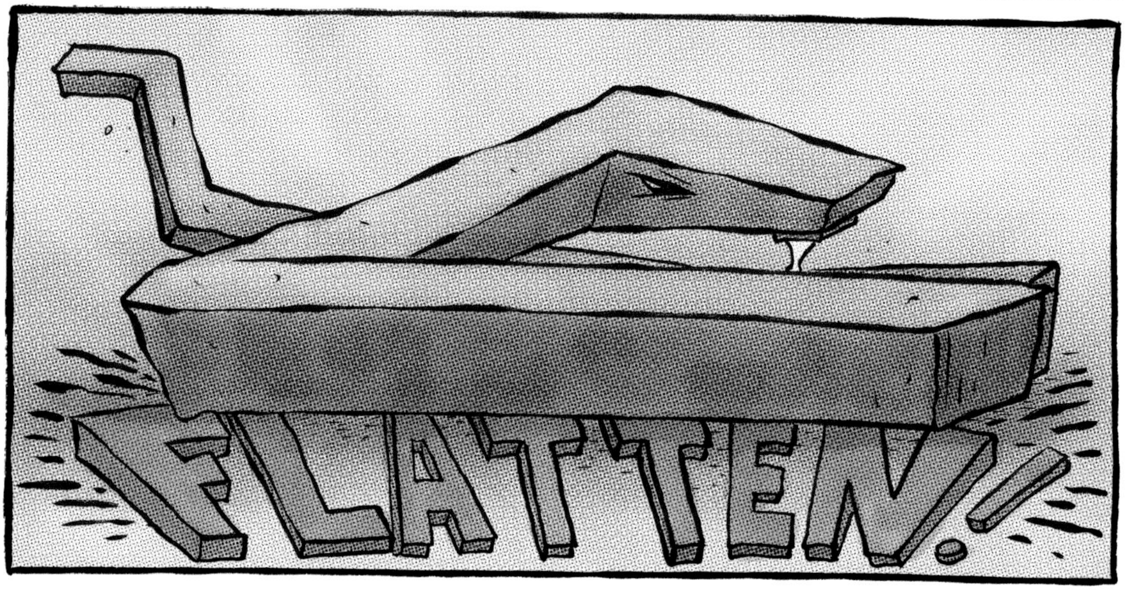
FLATTEN!

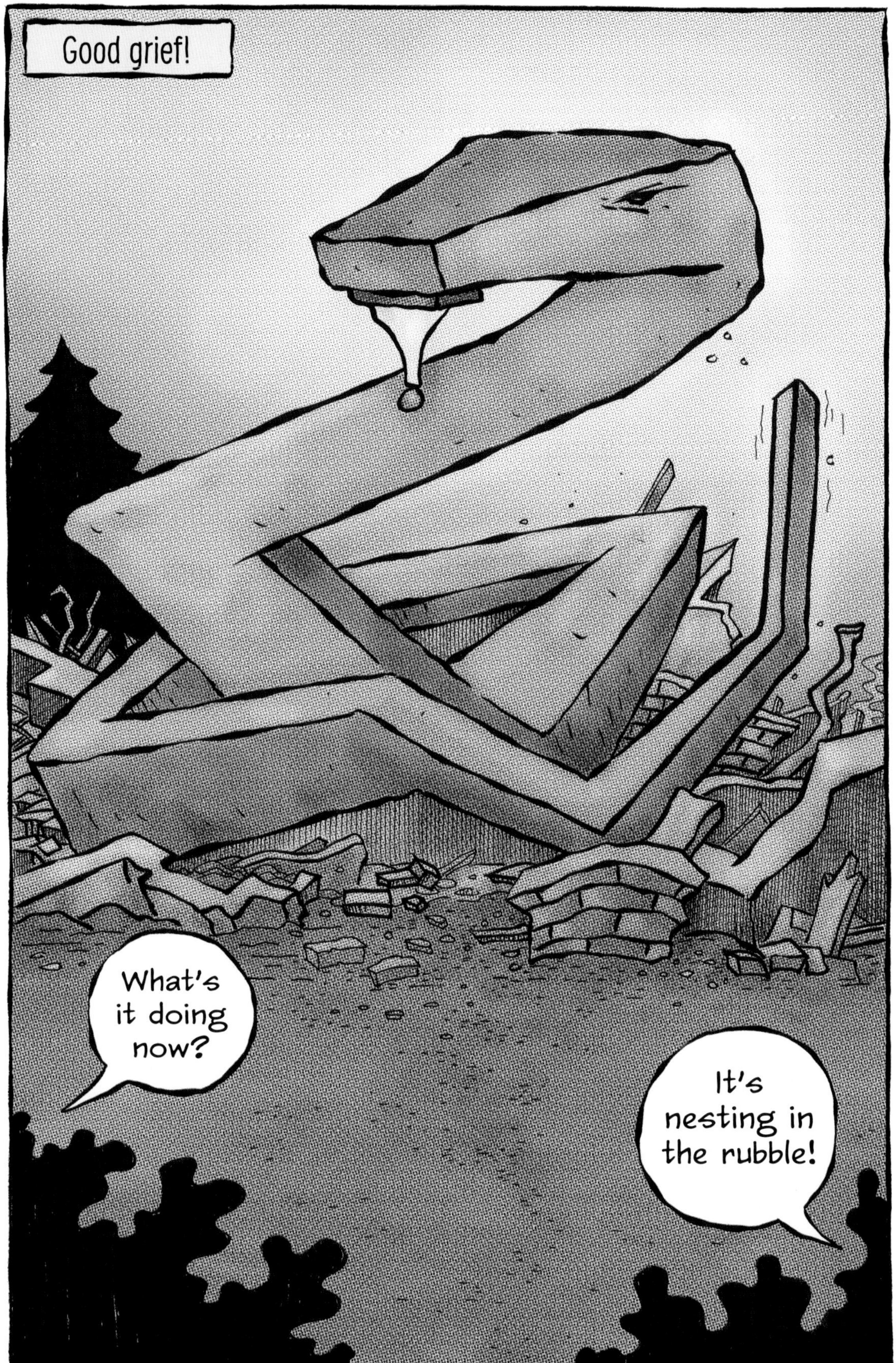
Good grief!
What's it doing now?
It's nesting in the rubble!

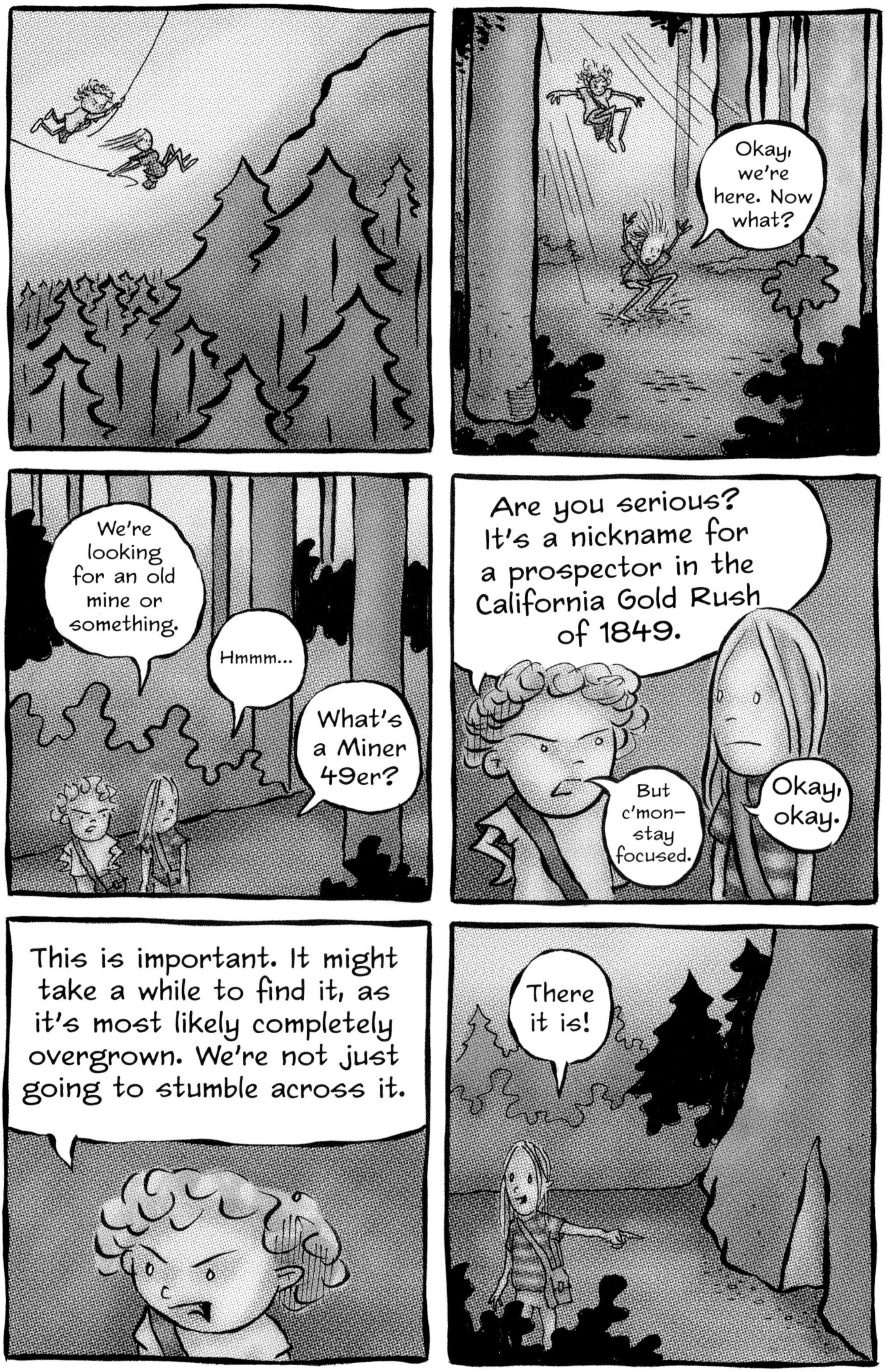
Okay, we're here. Now what?
We're looking for an old mine or something.
Hmmm...
What's a Miner 49er?
Are you serious? It's a nickname for a prospector in the California Gold Rush of 1849.
But c'mon–stay focused.
Okay, okay.
This is important. It might take a while to find it, as it's most likely completely overgrown. We're not just going to stumble across it.
There it is!

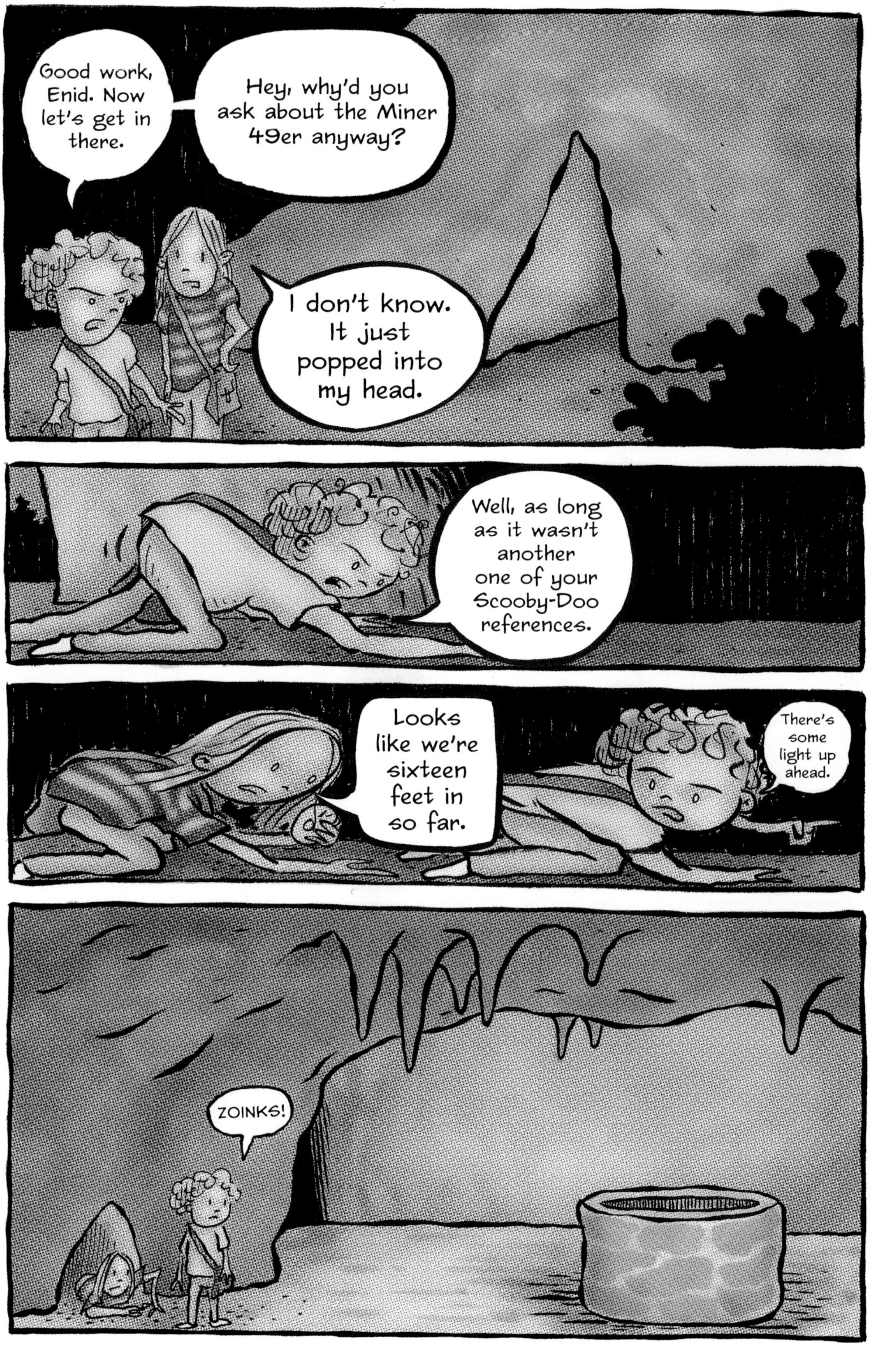
Good work, Enid. Now let's get in there.
Hey, why'd you ask about the Miner 49er anyway?
I don't know. It just popped into my head.
Well, as long as it wasn't another one of your Scooby-Doo references.
Looks like we're sixteen feet in so far.
There's some light up ahead.
ZOINKS!

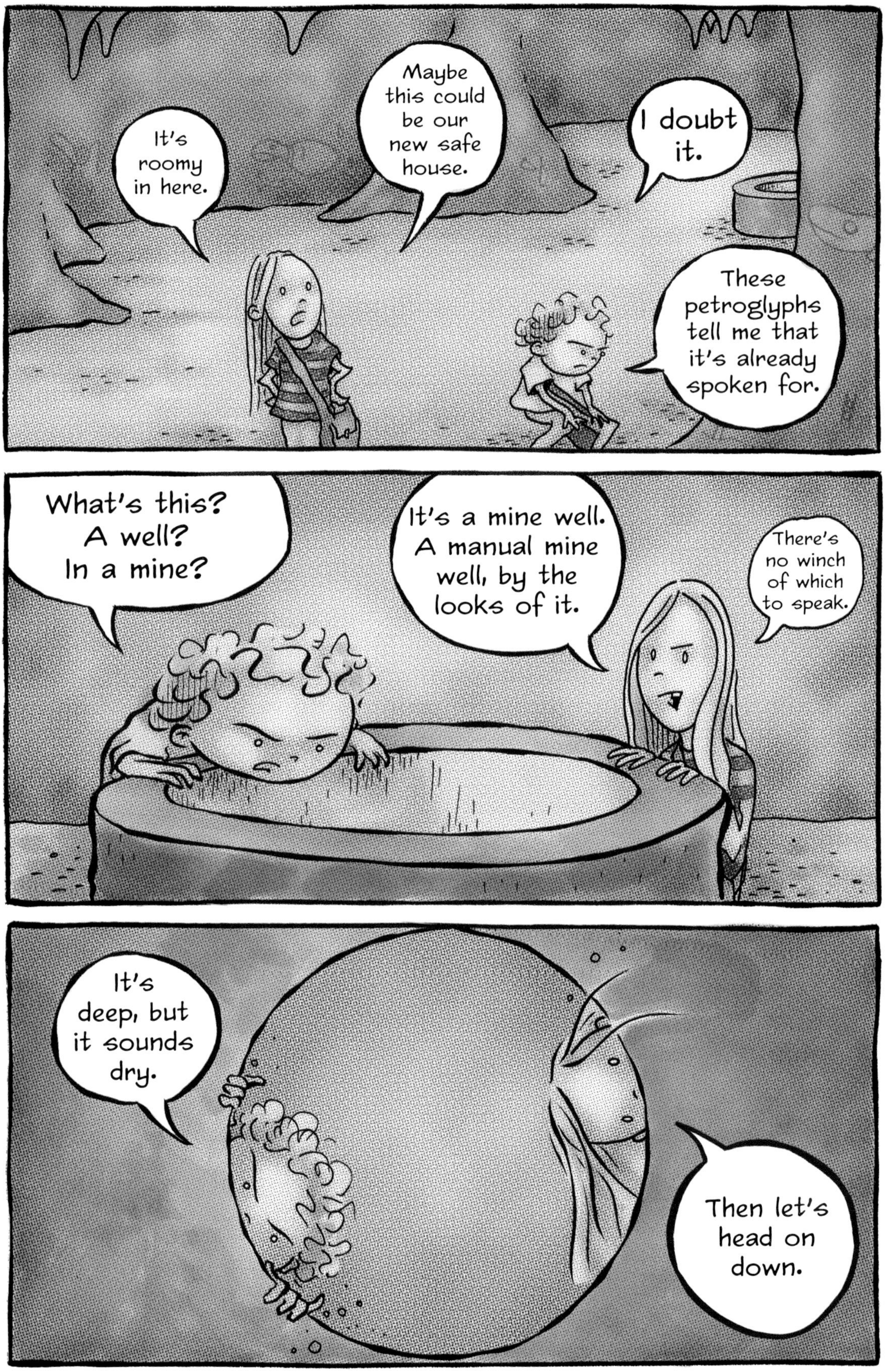
It's roomy in here.
Maybe this could be our new safe house.
I doubt it.
These petroglyphs tell me that it's already spoken for.
What's this? A well? In a mine?
It's a mine well. A manual mine well, by the looks of it.
There's no winch of which to speak.
It's deep, but it sounds dry.
Then let's head on down.

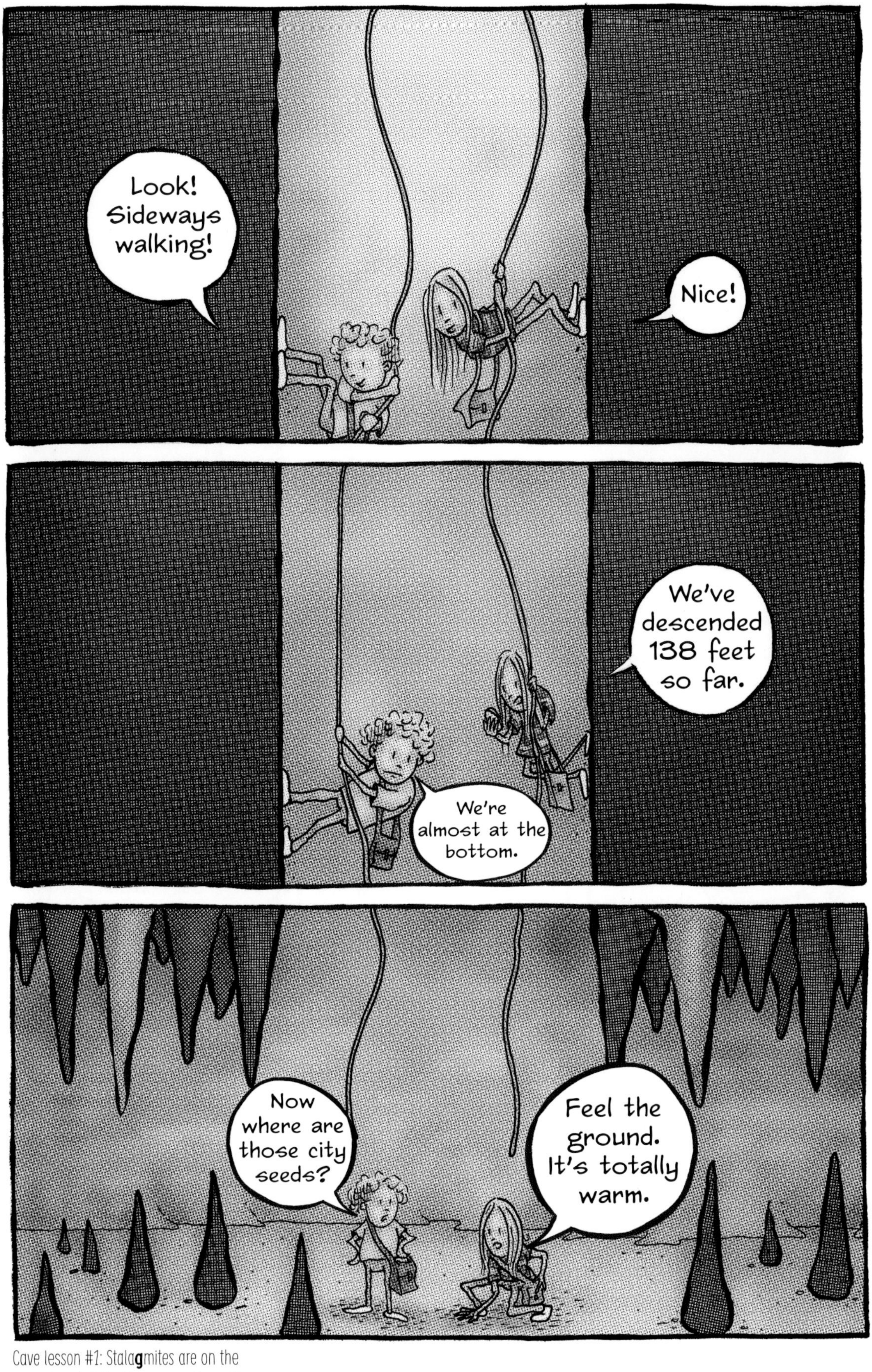
Look! Sideways walking!
Nice!
We've descended 138 feet so far.
We're almost at the bottom.
Now where are those city seeds?
Feel the ground. It's totally warm.

Cave lesson #1: Stala**g**mites are on the **g**round, and stala**c**tites are on the **c**eiling.

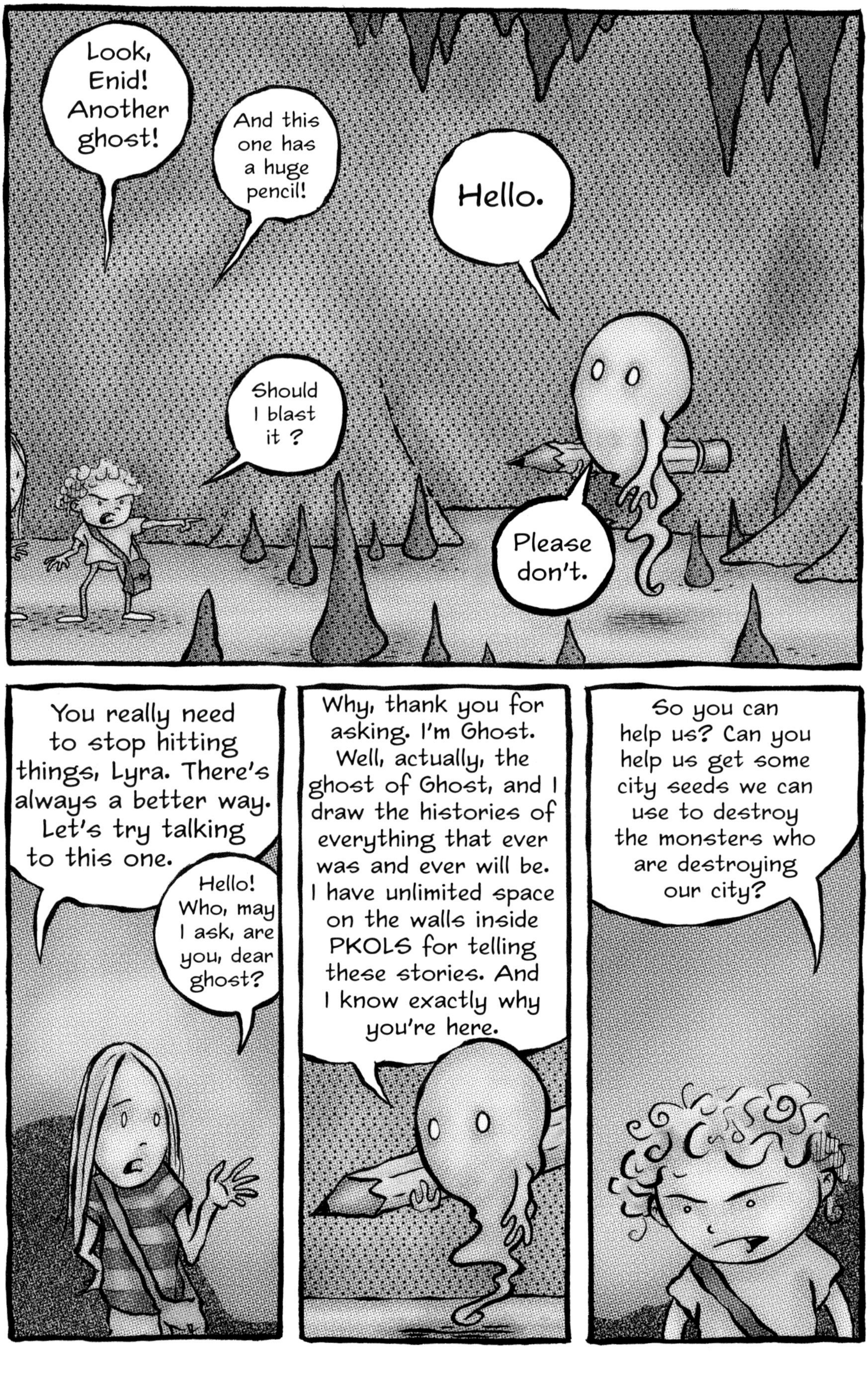
Look, Enid! Another ghost!
And this one has a huge pencil!
Hello.
Should I blast it ?
Please don't.
You really need to stop hitting things, Lyra. There's always a better way. Let's try talking to this one.
Hello! Who, may I ask, are you, dear ghost?
Why, thank you for asking. I'm Ghost. Well, actually, the ghost of Ghost, and I draw the histories of everything that ever was and ever will be. I have unlimited space on the walls inside PKOLS for telling these stories. And I know exactly why you're here.
So you can help us? Can you help us get some city seeds we can use to destroy the monsters who are destroying our city?

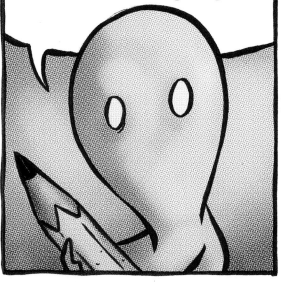

Yes, I can help you—but not yet. You came here searching for the seeds of a better idea, but you've approached your problem from the wrong angle.

Your problem is already a solution. Thus, your solution will undoubtedly become the problem. Go and do some more research, and only when you've seen the world as it really is, and not as you fear it will become, may you return.

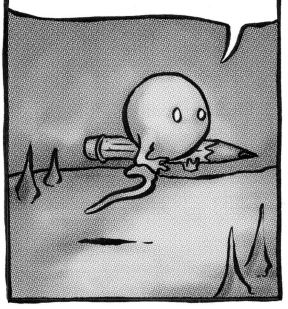

When you're pointed in the right direction, I'll give you the seeds. Go and find out WHY this is happening.

Return with a better understanding of what's actually going on out there. Good day, sisters.

Huh.

I guess it's back to the streets for us.

Is there an emergency exit, or do we have to climb back out of here?

PAUSE FOR CAVE EXTRACTION.

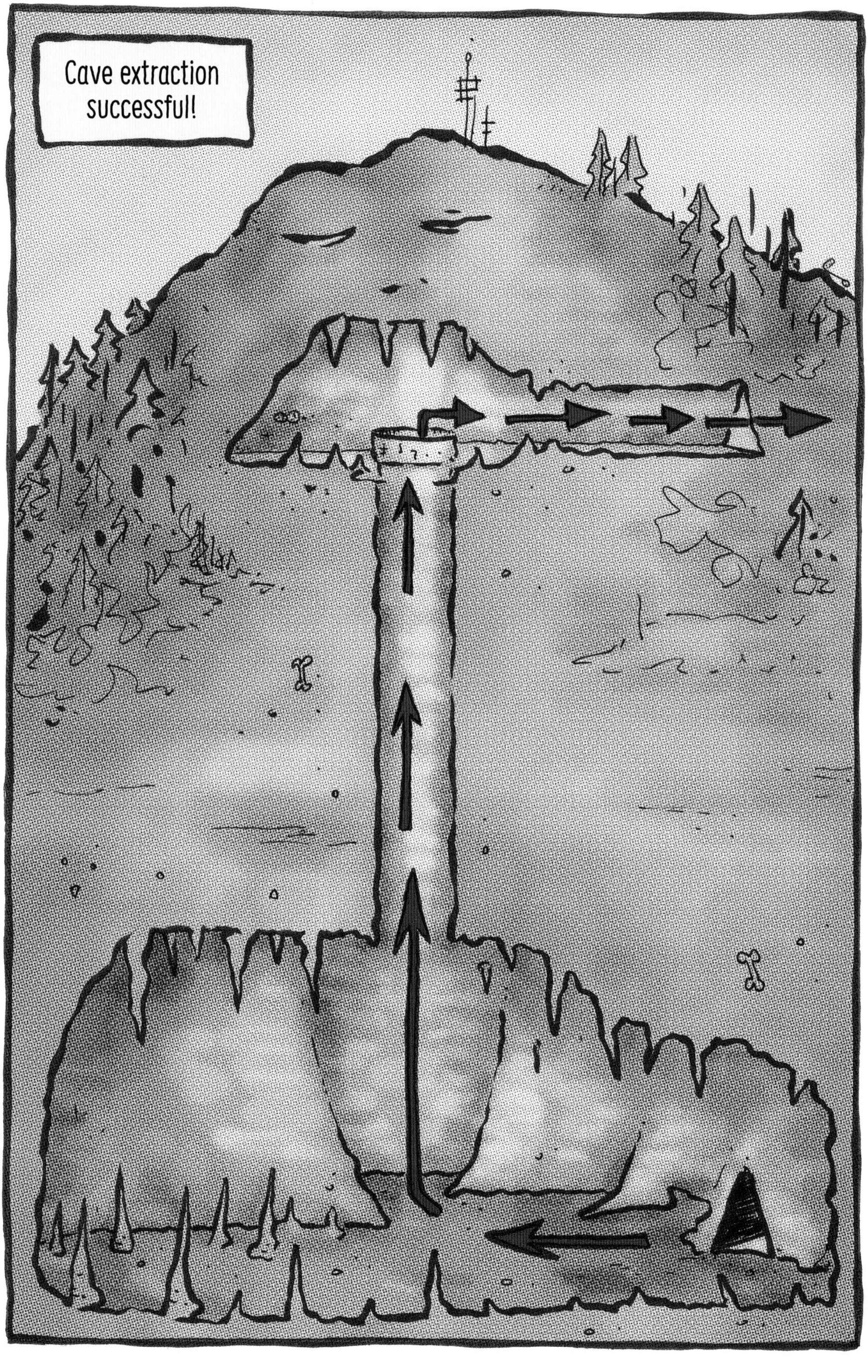
Cave extraction successful!

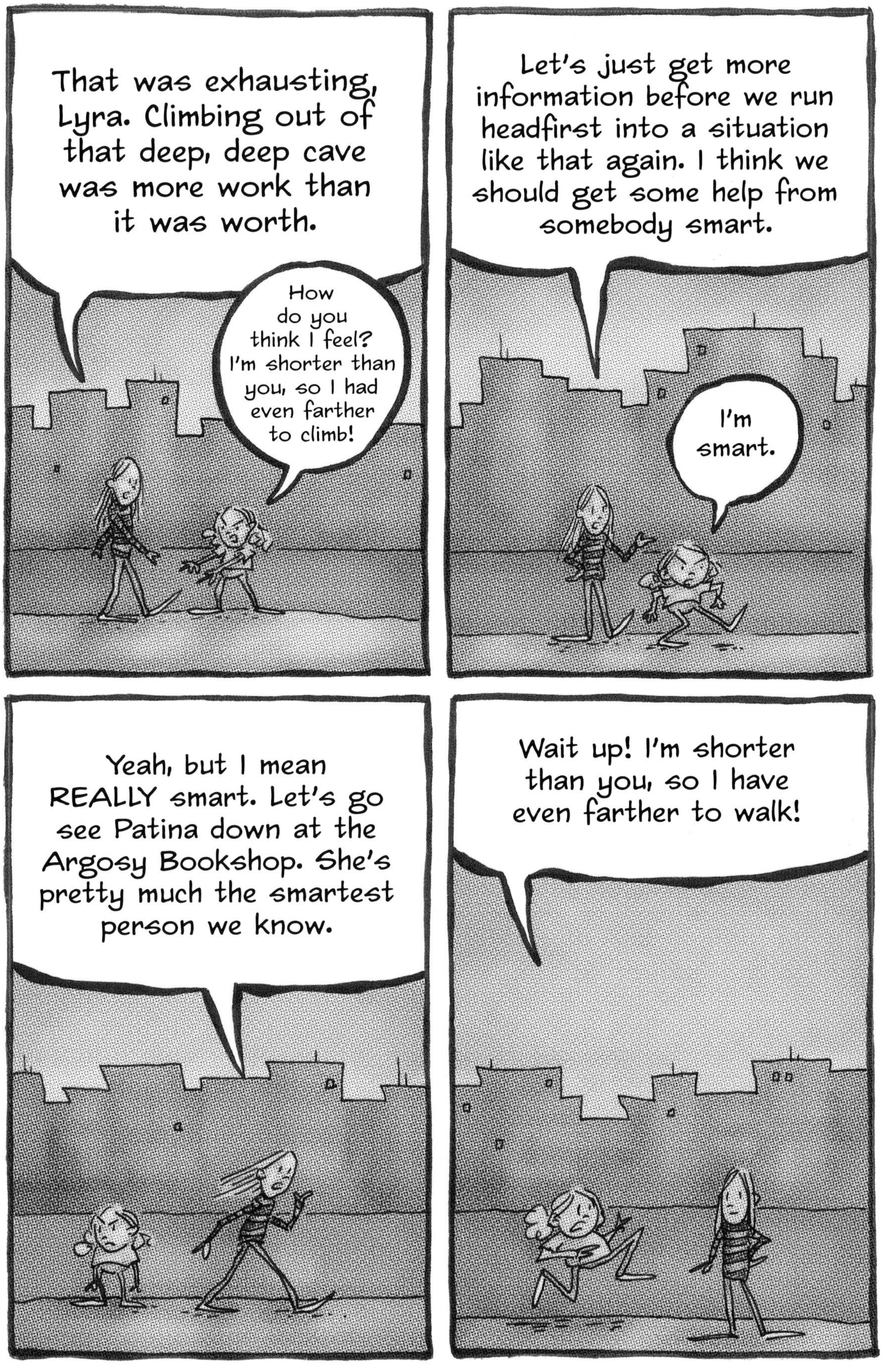
That was exhausting, Lyra. Climbing out of that deep, deep cave was more work than it was worth.
How do you think I feel? I'm shorter than you, so I had even farther to climb!
Let's just get more information before we run headfirst into a situation like that again. I think we should get some help from somebody smart.
I'm smart.
Yeah, but I mean REALLY smart. Let's go see Patina down at the Argosy Bookshop. She's pretty much the smartest person we know.
Wait up! I'm shorter than you, so I have even farther to walk!

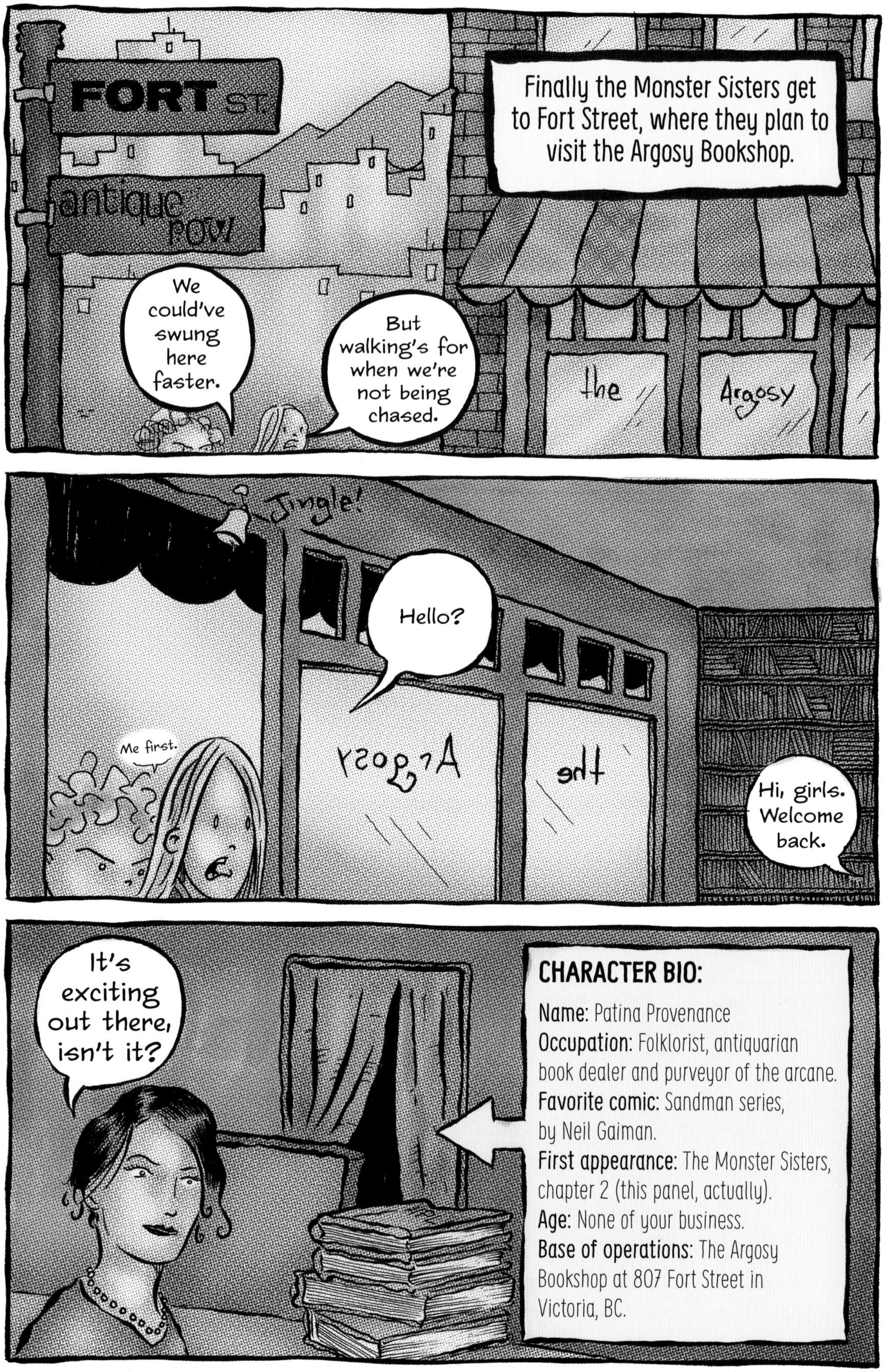
FORT ST.
antique row
Finally the Monster Sisters get to Fort Street, where they plan to visit the Argosy Bookshop.
We could've swung here faster.
But walking's for when we're not being chased.
the
Argosy
Jingle!
Hello?
Me first.
Hi, girls. Welcome back.
It's exciting out there, isn't it?
CHARACTER BIO:
Name: Patina Provenance
Occupation: Folklorist, antiquarian book dealer and purveyor of the arcane.
Favorite comic: Sandman series, by Neil Gaiman.
First appearance: The Monster Sisters, chapter 2 (this panel, actually).
Age: None of your business.
Base of operations: The Argosy Bookshop at 807 Fort Street in Victoria, BC.

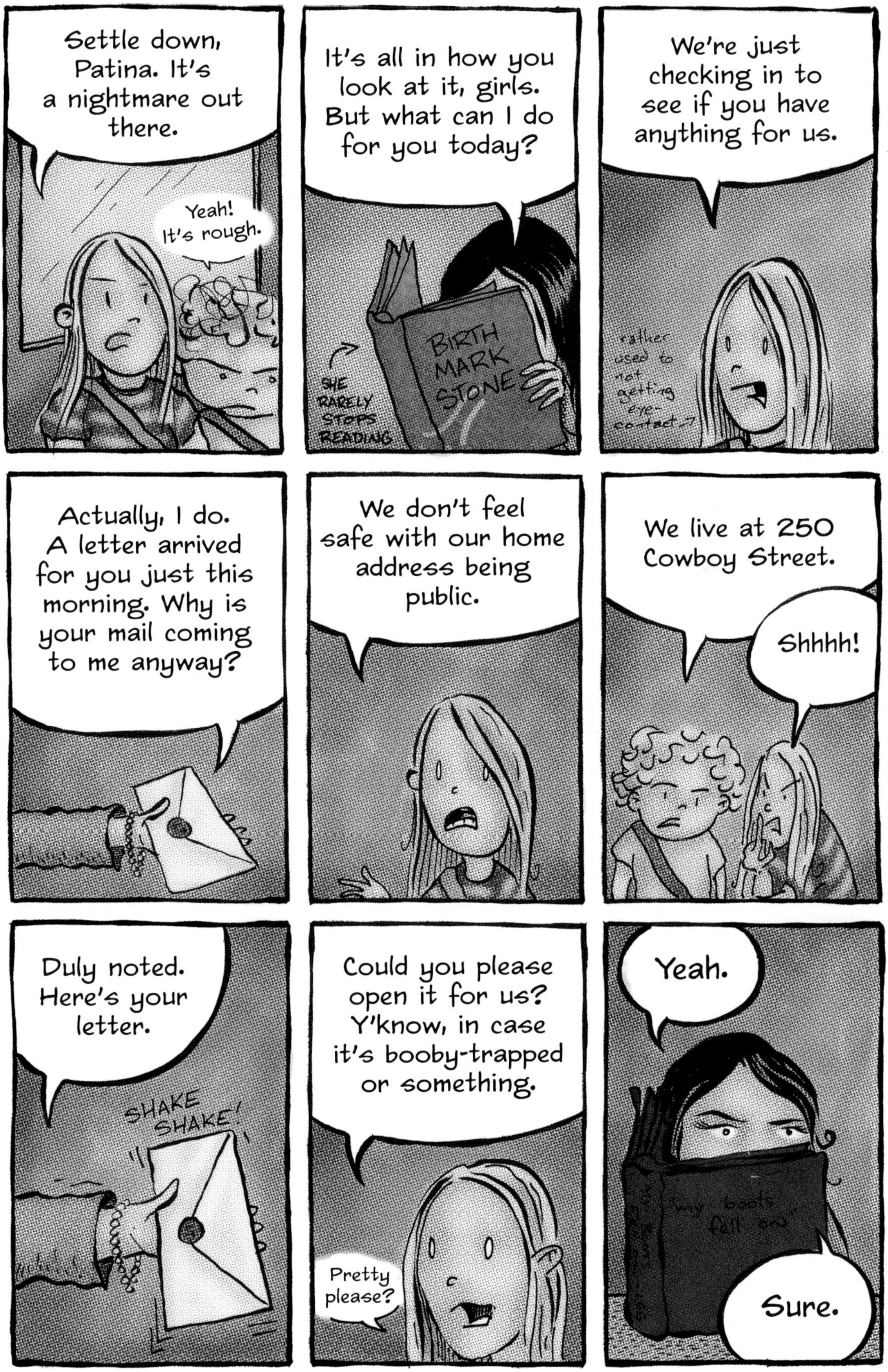

Settle down, Patina. It's a nightmare out there.
Yeah! It's rough.
It's all in how you look at it, girls. But what can I do for you today?
BIRTH MARK STONE
SHE RARELY STOPS READING
We're just checking in to see if you have anything for us.
rather used to not getting eye-contact
Actually, I do. A letter arrived for you just this morning. Why is your mail coming to me anyway?
We don't feel safe with our home address being public.
We live at 250 Cowboy Street.
Shhhh!
Duly noted. Here's your letter.
SHAKE SHAKE!
Could you please open it for us? Y'know, in case it's booby-trapped or something.
Pretty please?
Yeah.
"my boots
Sure.

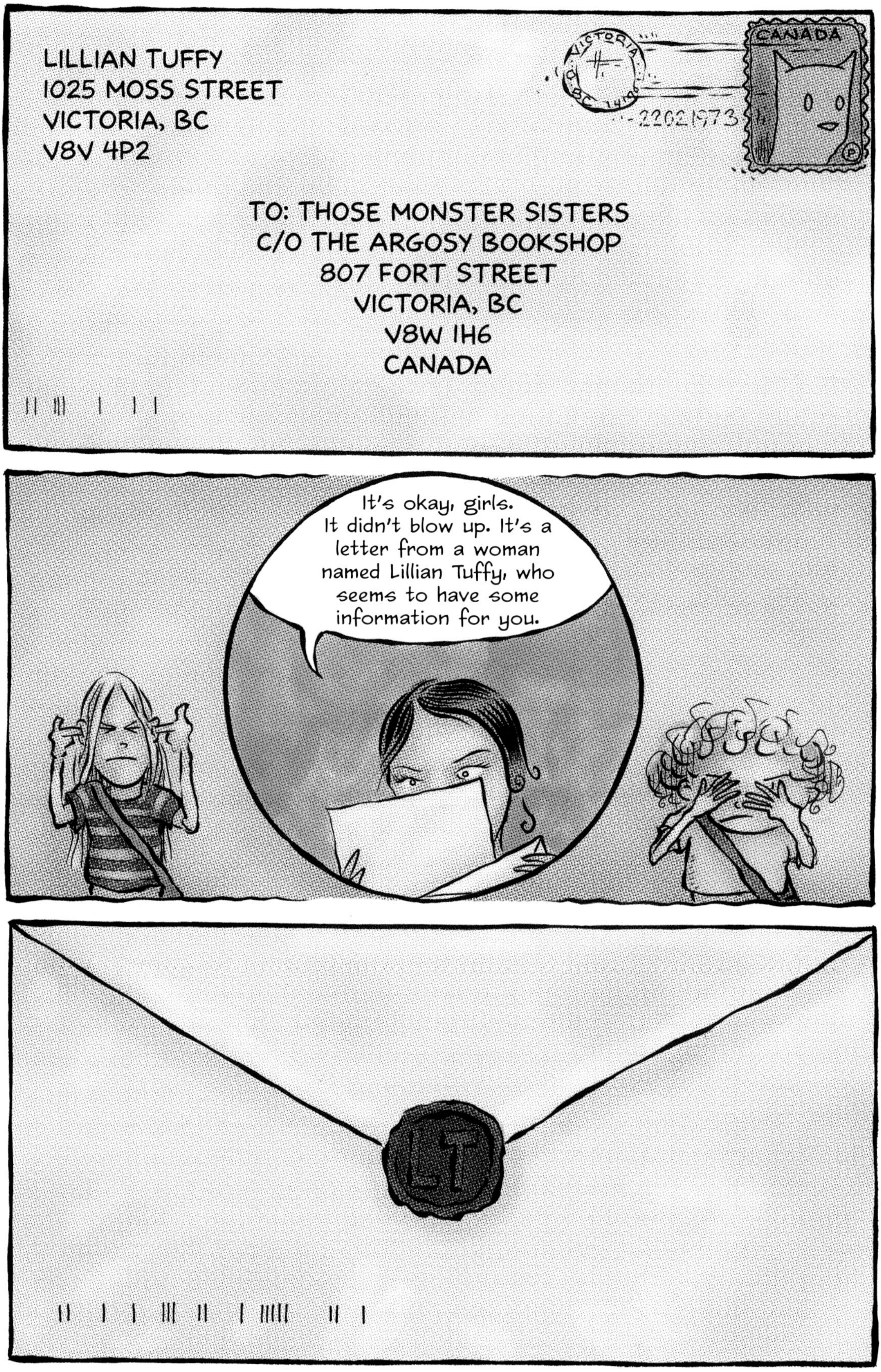
LILLIAN TUFFY
1025 MOSS STREET
VICTORIA, BC
V8V 4P2
CANADA
VICTORIA
22021973
TO: THOSE MONSTER SISTERS
C/O THE ARGOSY BOOKSHOP
807 FORT STREET
VICTORIA, BC
V8W 1H6
CANADA
It's okay, girls. It didn't blow up. It's a letter from a woman named Lillian Tuffy, who seems to have some information for you.
LT

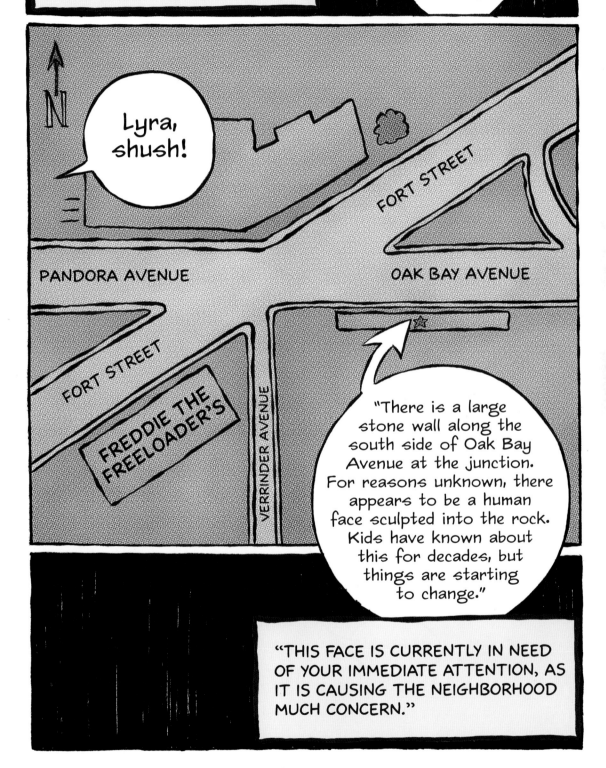

MONSTER SISTERS! PLEASE FORGIVE MY CRUDE MAP, BUT I THINK I HAVE A MYSTERY FOR YOU TO SOLVE.

As if we don't have enough of THOSE already!

Lyra, shush!

FORT STREET

OAK BAY AVENUE

PANDORA AVENUE

FORT STREET

FREDDIE THE FREELOADER'S

VERRINDER AVENUE

"There is a large stone wall along the south side of Oak Bay Avenue at the junction. For reasons unknown, there appears to be a human face sculpted into the rock. Kids have known about this for decades, but things are starting to change."

"THIS FACE IS CURRENTLY IN NEED OF YOUR IMMEDIATE ATTENTION, AS IT IS CAUSING THE NEIGHBORHOOD MUCH CONCERN."

65

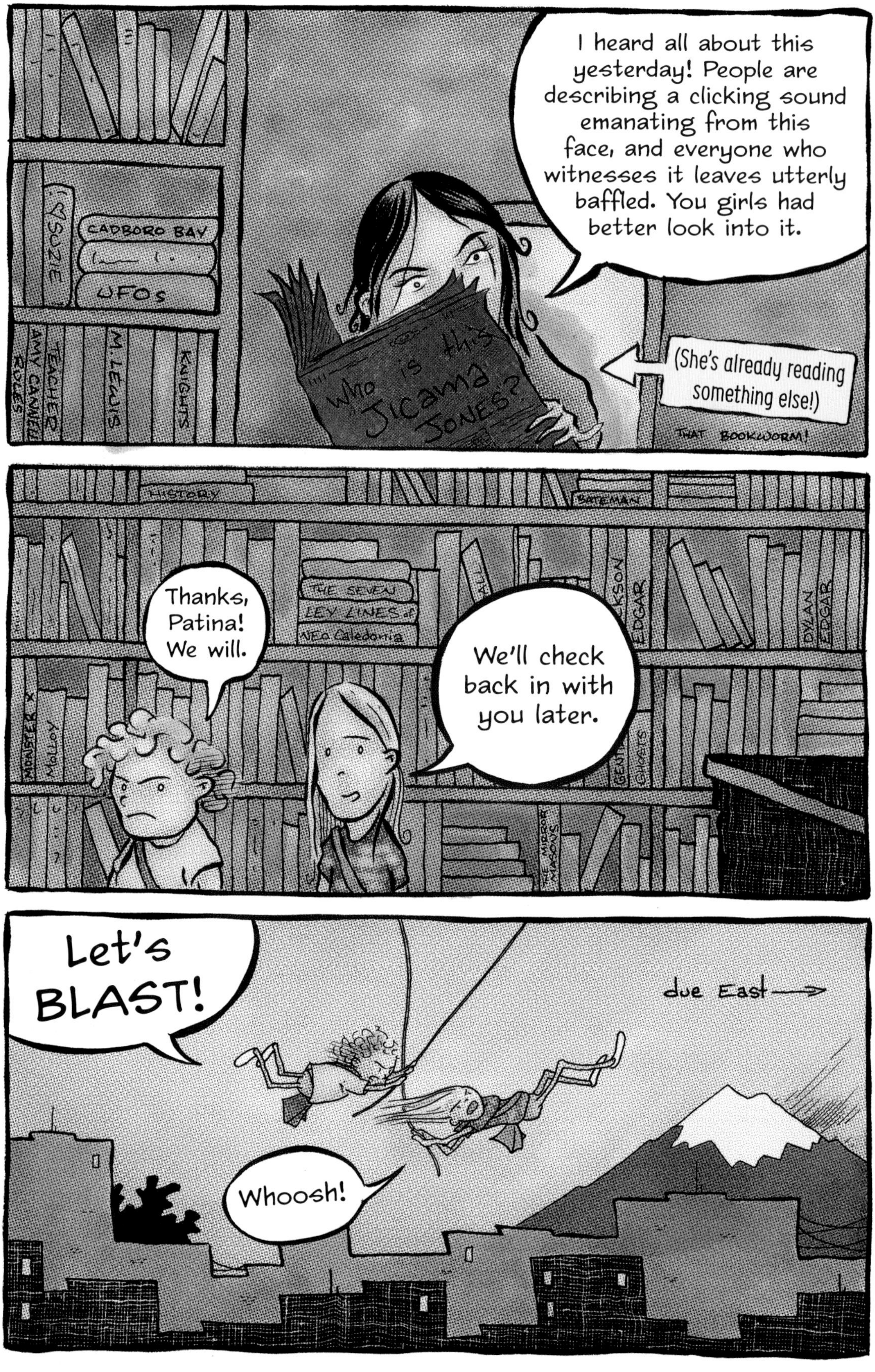
I heard all about this yesterday! People are describing a clicking sound emanating from this face, and everyone who witnesses it leaves utterly baffled. You girls had better look into it.
Who is this Jicama Jones?
(She's already reading something else!)
THAT BOOKWORM!
Thanks, Patina! We will.
We'll check back in with you later.
Let's BLAST!
due East
Whoosh!

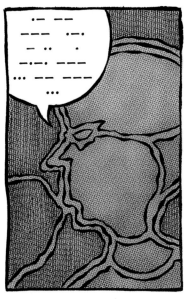

.- --
--- .-.
- .. .
-.-.- .- -
... -- ---
...

Patina was right!
The stones are
definitely clicking.

I think
it's
Morse
code.

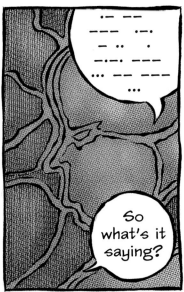

.- --
--- .-.
- .. .
-.-.- .- -
...

So
what's it
saying?

Hold
on...

.- --
--- .-.
- .. .
-.-.- ---
... -- ---
...

It just
keeps repeating
the phrase
"Amor De Cosmos."

.- --
--- .-.
- .. .
-.-.- ---
... -- ---
...

There
it goes
again!

"Love of the
universe?" This rock
wall not only speaks
Latin and Greek but
it's also a lover of
the universe?

Apparently.

But if my memory serves
me correctly, Amor De
Cosmos was also a
man. Born in 1825, he
went on to become the
second premier of British
Columbia.

Go
on.

He was also the
founder and publisher
of the *British Colonist*,
British Columbia's first
newspaper of any
permanence.

But why
would
this wall
care
about
any of
that?

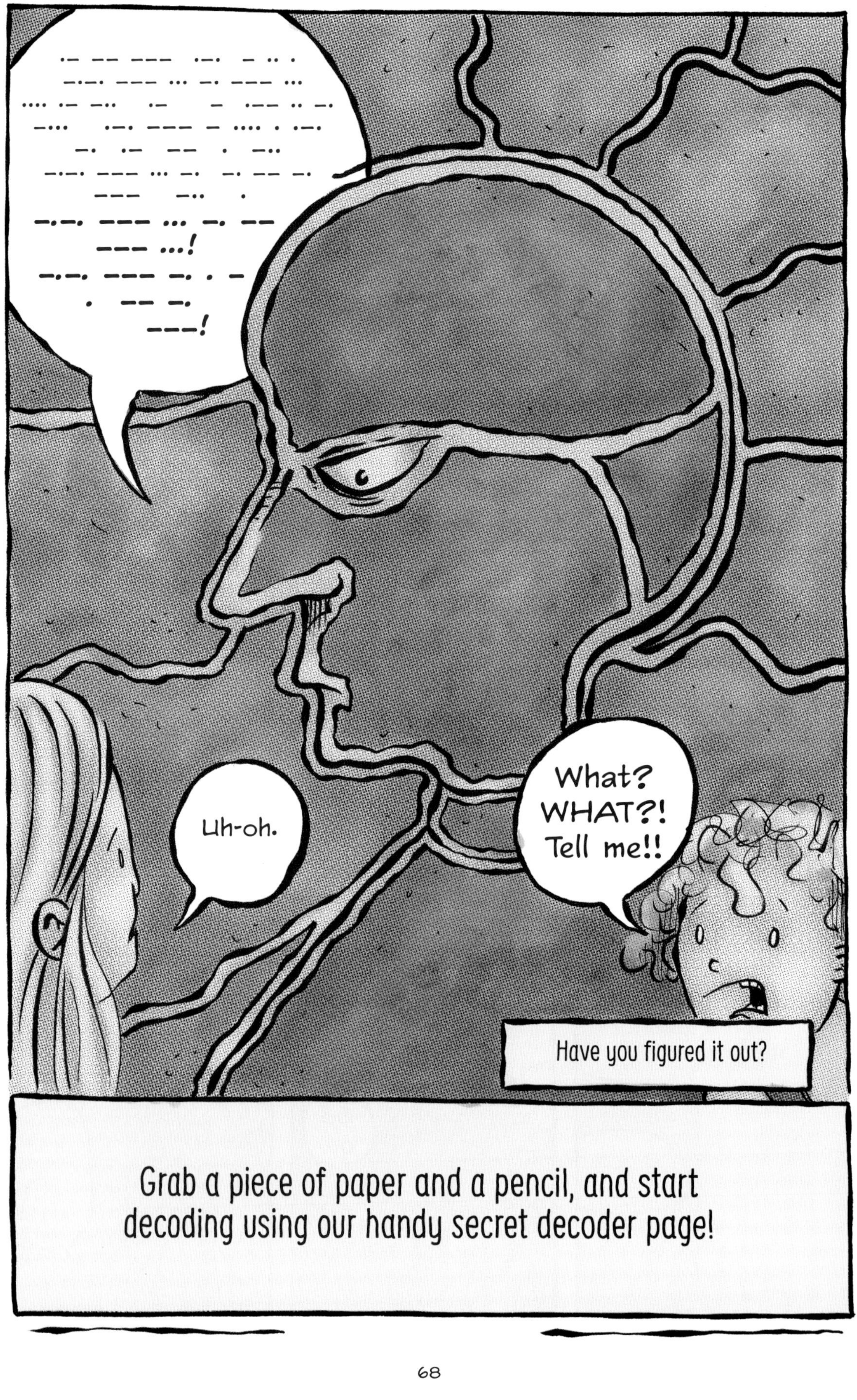
.- -- --- .-. - .. .
-.-. --- ... -. --- ...
.... .- -.. .- - .-- .. -.
-... .-. --- - .... . .-.
-. .- -- . -..
-.-. --- ... -. -. -- -.
--- -.. .
-.-. --- ... -. --
--- ...!
-.-. --- -. . -
. -- -.
---!
Uh-oh.
What? WHAT?! Tell me!!
Have you figured it out?
Grab a piece of paper and a pencil, and start decoding using our handy secret decoder page!

MORSE CODE
DECODER

A	· —		T	—
B	— · · ·		U	· · —
C	— · — ·		V	· · · —
D	— · ·		W	· — —
E	·		X	— · · —
F	· · — ·		Y	— · — —
G	— — ·		Z	— — · ·
H	· · · ·			
I	· ·		1	· — — — —
J	· — — —		2	· · — — —
K	— · —		3	· · · — —
L	· — · ·		4	· · · · —
M	— —		5	· · · · ·
N	— ·		6	— · · · ·
O	— — —		7	— — · · ·
P	· — — ·		8	— — — · ·
Q	— — · —		9	— — — — ·
R	· — ·		0	— — — — —
S	· · ·			

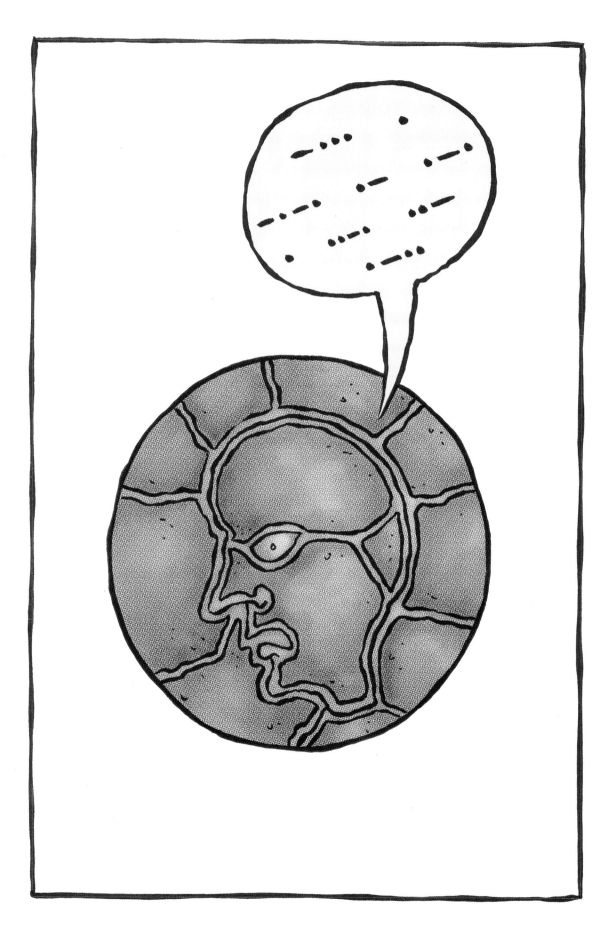

CHAPTER THREE
AFTER THE GOLD RUSH

3

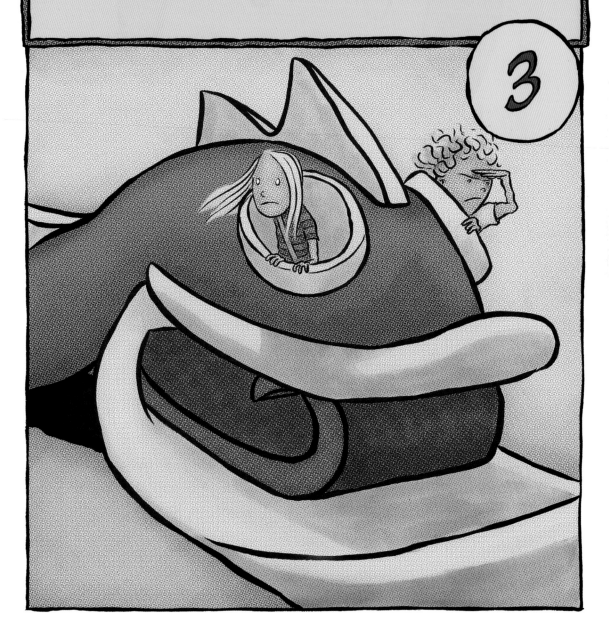

What a mystery, huh? So the girls are off again, racing to the provincial archives to find more clues. Along the way, Enid has a song in her head. It's "After the Gold Rush" by Canada's own Neil Young. I'd print the lyrics here for you if I could, but Neil Young hasn't given me permission yet. Maybe in a later printing. Just know that it's a really cool song and Enid has just figured out a connection between it and their current mission. Let's continue...

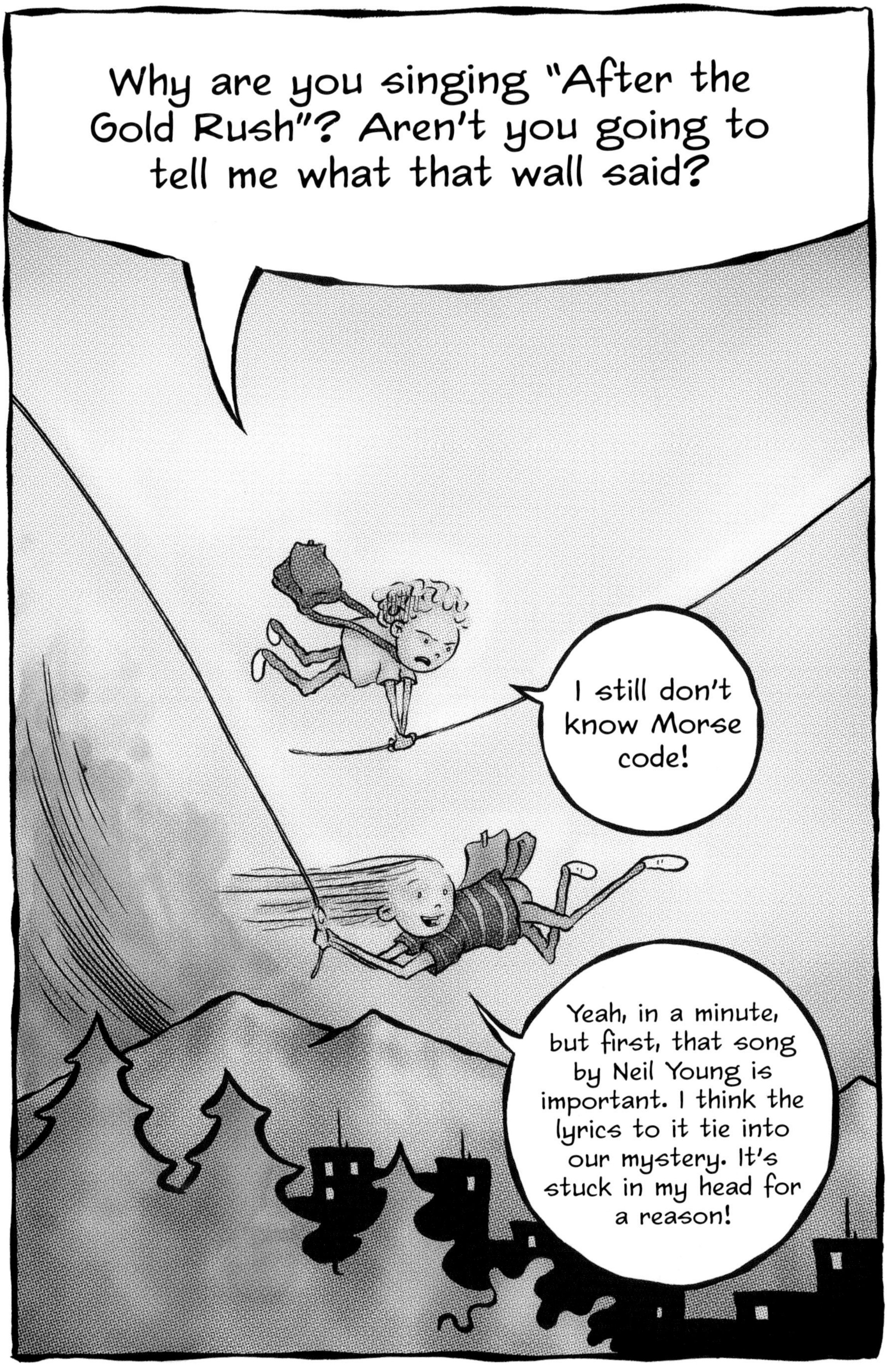
Why are you singing "After the Gold Rush"? Aren't you going to tell me what that wall said?
I still don't know Morse code!
Yeah, in a minute, but first, that song by Neil Young is important. I think the lyrics to it tie into our mystery. It's stuck in my head for a reason!

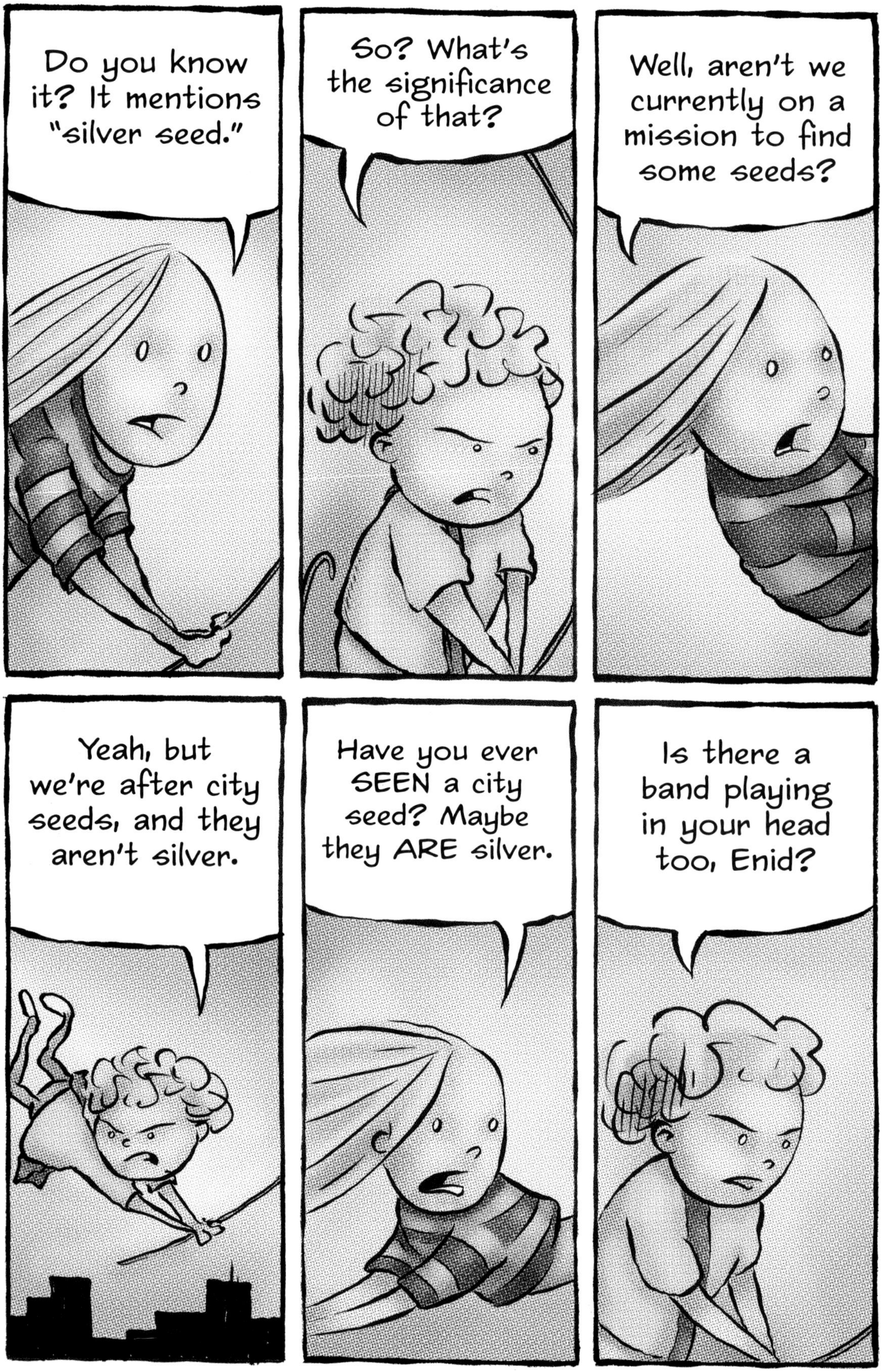
Do you know it? It mentions "silver seed."
So? What's the significance of that?
Well, aren't we currently on a mission to find some seeds?
Yeah, but we're after city seeds, and they aren't silver.
Have you ever SEEN a city seed? Maybe they ARE silver.
Is there a band playing in your head too, Enid?

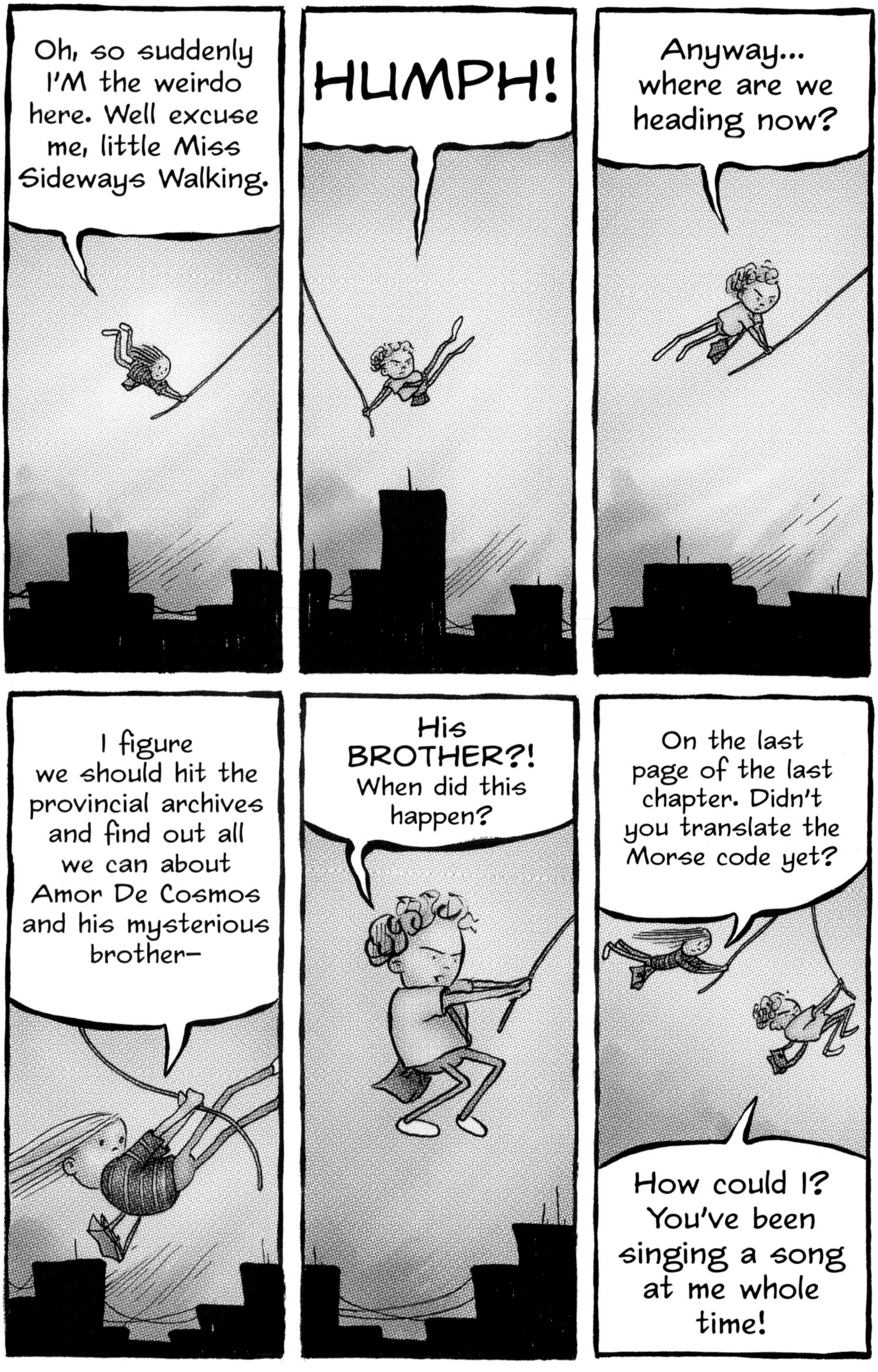
Oh, so suddenly I'M the weirdo here. Well excuse me, little Miss Sideways Walking.
HUMPH!
Anyway... where are we heading now?
I figure we should hit the provincial archives and find out all we can about Amor De Cosmos and his mysterious brother–
His BROTHER?! When did this happen?
On the last page of the last chapter. Didn't you translate the Morse code yet?
How could I? You've been singing a song at me whole time!

Oh yeah. The Morse code! Well, after the face in the rock wall kept saying "Amor De Cosmos" over and over, it then stated quite boldly:

"Amor De Cosmos had a twin brother named Contemno De Cosmos! CONTEMNO!"

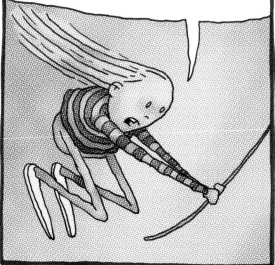

That doesn't bode too well for this having a cheerful ending. Amor De Cosmos's name means "love of the universe."

But his twin brother's name means "hate of the universe." Let's get to the archives quick.

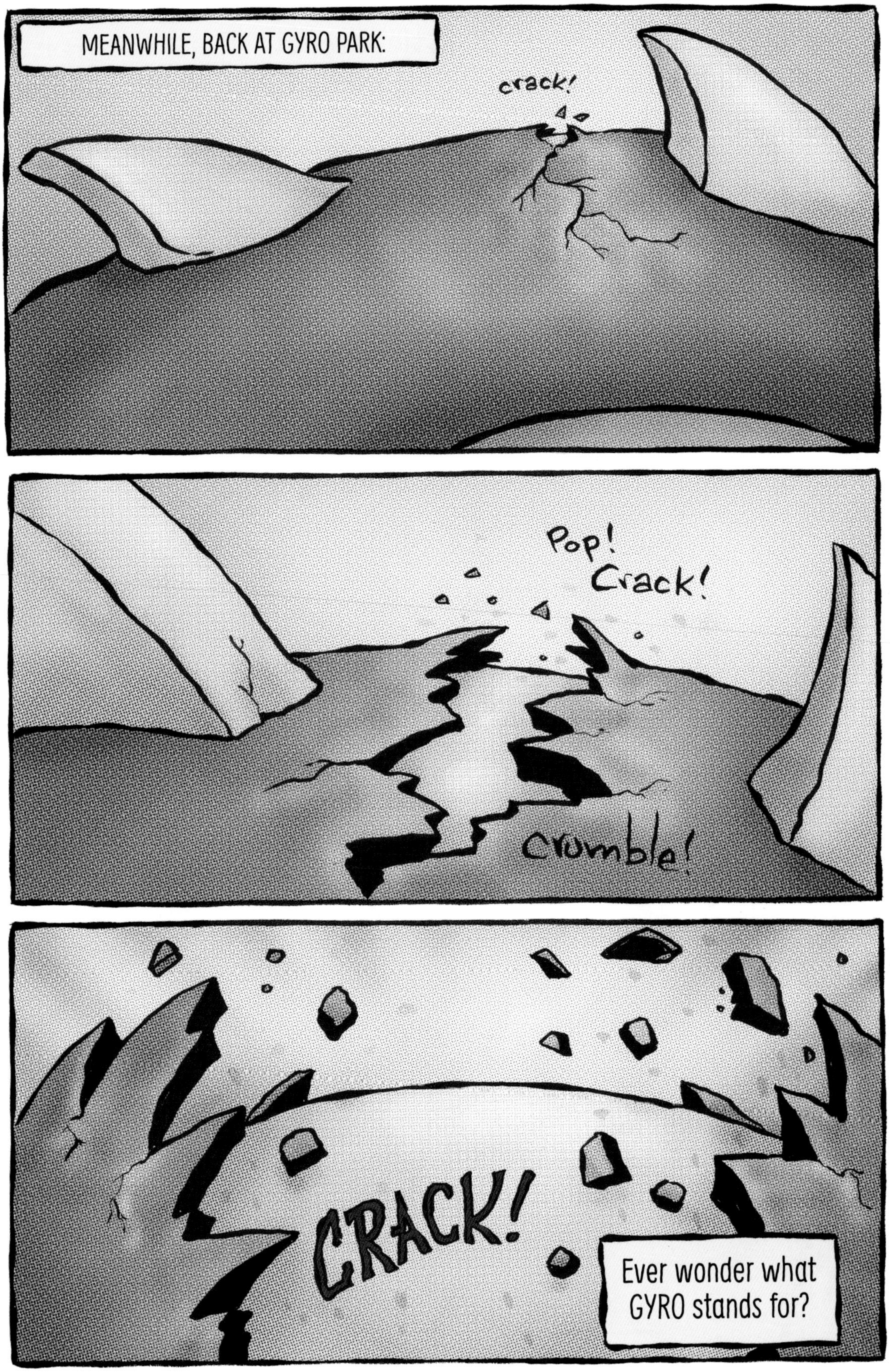
MEANWHILE, BACK AT GYRO PARK:
crack!
Pop!
Crack!
Crumble!
CRACK!
Ever wonder what GYRO stands for?

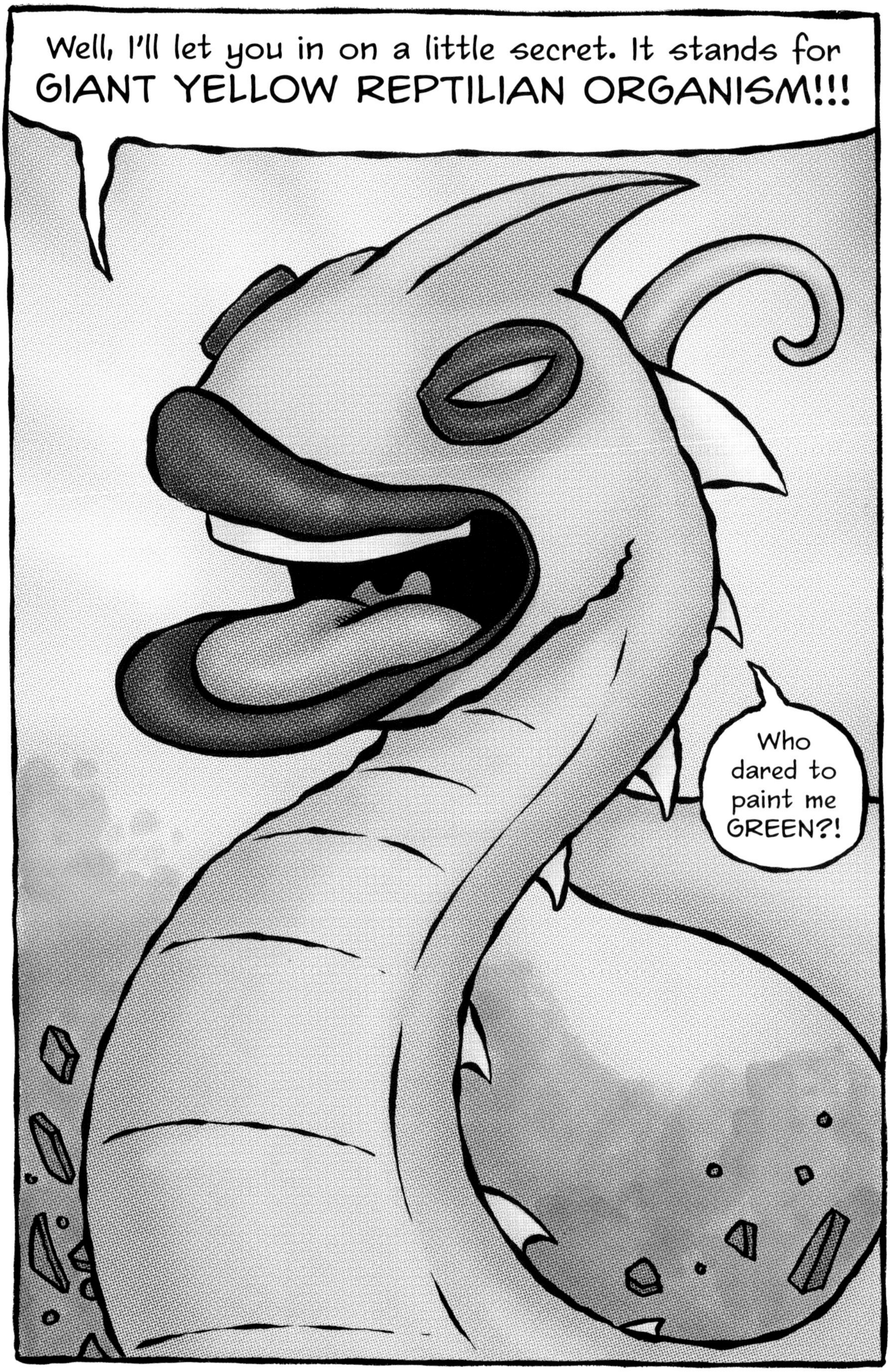
Well, I'll let you in on a little secret. It stands for GIANT YELLOW REPTILIAN ORGANISM!!!
Who dared to paint me GREEN?!

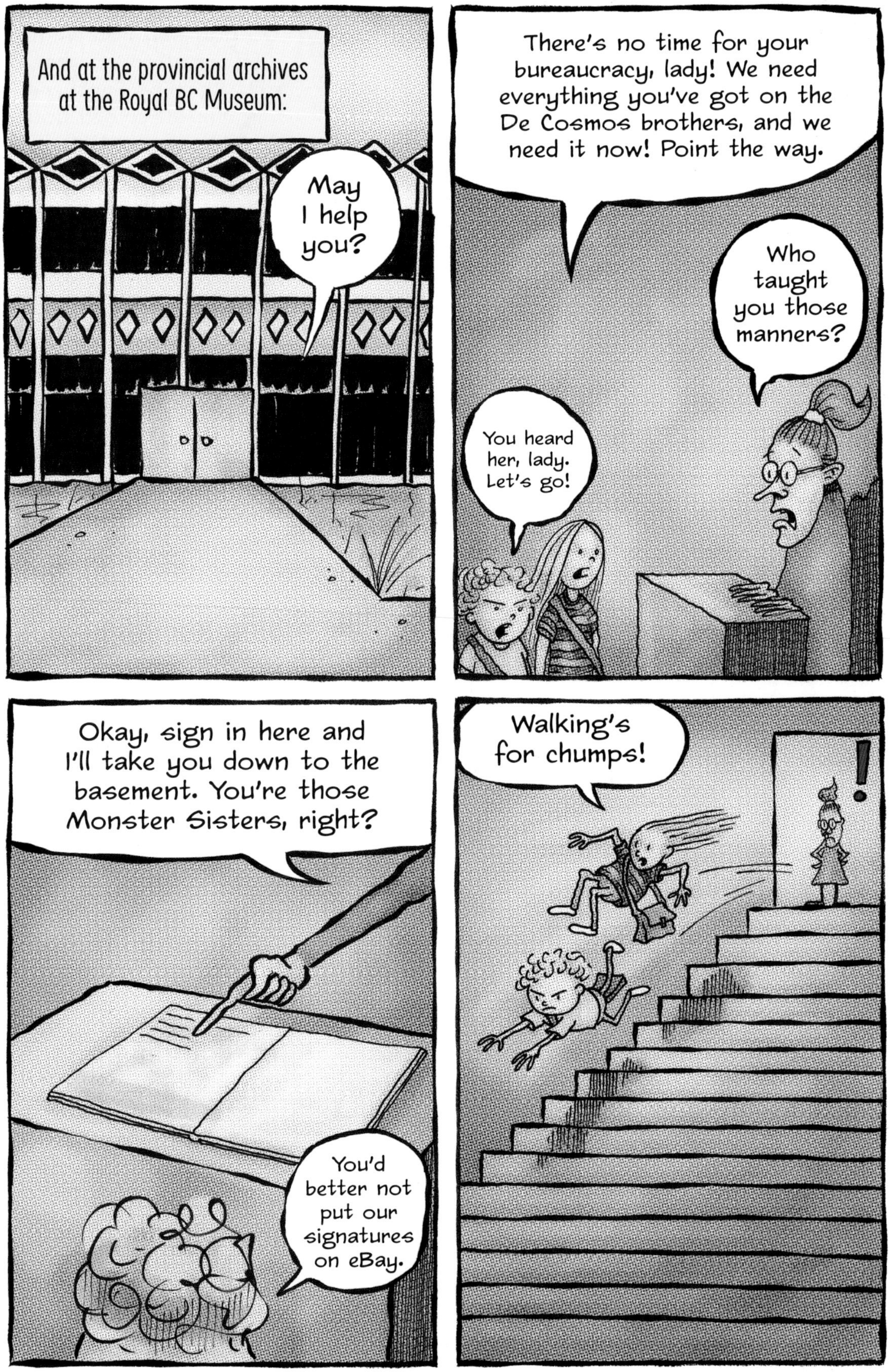
And at the provincial archives at the Royal BC Museum:
May I help you?
There's no time for your bureaucracy, lady! We need everything you've got on the De Cosmos brothers, and we need it now! Point the way.
Who taught you those manners?
You heard her, lady. Let's go!
Okay, sign in here and I'll take you down to the basement. You're those Monster Sisters, right?
You'd better not put our signatures on eBay.
Walking's for chumps!
!

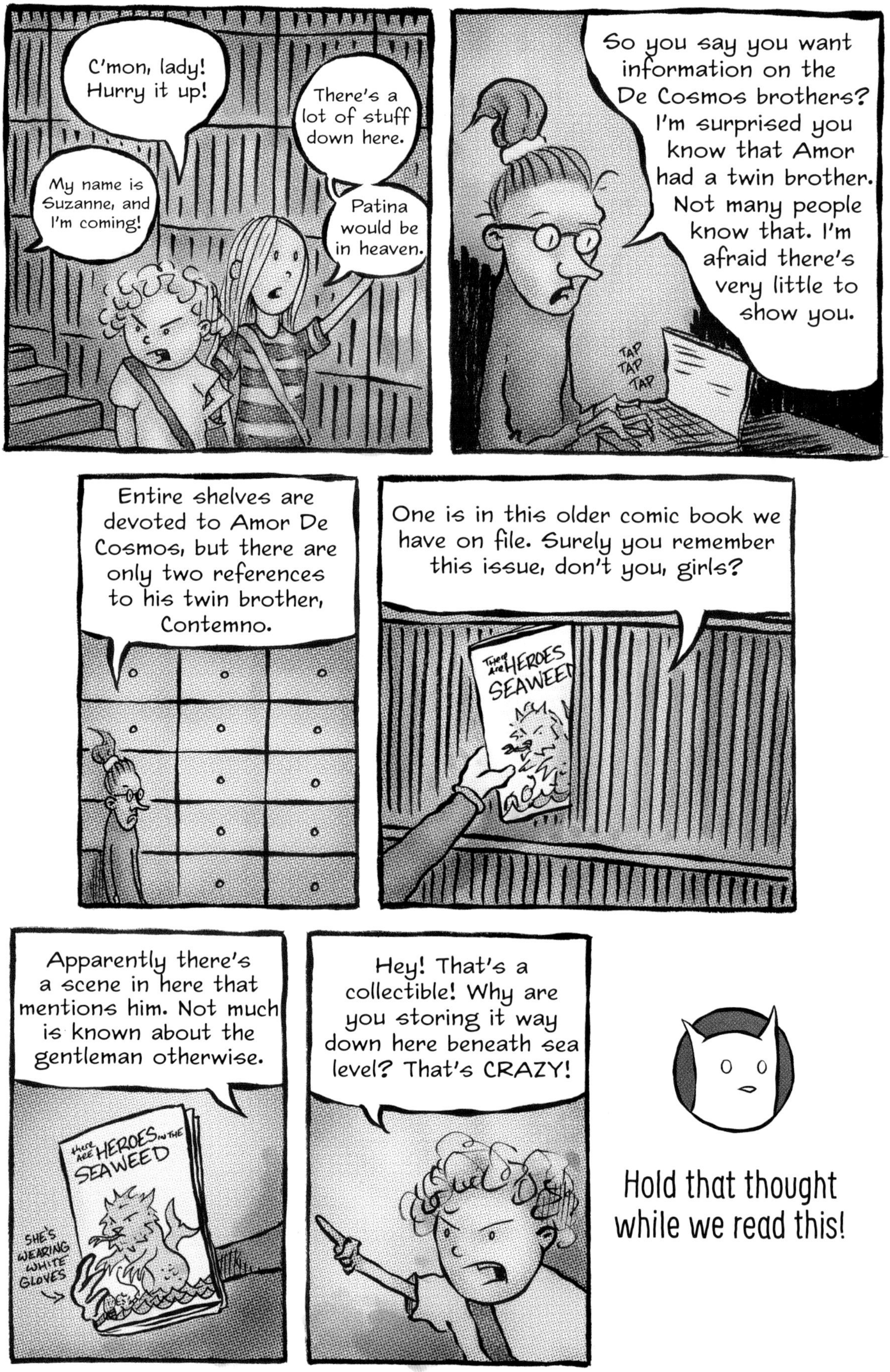
C'mon, lady! Hurry it up!
There's a lot of stuff down here.
My name is Suzanne, and I'm coming!
Patina would be in heaven.
So you say you want information on the De Cosmos brothers? I'm surprised you know that Amor had a twin brother. Not many people know that. I'm afraid there's very little to show you.
TAP TAP TAP
Entire shelves are devoted to Amor De Cosmos, but there are only two references to his twin brother, Contemno.
One is in this older comic book we have on file. Surely you remember this issue, don't you, girls?
There are HEROES in the SEAWEED
Apparently there's a scene in here that mentions him. Not much is known about the gentleman otherwise.
SHE'S WEARING WHITE GLOVES
Hey! That's a collectible! Why are you storing it way down here beneath sea level? That's CRAZY!
Hold that thought while we read this!

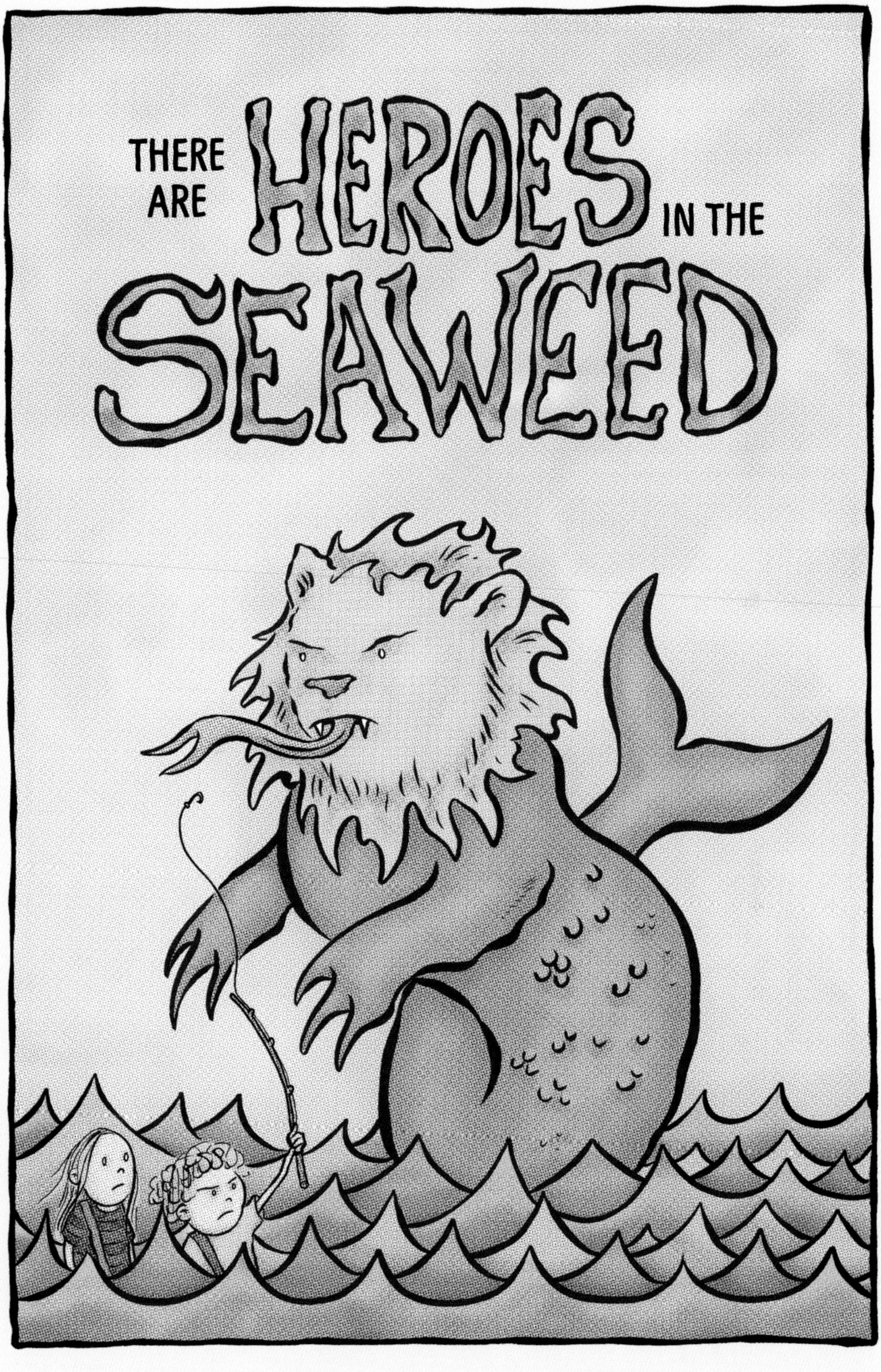
THERE ARE HEROES IN THE SEAWEED

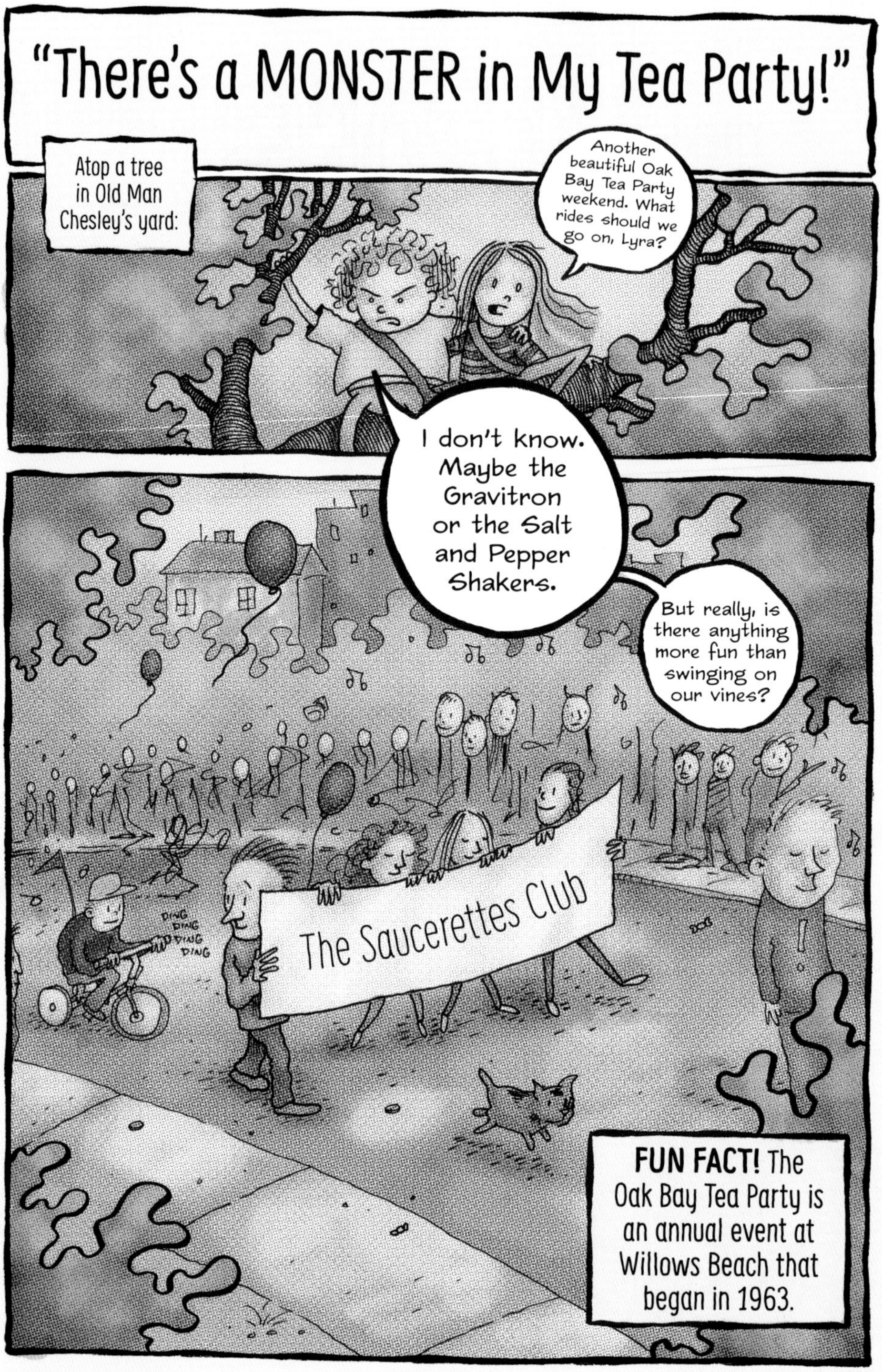
"There's a MONSTER in My Tea Party!"
Atop a tree in Old Man Chesley's yard:
Another beautiful Oak Bay Tea Party weekend. What rides should we go on, Lyra?
I don't know. Maybe the Gravitron or the Salt and Pepper Shakers.
But really, is there anything more fun than swinging on our vines?
The Saucerettes Club
DING DING DING DING
FUN FACT! The Oak Bay Tea Party is an annual event at Willows Beach that began in 1963.

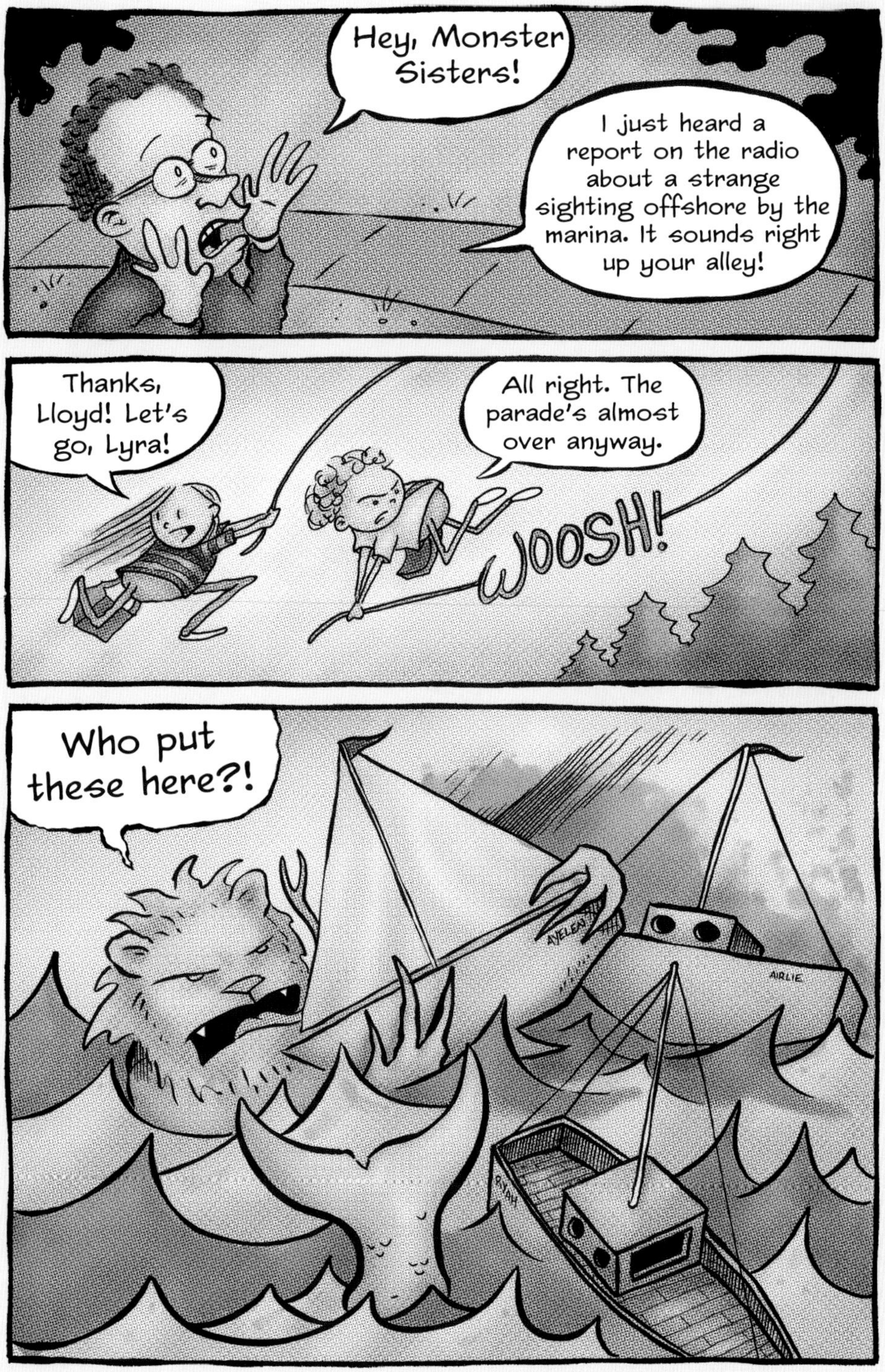
Hey, Monster Sisters!
I just heard a report on the radio about a strange sighting offshore by the marina. It sounds right up your alley!
Thanks, Lloyd! Let's go, Lyra!
All right. The parade's almost over anyway.
WOOSH!
Who put these here?!

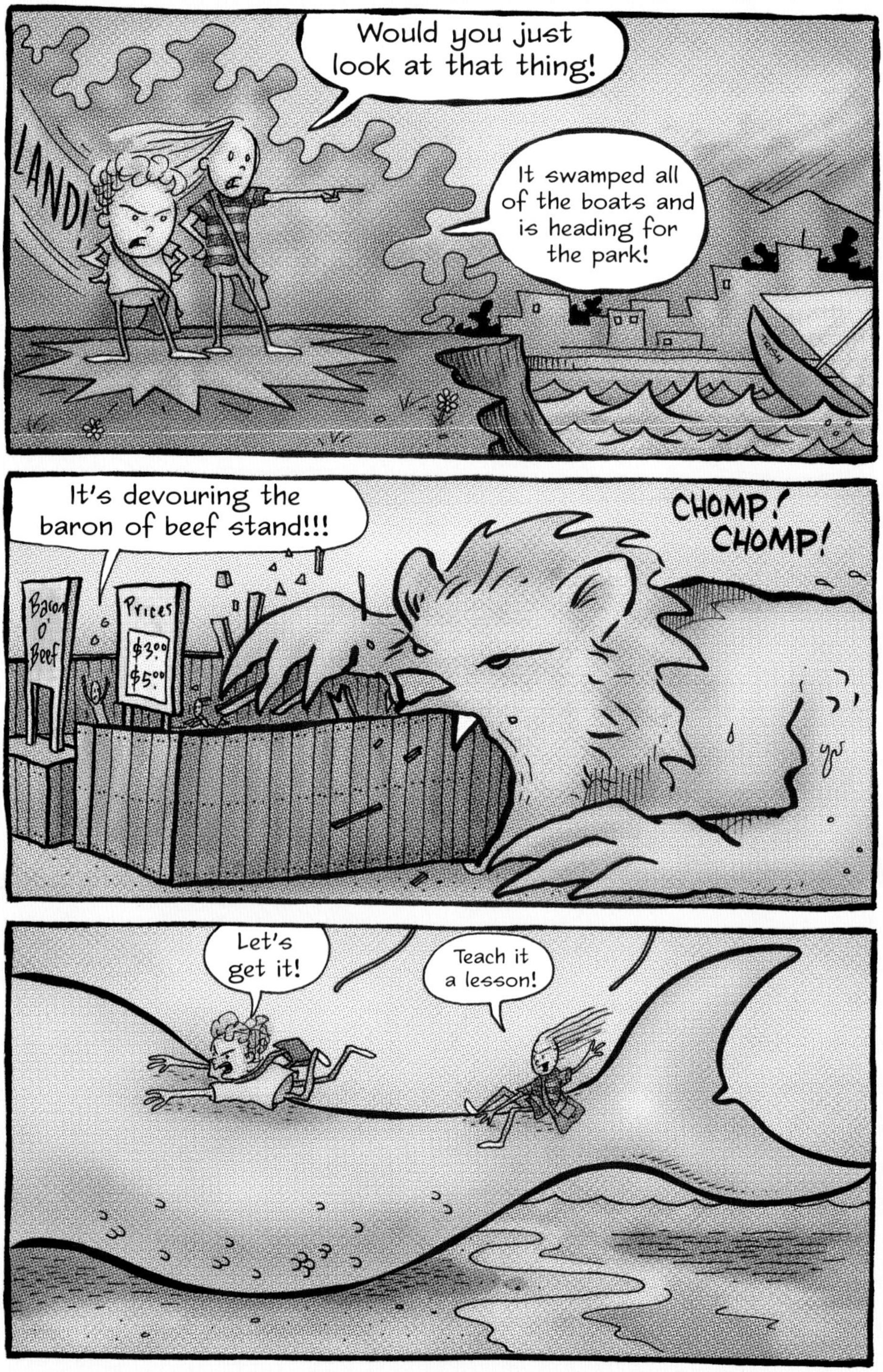
LAND!
Would you just look at that thing!
It swamped all of the boats and is heading for the park!
It's devouring the baron of beef stand!!!
Baron O' Beef
Prices
$3.00
$5.00
CHOMP! CHOMP!
Let's get it!
Teach it a lesson!

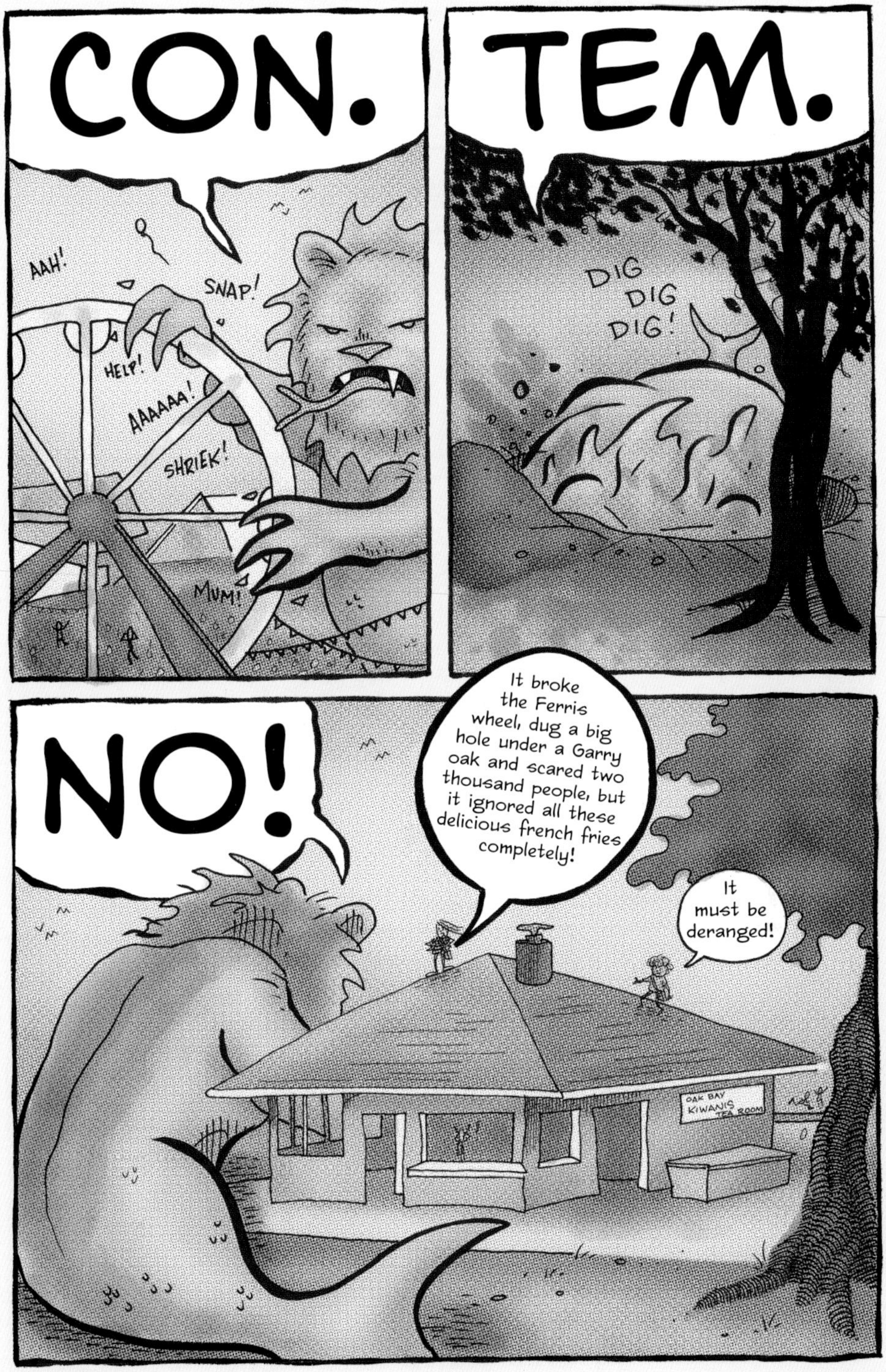
CON.
AAH!
SNAP!
HELP!
AAAAAA!
SHRIEK!
MUM!
TEM.
DIG
DIG
DIG!
NO!
It broke the Ferris wheel, dug a big hole under a Garry oak and scared two thousand people, but it ignored all these delicious french fries completely!
It must be deranged!
OAK BAY
KIWANIS
TEA ROOM

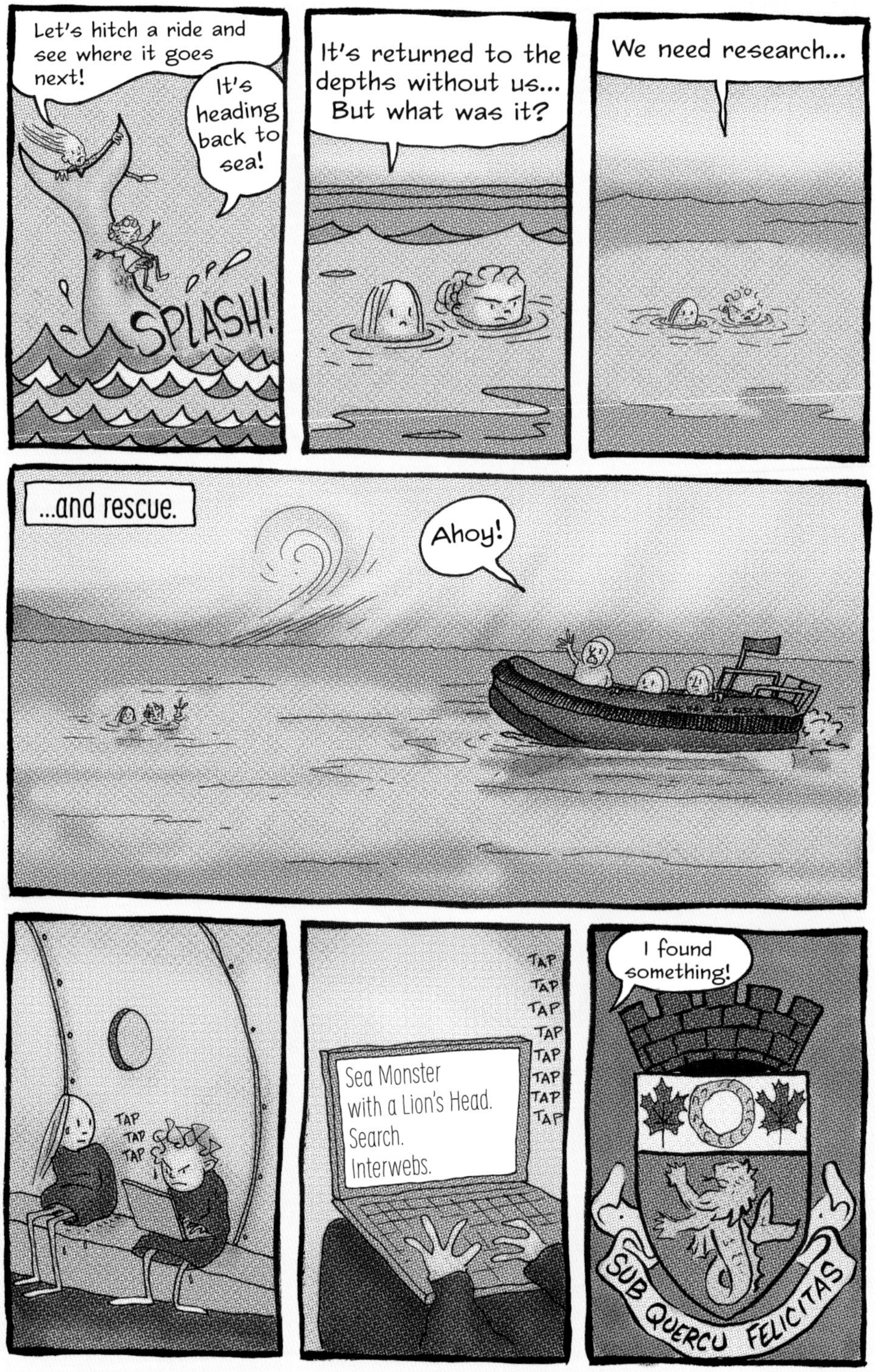
Let's hitch a ride and see where it goes next!
It's heading back to sea!
SPLASH!
It's returned to the depths without us... But what was it?
We need research...
...and rescue.
Ahoy!
TAP TAP TAP
TAP TAP TAP TAP TAP TAP TAP TAP
Sea Monster with a Lion's Head. Search. Interwebs.
I found something!
SUB QUERCU FELICITAS

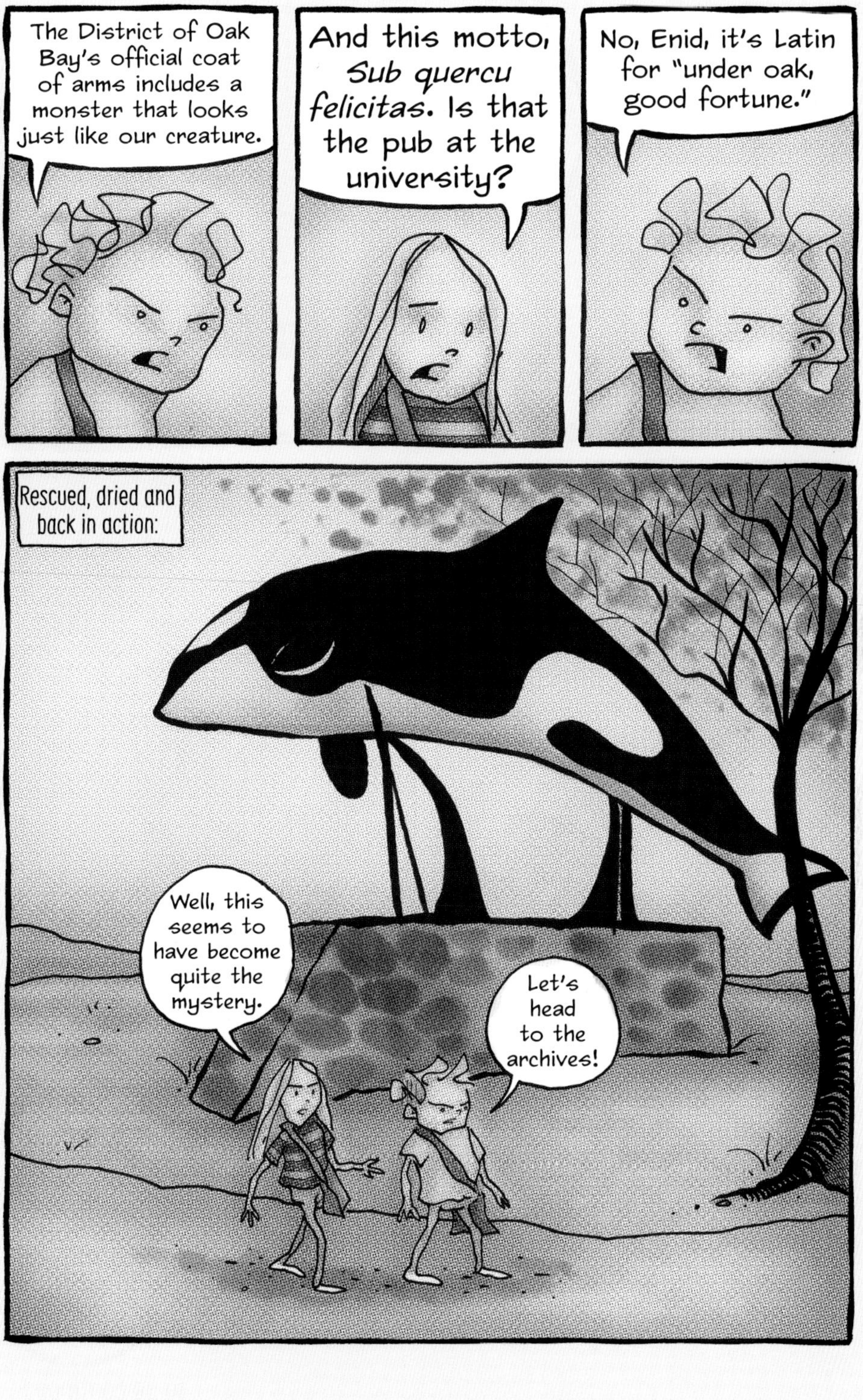
The District of Oak Bay's official coat of arms includes a monster that looks just like our creature.
And this motto, *Sub quercu felicitas*. Is that the pub at the university?
No, Enid, it's Latin for "under oak, good fortune."
Rescued, dried and back in action:
Well, this seems to have become quite the mystery.
Let's head to the archives!

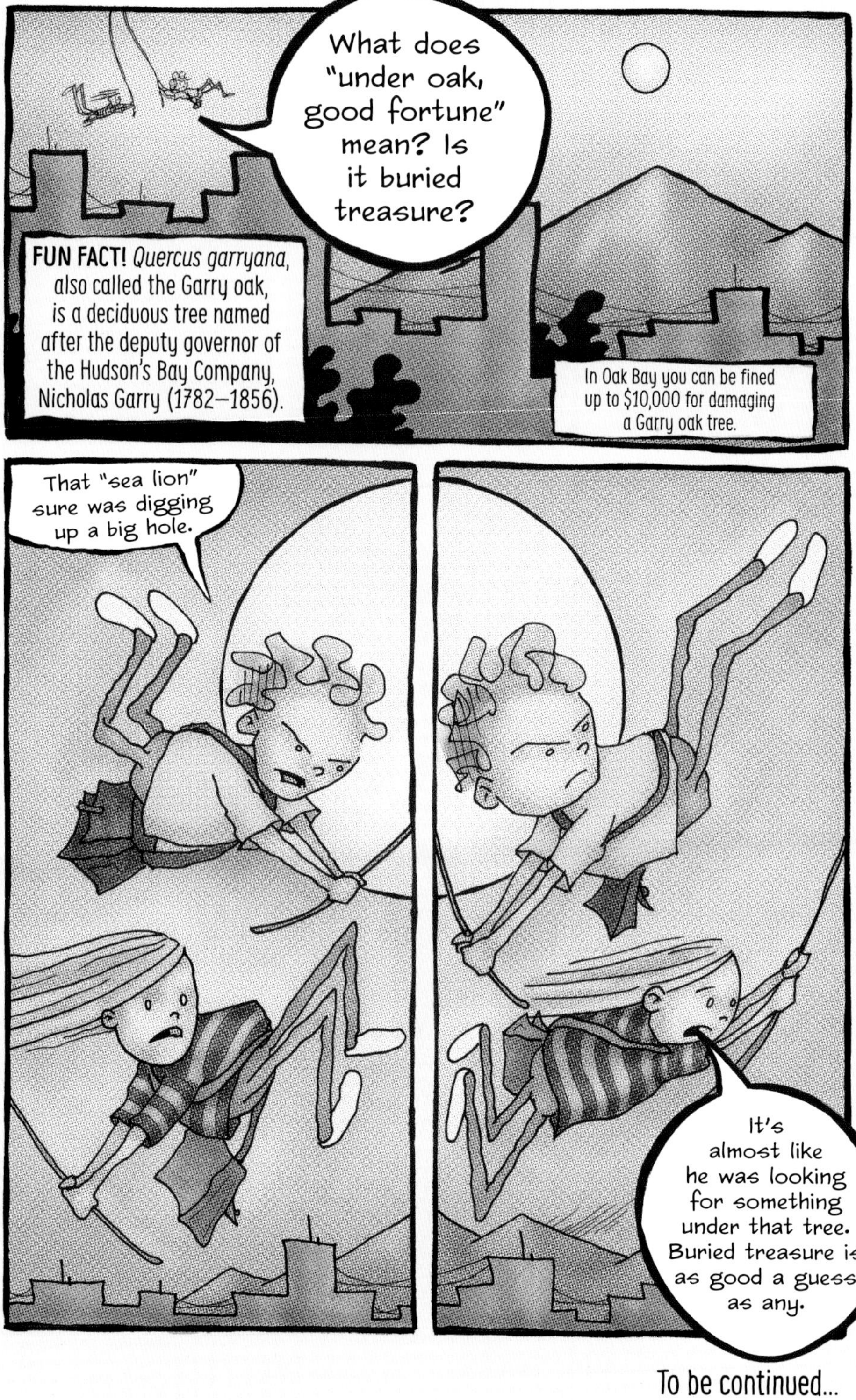
What does "under oak, good fortune" mean? Is it buried treasure?
FUN FACT! Quercus garryana, also called the Garry oak, is a deciduous tree named after the deputy governor of the Hudson's Bay Company, Nicholas Garry (1782–1856).
In Oak Bay you can be fined up to $10,000 for damaging a Garry oak tree.
That "sea lion" sure was digging up a big hole.
It's almost like he was looking for something under that tree. Buried treasure is as good a guess as any.

To be continued...

Huh. That was a cool issue.

You call that a reference to Contemno? The creature uttered his name over three panels in a comic book. Big deal.

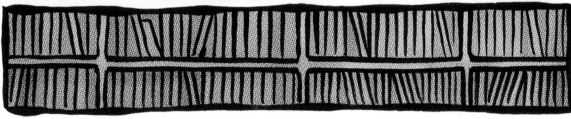

I didn't say it was a GOOD reference. Just the first one.

The second thing we have archived is the only known picture of him. It's right in here.

FLICK!

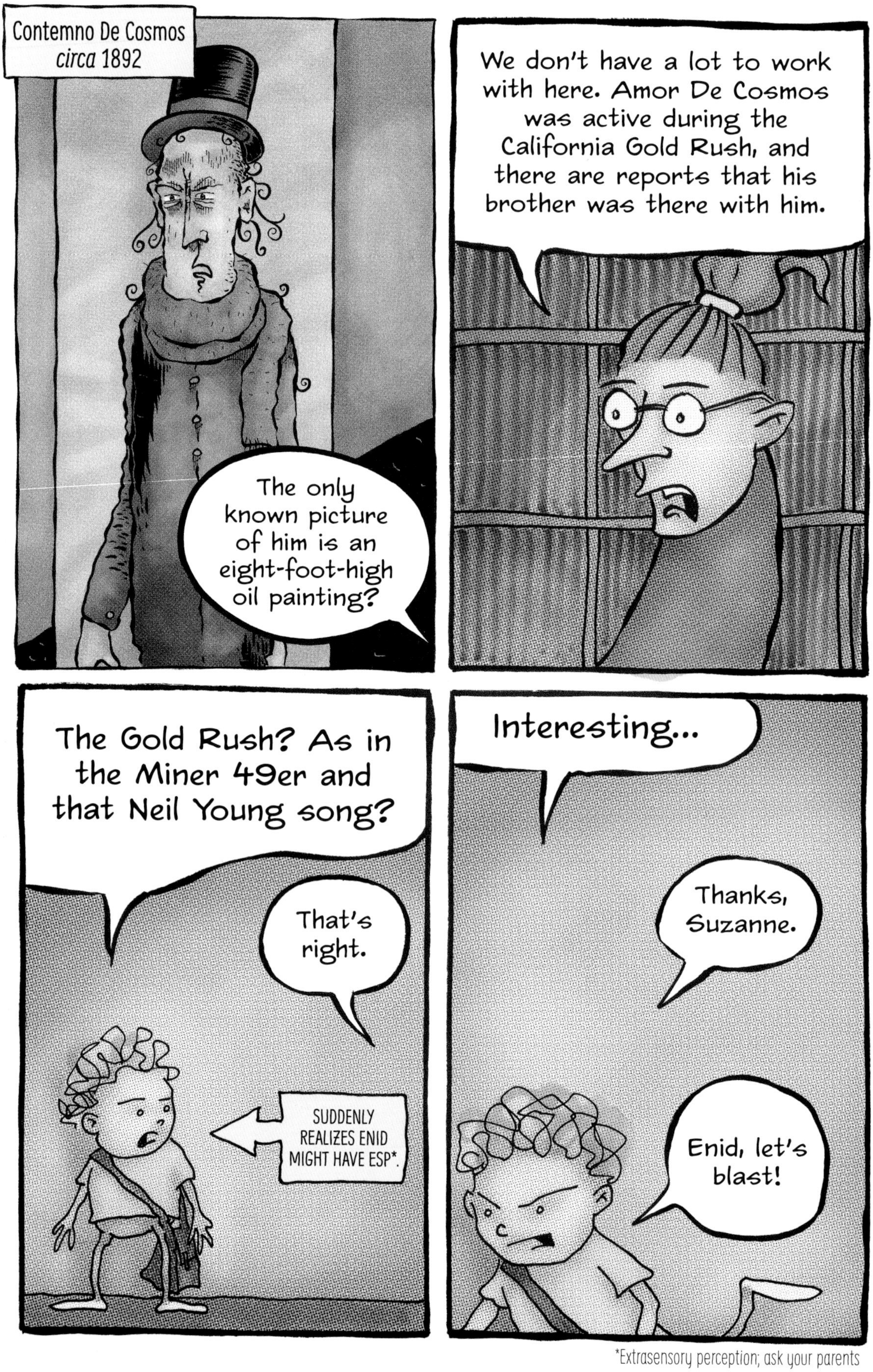
Contemno De Cosmos circa 1892
The only known picture of him is an eight-foot-high oil painting?
We don't have a lot to work with here. Amor De Cosmos was active during the California Gold Rush, and there are reports that his brother was there with him.
The Gold Rush? As in the Miner 49er and that Neil Young song?
That's right.
SUDDENLY REALIZES ENID MIGHT HAVE ESP*.
Interesting...
Thanks, Suzanne.
Enid, let's blast!

*Extrasensory perception; ask your parents

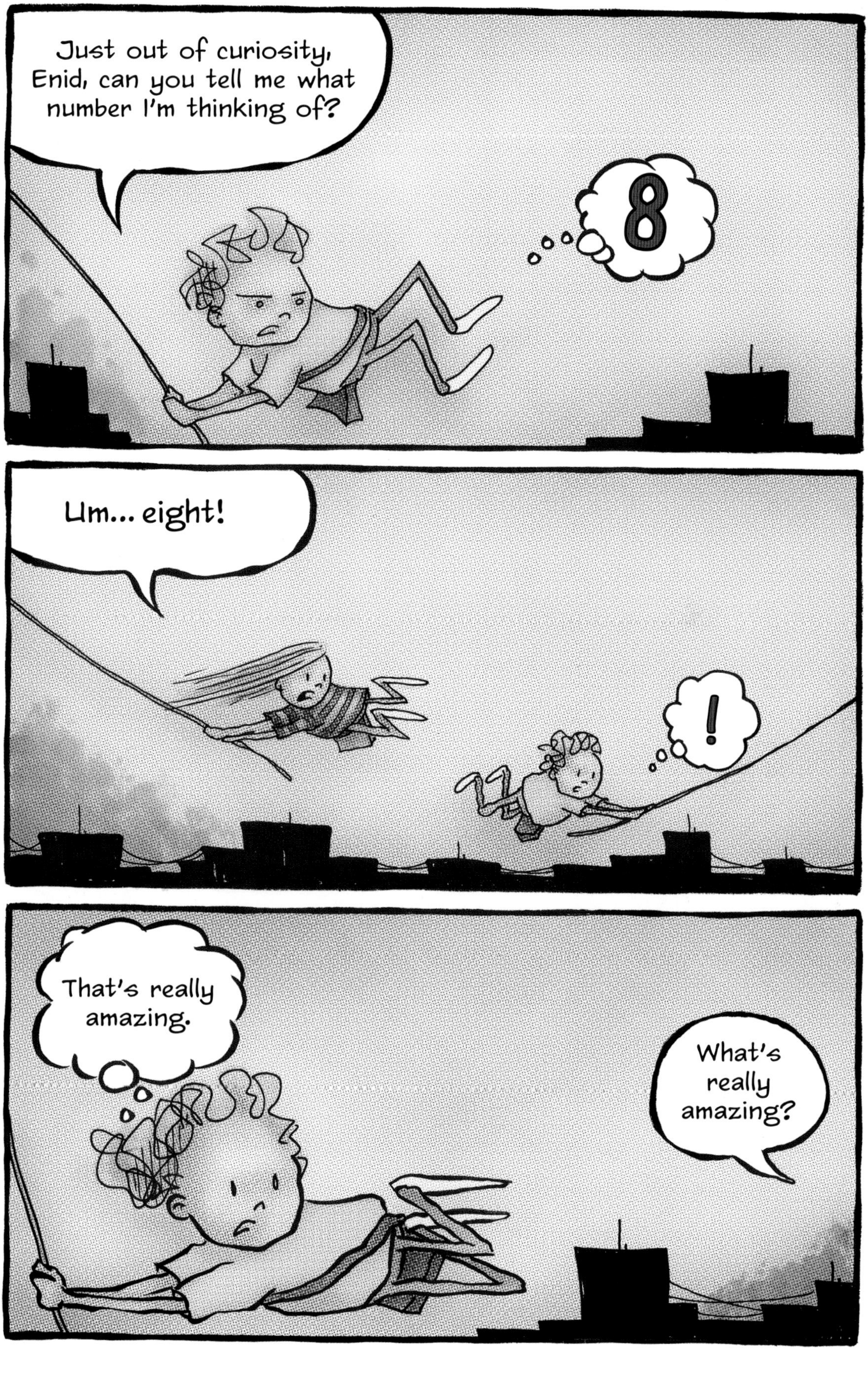
Just out of curiosity, Enid, can you tell me what number I'm thinking of?
8
Um... eight!
!
That's really amazing.
What's really amazing?

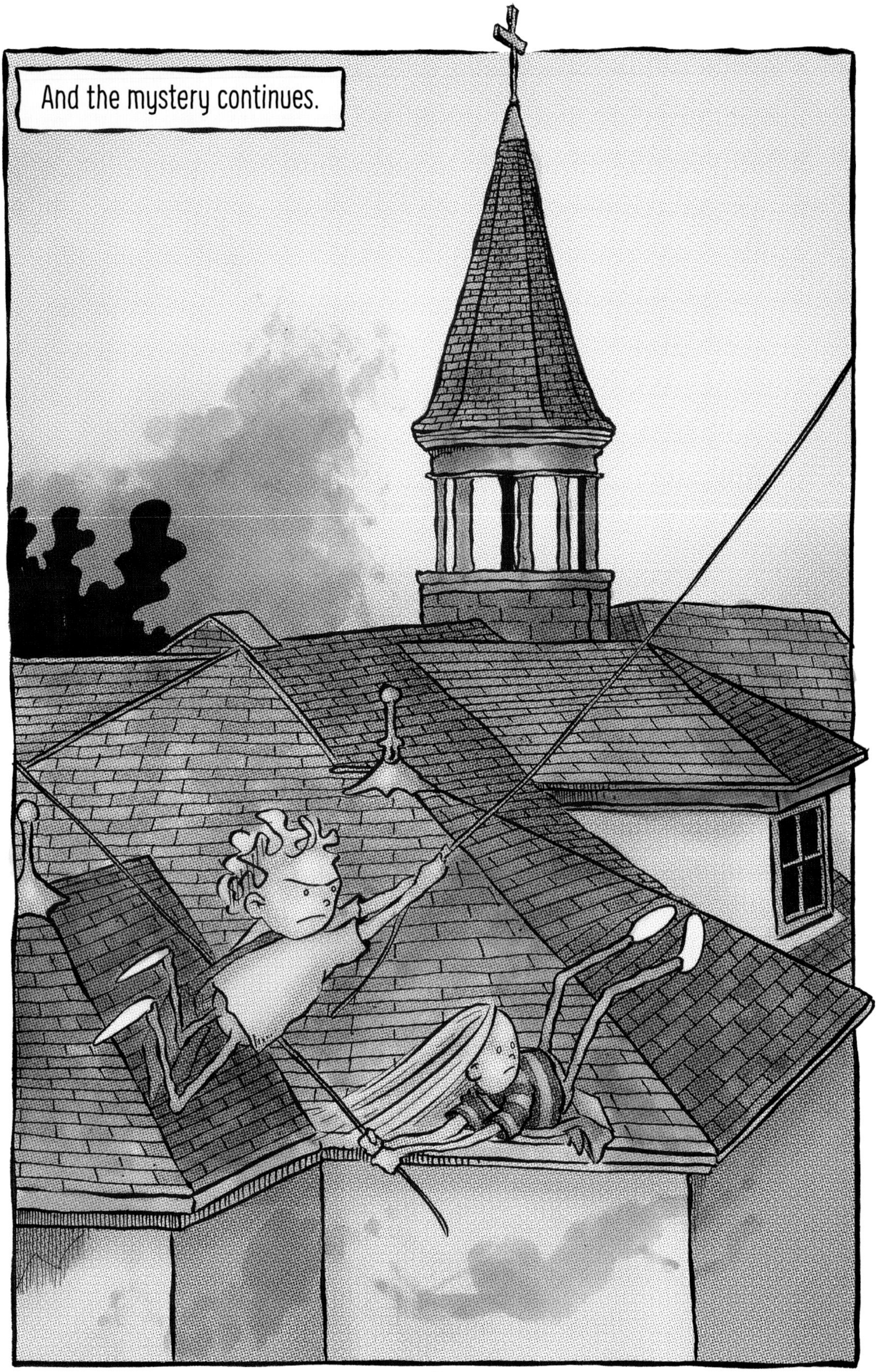
And the mystery continues.

CHAPTER FOUR

WE COME TO EAT VICTORIA

4

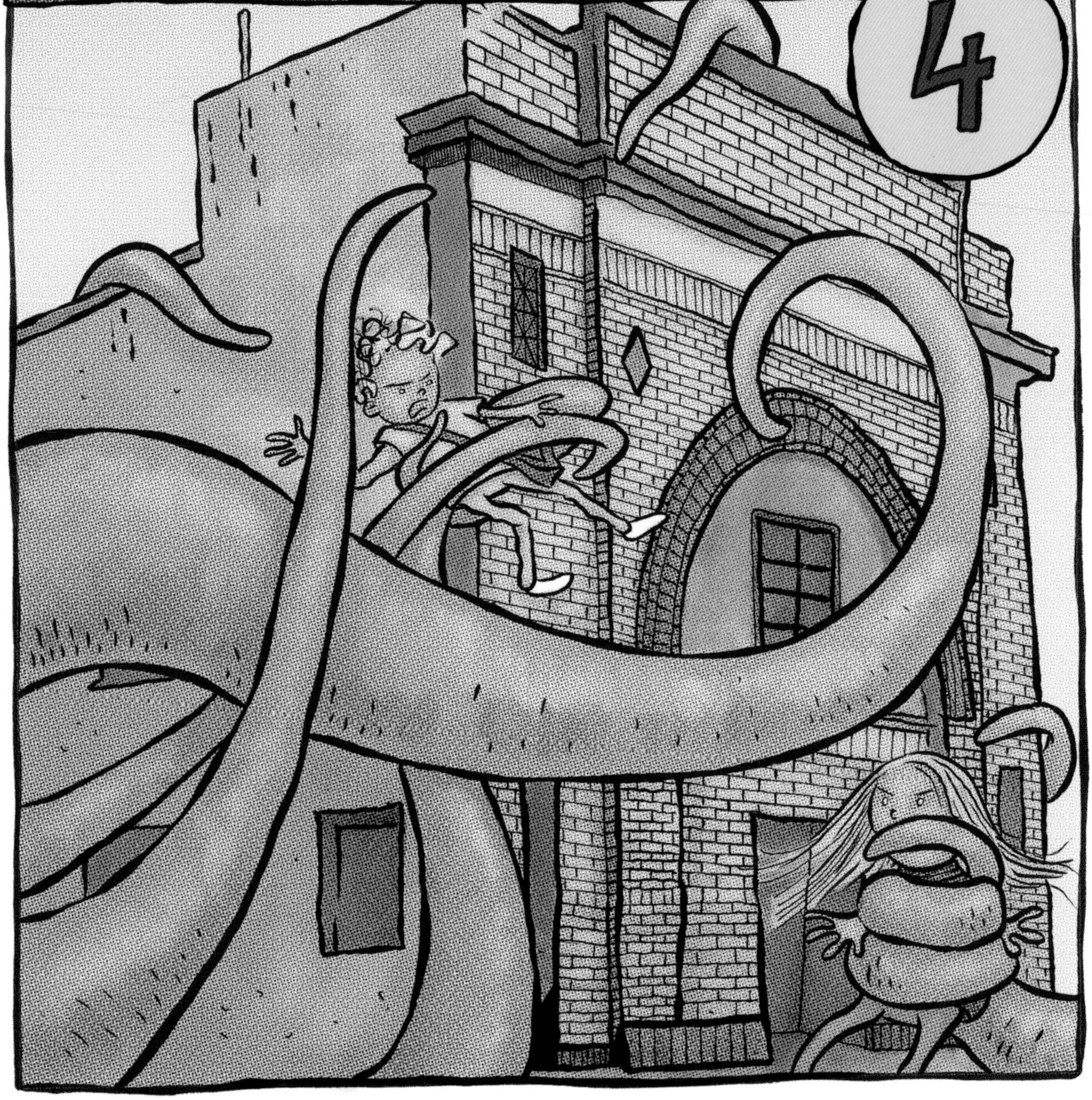

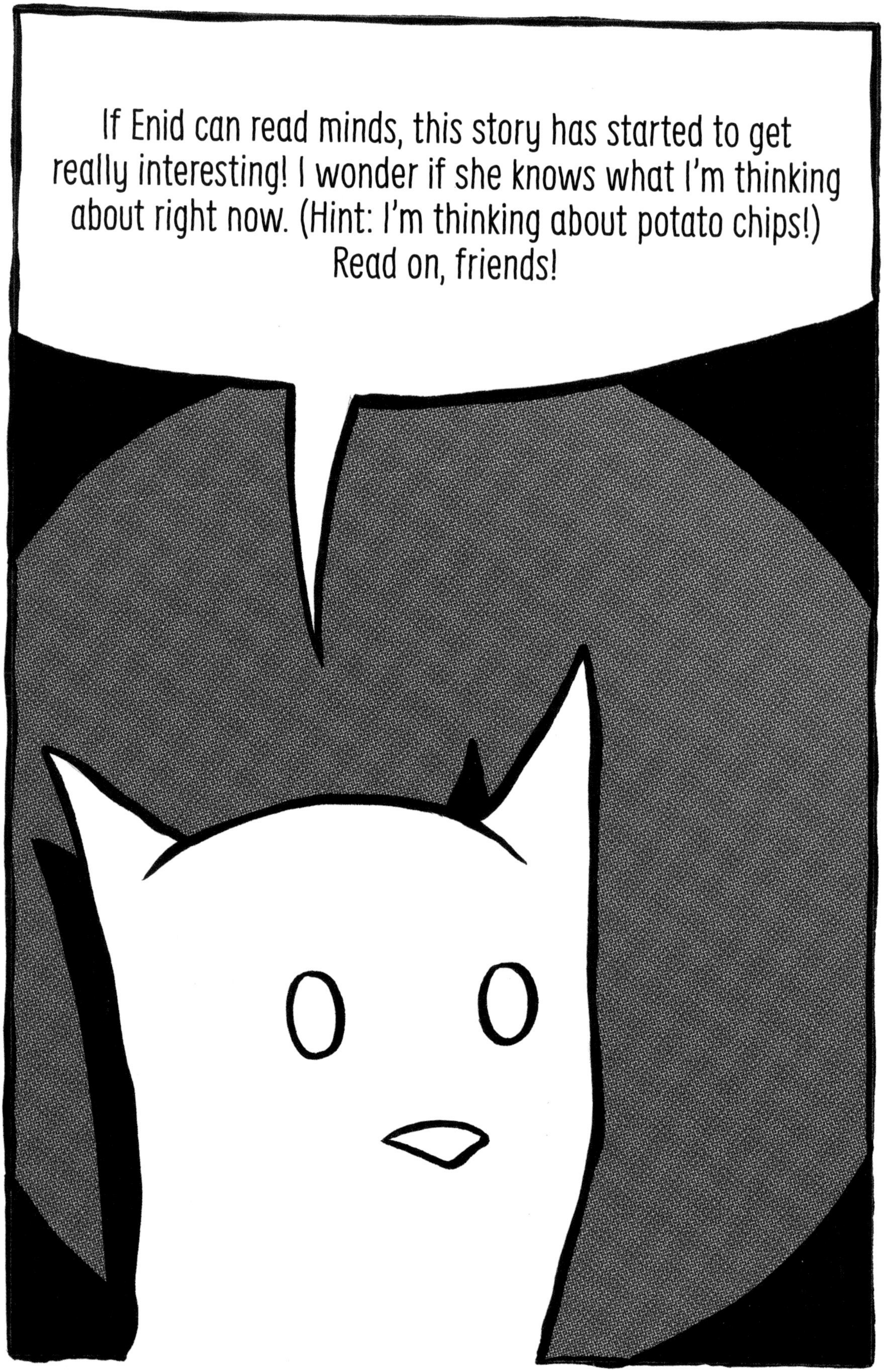
If Enid can read minds, this story has started to get really interesting! I wonder if she knows what I'm thinking about right now. (Hint: I'm thinking about potato chips!) Read on, friends!

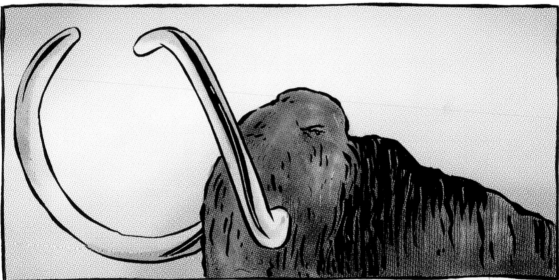

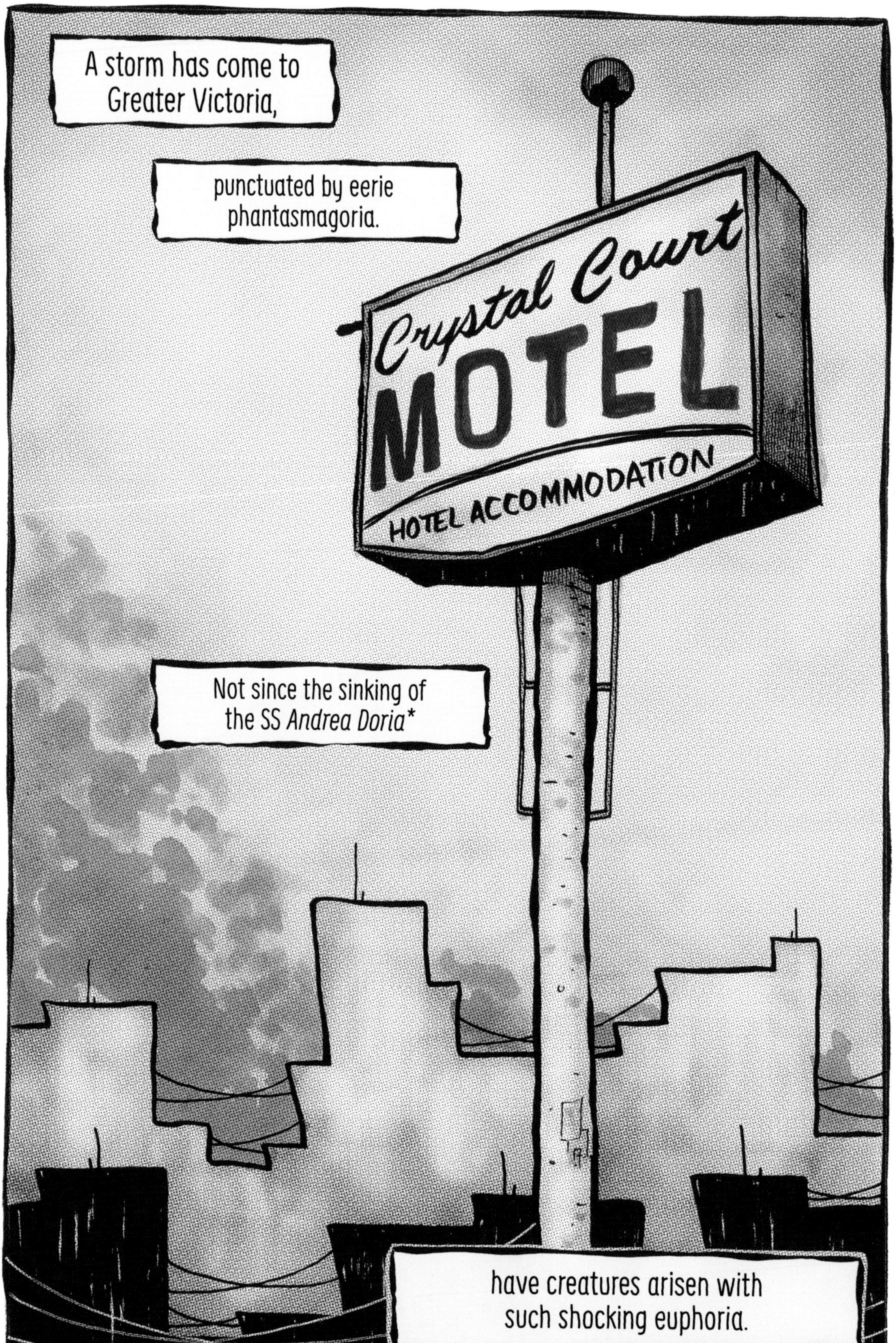
A storm has come to Greater Victoria,
punctuated by eerie phantasmagoria.
Crystal Court
MOTEL
HOTEL ACCOMMODATION
Not since the sinking of the SS *Andrea Doria**
have creatures arisen with such shocking euphoria.

* The SS *Andrea Doria* was an ocean liner that was part of one of the most infamous maritime disasters in history—it collided with the MS *Stockholm* while en route to New York City on July 25, 1956. Some people speculate that a sea serpent was involved. Others doubt this very much.

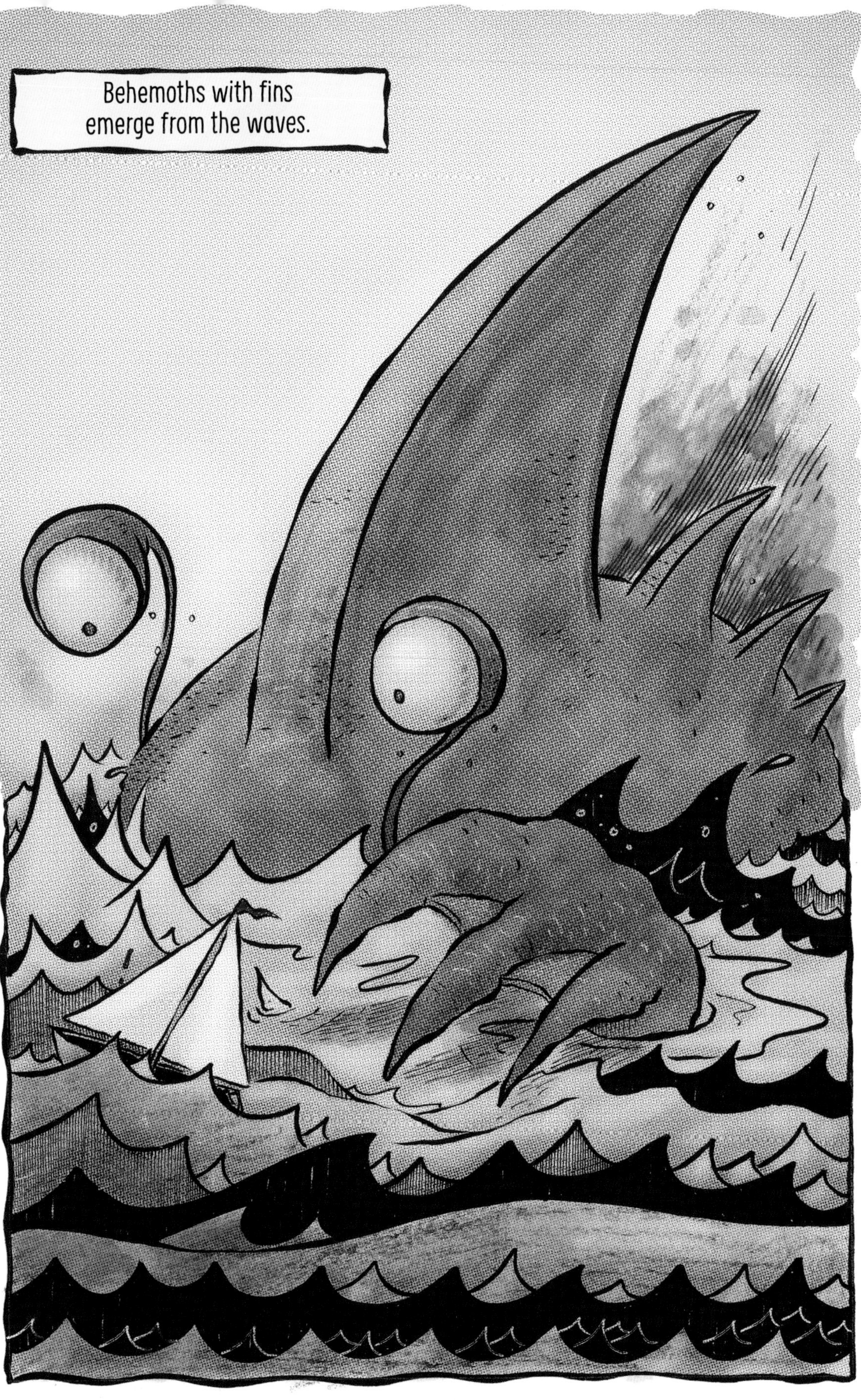
Behemoths with fins
emerge from the waves.

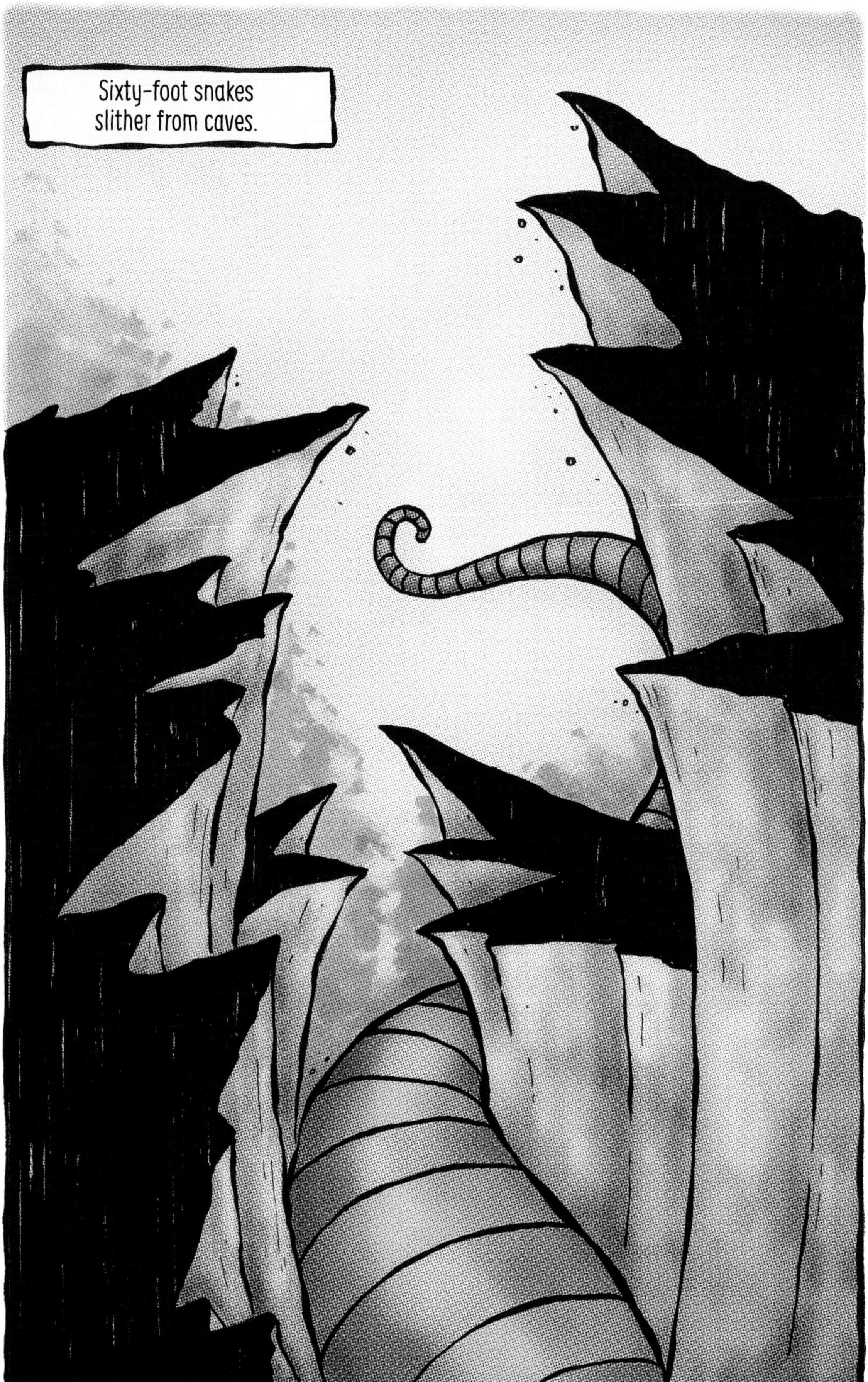
Sixty-foot snakes slither from caves.

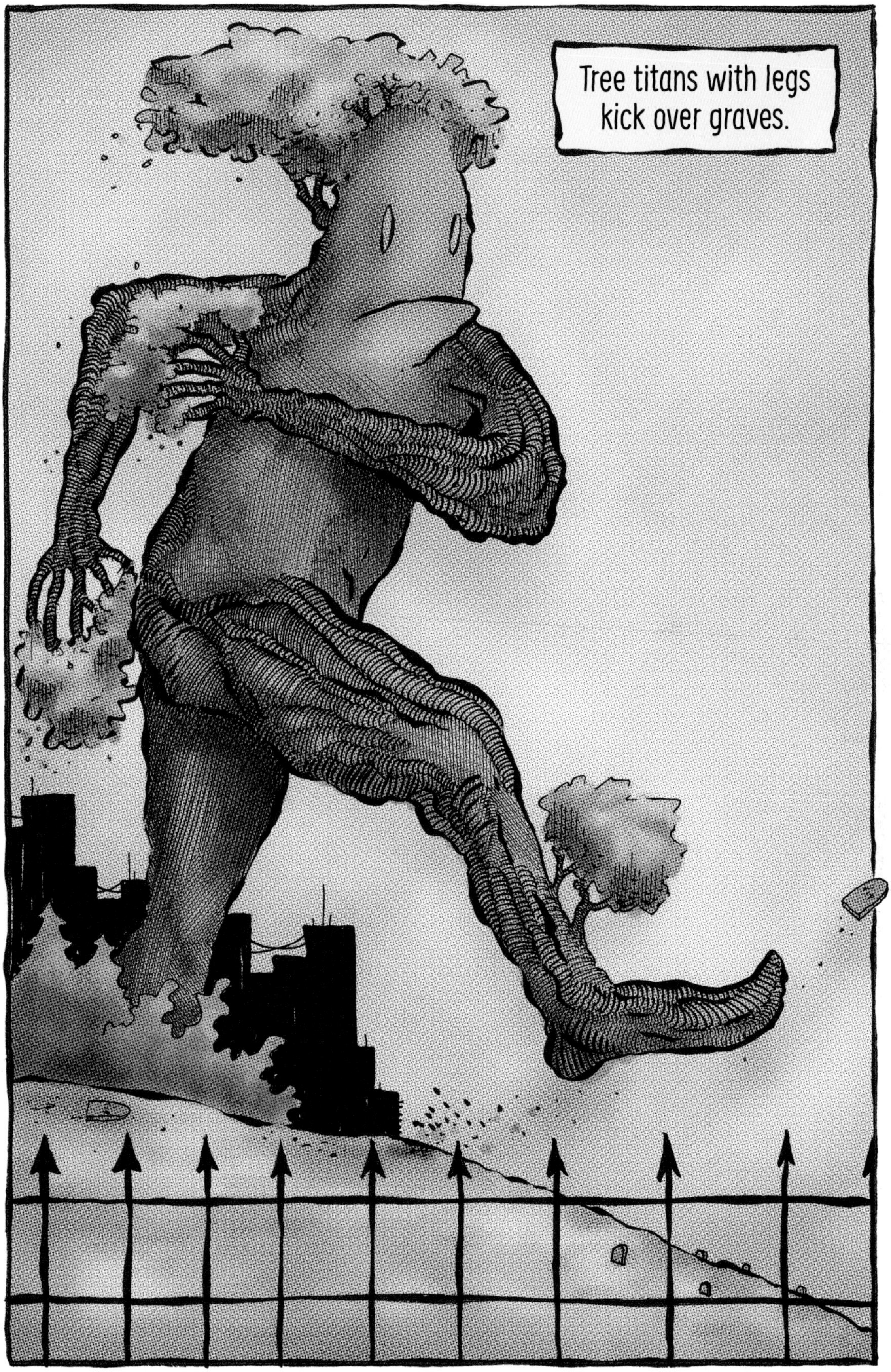
Tree titans with legs
kick over graves.

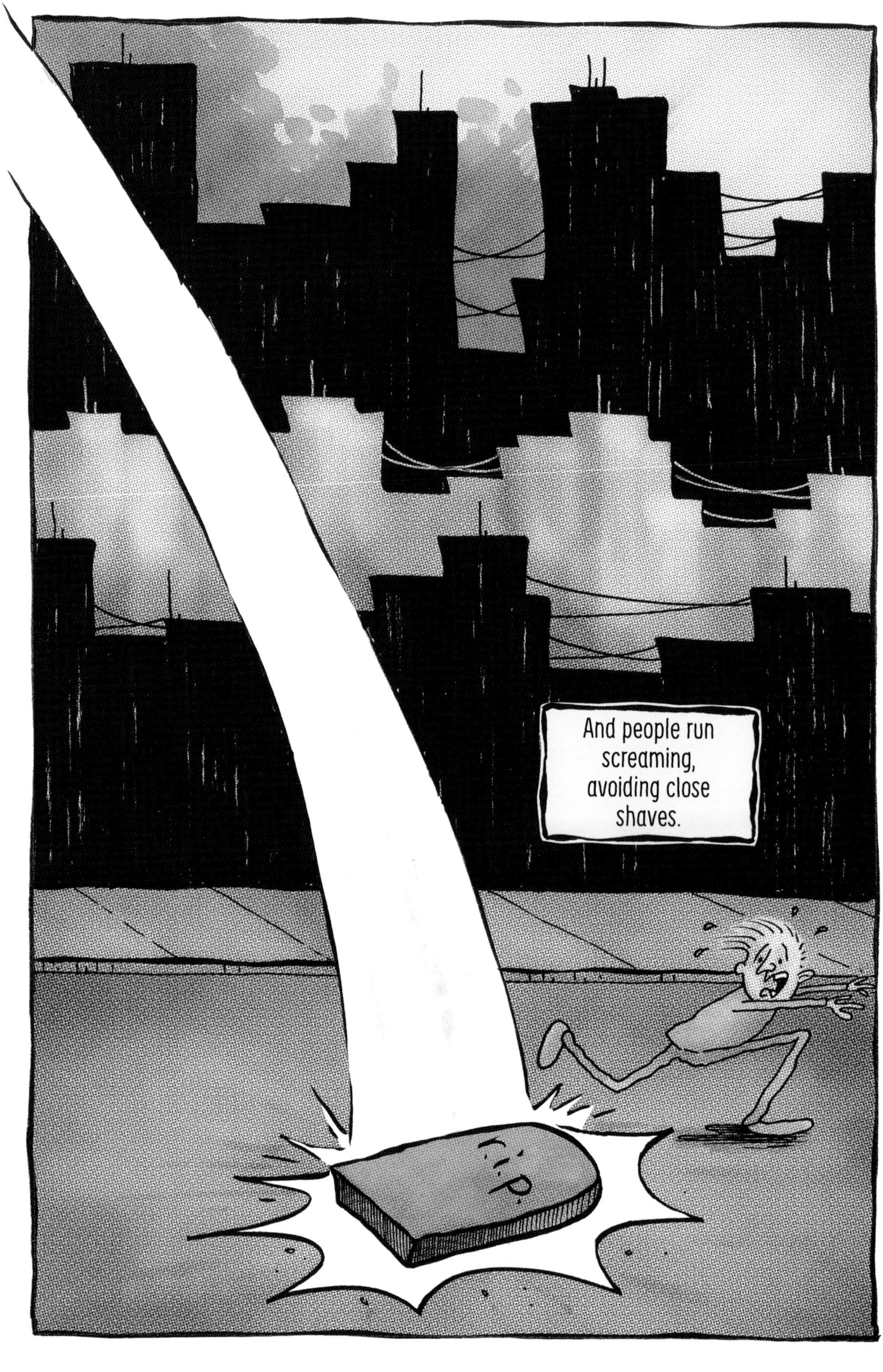
And people run screaming, avoiding close shaves.
r.i.p.

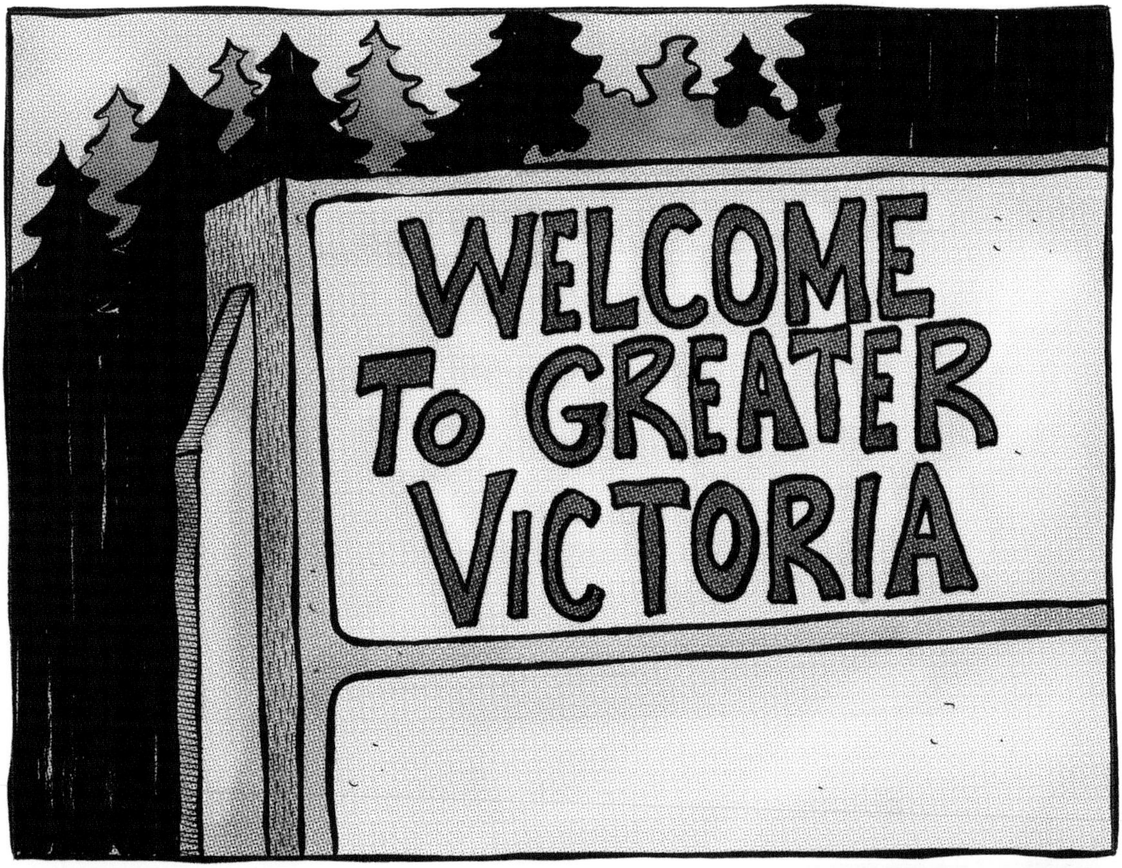
WELCOME
TO GREATER
VICTORIA

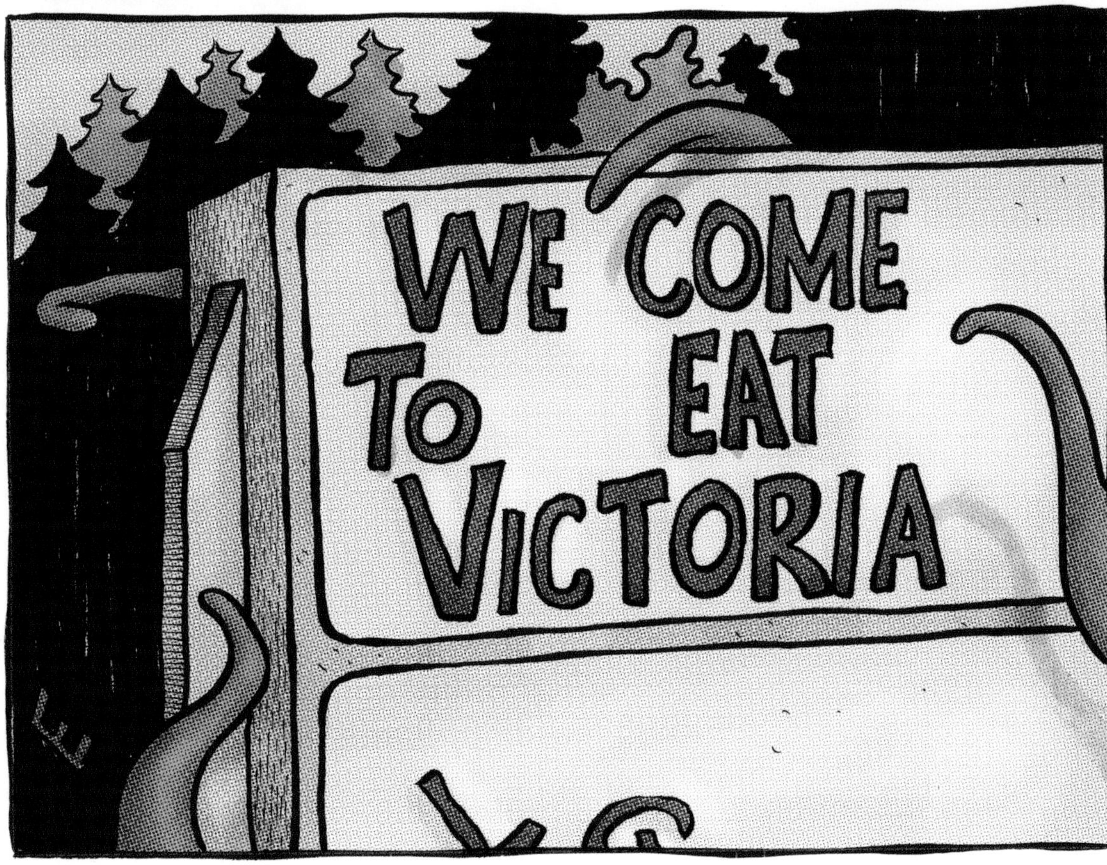
WE COME
TO EAT
VICTORIA

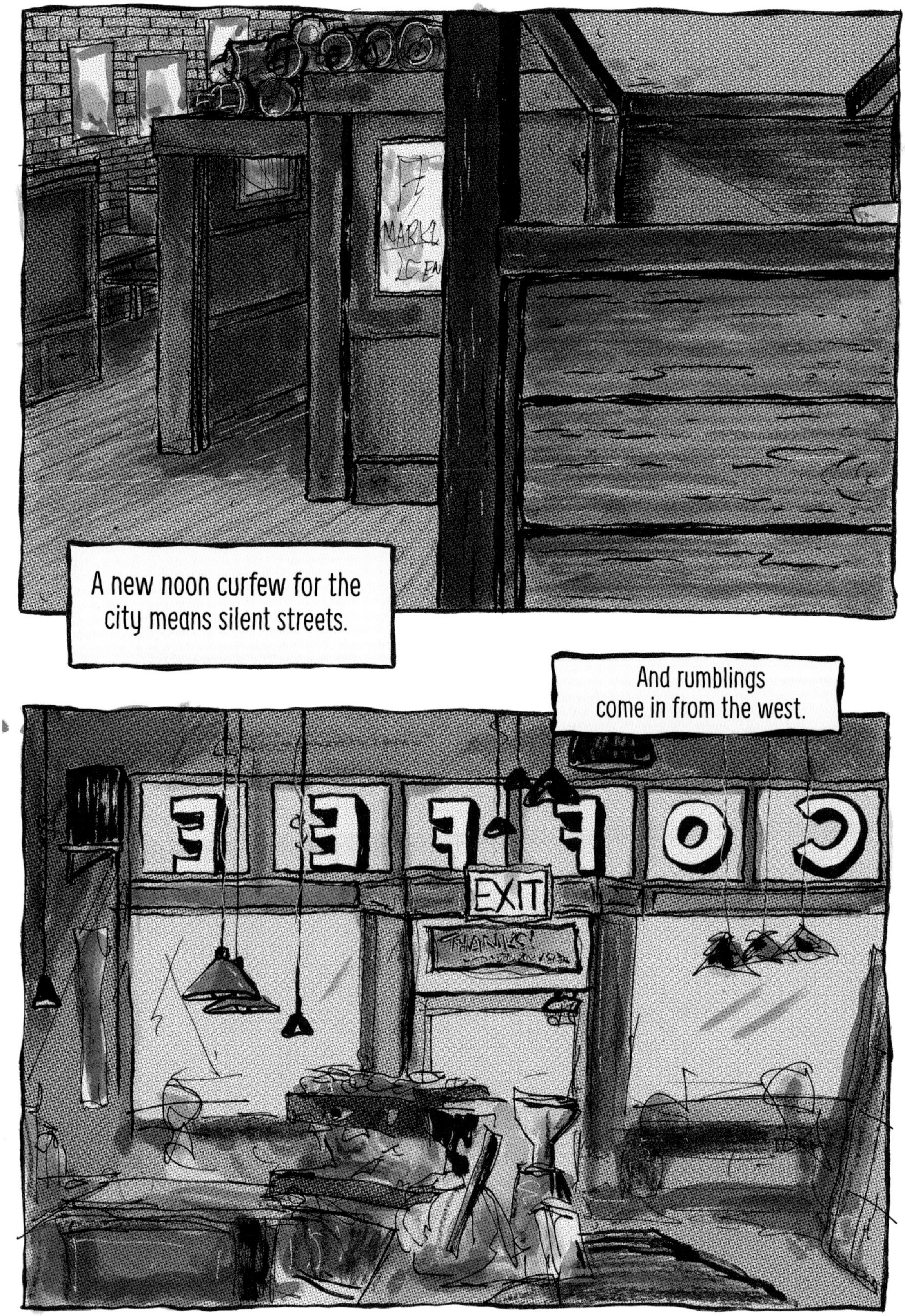
A new noon curfew for the city means silent streets.
And rumblings come in from the west.
EXIT
THANKS!

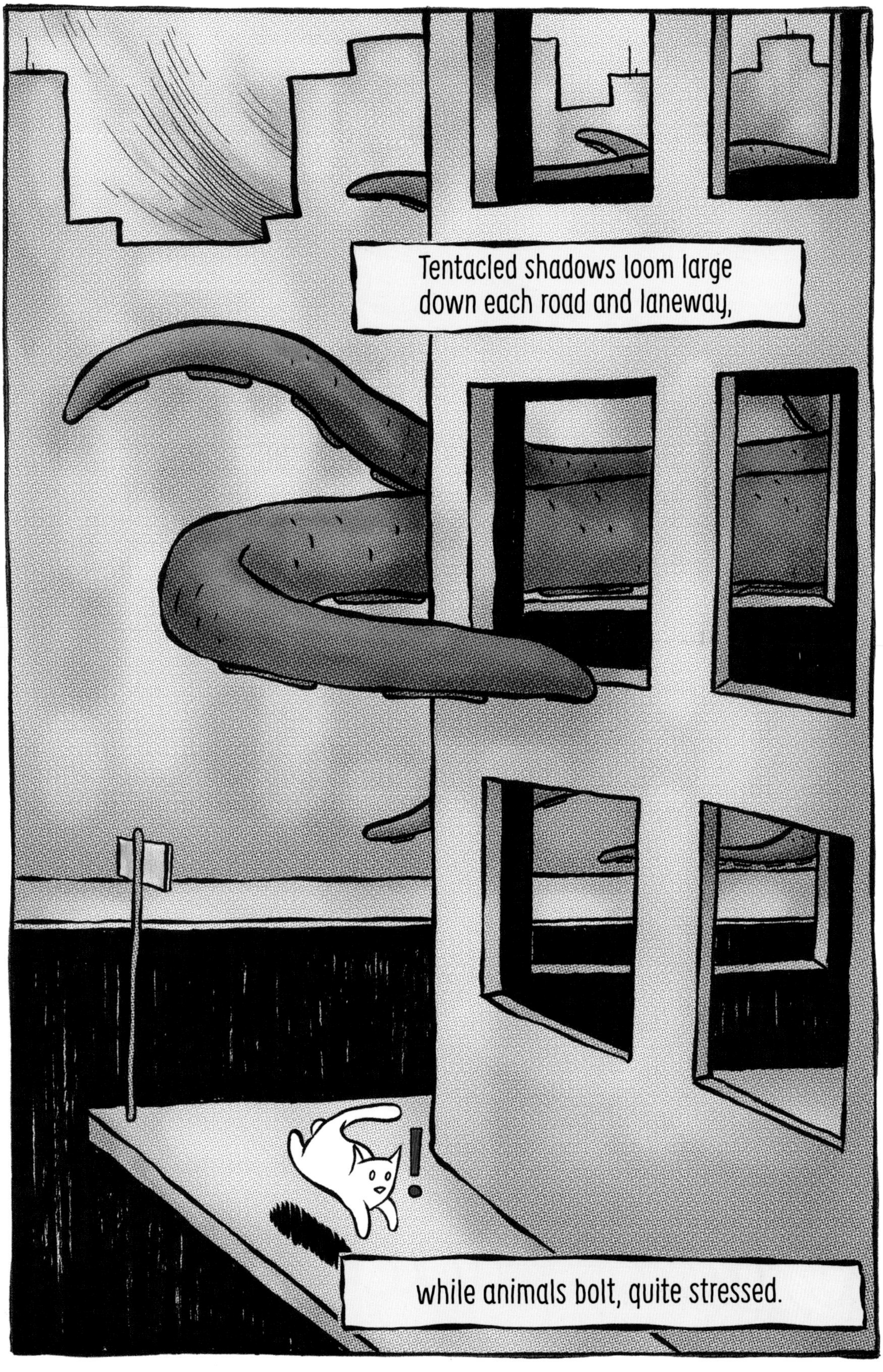
Tentacled shadows loom large down each road and laneway,
!
while animals bolt, quite stressed.

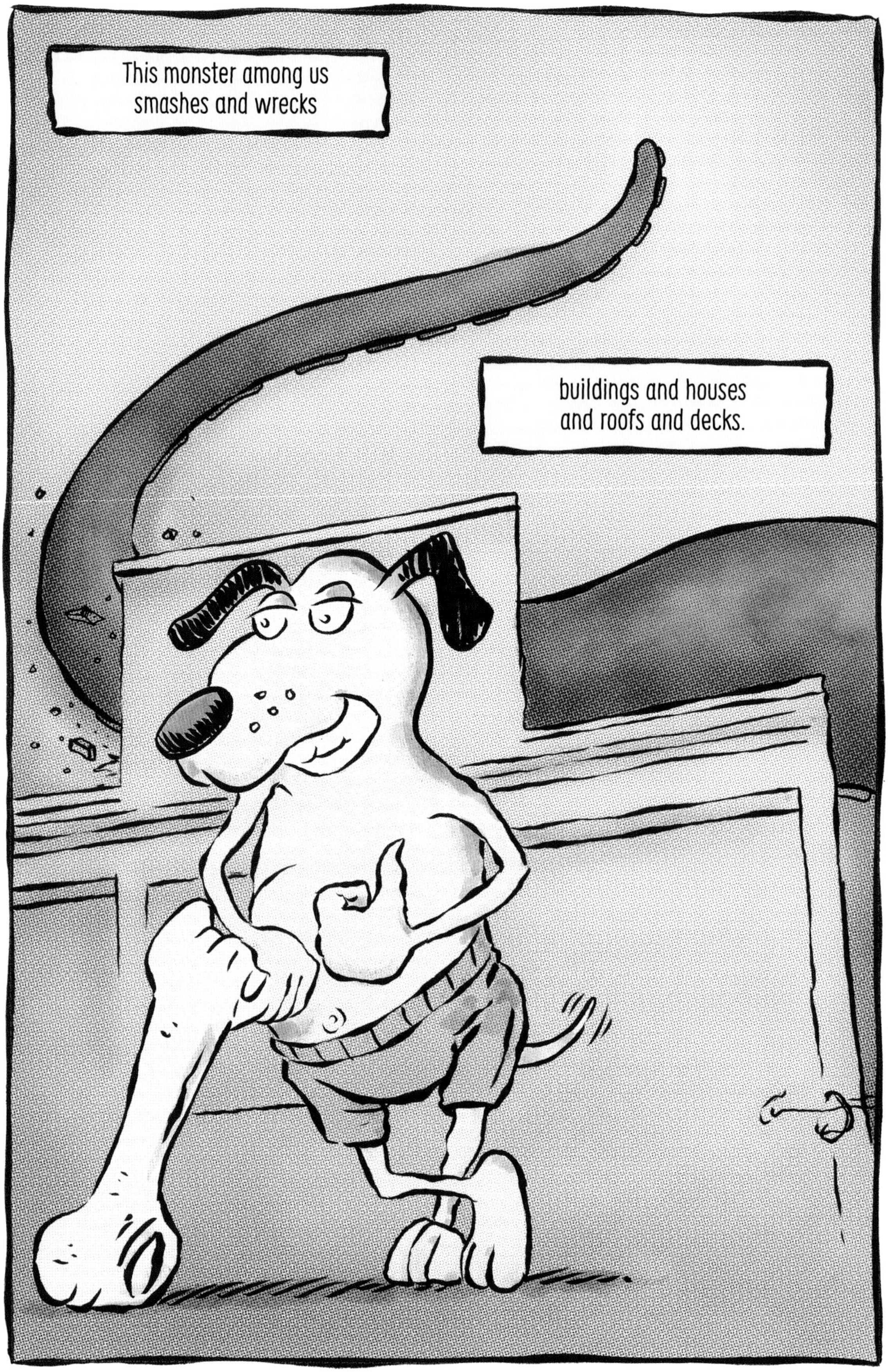
This monster among us
smashes and wrecks
buildings and houses
and roofs and decks.

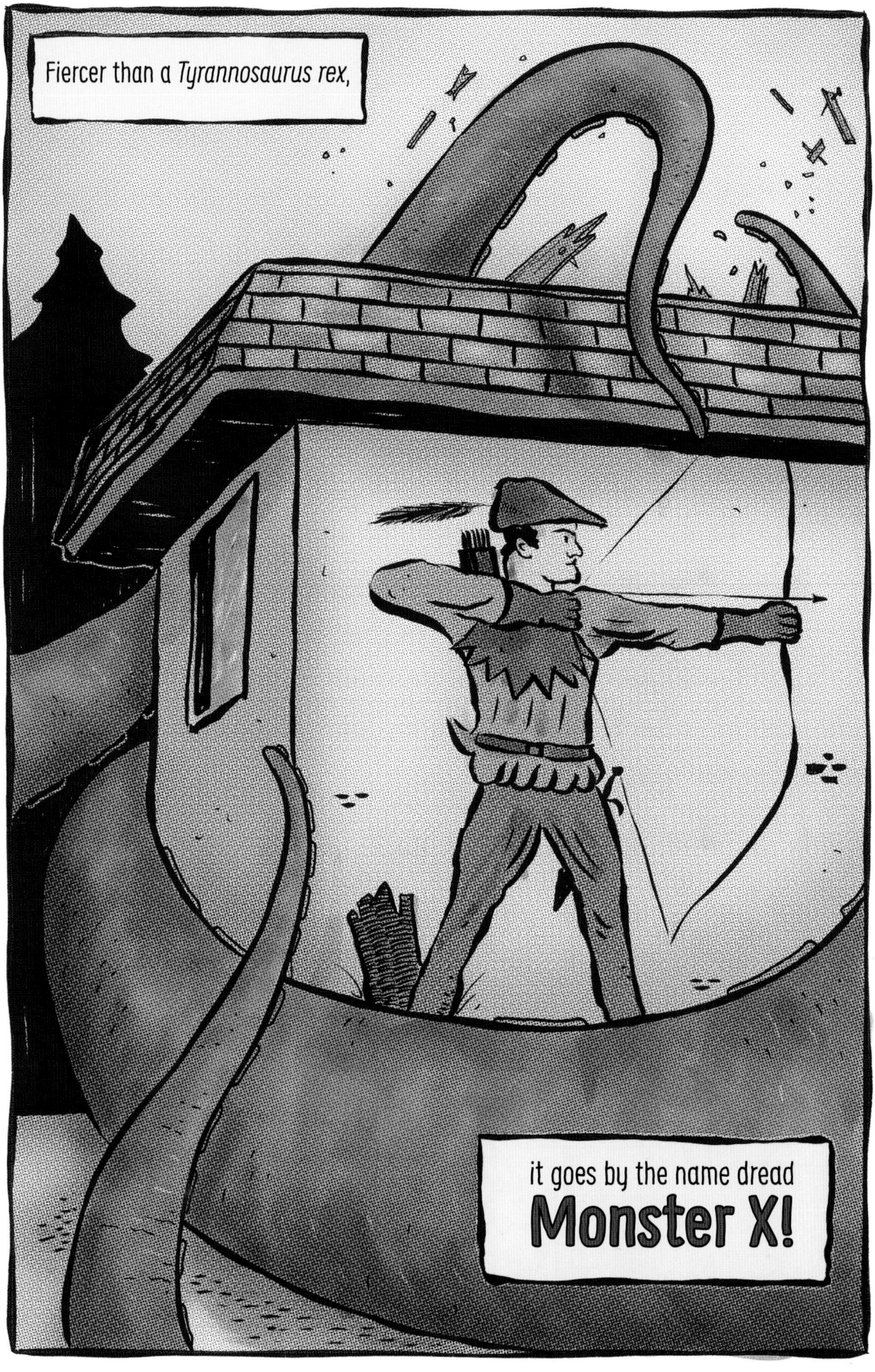
Fiercer than a *Tyrannosaurus rex*,
it goes by the name dread
Monster X!

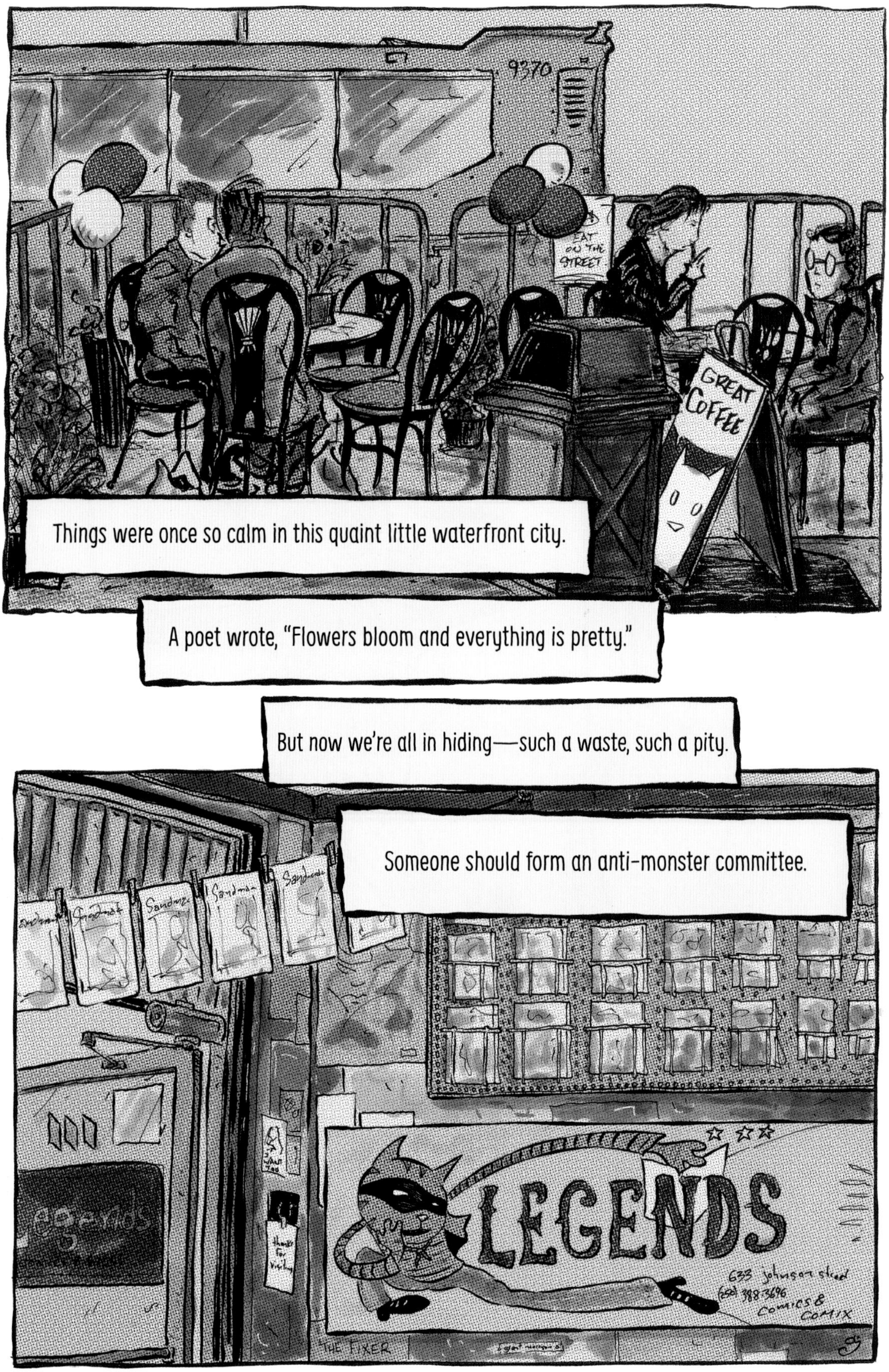
9370
GREAT COFFEE
Things were once so calm in this quaint little waterfront city.
A poet wrote, “Flowers bloom and everything is pretty.”
But now we’re all in hiding—such a waste, such a pity.
Someone should form an anti-monster committee.
LEGENDS
THE FIXER

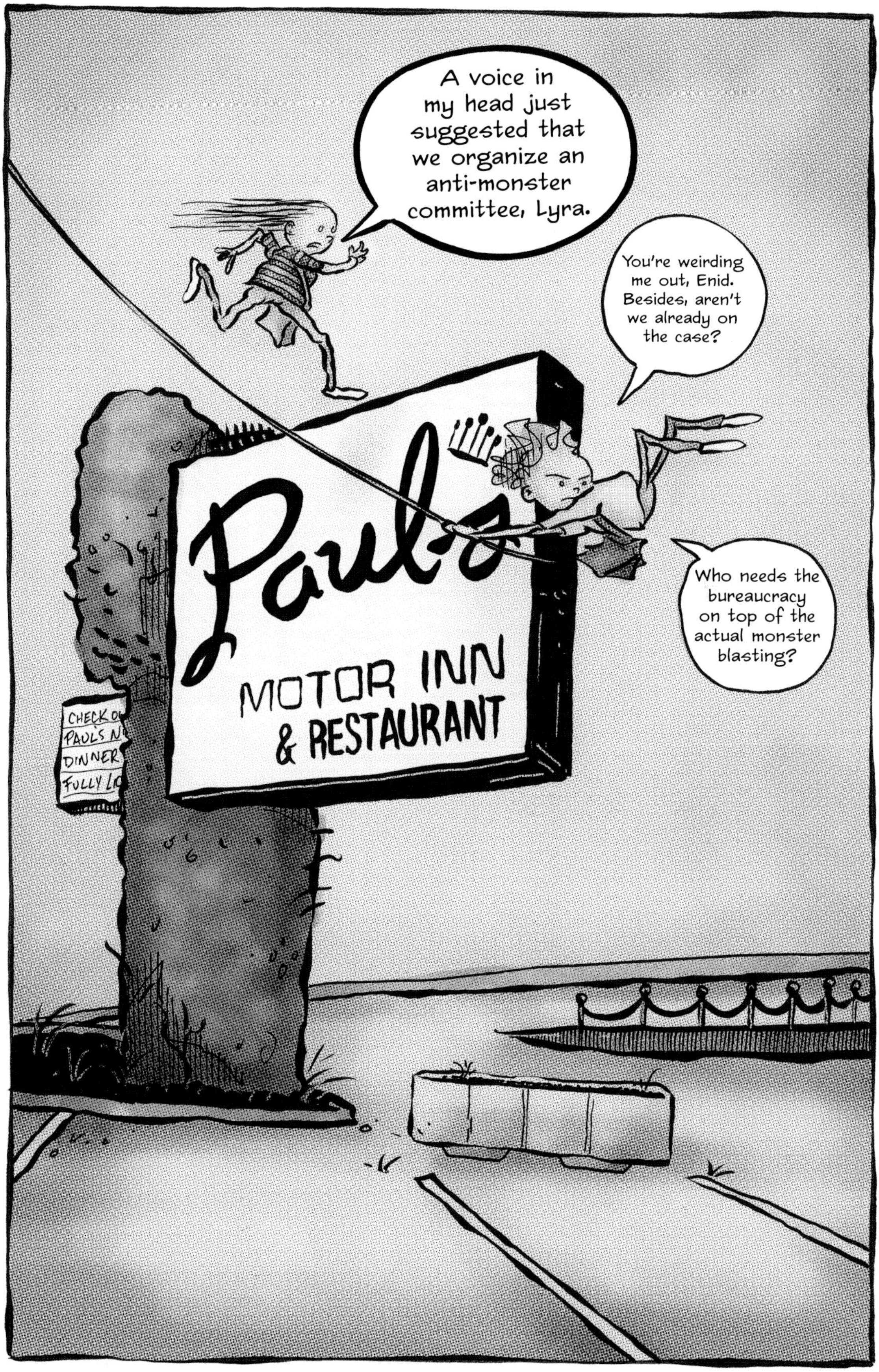
A voice in my head just suggested that we organize an anti-monster committee, Lyra.
You're weirding me out, Enid. Besides, aren't we already on the case?
Who needs the bureaucracy on top of the actual monster blasting?
Paul's
MOTOR INN
& RESTAURANT

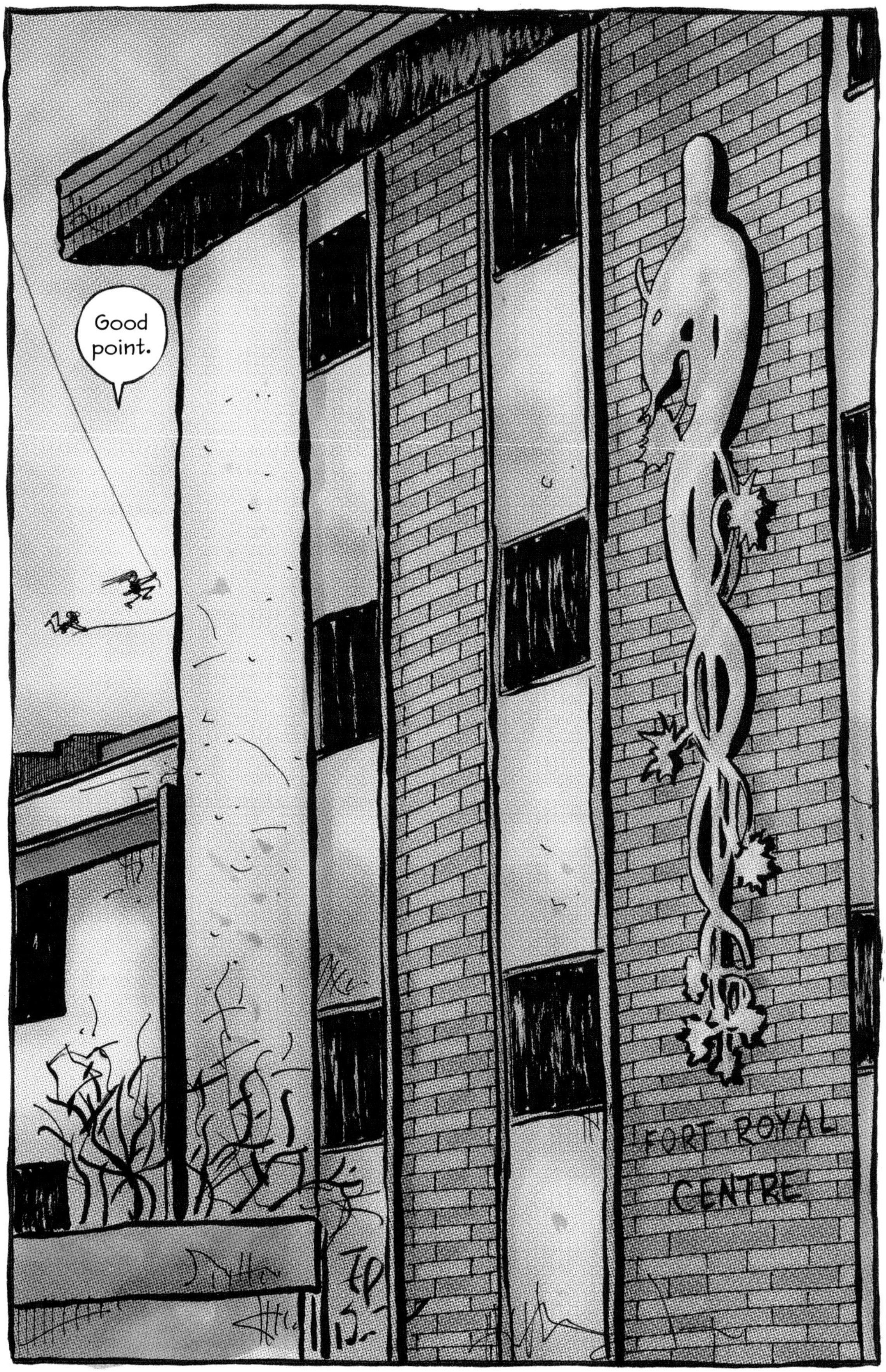
Good point.
FORT ROYAL CENTRE

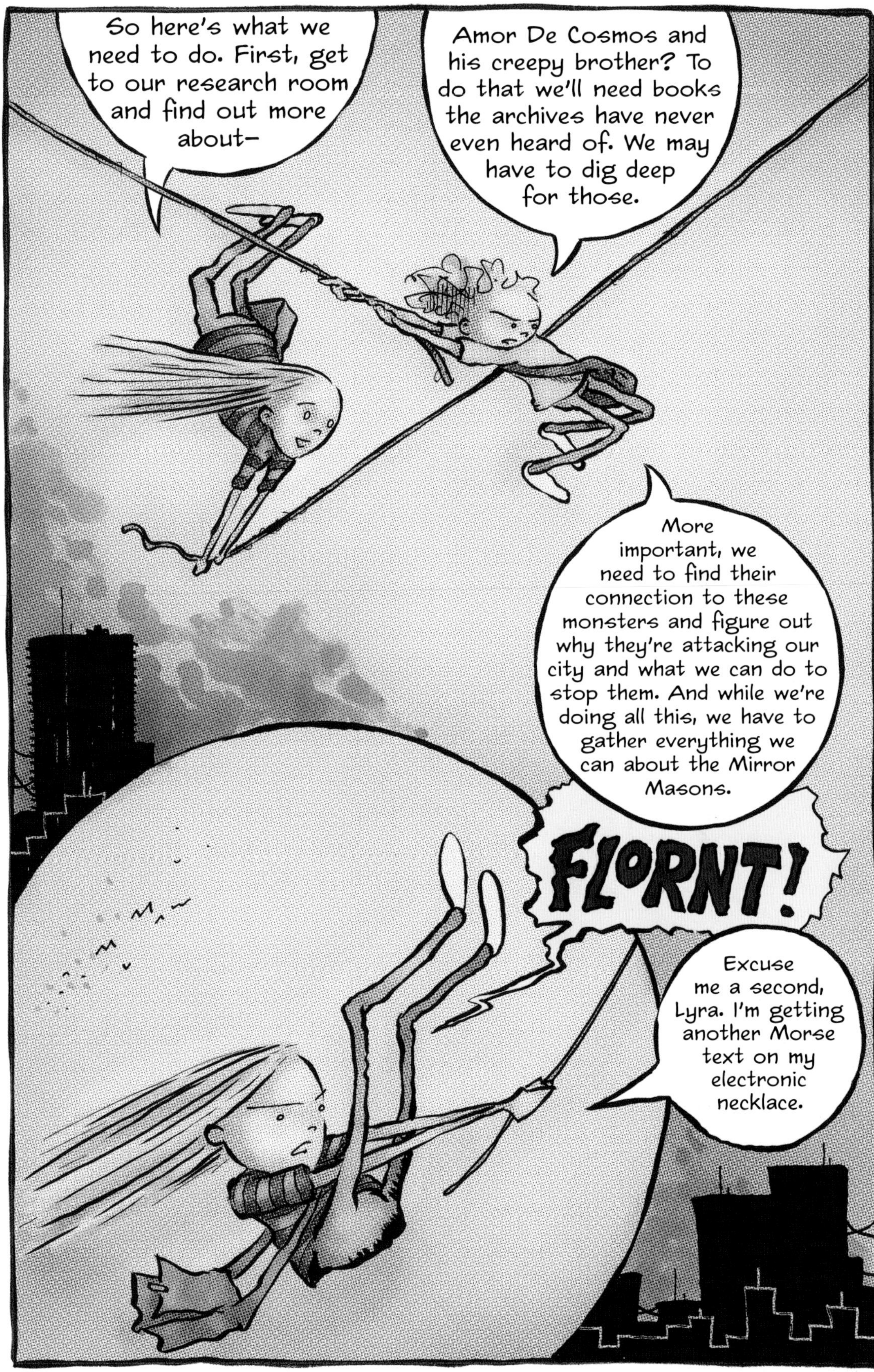
So here's what we need to do. First, get to our research room and find out more about–
Amor De Cosmos and his creepy brother? To do that we'll need books the archives have never even heard of. We may have to dig deep for those.
More important, we need to find their connection to these monsters and figure out why they're attacking our city and what we can do to stop them. And while we're doing all this, we have to gather everything we can about the Mirror Masons.
FLORNT!
Excuse me a second, Lyra. I'm getting another Morse text on my electronic necklace.

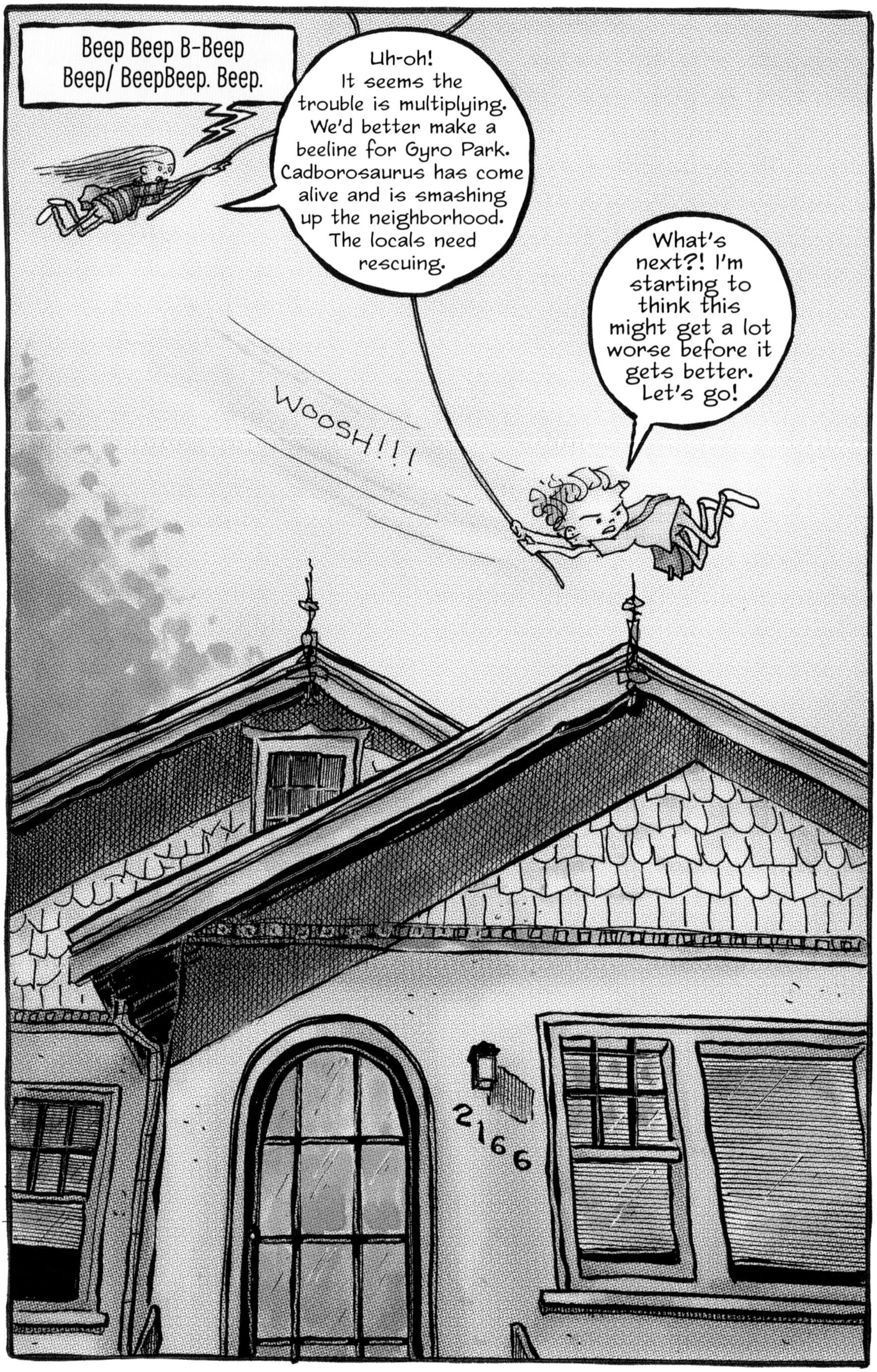
Beep Beep B-Beep Beep/ BeepBeep. Beep.
Uh-oh! It seems the trouble is multiplying. We'd better make a beeline for Gyro Park. Cadborosaurus has come alive and is smashing up the neighborhood. The locals need rescuing.
What's next?! I'm starting to think this might get a lot worse before it gets better. Let's go!
WOOSH!!!
2166

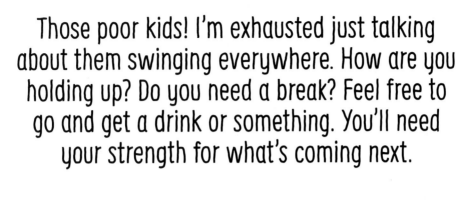

Those poor kids! I'm exhausted just talking about them swinging everywhere. How are you holding up? Do you need a break? Feel free to go and get a drink or something. You'll need your strength for what's coming next.

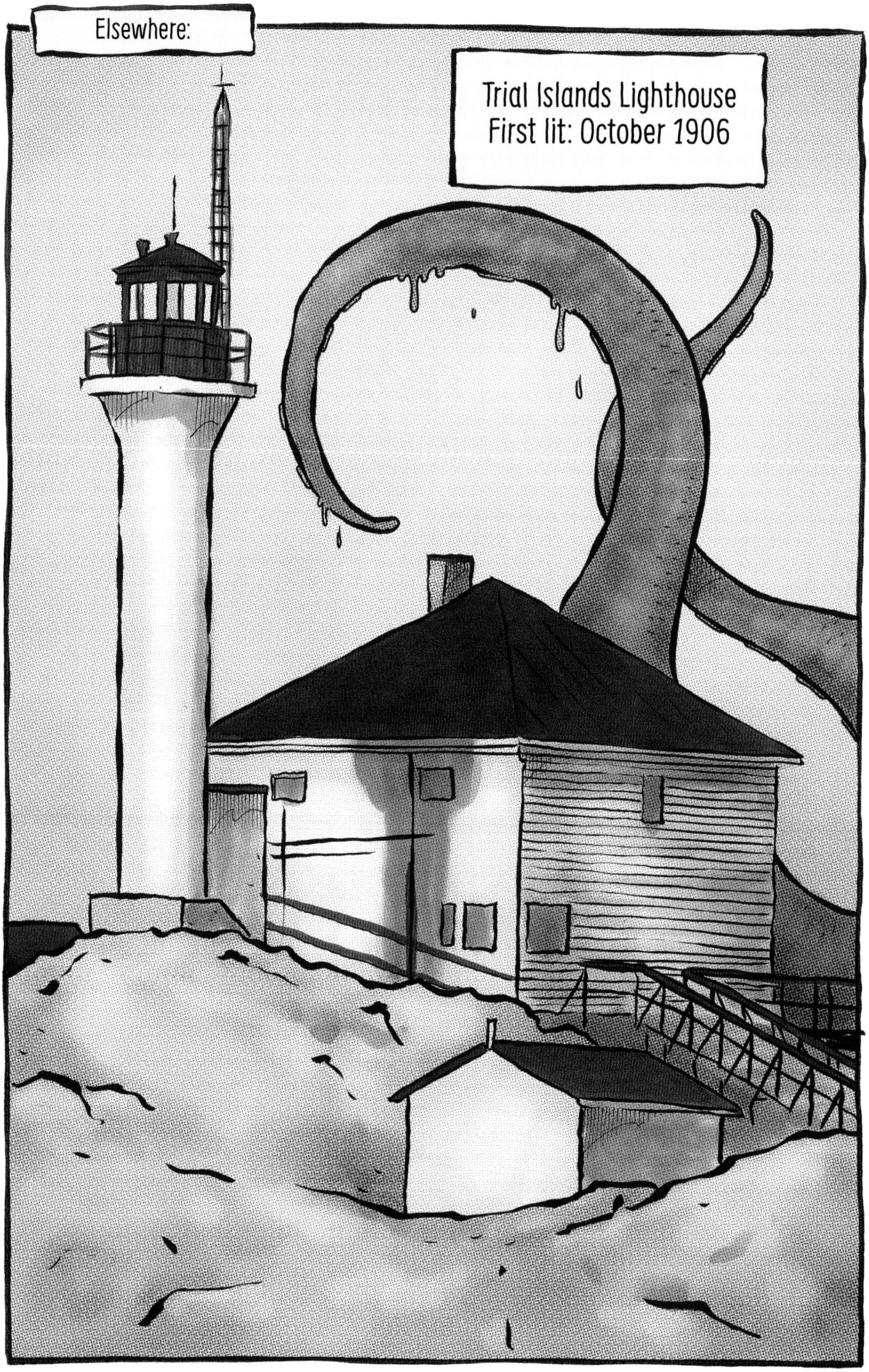
Elsewhere:
Trial Islands Lighthouse
First lit: October 1906

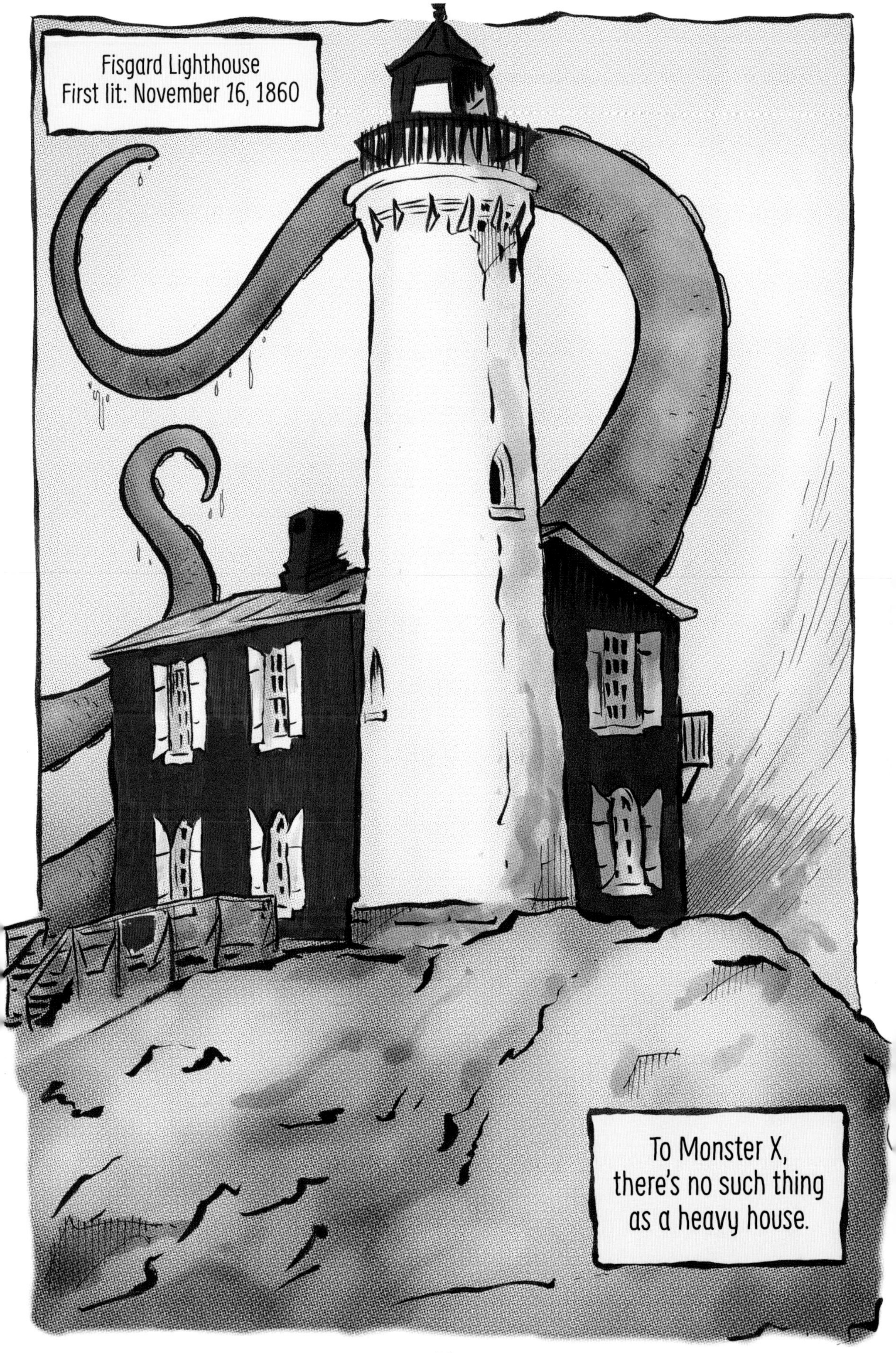
Fisgard Lighthouse
First lit: November 16, 1860
To Monster X,
there's no such thing
as a heavy house.

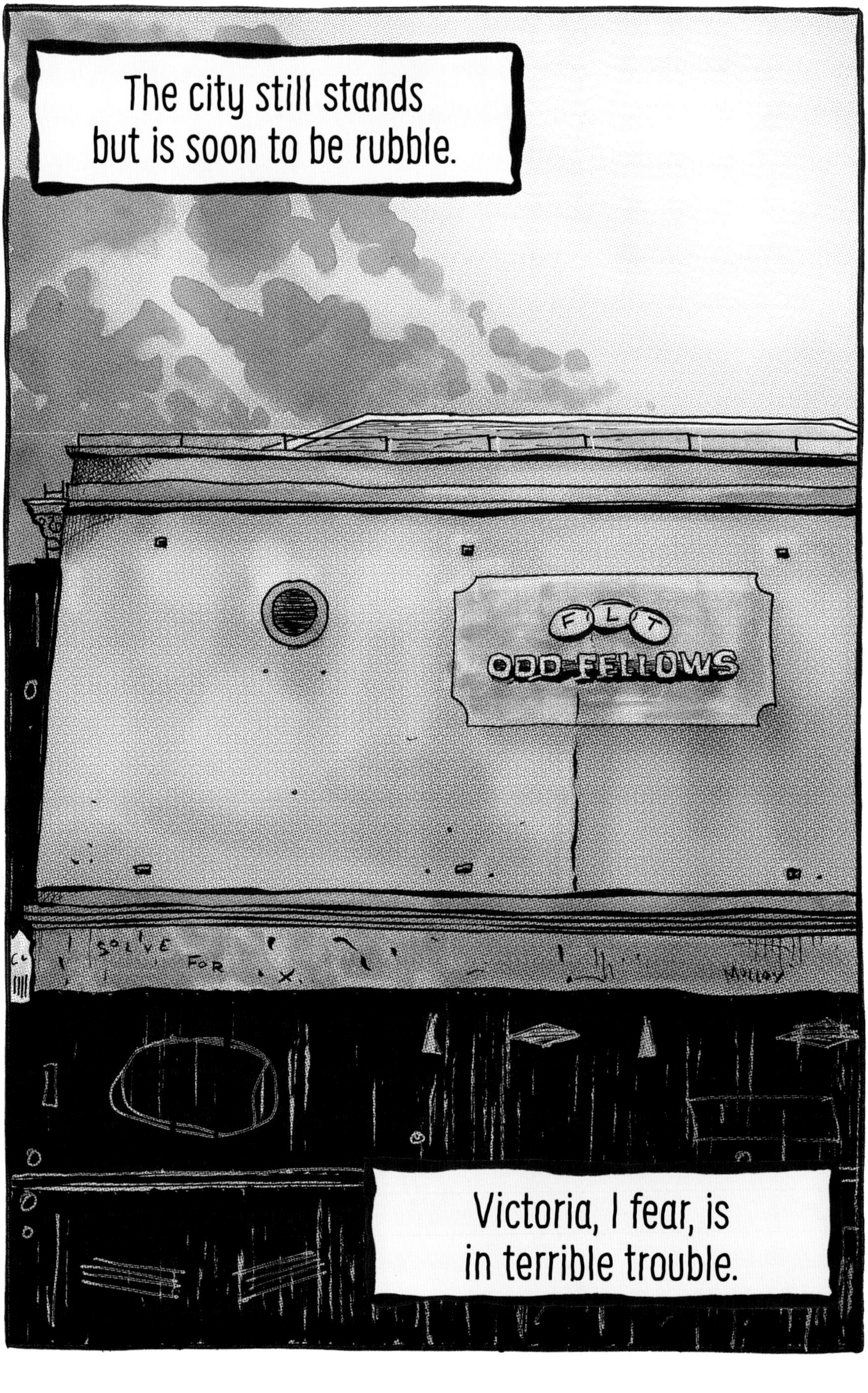
The city still stands
but is soon to be rubble.
F L T
ODD FELLOWS
SOLVE FOR X
Victoria, I fear, is
in terrible trouble.

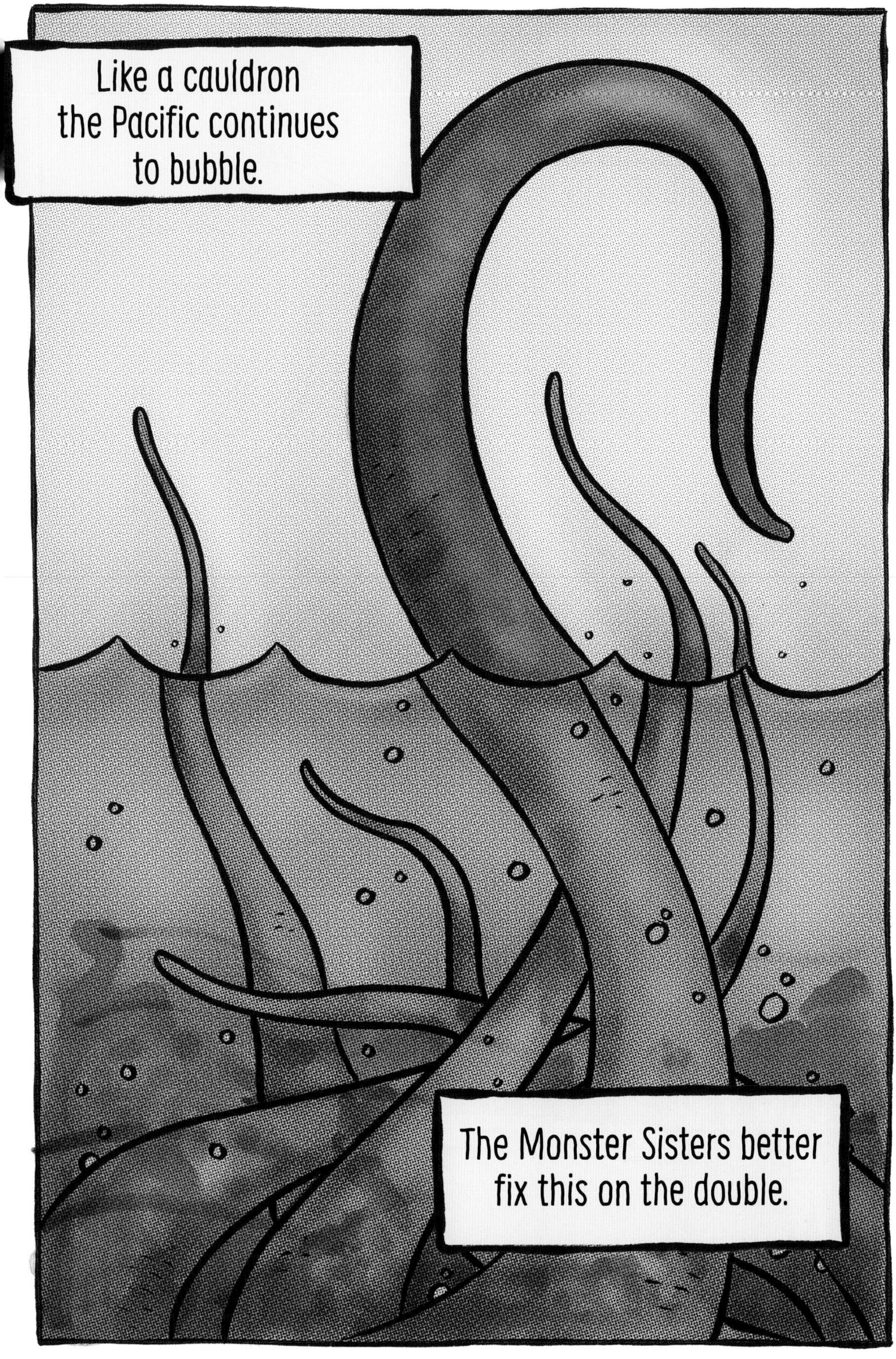
Like a cauldron the Pacific continues to bubble.
The Monster Sisters better fix this on the double.

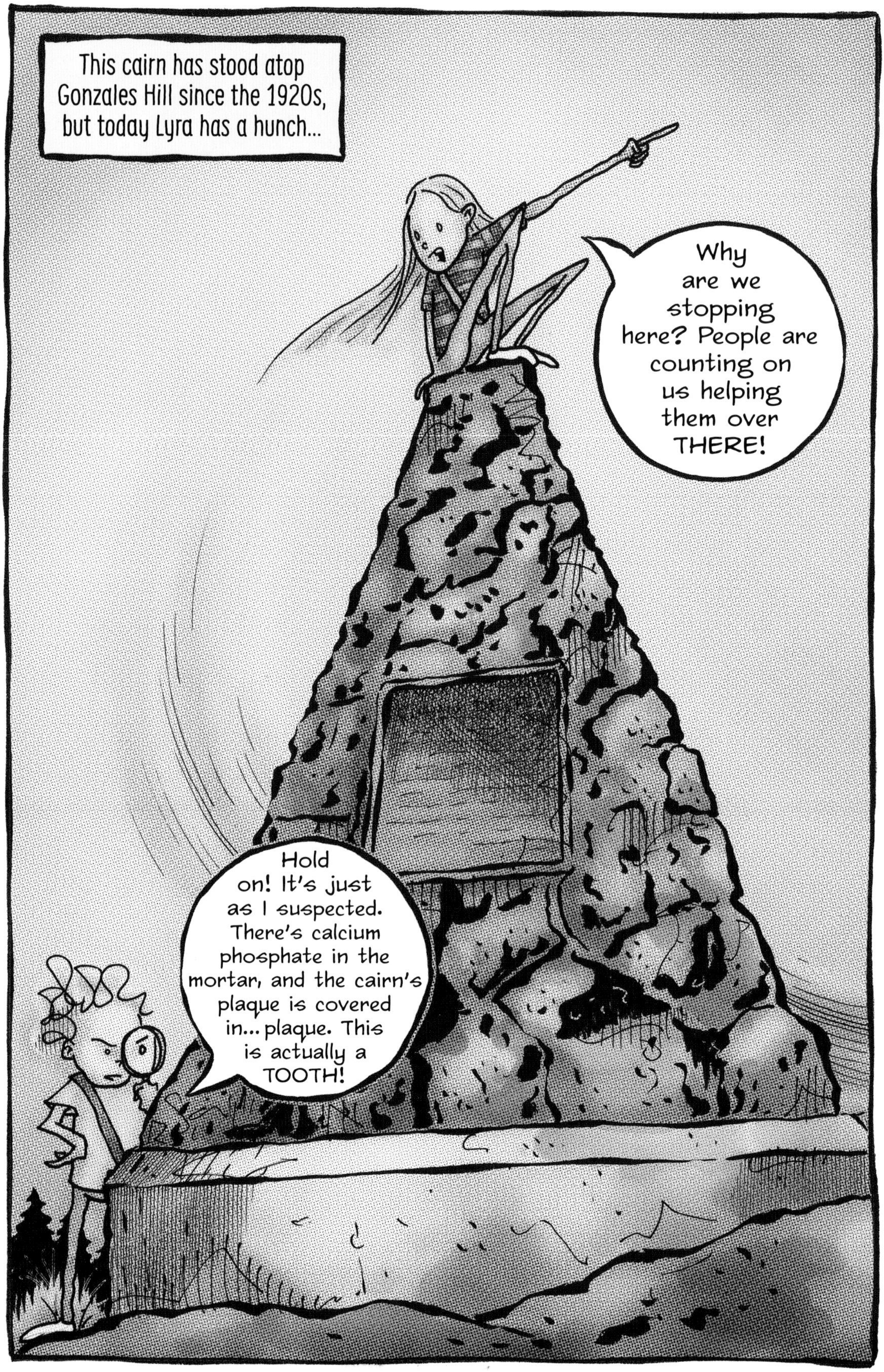
This cairn has stood atop Gonzales Hill since the 1920s, but today Lyra has a hunch...
Why are we stopping here? People are counting on us helping them over THERE!
Hold on! It's just as I suspected. There's calcium phosphate in the mortar, and the cairn's plaque is covered in... plaque. This is actually a TOOTH!

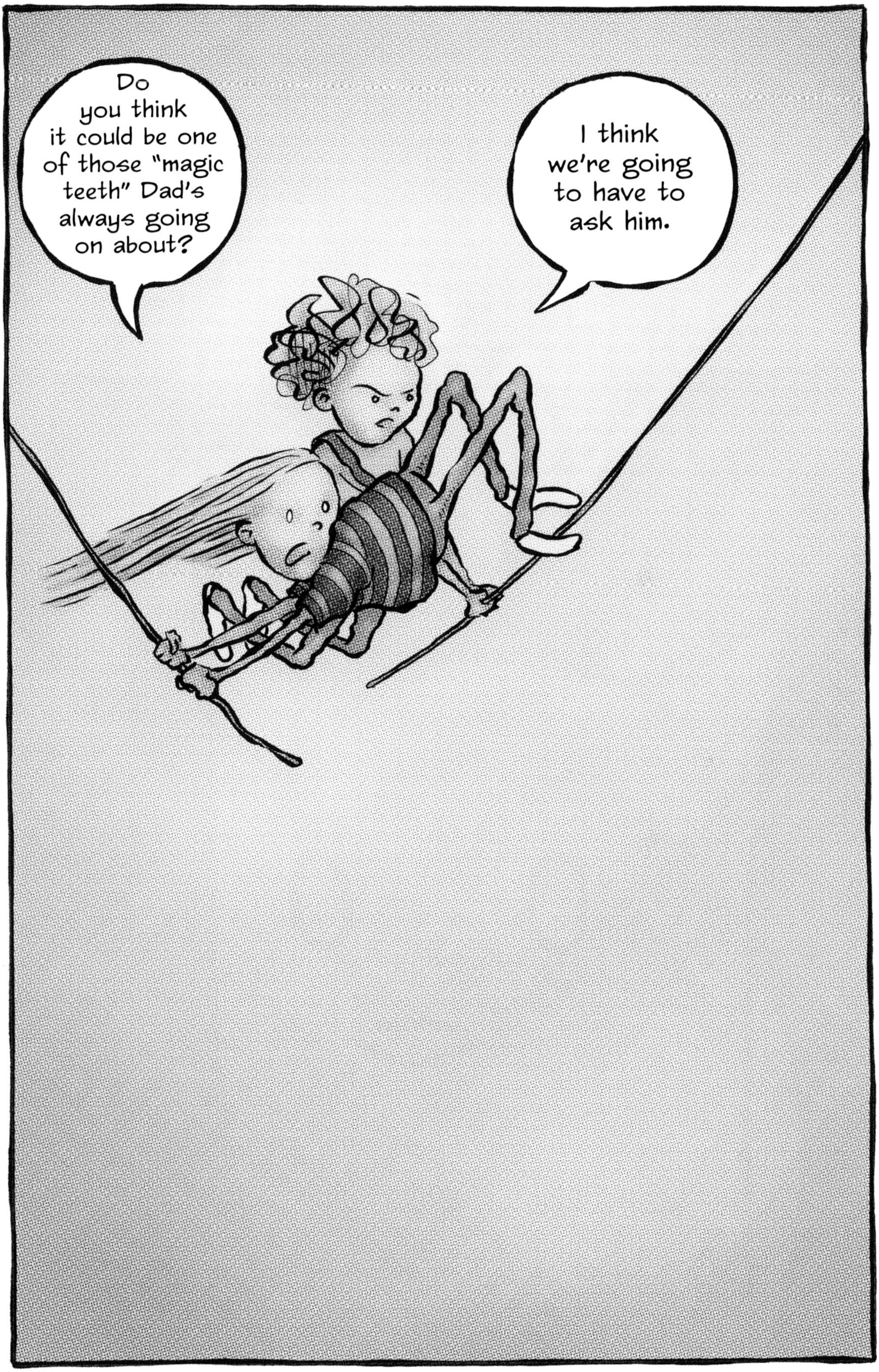
Do you think it could be one of those "magic teeth" Dad's always going on about?
I think we're going to have to ask him.

To be continued...

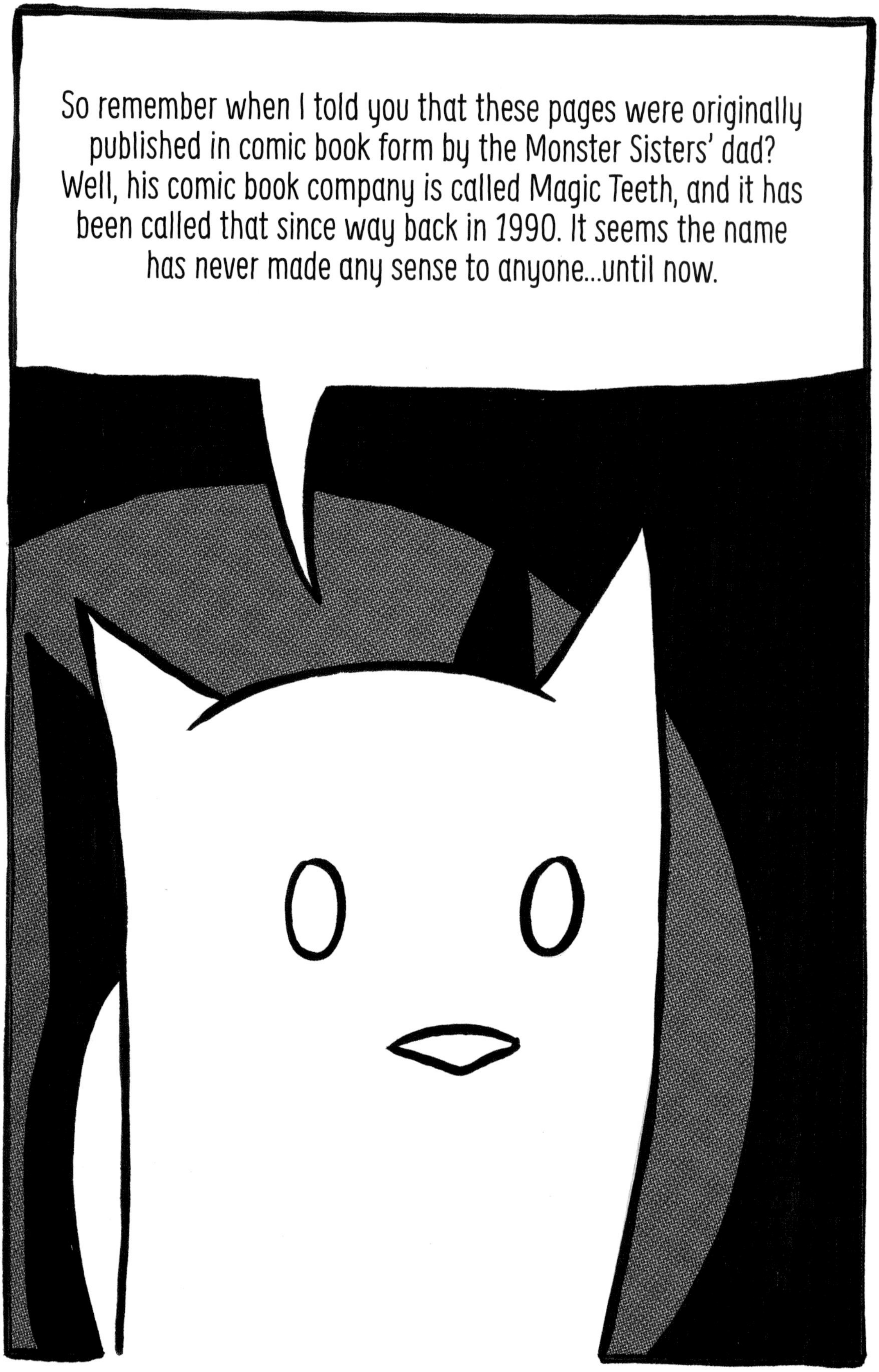
So remember when I told you that these pages were originally published in comic book form by the Monster Sisters' dad? Well, his comic book company is called Magic Teeth, and it has been called that since way back in 1990. It seems the name has never made any sense to anyone...until now.

CHAPTER FIVE

THE ORIGIN OF THE MONSTER SISTERS

5

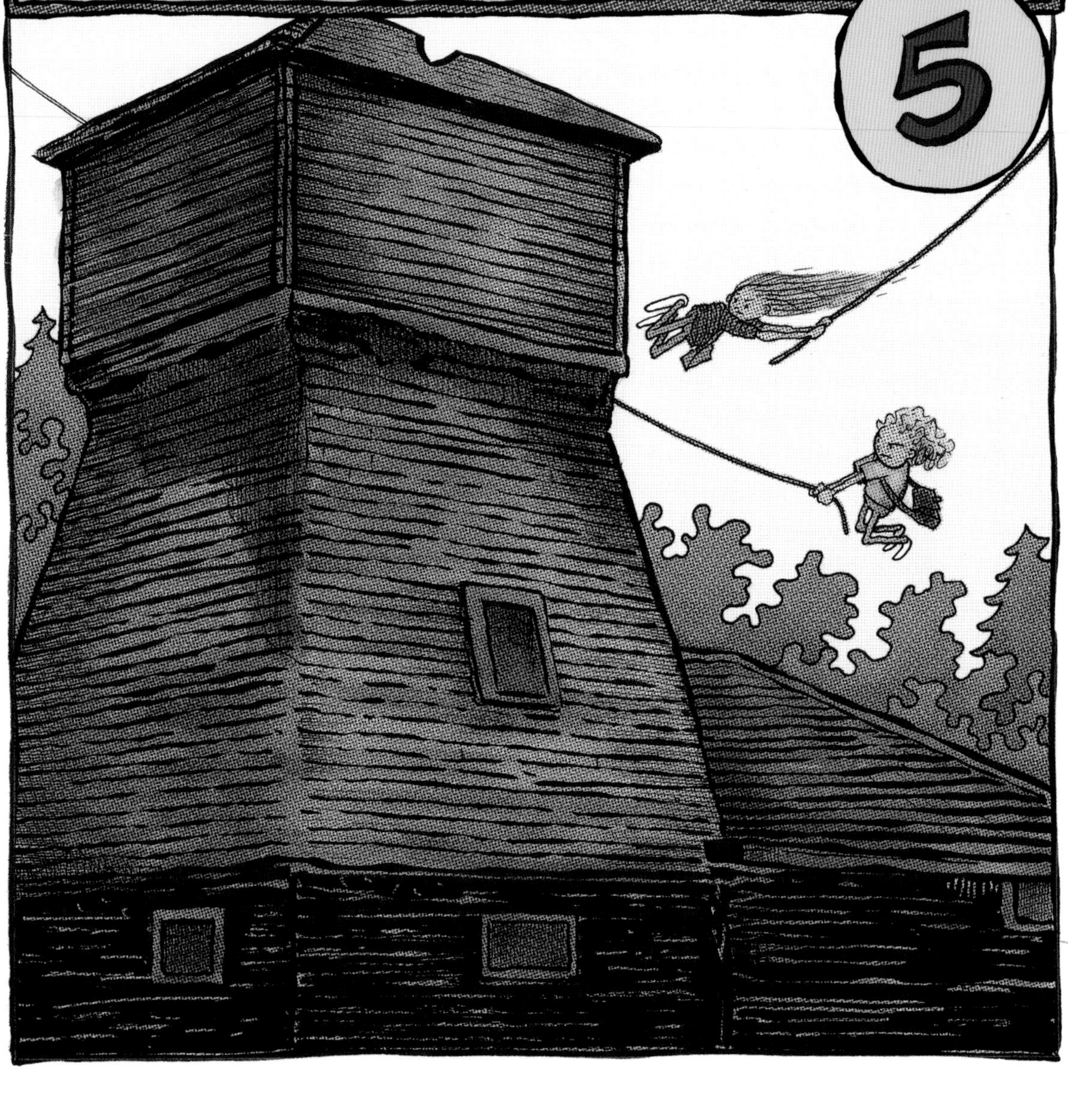

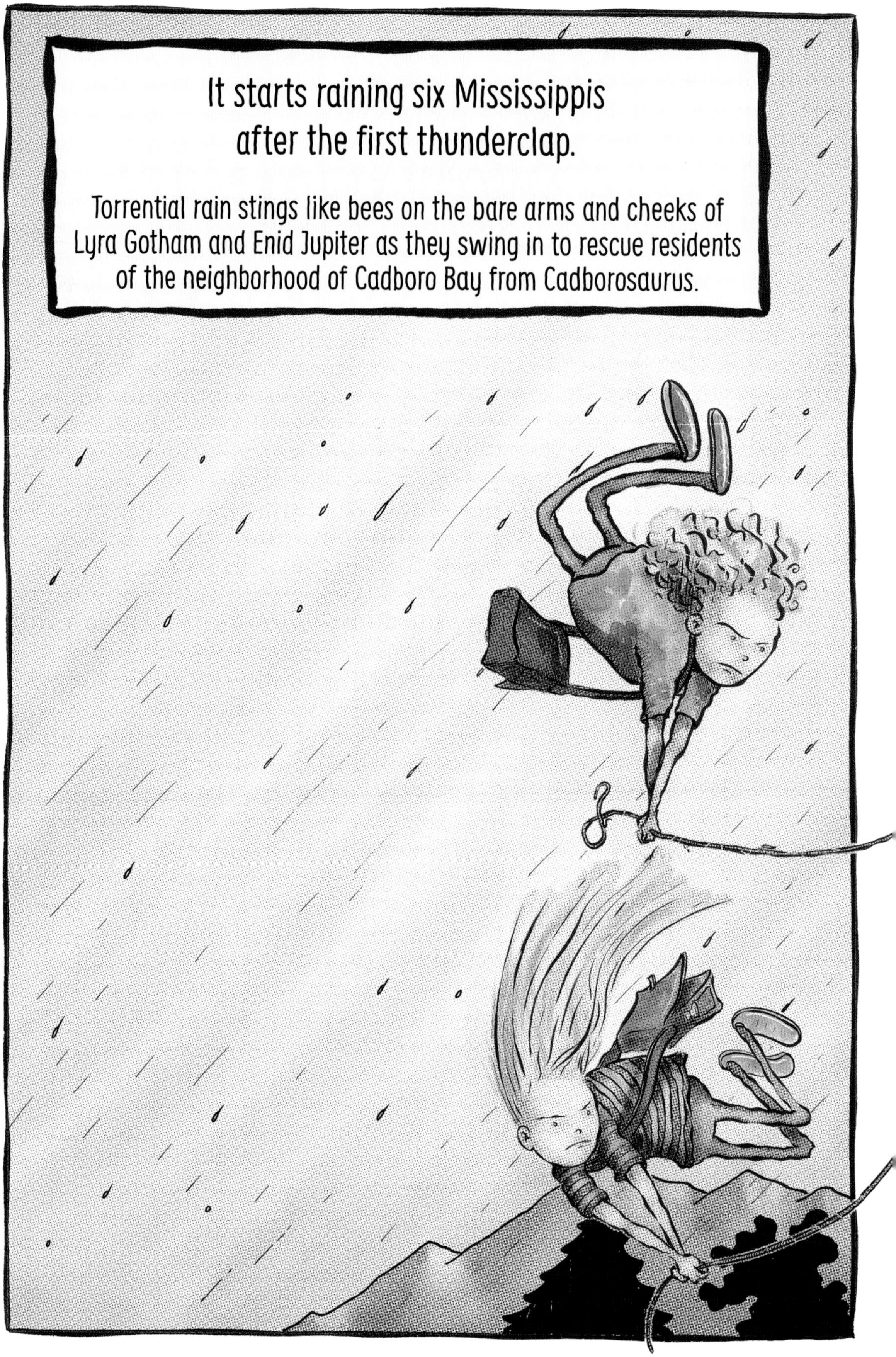
It starts raining six Mississippis after the first thunderclap.
Torrential rain stings like bees on the bare arms and cheeks of Lyra Gotham and Enid Jupiter as they swing in to rescue residents of the neighborhood of Cadboro Bay from Cadborosaurus.

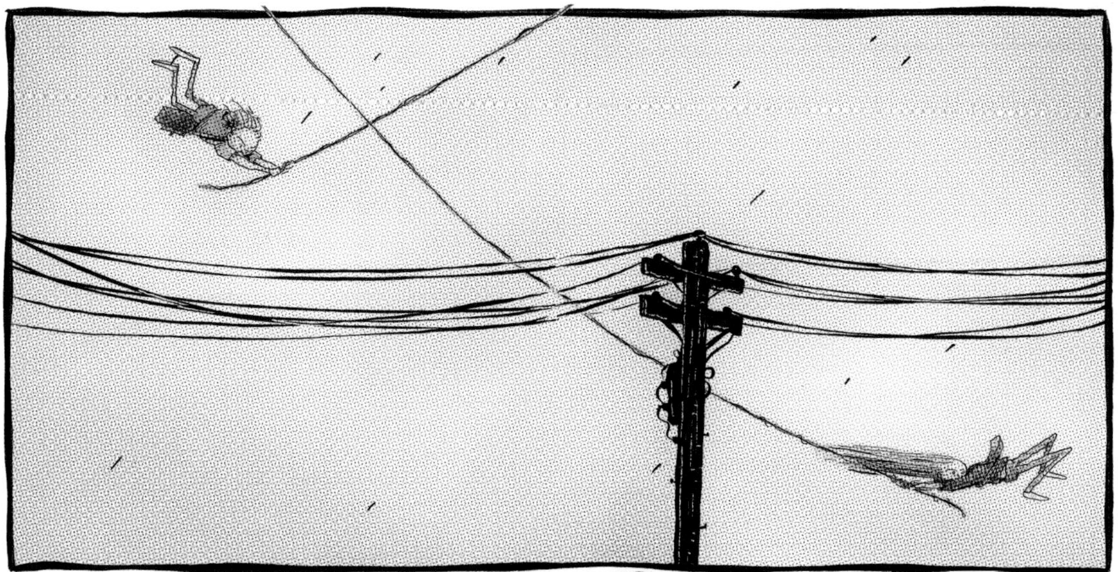

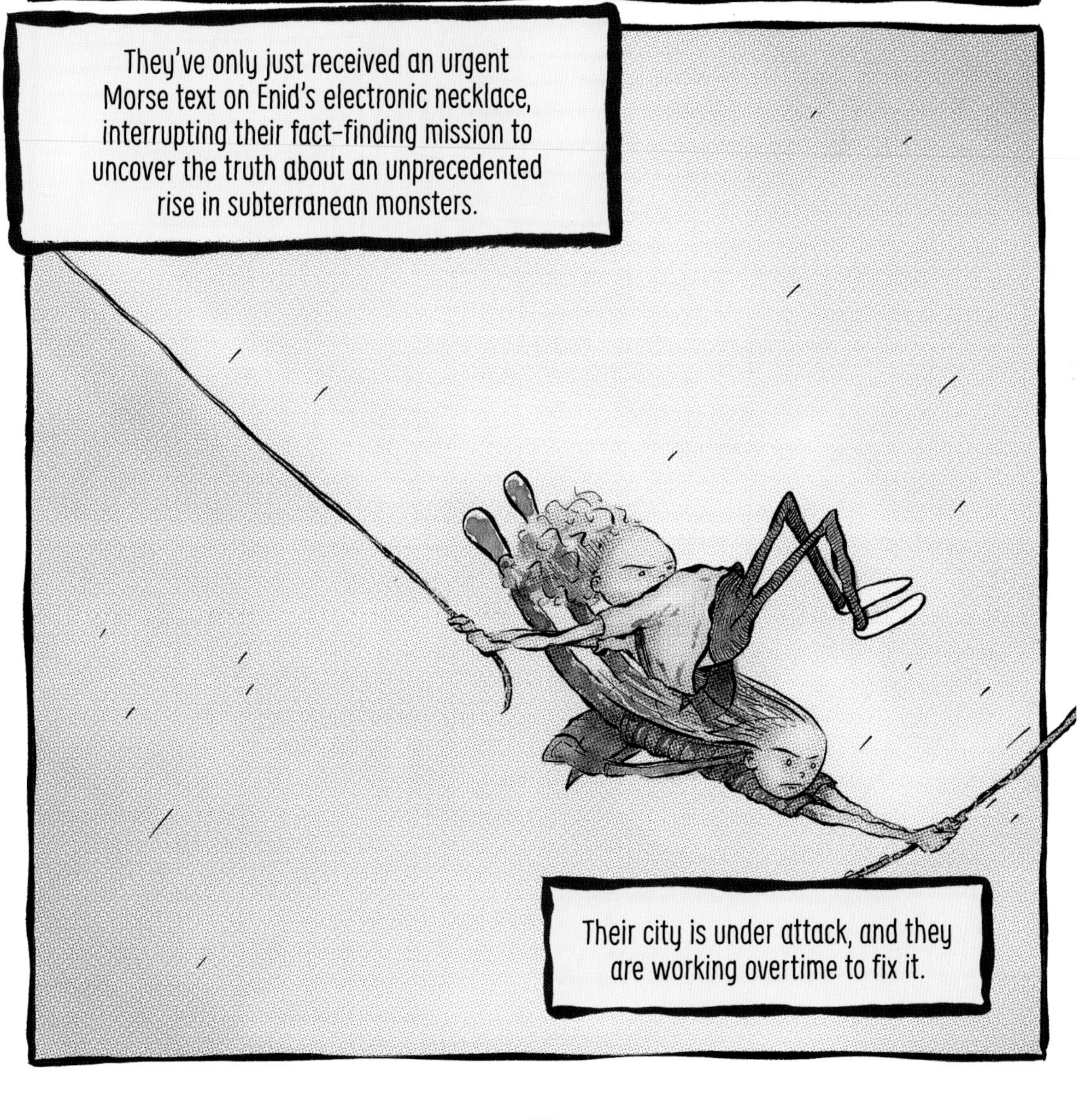
They've only just received an urgent Morse text on Enid's electronic necklace, interrupting their fact-finding mission to uncover the truth about an unprecedented rise in subterranean monsters.
Their city is under attack, and they are working overtime to fix it.

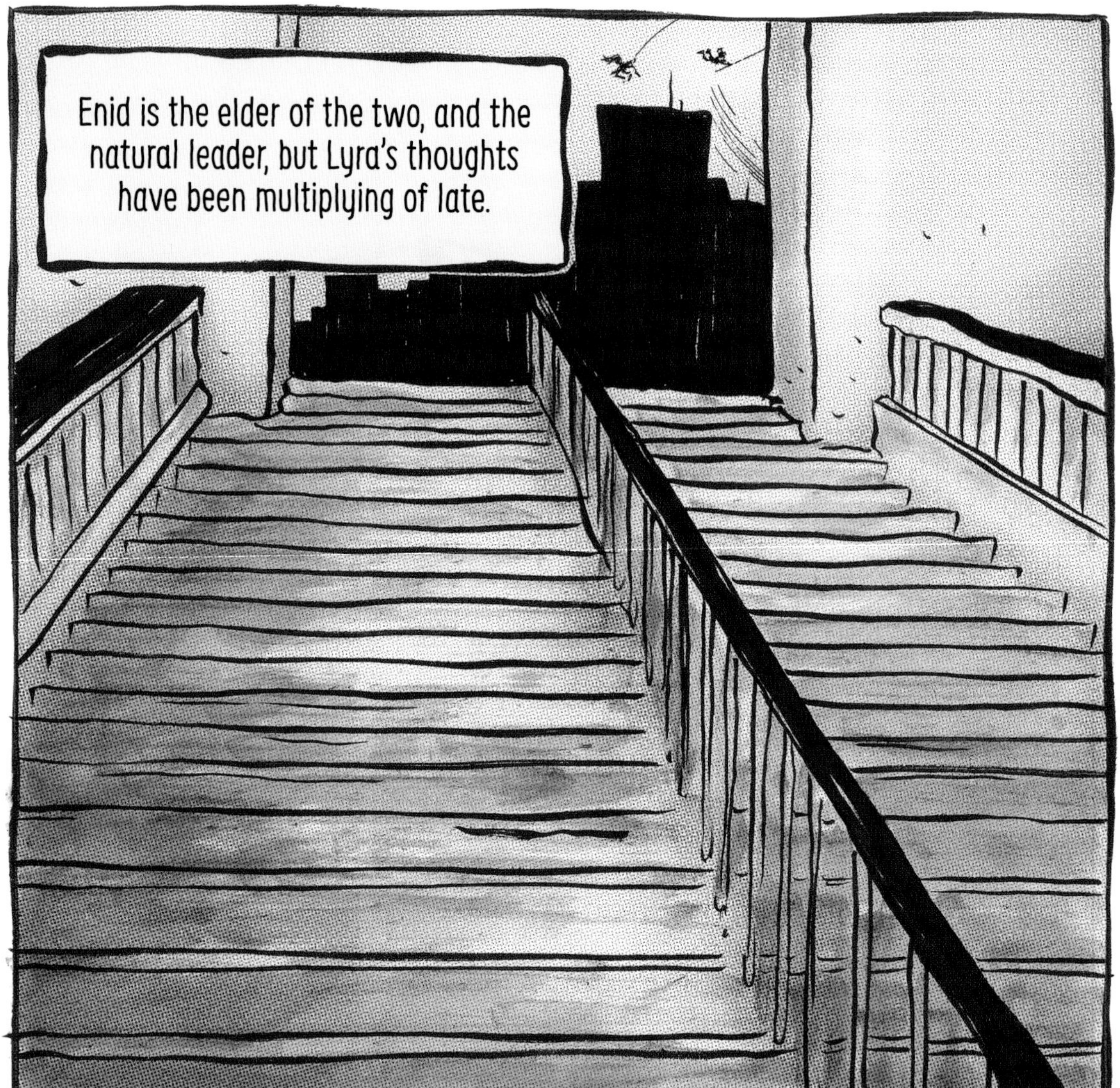
Enid is the elder of the two, and the natural leader, but Lyra's thoughts have been multiplying of late.

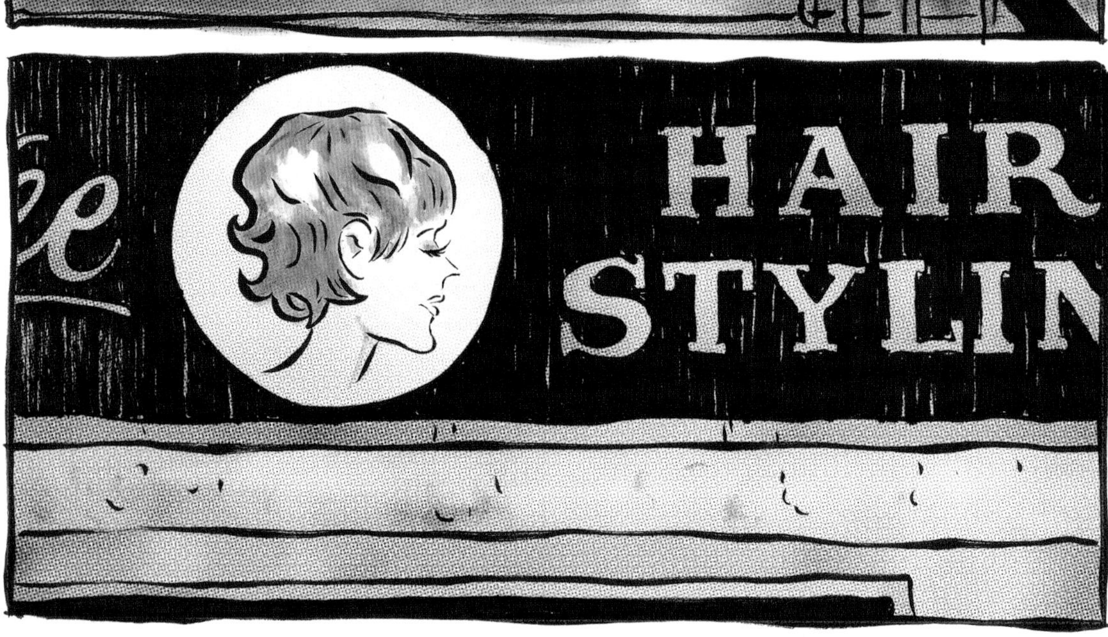
HAIR
STYLIN

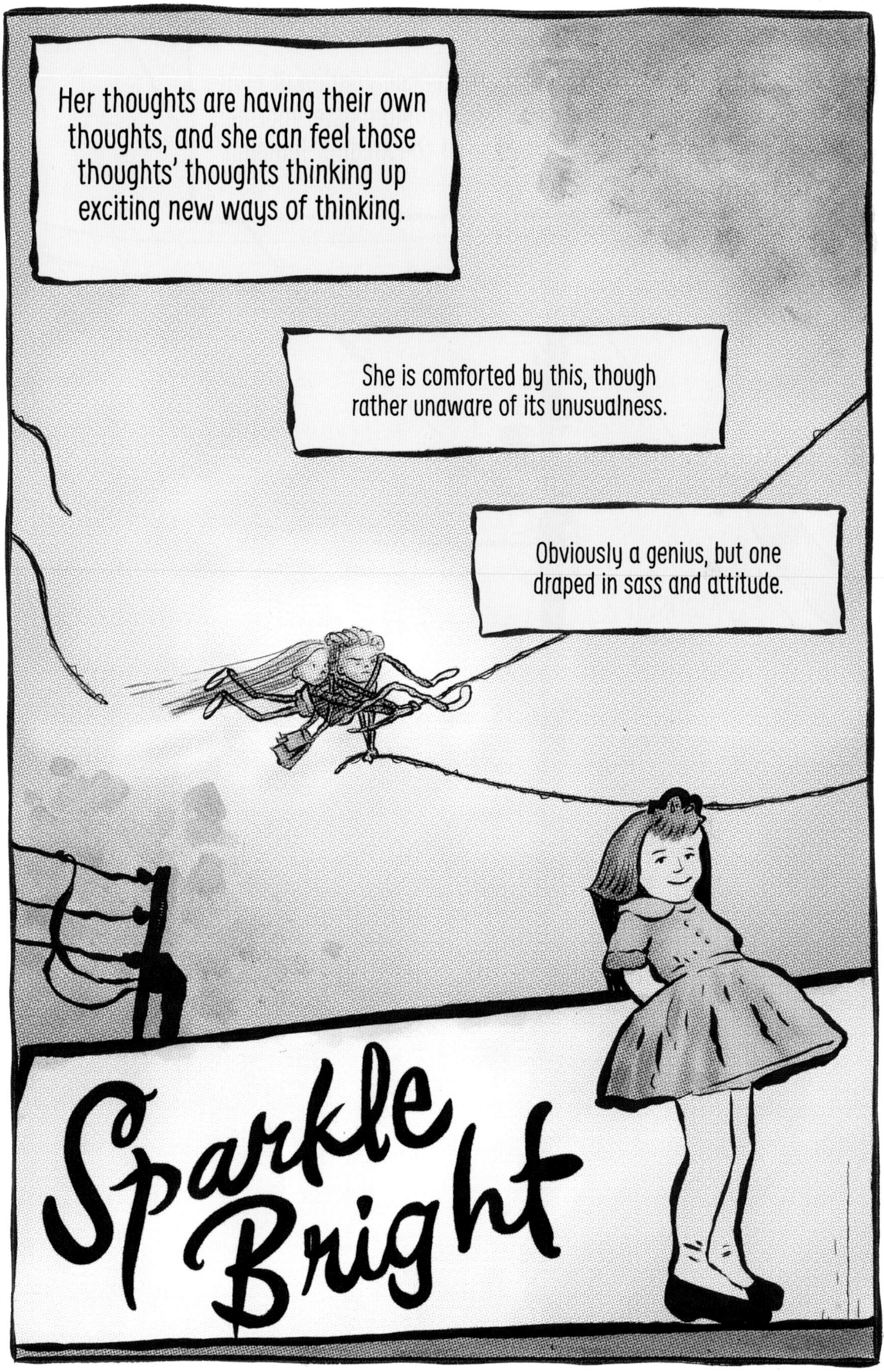
Her thoughts are having their own thoughts, and she can feel those thoughts' thoughts thinking up exciting new ways of thinking.
She is comforted by this, though rather unaware of its unusualness.
Obviously a genius, but one draped in sass and attitude.
Sparkle Bright

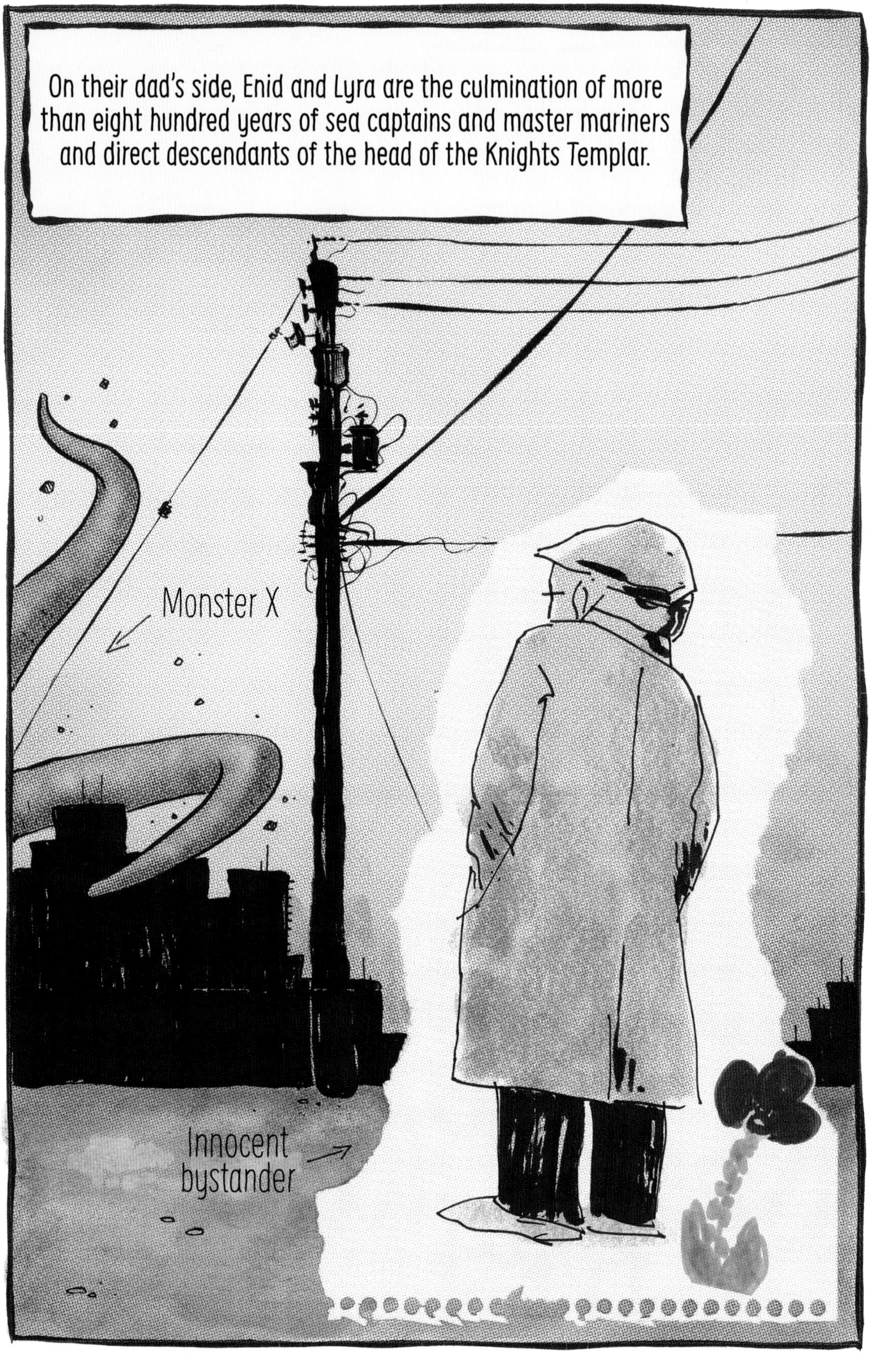
On their dad's side, Enid and Lyra are the culmination of more than eight hundred years of sea captains and master mariners and direct descendants of the head of the Knights Templar.
Monster X
Innocent bystander

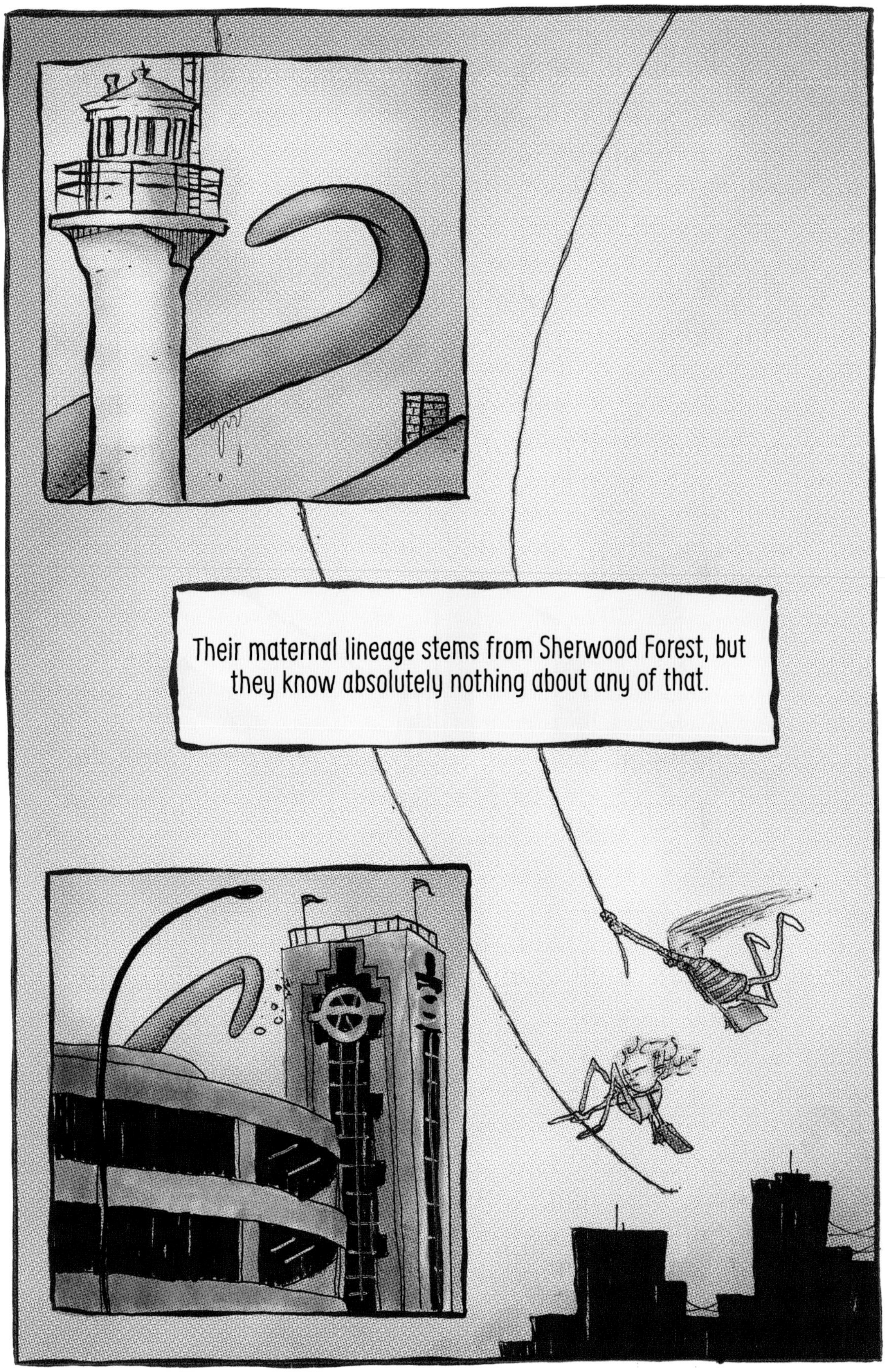
Their maternal lineage stems from Sherwood Forest, but they know absolutely nothing about any of that.

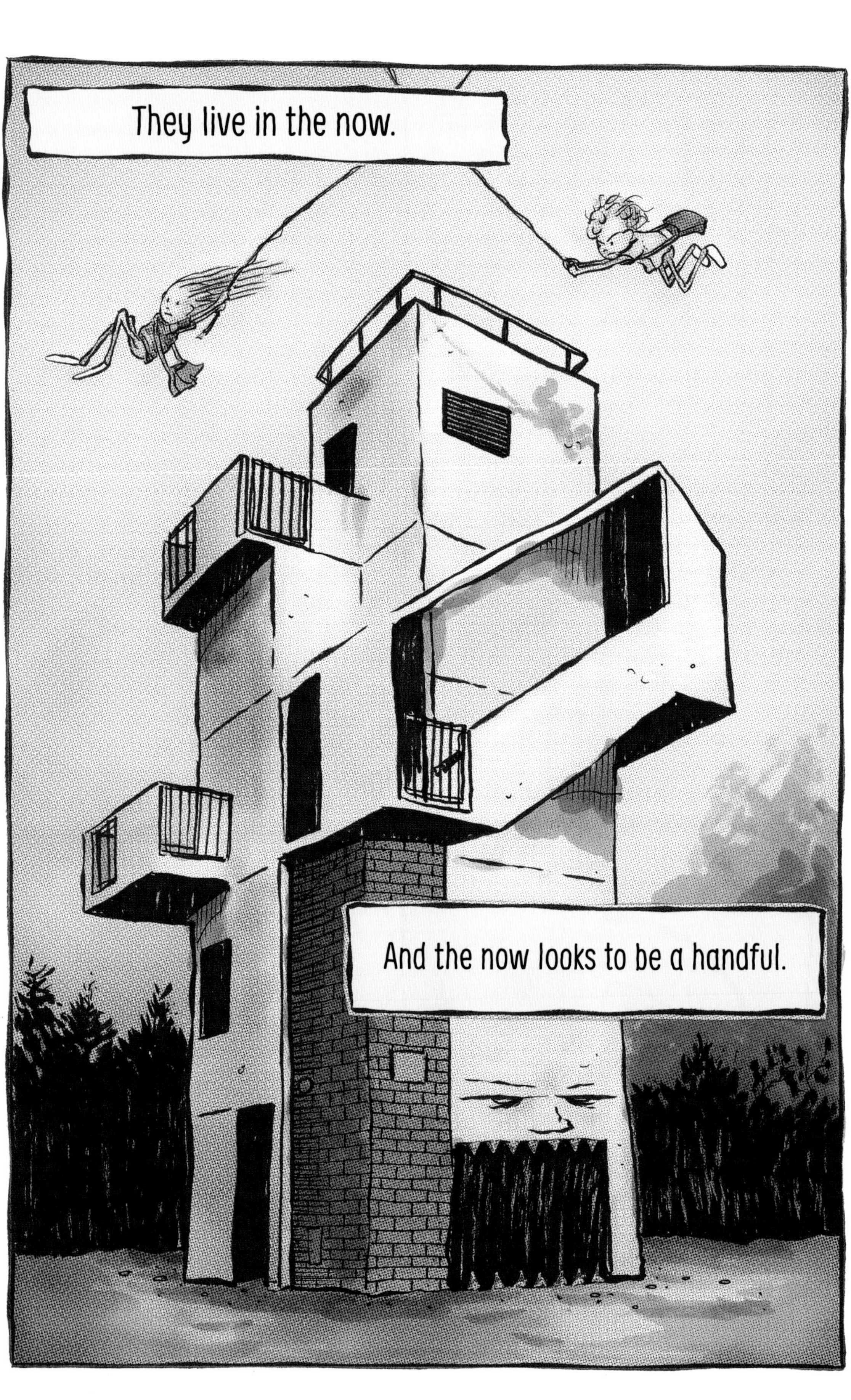
They live in the now.
And the now looks to be a handful.

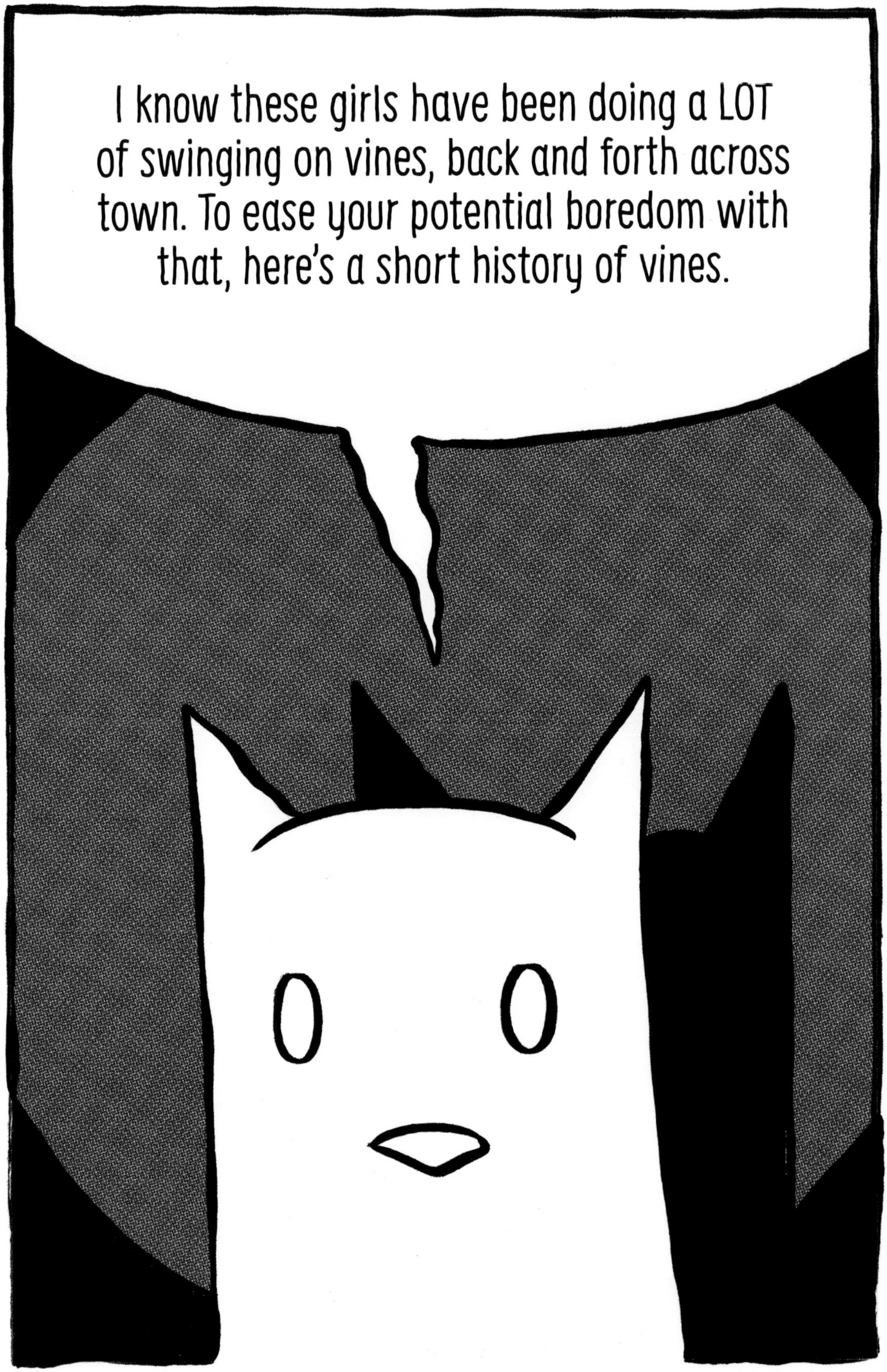
I know these girls have been doing a LOT of swinging on vines, back and forth across town. To ease your potential boredom with that, here's a short history of vines.

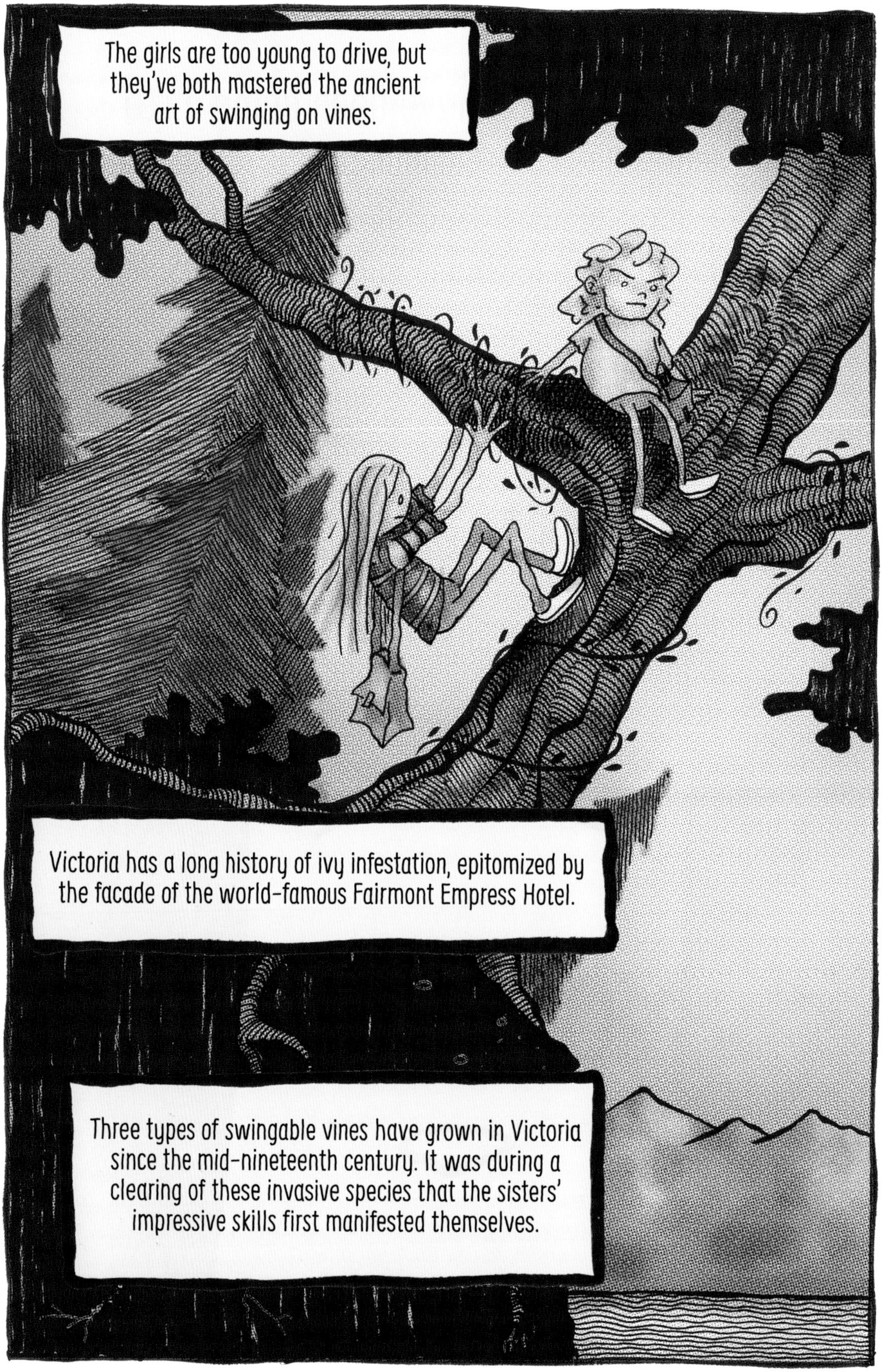
The girls are too young to drive, but they've both mastered the ancient art of swinging on vines.
Victoria has a long history of ivy infestation, epitomized by the facade of the world-famous Fairmont Empress Hotel.
Three types of swingable vines have grown in Victoria since the mid-nineteenth century. It was during a clearing of these invasive species that the sisters' impressive skills first manifested themselves.

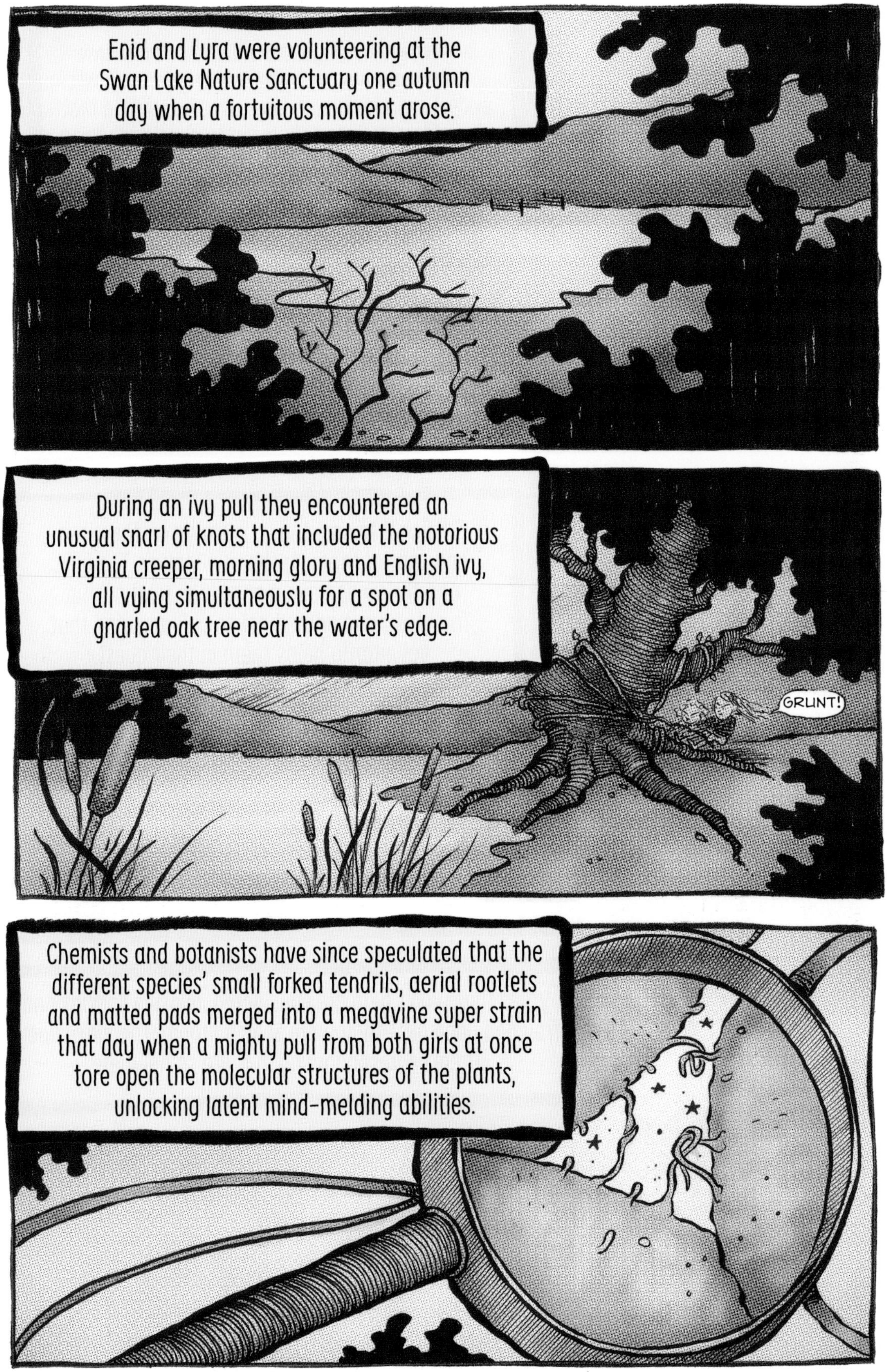
Enid and Lyra were volunteering at the Swan Lake Nature Sanctuary one autumn day when a fortuitous moment arose.
During an ivy pull they encountered an unusual snarl of knots that included the notorious Virginia creeper, morning glory and English ivy, all vying simultaneously for a spot on a gnarled oak tree near the water's edge.
GRUNT!
Chemists and botanists have since speculated that the different species' small forked tendrils, aerial rootlets and matted pads merged into a megavine super strain that day when a mighty pull from both girls at once tore open the molecular structures of the plants, unlocking latent mind-melding abilities.

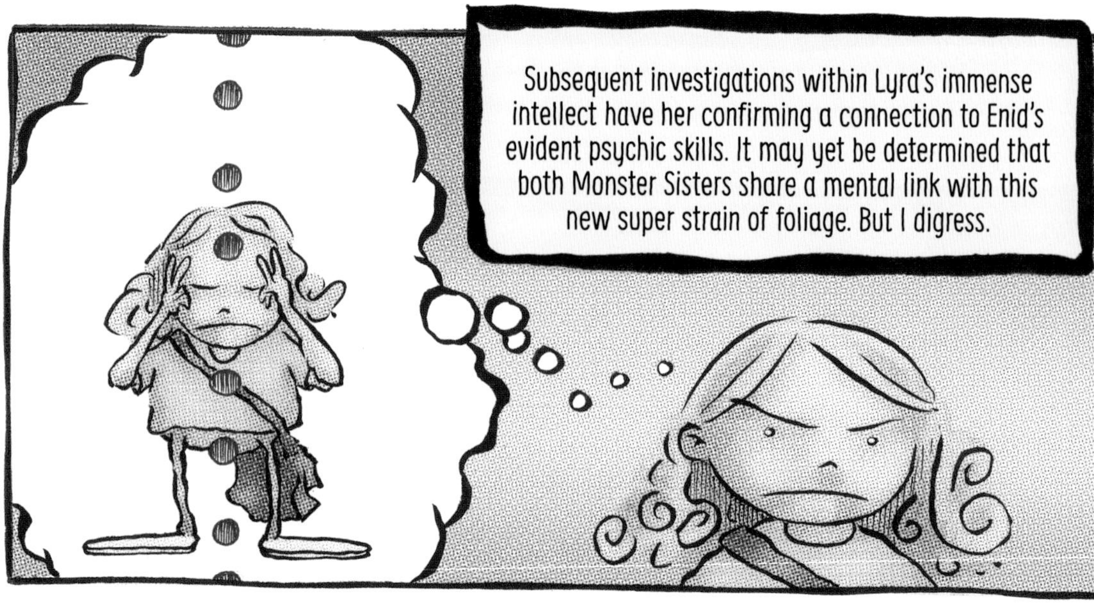
Subsequent investigations within Lyra's immense intellect have her confirming a connection to Enid's evident psychic skills. It may yet be determined that both Monster Sisters share a mental link with this new super strain of foliage. But I digress.

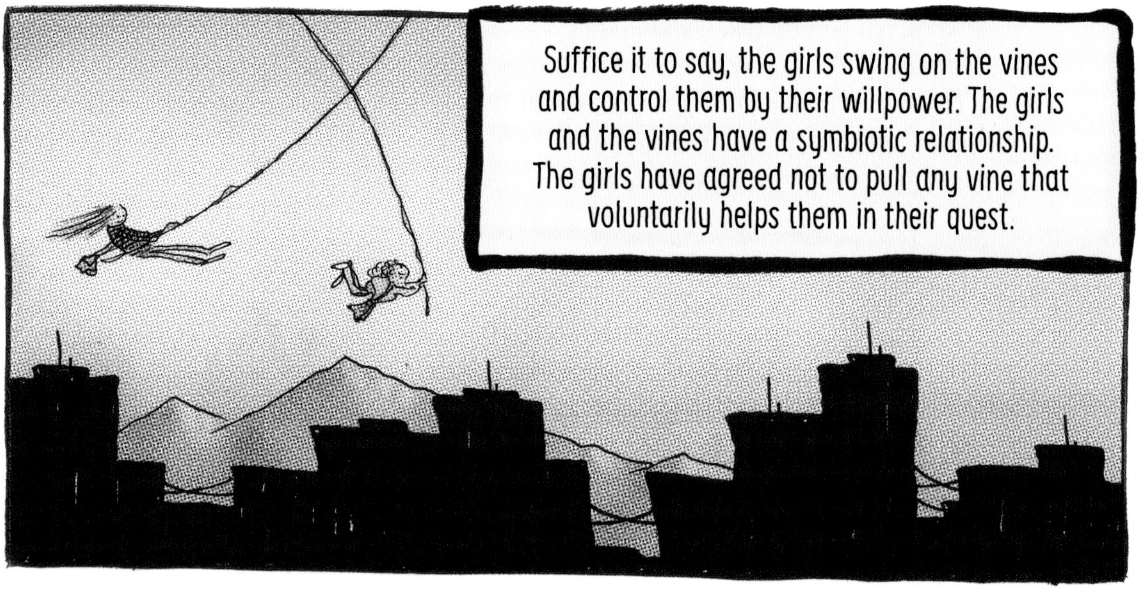
Suffice it to say, the girls swing on the vines and control them by their willpower. The girls and the vines have a symbiotic relationship. The girls have agreed not to pull any vine that voluntarily helps them in their quest.

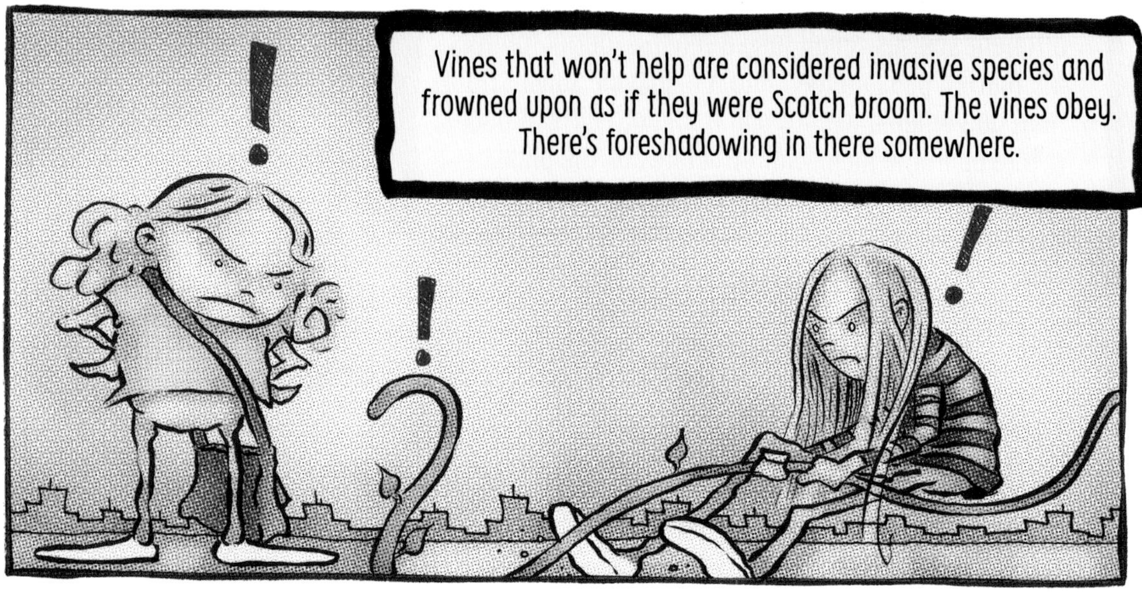
Vines that won't help are considered invasive species and frowned upon as if they were Scotch broom. The vines obey. There's foreshadowing in there somewhere.
!
!
!

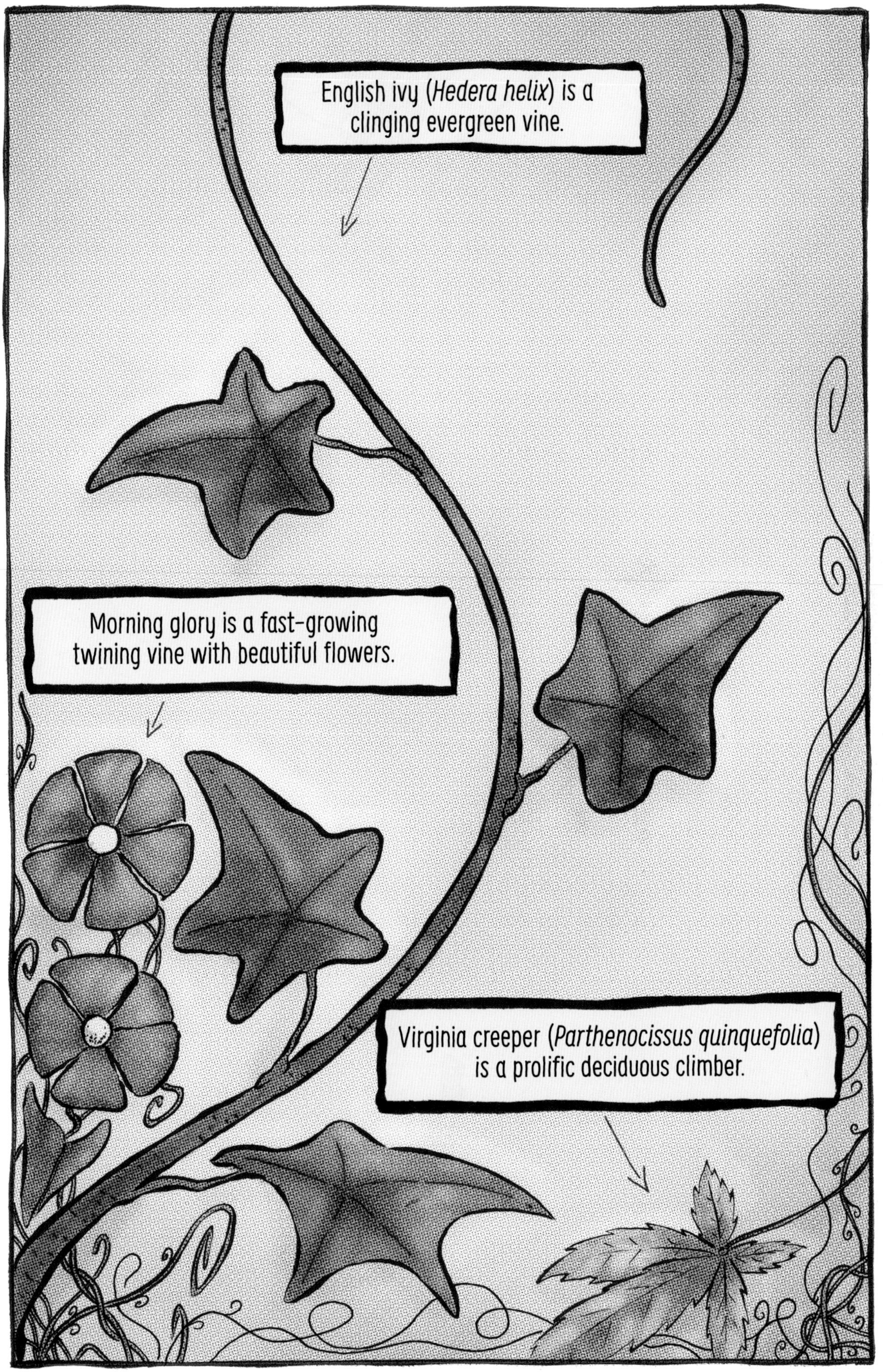
English ivy (*Hedera helix*) is a clinging evergreen vine.
Morning glory is a fast-growing twining vine with beautiful flowers.
Virginia creeper (*Parthenocissus quinquefolia*) is a prolific deciduous climber.

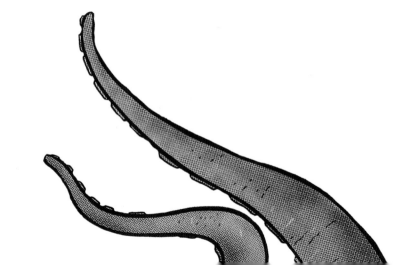

CHAPTER SIX

OCTOPUS

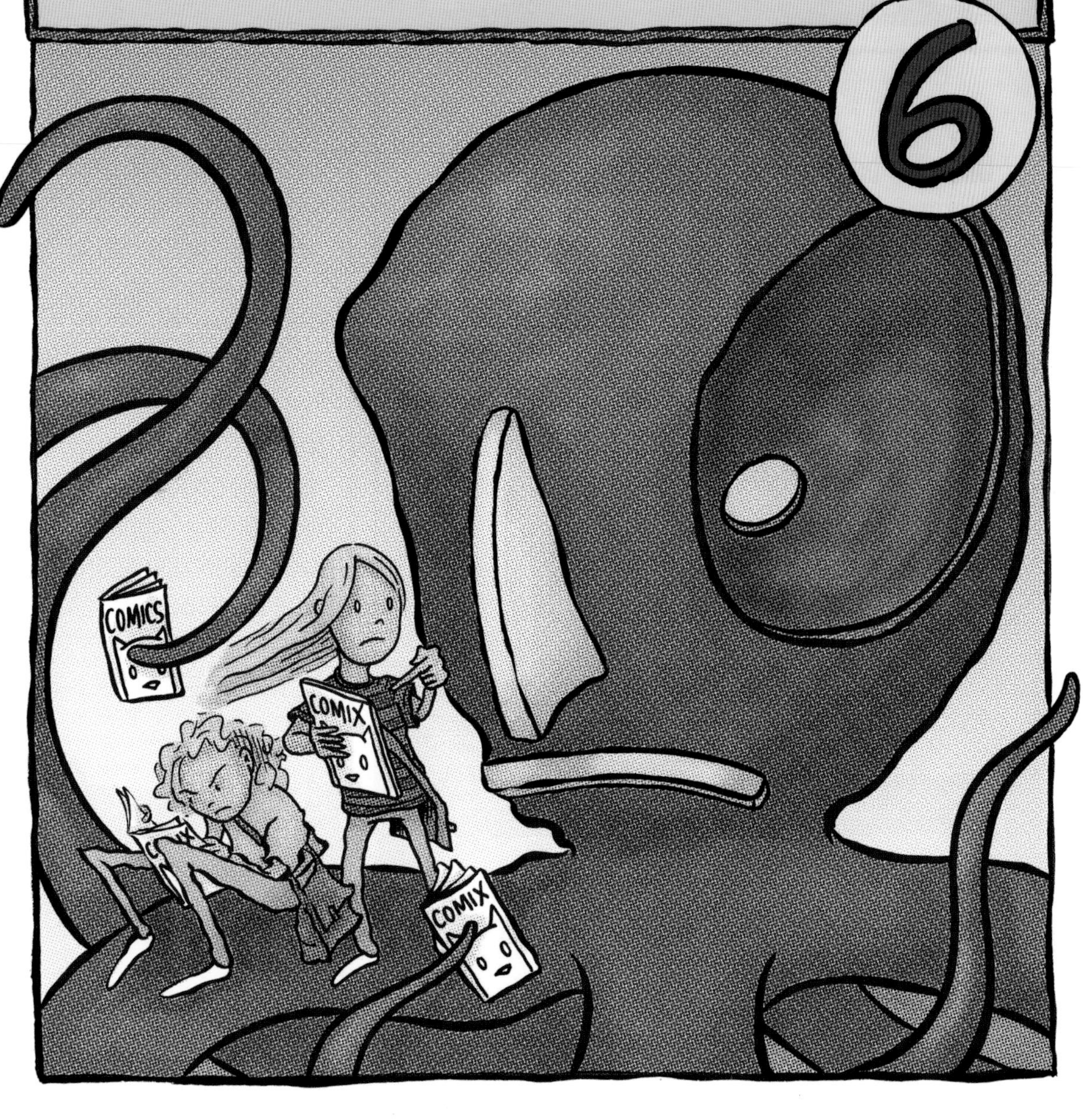
6
COMICS
COMIX
COMIX

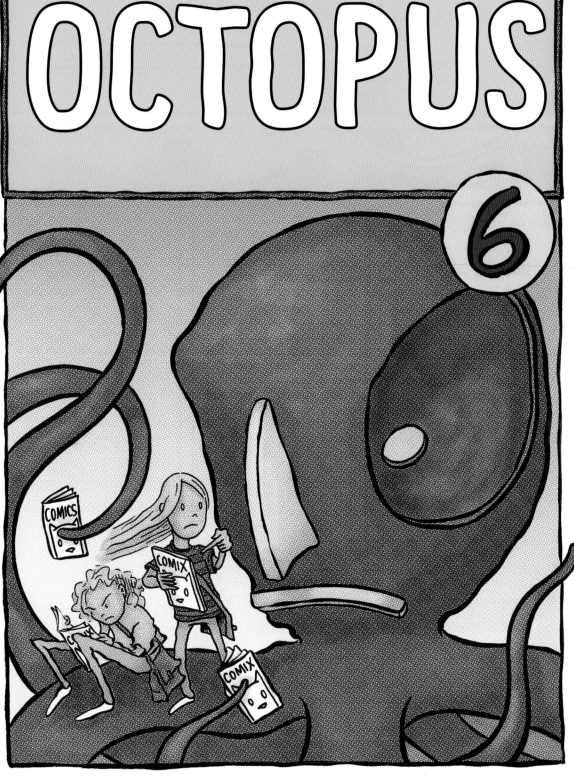

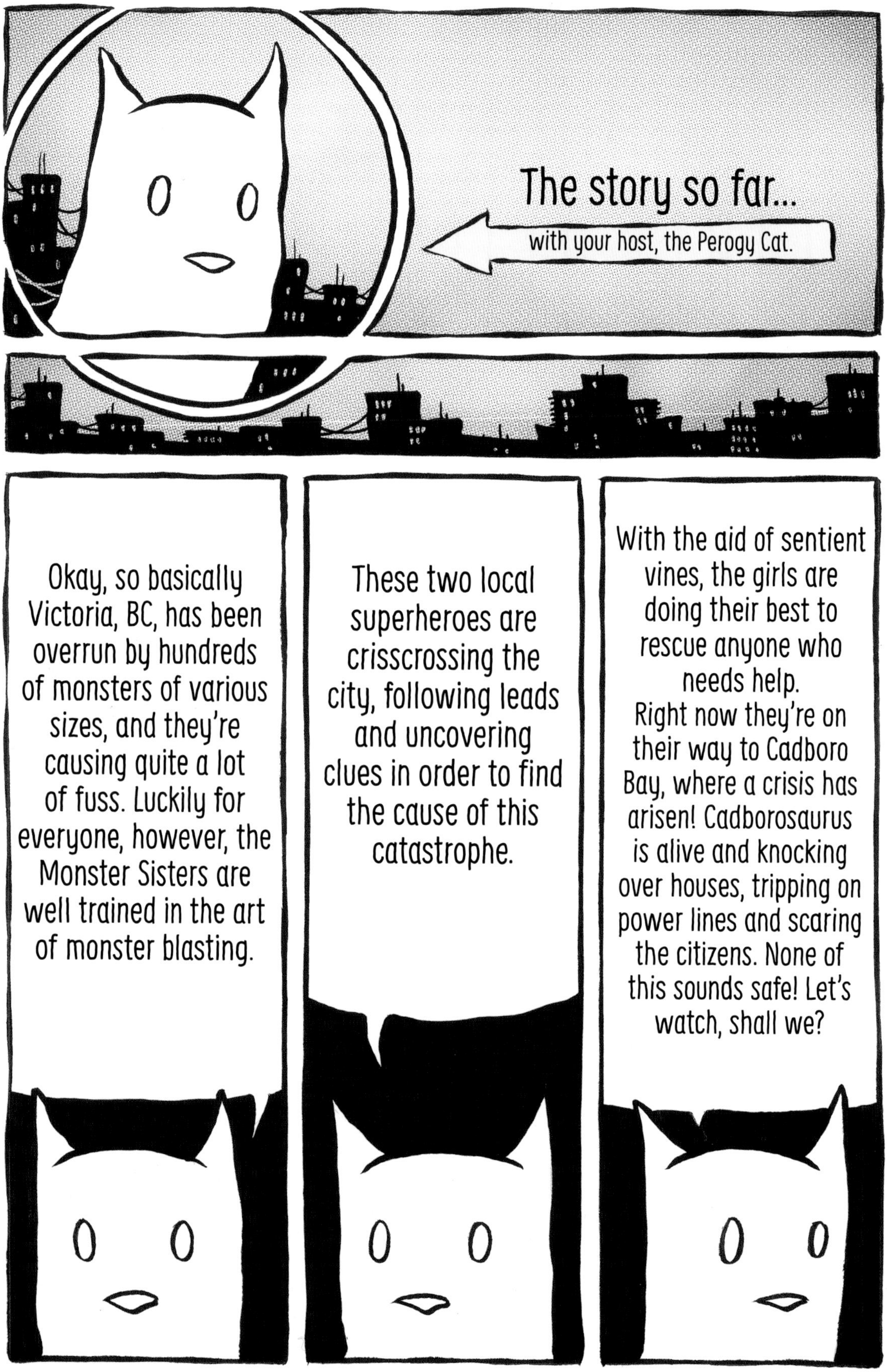

The story so far...
with your host, the Perogy Cat.
Okay, so basically Victoria, BC, has been overrun by hundreds of monsters of various sizes, and they're causing quite a lot of fuss. Luckily for everyone, however, the Monster Sisters are well trained in the art of monster blasting.
These two local superheroes are crisscrossing the city, following leads and uncovering clues in order to find the cause of this catastrophe.
With the aid of sentient vines, the girls are doing their best to rescue anyone who needs help. Right now they're on their way to Cadboro Bay, where a crisis has arisen! Cadborosaurus is alive and knocking over houses, tripping on power lines and scaring the citizens. None of this sounds safe! Let's watch, shall we?

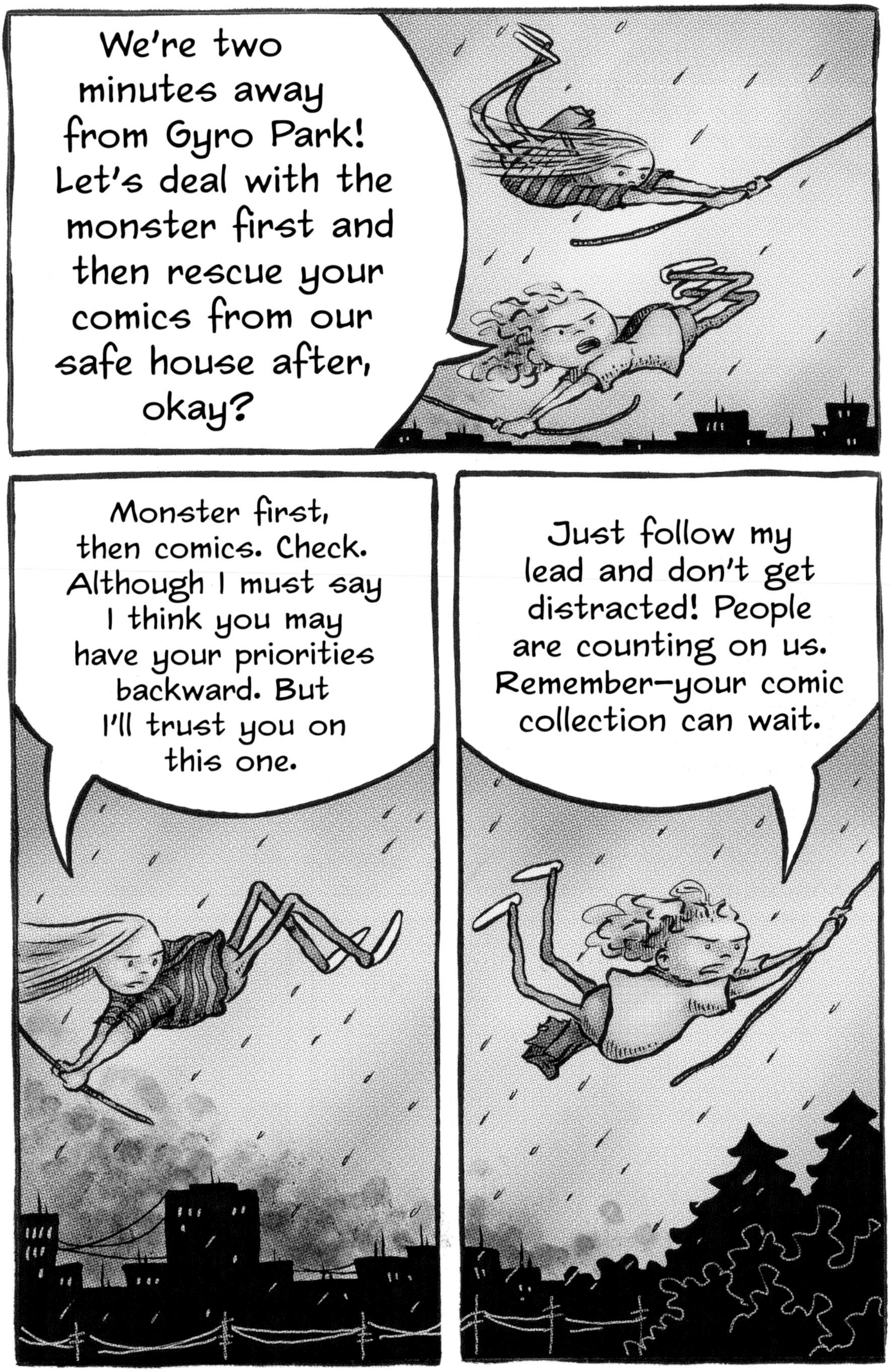
We're two minutes away from Gyro Park! Let's deal with the monster first and then rescue your comics from our safe house after, okay?
Monster first, then comics. Check. Although I must say I think you may have your priorities backward. But I'll trust you on this one.
Just follow my lead and don't get distracted! People are counting on us. Remember—your comic collection can wait.

But just then:

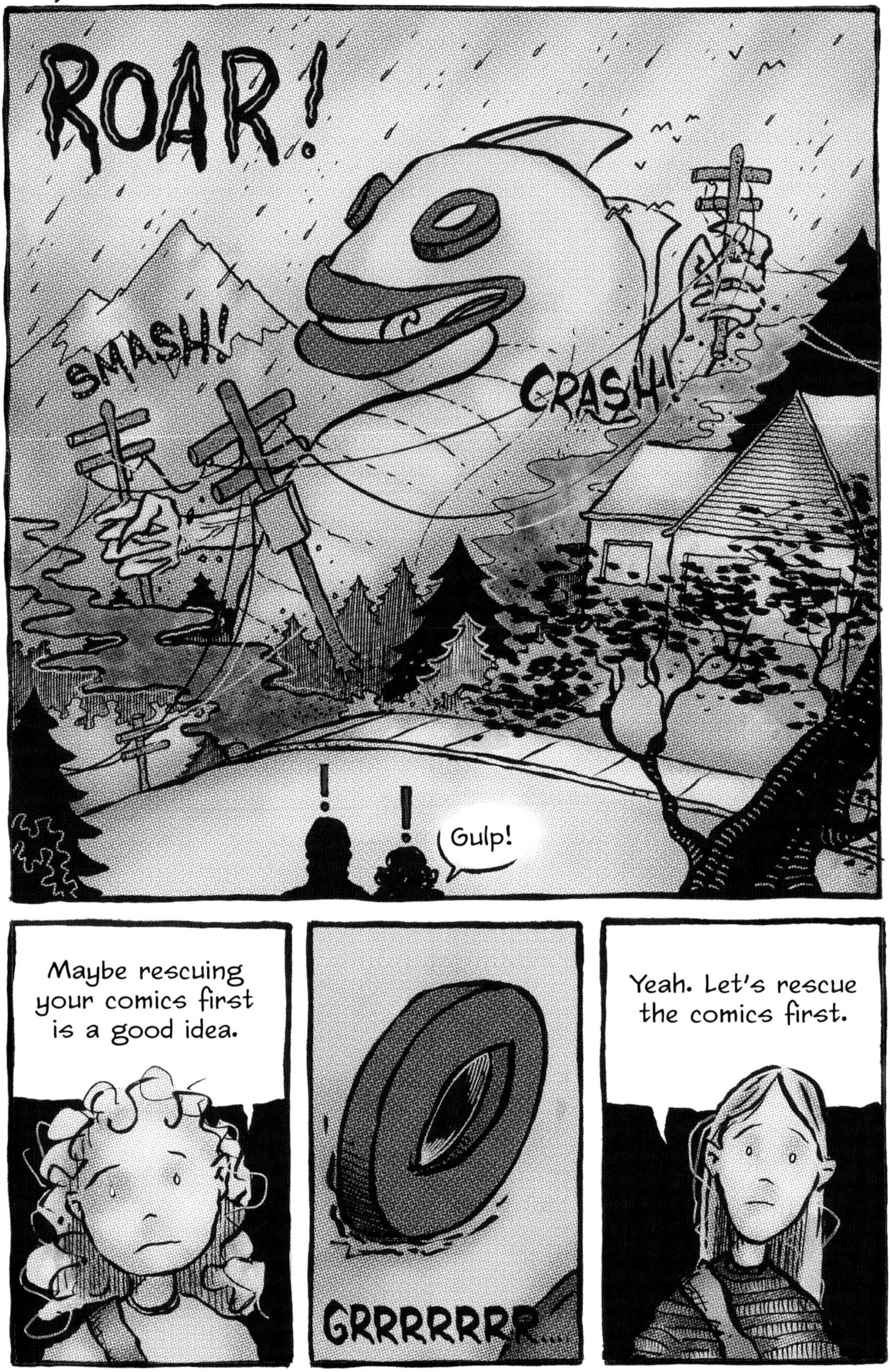
ROAR!
SMASH!
CRASH!
!
!
Gulp!
Maybe rescuing your comics first is a good idea.
GRRRRRRR...
Yeah. Let's rescue the comics first.

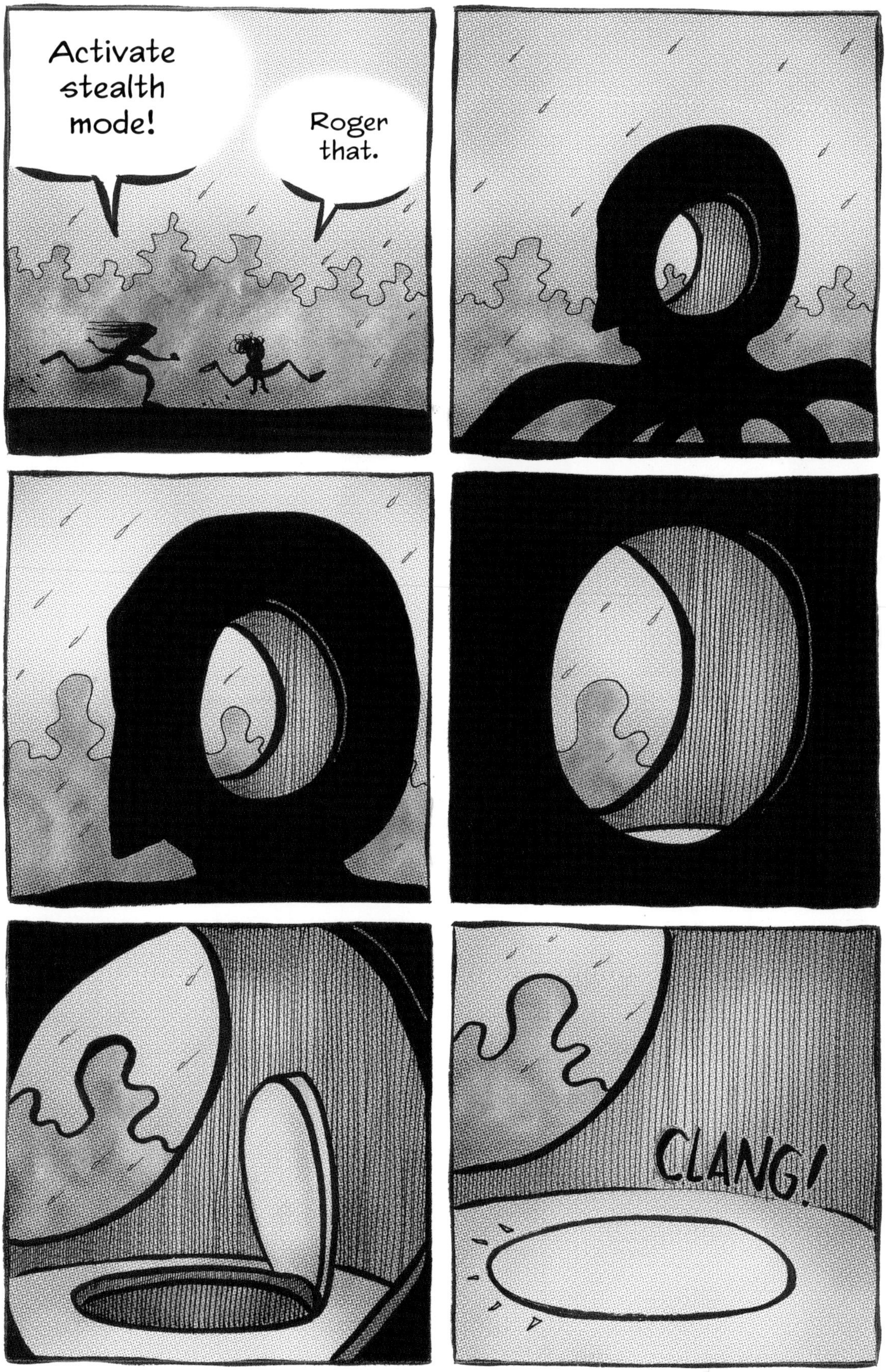
Activate stealth mode!
Roger that.
CLANG!

Stealth mode: successful!

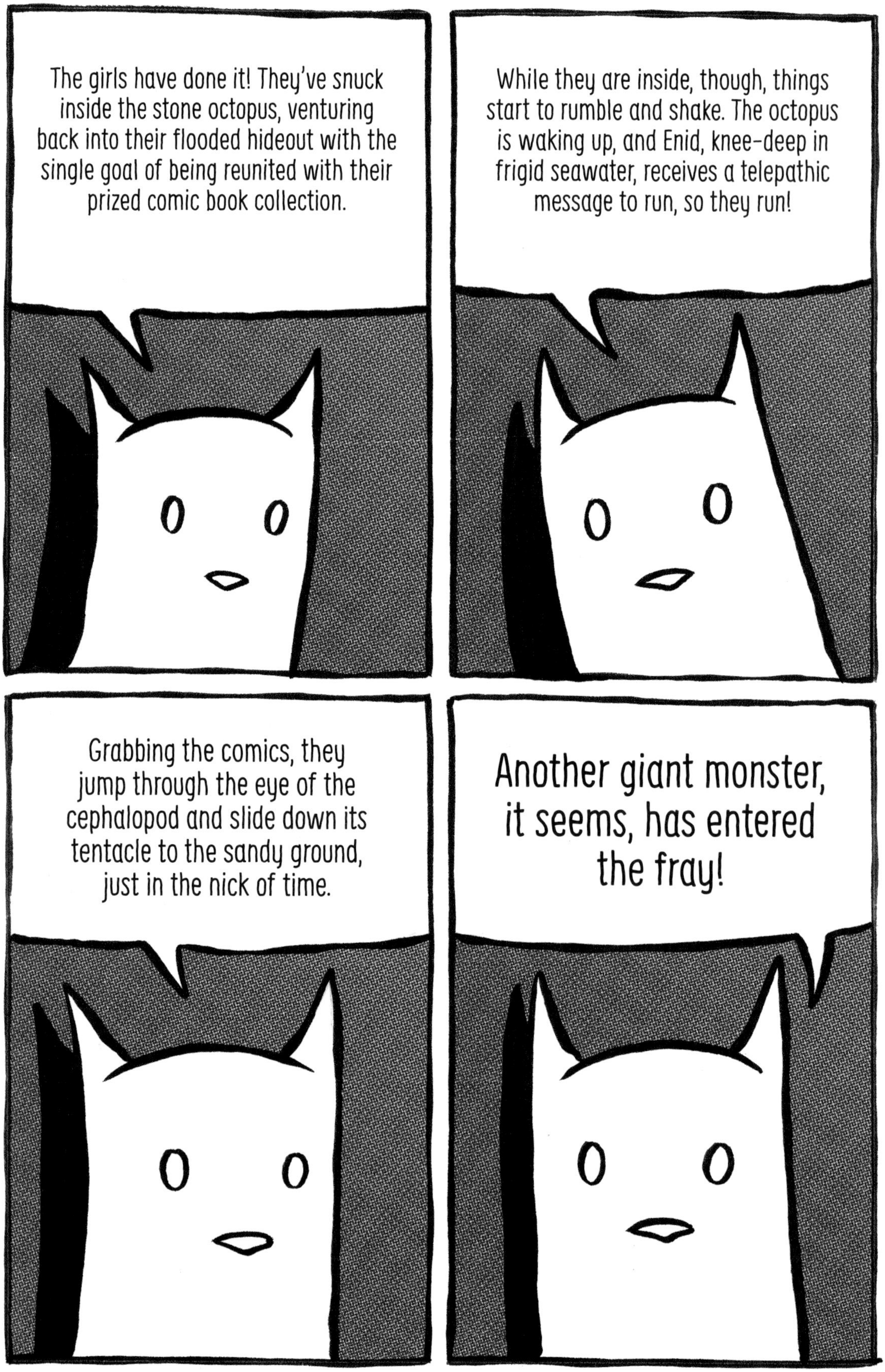

The girls have done it! They've snuck inside the stone octopus, venturing back into their flooded hideout with the single goal of being reunited with their prized comic book collection.
While they are inside, though, things start to rumble and shake. The octopus is waking up, and Enid, knee-deep in frigid seawater, receives a telepathic message to run, so they run!
Grabbing the comics, they jump through the eye of the cephalopod and slide down its tentacle to the sandy ground, just in the nick of time.
Another giant monster, it seems, has entered the fray!

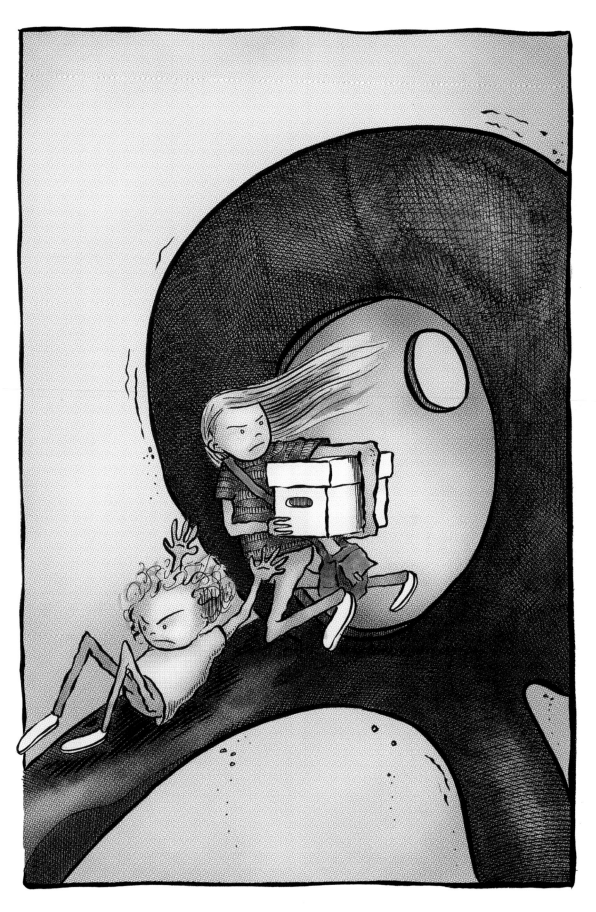

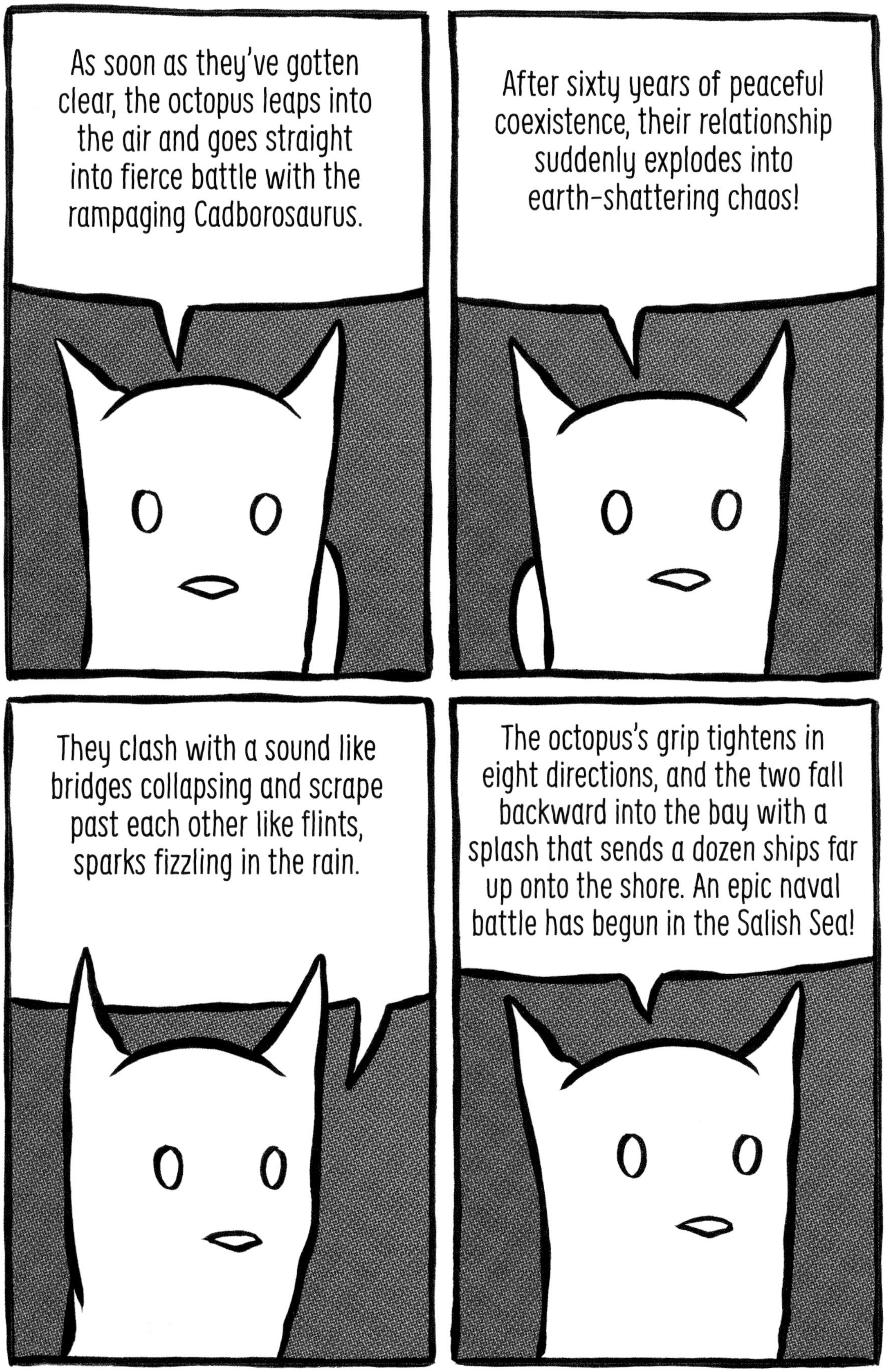
As soon as they've gotten clear, the octopus leaps into the air and goes straight into fierce battle with the rampaging Cadborosaurus.
After sixty years of peaceful coexistence, their relationship suddenly explodes into earth-shattering chaos!
They clash with a sound like bridges collapsing and scrape past each other like flints, sparks fizzling in the rain.
The octopus's grip tightens in eight directions, and the two fall backward into the bay with a splash that sends a dozen ships far up onto the shore. An epic naval battle has begun in the Salish Sea!

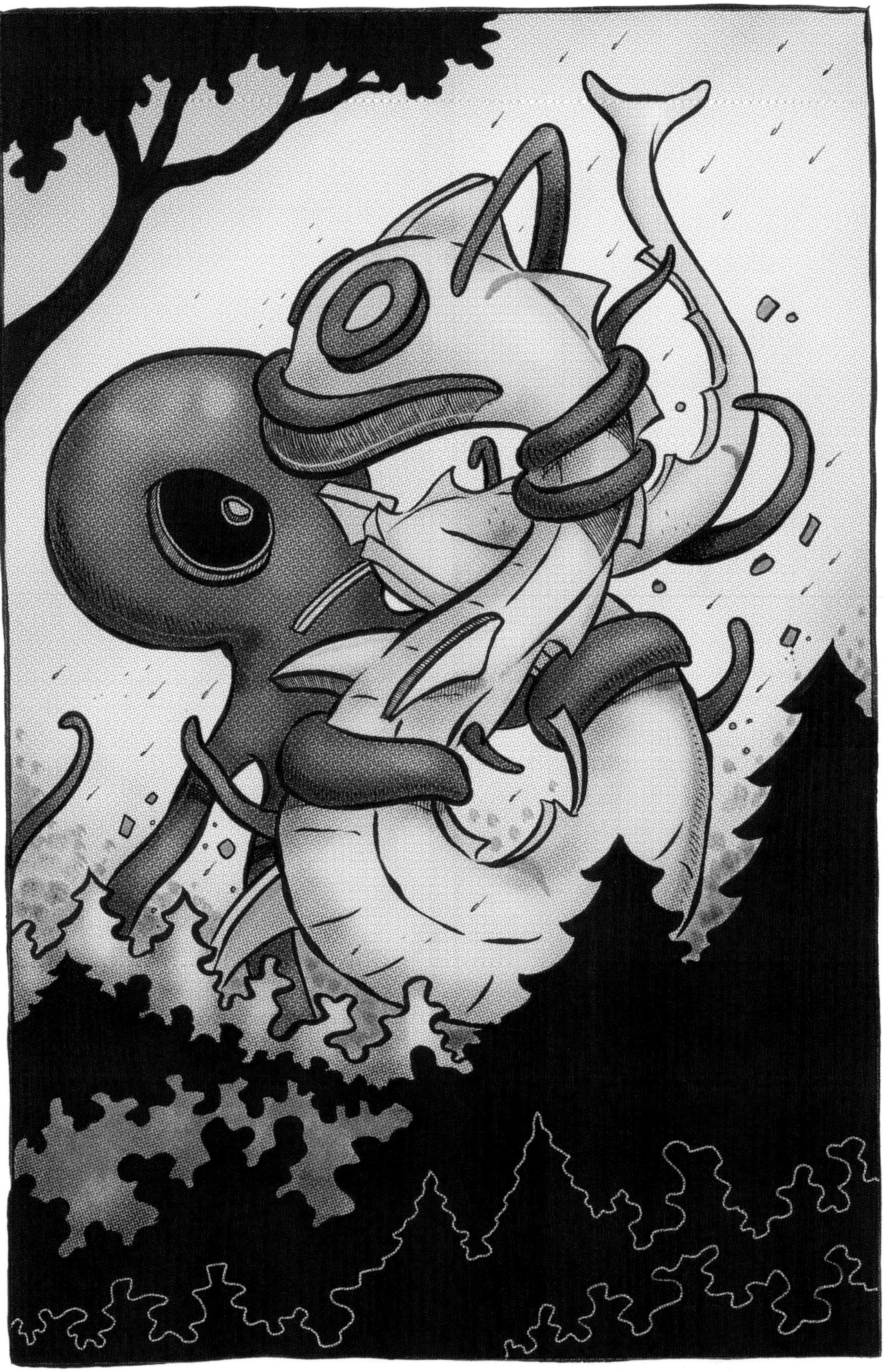

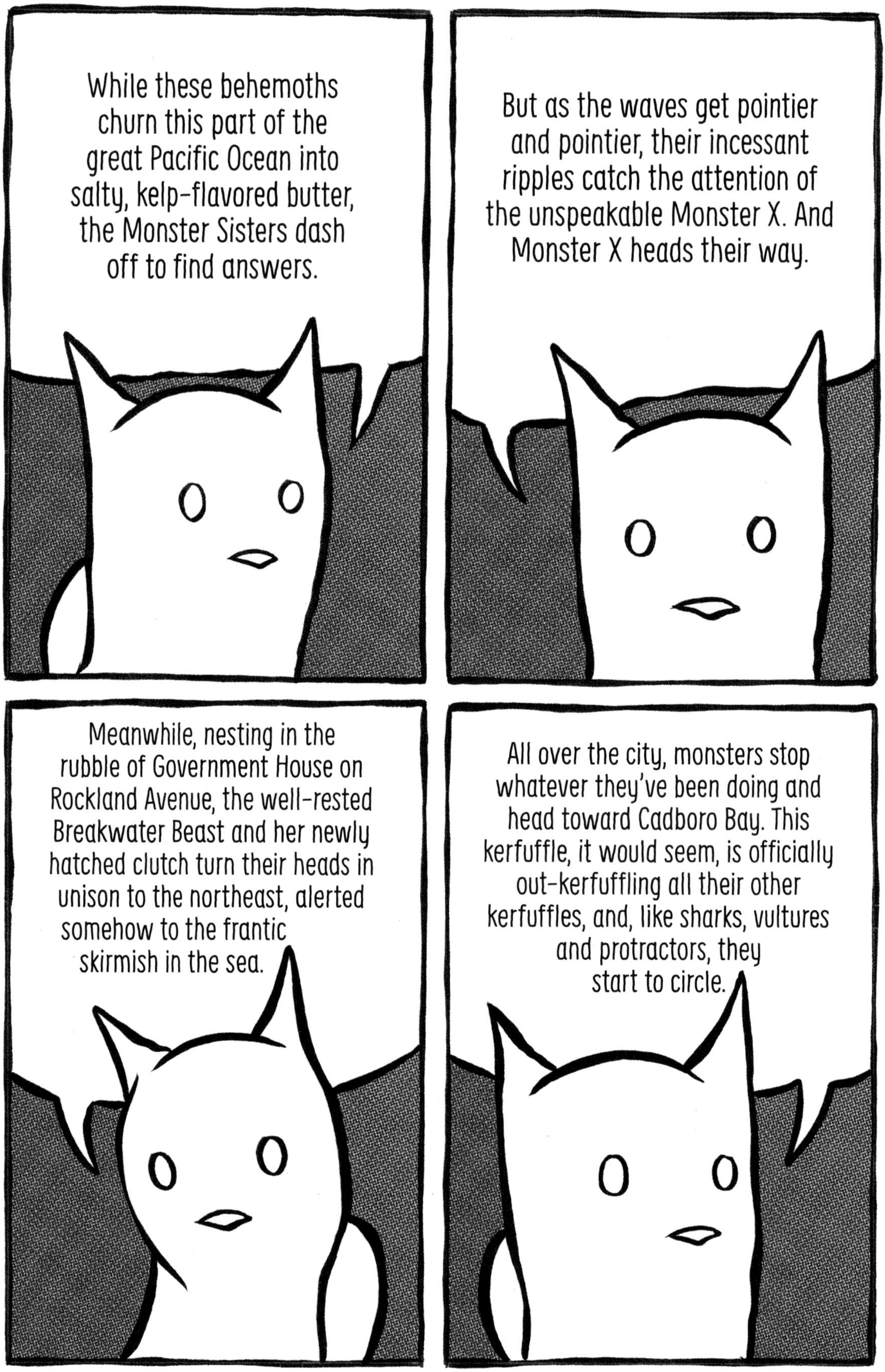
While these behemoths churn this part of the great Pacific Ocean into salty, kelp-flavored butter, the Monster Sisters dash off to find answers.
But as the waves get pointier and pointier, their incessant ripples catch the attention of the unspeakable Monster X. And Monster X heads their way.
Meanwhile, nesting in the rubble of Government House on Rockland Avenue, the well-rested Breakwater Beast and her newly hatched clutch turn their heads in unison to the northeast, alerted somehow to the frantic skirmish in the sea.
All over the city, monsters stop whatever they've been doing and head toward Cadboro Bay. This kerfuffle, it would seem, is officially out-kerfuffling all their other kerfuffles, and, like sharks, vultures and protractors, they start to circle.

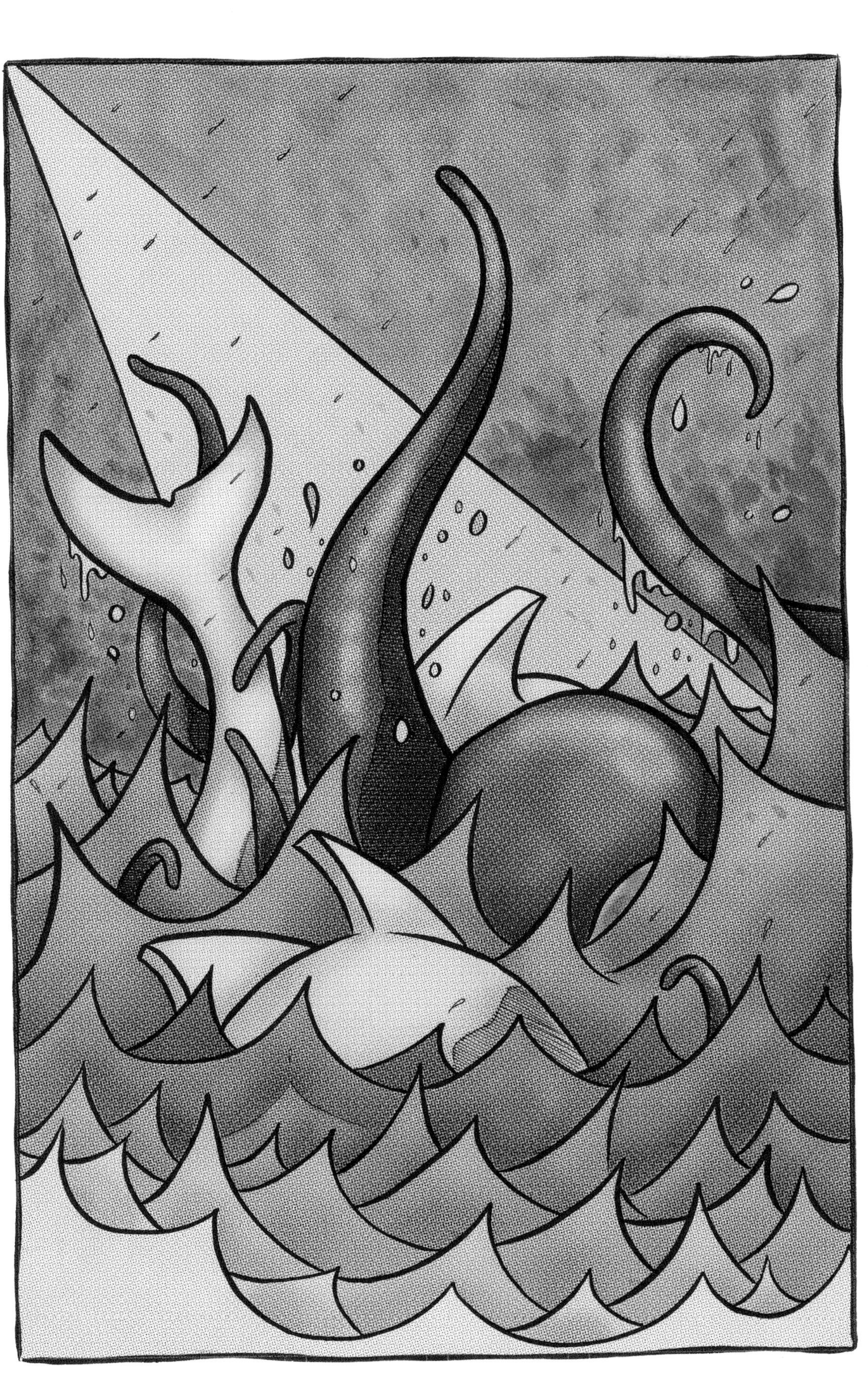

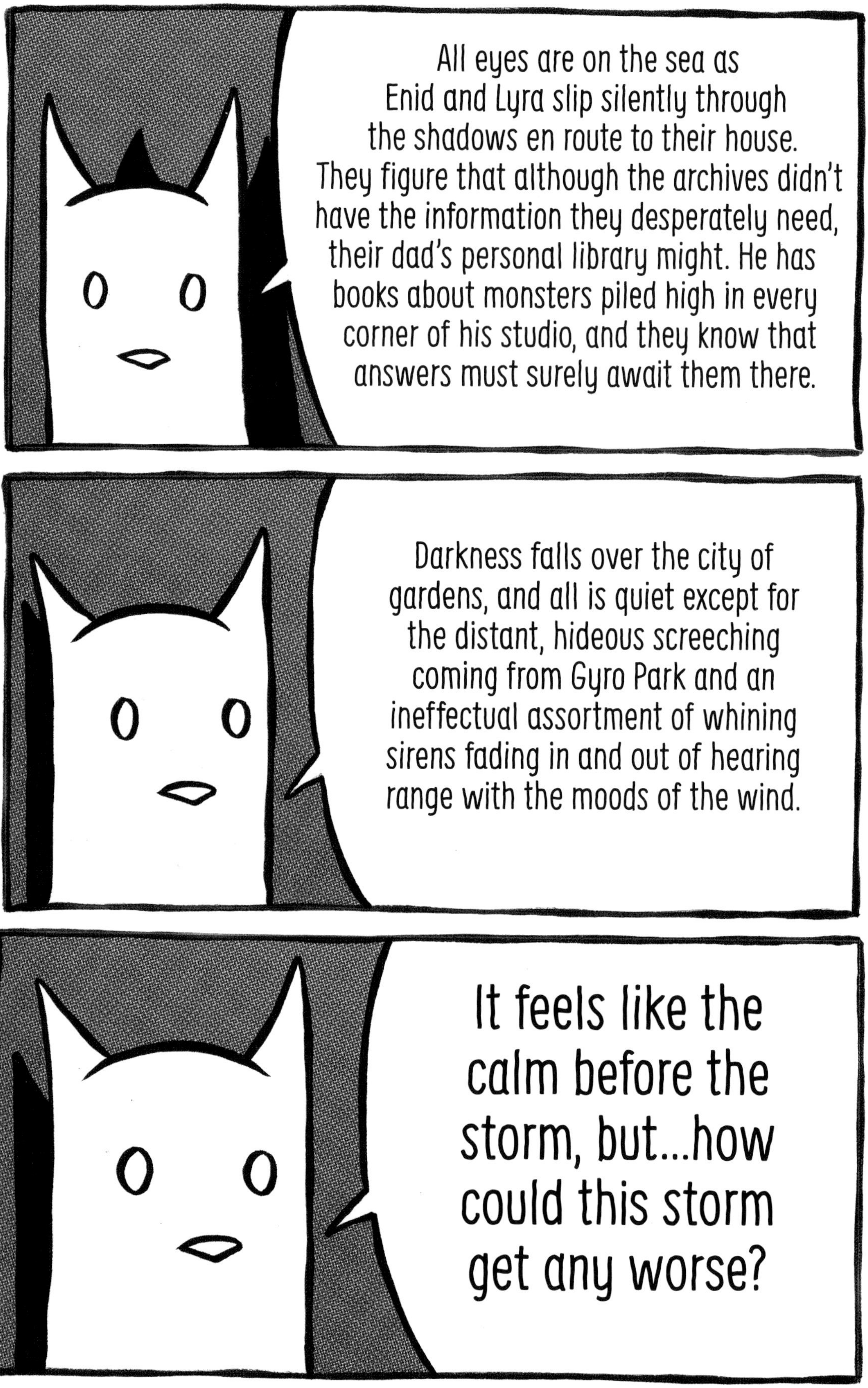
All eyes are on the sea as Enid and Lyra slip silently through the shadows en route to their house. They figure that although the archives didn't have the information they desperately need, their dad's personal library might. He has books about monsters piled high in every corner of his studio, and they know that answers must surely await them there.
Darkness falls over the city of gardens, and all is quiet except for the distant, hideous screeching coming from Gyro Park and an ineffectual assortment of whining sirens fading in and out of hearing range with the moods of the wind.
It feels like the calm before the storm, but...how could this storm get any worse?

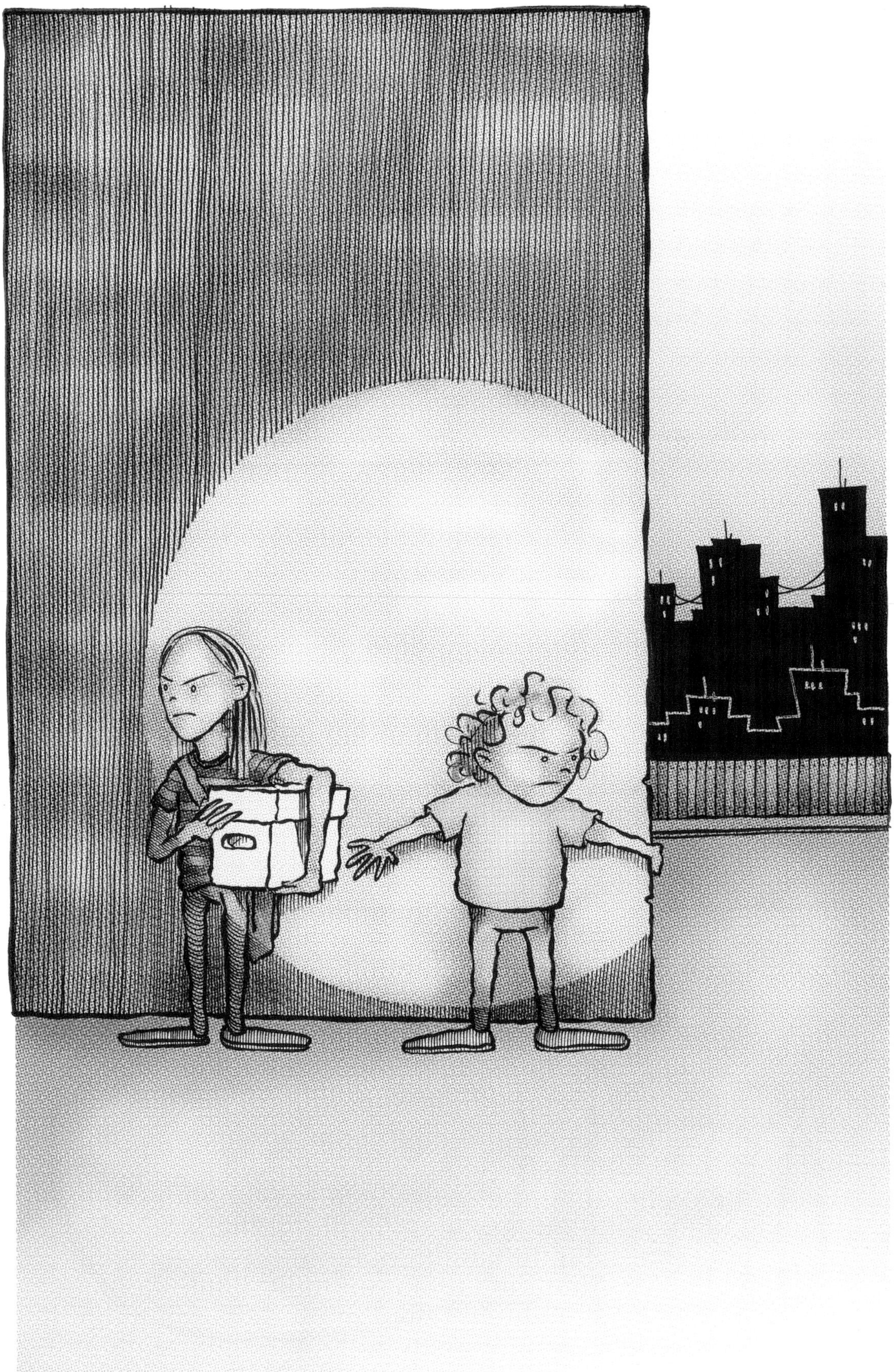

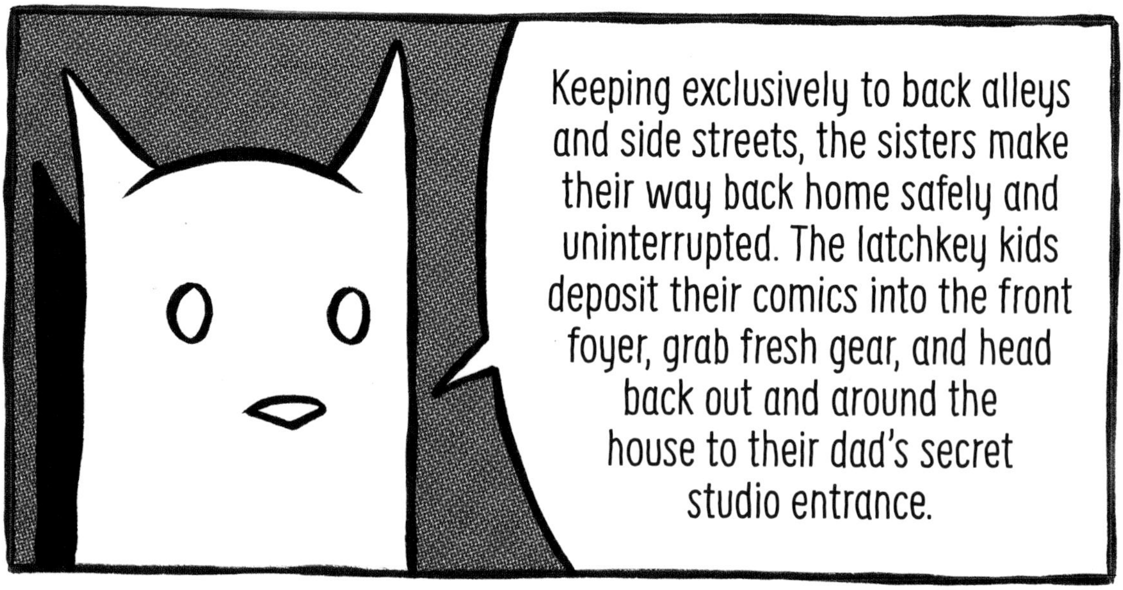
Keeping exclusively to back alleys and side streets, the sisters make their way back home safely and uninterrupted. The latchkey kids deposit their comics into the front foyer, grab fresh gear, and head back out and around the house to their dad's secret studio entrance.

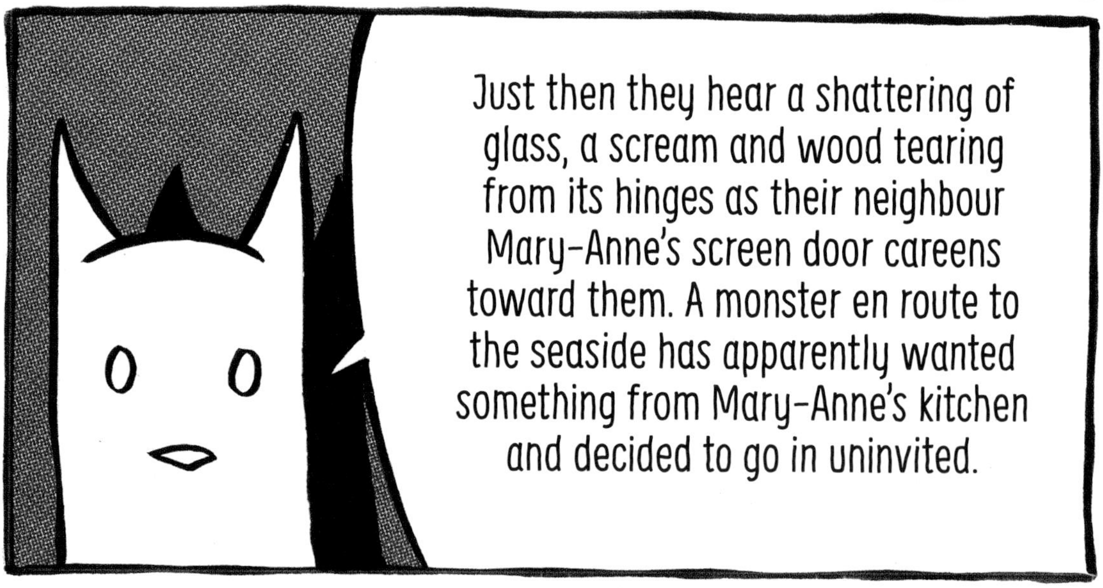
Just then they hear a shattering of glass, a scream and wood tearing from its hinges as their neighbour Mary-Anne's screen door careens toward them. A monster en route to the seaside has apparently wanted something from Mary-Anne's kitchen and decided to go in uninvited.

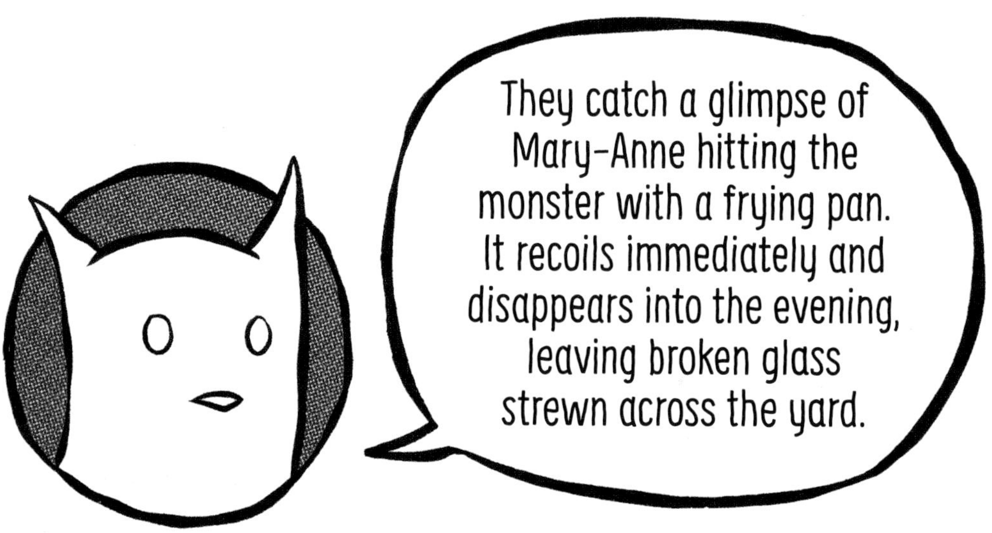
They catch a glimpse of Mary-Anne hitting the monster with a frying pan. It recoils immediately and disappears into the evening, leaving broken glass strewn across the yard.

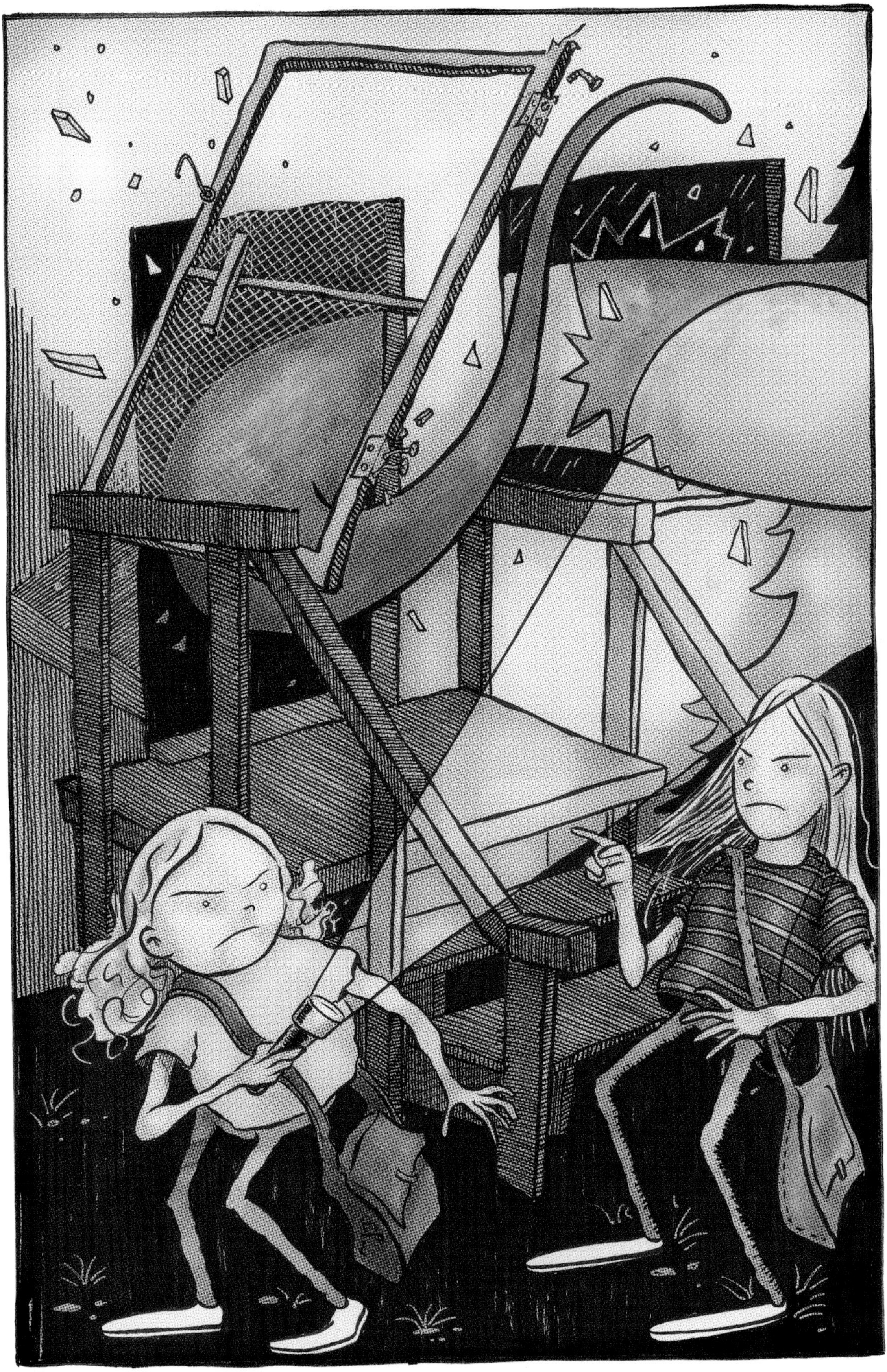

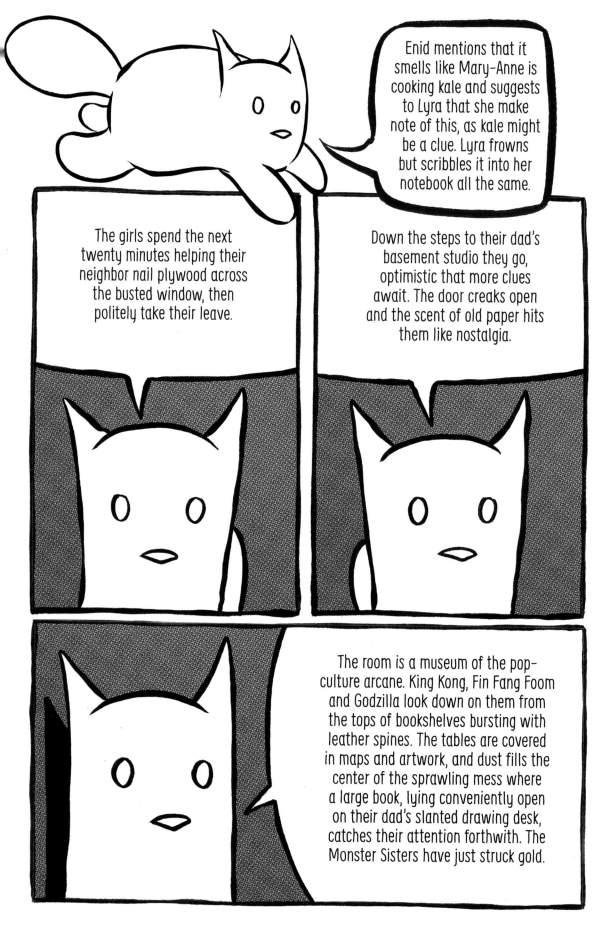

Enid mentions that it smells like Mary-Anne is cooking kale and suggests to Lyra that she make note of this, as kale might be a clue. Lyra frowns but scribbles it into her notebook all the same.

The girls spend the next twenty minutes helping their neighbor nail plywood across the busted window, then politely take their leave.

Down the steps to their dad's basement studio they go, optimistic that more clues await. The door creaks open and the scent of old paper hits them like nostalgia.

The room is a museum of the pop-culture arcane. King Kong, Fin Fang Foom and Godzilla look down on them from the tops of bookshelves bursting with leather spines. The tables are covered in maps and artwork, and dust fills the center of the sprawling mess where a large book, lying conveniently open on their dad's slanted drawing desk, catches their attention forthwith. The Monster Sisters have just struck gold.

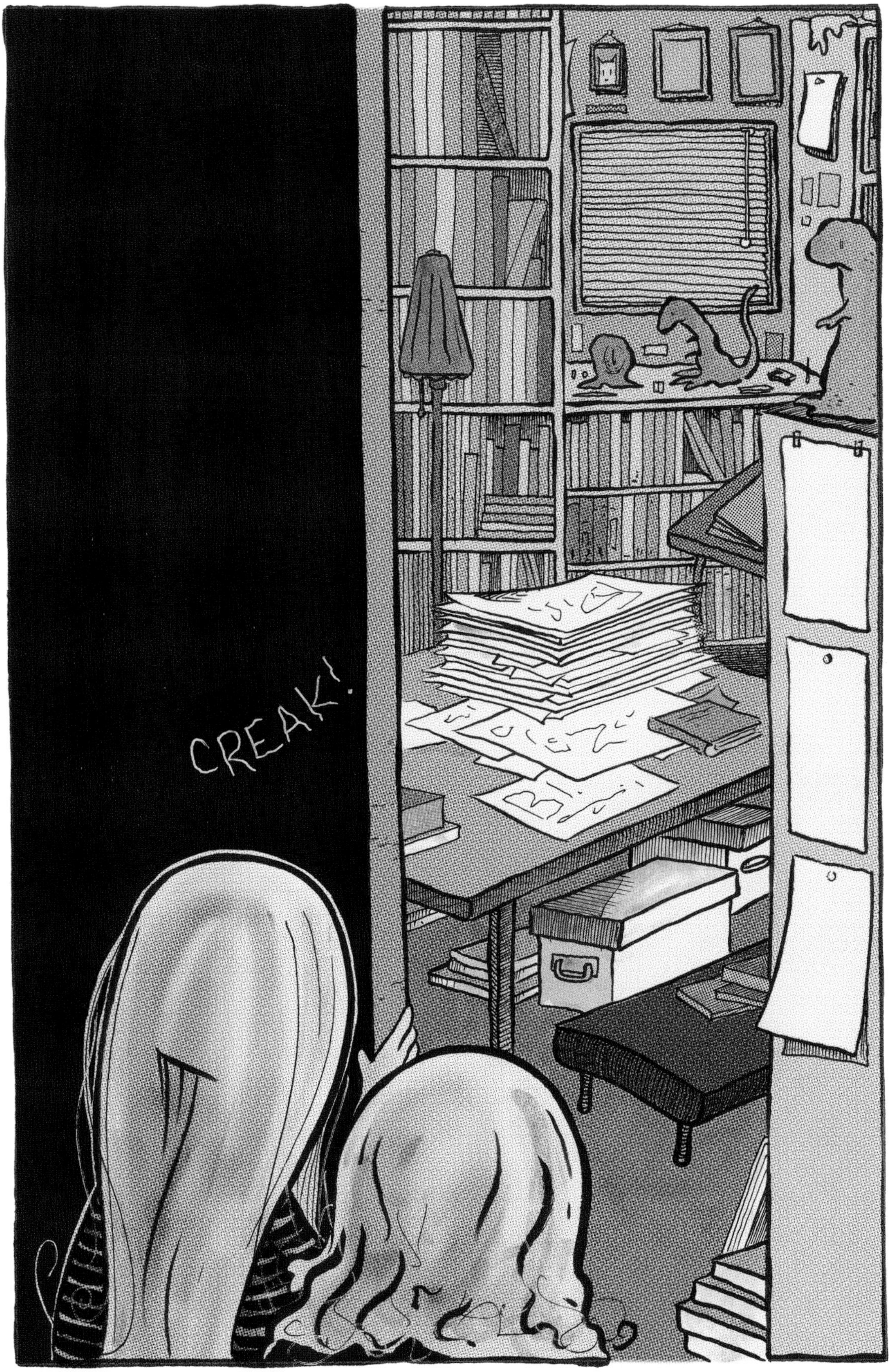
CREAK!

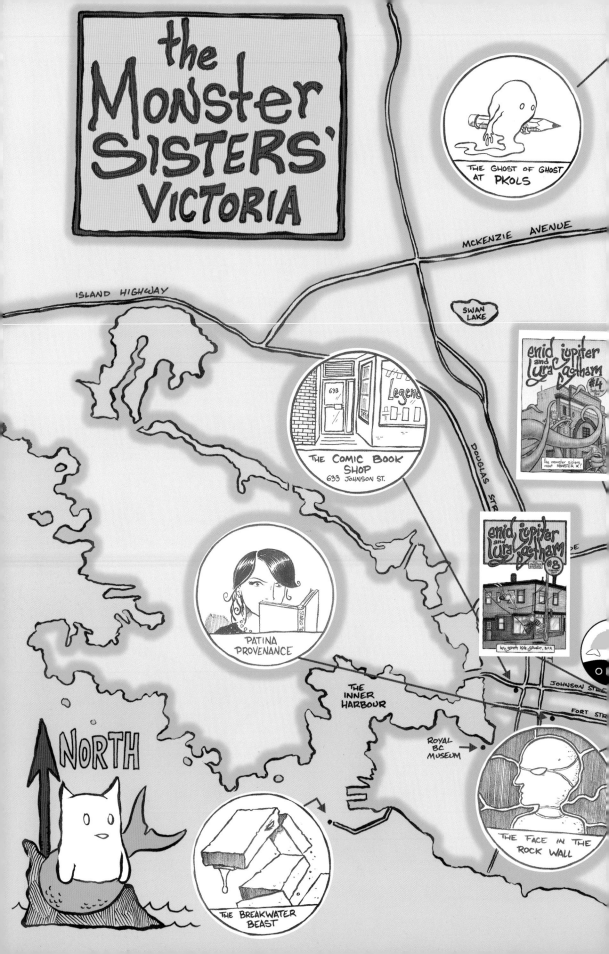

the **Monster SISTERS'** VICTORIA

THE GHOST OF GHOST AT PKOLS

MCKENZIE AVENUE

ISLAND HIGHWAY

SWAN LAKE

633

Legend

THE COMIC BOOK SHOP
633 JOHNSON ST.

enid and lura jupiter gotham #4

the monster sisters meet MONSTER X!

enid and lura jupiter gotham #8

PATINA PROVENANCE

DOUGLAS STREET

JOHNSON STREET

FORT STREET

THE INNER HARBOUR

ROYAL BC MUSEUM

NORTH

THE FACE IN THE ROCK WALL

THE BREAKWATER BEAST

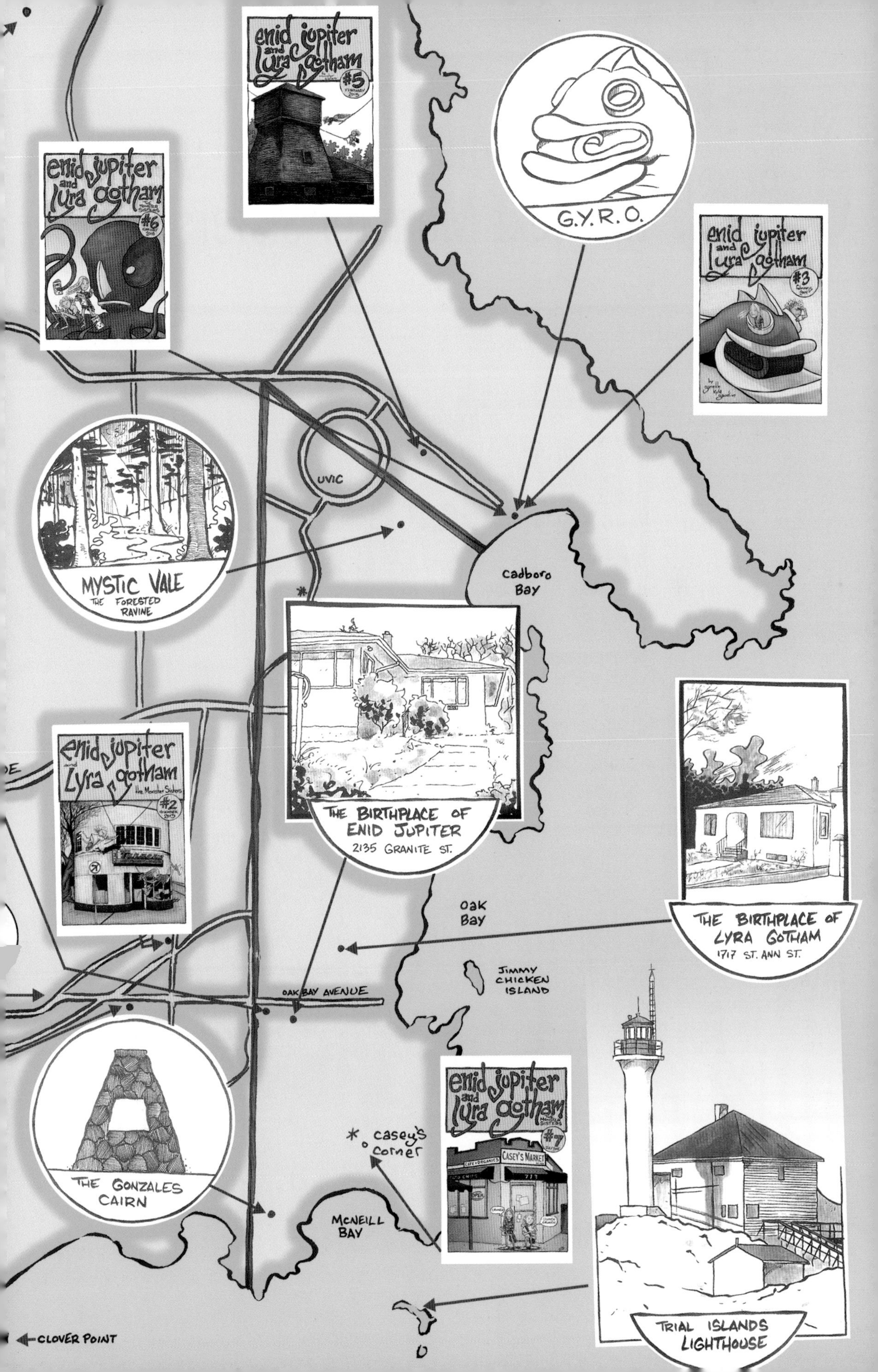
enid jupiter and lyra gotham
#5
FEBRUARY 2016
enid jupiter and lyra gotham
the monster sisters
#6
G.Y.R.O.
enid jupiter and lyra gotham
#3
UVIC
MYSTIC VALE
THE FORESTED RAVINE
Cadboro Bay
THE BIRTHPLACE OF ENID JUPITER
2135 GRANITE ST.
enid jupiter and lyra gotham
the monster sisters
#2
THE BIRTHPLACE OF LYRA GOTHAM
1717 ST. ANN ST.
Oak Bay
JIMMY CHICKEN ISLAND
OAK BAY AVENUE
enid jupiter and lyra gotham
the monster sisters
#7
CASEY'S MARKET
casey's corner
THE GONZALES CAIRN
McNEILL BAY
TRIAL ISLANDS LIGHTHOUSE
CLOVER POINT

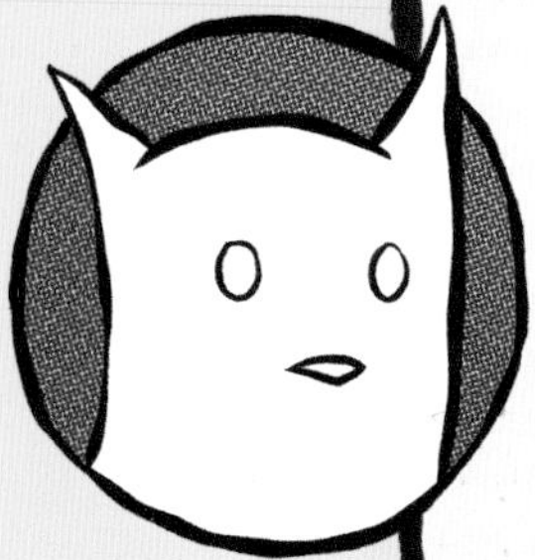

Don’t miss Enid and Lyra in the next Monster Sisters book!

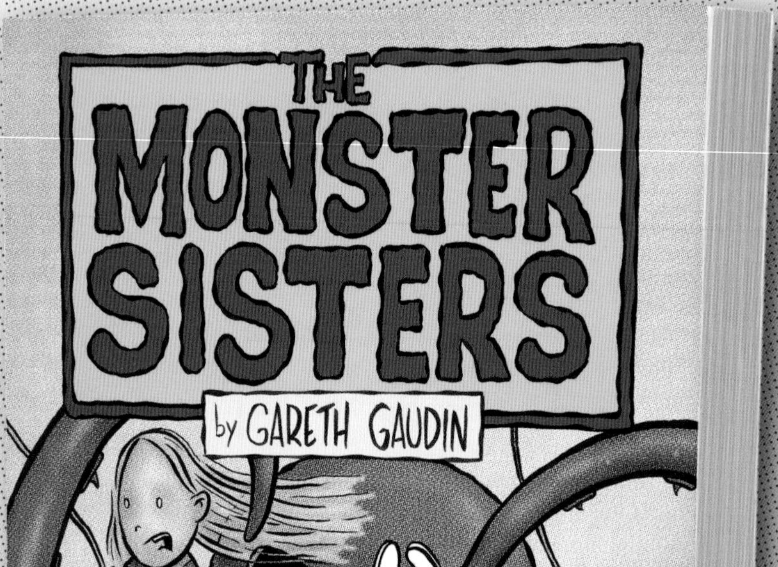
THE MONSTER SISTERS
by GARETH GAUDIN
The Mystery of the Stone Octopus

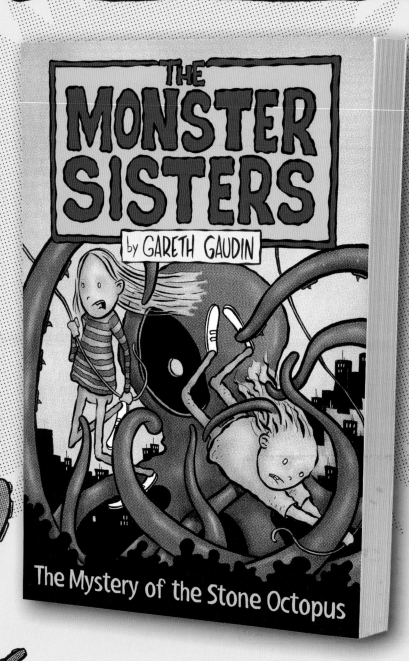